The Mereleigh Record Club Tour of Japan

The Mereleigh Record Club Tour of Japan

Lost in Japan

by Roy Vaughan

Strategic Book Publishing and Rights Co.

Strategic Book Publishing and Rights Co.
12620 FM 1960, Suite A4-507
Houston, TX 77065
www.sbpra.com

ISBN 978-1-62212-928-7

Dedication

Dedicated to many fine friends in
Fukuoka City, Japan including

The Fukuoka Auckland Friendship Association at
Fukuoka, the Fukuoka Association of Independent
Entrepreneurs, and the Marlow Record Club in Britain,
which inspired the Mereleigh Record Club series; and to
the Auckland Fukuoka Friendship Society at Auckland
for shared fun and experiences in Japan.

Thanks to Peter Scherer and Amanda Vaughan
for their interest and support.

*All the events and characters portrayed in this novel
are fictional and any resemblance to real people
and events are purely coincidental*

About the author

Roy Vaughan was born in Wales and spent most of his childhood in Jersey, and Marlow on Thames before he went to sea in the British Merchant Navy as a deck officer. He migrated to New Zealand to continue a career at sea but later became a writer on maritime affairs as a journalist for the New Zealand Herald and part time correspondent for Lloyds List in London.

His involvement with Japan was first as a journalist covering Japanese affairs and later as the chief executive of an incorporated society involved in cultural and trade exchanges with Japan. He spent some years with the regional aid and development organisation The South Pacific Forum in Fiji and now runs his own travel agency in New Zealand.

He professes a strong interest in the sea and sailing, travel and cultural relationships and writing.

This is the second of a trilogy about the Mereleigh Record Club. The first book The Mereleigh Record Club Tour of New Zealand has been strongly recommended by a number of critics as being an excellent subject for a movie or television series.

SYNOPSIS

In this fast moving novel 'could happen type story' about The Mereleigh Record Club, a British group, who were first drawn together by their shared love of the Sixties pop music, get an unexpected invitation to visit Japan, all expenses paid, to assist in a charity fund raising gig. The invite was just too good to be true, but irresistible.

It involves a roller coaster clash of cultures with on again off again relationships and a glimpse of the sordid underworld of glitzy Japanese night life.

Travel agent, and Record Club member, Rick Foster, from New Zealand, gets the assignment to make it happen, he knows the territory but has no idea what is in store for his pals. To make matters worse he is asked by a Welsh cousin to check the location of a missing actress last heard of working at a Tokyo night club.

CHAPTER 1

The mid-Wales guest house looked ok, judging from the pictures on its website. It was portrayed as small old coaching inn tastefully converted with modern facilities, boasting a good table for dinner and an ample private car park set back from the road. There were not a lot of accommodation choices at Newtown, Powys anyway, so Rick Foster had no real hesitation about booking a few nights there.

It was not a big deal for a travel agent used to making hundreds of bookings a year for others. It was easier: in fact, he had only he to please, not some picky tourists, but he was tired and annoyed at having to make a late change to his accommodation. Newtown was his old home town. It was one of those dull, nondescript overcast days, good for trout fishing and having a few beers with friends in a country pub or getting out with a gun and shooting rabbits or pheasants.

Even after three decades of life in New Zealand, having a large Welsh family had meant he had never had to stay in paid accommodation in Newtown before. The Grim Reaper had taken a heavy toll of his relations over the years and he was now down to one or two who he could stay with. As he typed in his acceptance of the booking on an internet café computer he could not help feeling annoyed and rejected. Through no fault of his own his Welsh cousin suddenly could not take him in as a guest. At the last minute he had to accommodate a sick uncle who had to attend the local Hospital for a series of abdominal tests. The sick uncle had nowhere else to stay.

With a degree of embarrassment the cousin reluctantly told Rick he had no room for him but to come over every day and have a few beers as usual. Rick picked up the concern in his cousin's voice, and did not wish to offend him, realising he was very embarrassed by the situation. He readily agreed, and said it would be no problem to find a place in Newtown as he had a couple of other old friends to catch up on as well, and it could work out ok.

He prided himself on being able to match up suitable accommodation for his customers and had acquired a deserved reputation for this talent. Regardless of whether the hotel was good or bad, the real downside was not being able to burn the midnight oil with his cousin over a few beers. Probably a bloody soulless dump for commercial travellers with boring bastards boasting their prowess bedding women and making sales, he mused.

It was called 'The Rising Sun', and was just a ten

minute drive from the internet café, and then suddenly there it was with a large old-style inn sign hanging out, looking like a P & O Shipping Company house flag with a rising sun complete with sunbeams rising up from the sea. What could be more out of place in Newtown! The brick building had been around for probably nearly two centuries at least. It was neat and tidy on the outside and boasted a discreet car park with high hedged boundaries out of sight of the main road.

He parked his rental car and walked to the reception office, wondering what the place used to be called. It was damned annoying not to be able to remember its earlier name but it was probably a good Welsh name. He sighed and pushed the inn's reception door open, a bell tinkled and a rather careworn middle-aged woman with a Midlands accent greeted him with an insincere electric light bulb smile that could be turned on and off in a flash.

He noted a popular reproduction of a sultry, scantily clad Chinese woman on a black velvet background hanging in the hallway which did not fit the image of the place he had in mind when making his internet booking.

'I emailed a booking earlier about a room for three nights, I am Rick Foster.'

'Yes luv, I just downloaded it. I guessed who you were. It's for three nights, right, correct?' Her tone was that of a hard-nosed businesswoman, though she seemed to be overly concerned that she had got it right over the number of nights he wanted to stay.

'Yes. Three.'

Rick was sure she had heard him correctly the first

time. Did she want him to stay longer or was it unusual for her normal customers to stay longer than a night?

'OK that is fine, we have just one room left, it has just become available. You wouldn't believe it. It's been like Piccadilly Circus here today. Is your lady with you?' she added.

'No, I am alone, it's just for me,' he replied.

'Are you expecting some company?' she asked.

'No, as I said it's just for me.' He was annoyed by this quizzing.

'Oh. Well that's all right,' she paused, obviously a little surprised by his reply.

'How will you pay?'

'By credit card,' He produced his Master Card for an imprint.

'Most of our customers pay cash but your card's fine, and I like your Australian accent,' she added while imprinting his card. He winced.

'No, I am not Australian. I was born just down the road, I have never lived in Australia and I suppose now I am well and truly a New Zealander.' He laid it on to indicate his annoyance.

'Oh yes of course, but it's very close to Australia isn't it, do you have friends here?' she probed speculatively with emphasis on 'friends'.

He resented the tone of her voice. She was brassy and tough: the less she knew about his life the better. He just shrugged in a non-committal sort of way. He liked Australians, but just as Scotsmen don't like being identified as Englishmen, neither did Rick like being mistaken for an Aussie.

'New Zealand is about as close to Australia as Ireland is to Canada,' he said sarcastically as he completed the guest form. He now had a distinct feeling that most visitors did not stay very long at this place. One night could probably be more than enough, and he was annoyed that he had committed himself to three nights.

She caught his drift and with a worldly ability not to waste time on things that did not pay money she switched off her light bulb smile. A man dressed in a regulation black business suit with a small attaché case brushed past him in a hurry after nodding at the receptionist on his hurried way out.

'See you next time and I will make sure Julie is around for you then,' she promised him.

'What's up with him? Has he got a train to catch? He nearly knocked me off my feet,' Rick protested.

'No dear, he is just shy. You know some men are about these things.'

Rick was about to ask 'about what things?' when a bottle blonde with a barely clad and constrained busty body within an extremely tight low-cut dress cat-minced past him, casting a long seductive look in his direction.

'I've put the room on your account dear, you can fix me up later if you are in a rush,' said the receptionist.

'Oh that would be fine,' said the busty bird fluttering her false eyelashes speculatively at Rick.

'Sophie is a regular, a very honest girl, not many like her, and good company I am told' the receptionist added.

Rick got the drift all too clearly now as he watched her move, ass tits, ass tits, ass tits all the way to the door, advertising her physical assets to best effect.

'Christ! I've booked into a bloody brothel! How bloody stupid.' He shrugged off the thought in self-annoyance.

'Here are your keys. Sophie will be free in about an hour if you change your mind. The room is up the stairs, number five, third on the right, just give me a call if you need anything, or anyone.'

She turned on her heel and click-clacked out of the reception office faster than he could pick up his bags. Bitch, probably a retired tart, she has seen it all before. Only interested in money, he surmised. What was the 'anyone' supposed to mean, Sophie for a 60 minute romp? She certainly had a body many men would die for and probably a matching price tag.

The stairway was cramped and tortuous and his suit-case bumped against the walls as he struggled up the stairs. As he unlocked his room door he got a strong dose of the mixed smells of disinfectant and canned fresh air. Though it was still summer time the room was rather dark, and a touch chilly. It faced north! His window looked out into the backyard of an amateur junk dealer of some sort, clearly working from home. It stinks of cheap perfume like some Hong Kong brothel, he mused.

There was no phone in the room, but at least he had his mobile. It would mean he would have to go to reception for any incoming land line calls though. To his dismay he discovered the bathroom was shared and down the hall and he only had a hand basin in the room. He had no dressing gown with him and it would mean wearing clothes to go to and from the shower and toilet and probably waiting for other guests to vacate the ablutions room in the morning before he could get in.

'This is a brothel and there are no showers in the rooms and the bloody bathroom will be in use 24 hours a day.' He groaned at the thought.

There were no towels in the room. He would have to go downstairs to collect some from reception. A very faded and probably seldom used card on the sideboard gave succinct details of meal times and procedures to order several hours in advance, breakfasts before 9 pm the day before. A recently well scrubbed stain on the carpet caught his eye and seemed to be the epicentre of hospital type disinfectant smell.

'Very nice, the last occupant probably had a Technicolor yawn on the carpet or pissed his pants. Who knows?' Rick thought, and started to toy with the idea of doing an immediate check out and going elsewhere. There were a dozen or so far better places to stay in and around Newtown where you could count on good Welsh hospitality, a nice lamb roast and feeling welcome.

'I must be suffering from dementia,' Rick realised. 'The name "The Rising Sun", of course it's from the Animals' hit 'The House of the Rising Sun':

'There is a house in New Orleans

They call the Rising Sun

And it's been the ruin of many a poor boy

And God I know I'm one.'

There would be doors banging and hushed drunken whispers all night, along with the feigned groans of ecstasy designed to extract a tip from the customers at the end of each session.

The room contained a mean little TV set and a large box of tissues next to the bed. The bed had a well-used slump in the centre indicating its springs were well past their use-by date. An involuntary shiver ran through his body, the sort that prompts people to say someone has walked over their graves.

'It's a mean dump where hard cash and no real names were used,' he reflected.

Tiredness had got the better of his judgment, he knew it would have been best to case this joint first rather than commit himself to an internet booking, but he decided he would be so tired when he hit the sack he could sleep through an air raid. Provided no one he knew saw him leave in the morning, he might as well stay put.

He chucked his suitcase on the bed, and started to unpack a few things. Then his credit and business card holder flipped out of his top pocket onto the floor. Bloody hell, his patience was at an end.

He could not see it on the floor, how the hell it could vanish into thin air? He bent down to feel under the bed. He lifted the bed cover and groped beneath the bed hoping to find it without bending down any further and looking. His hand touched something that froze him in his tracks, and made his hair stand on end. It was a rather cold and lifeless rigid hand.

'Jesus Christ!' he rapidly retracted his hand in disgust

and fear. Then, very cautiously, he lifted the cover and took a look beneath the bed. The body of a short, stocky, suited man was jammed beneath the bed and was clearly in a state of rigor mortis with one arm outstretched almost as though he was about to shake hands or hand something to someone, and another at his throat as though choking.

'For God's sake! What next?'

The face was oriental — Japanese, or possibly Korean or Chinese. He paused and took a breath trying to decide if it was a very dead person or someone still alive. He touched the hand. Rigor mortis had set in. There was no sign of breathing. No one would die naturally under a bed unless they had some weird fetish of hiding under beds when others had sex above. This poor bastard had probably been pushed there.

I could just walk out of here but it would be the dumbest thing in the world to do, someone would be on to me very soon and then I would be number one suspect, I can contact the front desk but shit she would only ring the cops, maybe, or maybe she would not. Rick made a quick decision and rang the police directly from his mobile, that way he would avoid time wasting with the receptionist.

The police were there in about ten minutes. He heard a couple of cars draw up outside, a few gruff words said downstairs to a surprised receptionist and shortly afterwards he gave entry to three plain clothes policemen, and noted one remained out in the courtyard and was busy checking all the vehicles . Inspector Roberts, CID, the grim-faced elder member of the trio raced up the stairs to Rick's room where Rick already had the door ajar ready for his entry.

'Detective Inspector Roberts,' he said as he thrust out a rugby player's battle-scarred large leathery hand. The hand was matched by an equally battered and scarred face, broken nose and a cauliflower ear. Rick tried to introduced himself and was also about to mention the smell and stain.

'Where's the body?' the Inspector quickly scanned the room with the gimlet eye of an experienced stalker taking in every detail, and noting everything that might be out of place. Before Rick could answer he asked, 'What's the stain on the carpet, it looks pretty recent and it pongs of disinfectant?'

'Oh ... well first I am Rick Foster and I have only just arrived here, probably just 20 minutes or so before you came. The stain was here when I arrived and the body is under the bed.' Rick shook himself out of a bit of a daze caused by the shock of finding the body and realised he was dealing with a professional used to working very hard and fast when needed.

'Right, first concern, don't touch anything if you can help it, but if you have any tissues or hand towels, we will use them to lift the bed off the body so as not to leave any of our fingerprints.' Rick found a box of tissues, and handed them round to the cops, and they carefully lifted the bed clear of the body and dumped it on the floor near the window.

'Hummm, looks like he is still in rigor mortis, and Oriental to boot. Yeah, a stiff stiff ! Eh. What's that?' Inspector Roberts spotted a small card near the body.

'Oh, it could be mine. I just dropped my card holder on the floor before I found the body, and it was only because of that that I found the body.' Rick went to pick it up.

'No, no, leave it. There could be finger prints.' The inspector pulled out a pair of surgical rubber gloves and gave Rick a set.

'Don't touch anything from now on if you can avoid it.'

Rick explained he had managed to lift up the business card by carefully holding the edges of the card between his fingers and left it where he found it.

'It's not one of mine. It's Japanese, and it's a nightclub membership card from a club at Nakasu, Fukuoka!' Rick was surprised, and shocked at this discovery.

'How the bloody hell do you know that? Do you know this man?' The inspector smelled blood and a hot trail.

'No I haven't seen him before in my life, but I am a travel agent and have done a lot of business in Japan, particularly Fukuoka. I can read a bit of Japanese. It's an amazing coincidence,' Rick said innocently, before realising that the inspector might not think it such a coincidence.

The inspector frowned, sighed, and told a junior colleague, 'I don't think our dead Asian friend was over here to study Welsh at the University of Wales' Gregynog Hall campus. People don't just die and roll under a bed so best get the forensics team over, and emphasize it looks like a recent death, and is very suspicious.'

Once he was shown the body Inspector Roberts

detailed one of the other detectives to organise the place as an official investigation site with the usual tape barriers, detain anyone who wanted to leave so they could be interviewed, and to instruct the receptionist not to talk about this to anyone at that point. She had to be told to stay put so they could talk to her later.

The detective was back within minutes to report to the Inspector the result of his conversation with the receptionist. She told him that she had checked out room 5, where the body was found, earlier that day. Some foreign European men had visited the oriental guest and there were a few comings, and she had not seen any girls use the room while they were there.

'I told her we would talk to her later,' the detective replied. 'And get a statement from her.' She was cautioned to keep mum.' Turning to Rick he added, 'Bloody forensics can keep you hanging about for ages their motto seems to be, why rush to a dead body when it's not going anywhere.'

'I am going to need a statement from you right now Mr Foster, proof of identity, and also a set of dabs so we can eliminate you from our inquiries, if you are innocent, of course!' Inspector Roberts allowed himself a teasing smile at Rick. Rick felt a bit weak at the knees and uttered a sickly laugh in reply. It would be easy to fall under suspicion in such circumstances.

'Oh, also your permanent address. To my ears you sound like a Kiwi, I have played rugby against a few of your fellow-countrymen over the years.'

Rick nodded in reply, a bit stuck for words, thinking

how quickly things in life can change, and hoping he could pick up his schedule as soon as possible and not get mired down in some exhaustive police investigation.

'But maybe a trace of a Welsh accent?' Inspector Roberts added.

'My family is from around here.'

'I have seen you before I think, or maybe it's your name. No, don't tell me, I like to remember myself.' The inspector paused for a moment.

'Yes, it's both, are you part of that Mereleigh Record Club group that had strife in New Zealand on the tour that was turned into film?'

'Not the film star. I am the real person, not the film star, I organised that tour. I think my photograph was in 'The County Times' but I was never in the film,' he explained.

'I doubt your pals would have thanked you for the mayhem during the trip,' the Inspector added with a touch of sarcasm.

'No, but they enjoyed the happy ending, and all the publicity and money that came from the film rights,' Rick added. 'The maternal side of my family is originally from Tregynon.'

The atmosphere instantly lightened up, and it was almost all plain sailing. The inspector knew half of Rick's cousins and he relaxed bit hoping the Inspector felt he was dealing with a friendly witness rather than a suspect.

'I do have to ask one more question, you understand, I am satisfied with everything you have given me so far, so take no offence, it's my job. Do you think there could be any link between the last tour you did with that group and this man, or between your business connections in Japan and this man?'

'Definitely not, there is no connection between that group and Japan at all, in any shape or form. Also no link between my business in Japan, and this man either. He is a total stranger. I have some travel agency contacts in Japan you can check out, but to me, at first glance, this man looks like a Yakuza, you know, Japanese mafia. He has a spivvy Italian kind of Oriental dress. Check his hands to see if he has any finger tips missing,' Rick joked.

'Yeah that's a point; let's carefully look at his left hand just under his body.'

Rick was not over-eager to help. He had always been a bit squeamish about dead bodies and he was not being serious when he made the suggestion but, as they rolled the body slightly, to his surprise he noted the smallest finger on his left hand was missing.

'Well, there you are now, boyo. I have got a dead Yakuza on my patch. I don't believe we have had one of those in these remote parts of Mid-Wales.'

'Phew, it's a surprise to me. I was only joking. What the hell would he be doing here?'

'It's anyone's guess at this point. The only foreign gangs we have about here are some of those Slav gangs and Albanians who are into prostitution and drugs, one or two of whom have on odd occasions been known to stay at this establishment. So what is a nice boy like you doing in a place like this?'

The inspector said almost as a joke but Rick was seriously embarrassed, and told him about his cousin's sudden inability to put him up.

'Well, what do you think, with your Japanese experience, would a Yakuza be doing here?' The Inspector gave him pleading look, scratching his greying head at the same time.

'I can't even guess, the Yakuza are a bit like hot house plants. They thrive in Japan and are part of the culture but you don't really see them beyond Japan.'

'So what sort of crime do they get involved in?' The inspector needed something even just a hint at what sort of crime the dead criminal could be involved in.

Rick though long drew a breath. 'Well, they are in the usual stuff, prostitution, night clubs, gambling , loan sharks, enforcers for others, every Japanese street stall, or yati, has to pay regular protection money for their pitch on a street. Crickey, there are about 85,000 Yakuzas in Japan. I read some statistics a couple of weeks ago and something like two dozen major gangs, mostly regional so they don't conflict within Japan,' Rick warmed to his theme. 'Their connections go up to some of the highest political levels in Japan's Diet.'

'It what?' The Inspector asked.

'The Diet is their Parliament. They also have close connections to rogue property developers and pressure people out of their homes if a developer wants a property cleared for some reason. They would also be into drugs I imagine, but I have to add the Yakuza are not noted for senseless crime.'

'What do you mean senseless, all crime is bloody

senseless, if you ask me.'

'Yes, you're a cop, I agree but what I mean is that they don't go around bashing up old ladies and beating the crap out of ordinary folk for no reason like some dumb drunken skinheads do. And they are all usually very visible with tidy crew cuts and black suits,' Rick explained.

'I see you mean intelligent professional crims, like.'

'Yes inspector, exactly.' Rick thrust his hands into his pockets wondering where this would lead and hoping the gruesome find would not upset or delay his own plans too much.

'If I had to pick a possible motive for this Jap to be here on my bloody doorstep what kind of crime do you think he would most likely be involved in?'

'Well, as you said, he is probably not in Wales to learn Welsh, or to sing in the local male voice choir, or play rugby. It's unusual to find a Yakuza gangster by himself. The Japanese like to do things in numbers, whether it is business or holidays, so where are his mates if he has any?

'If he is by himself I would guess he is under some punishment threat from his boss. He may have stuffed up something and has to do some sort of job to clear himself of an obligation. In those circumstances he would not have a mate with him as he probably could not afford to pay any other Yakuza to come with him.'

'And..?' the Inspector interjected.

'And I would think he is working with some local criminals, or against them, if your local crims have had some sort of dealing with his boss in Japan.' Rick was quite pleased with his process of deduction, as was the

Inspector who hung on almost every word.

'OK then, all I have to do is to go around my manor and check out all the crims and prostitutes and ask them if they have been doing business with Japan recently and show them a mug shot of Mr Yakuza to see if they know him. It would be nice to think I could have it all wrapped up by the weekend in time to duck down to the Millennium Stadium in Cardiff for the rugby international on Saturday. I got a season ticket but that is not going to happen now is it?'

Rick was a bit embarrassed by it all and shifted his feet like schoolboy before being punished by his teacher 'Well, I know it sounds pretty simple, I am not a cop and you asked me. Sorry you have to miss the big game.'

'No, no, Rick your knowledge and ideas are most welcome, probably saved me a day's research on the computer. I like the loner under punishment or obligation angle, it fits, but to misquote Gilbert and Sullivan before we can make the punishment fit the crime, we must first find the crime.

'By international standards Mid-Wales is a pretty low key rather petty crime area really, so what on earth would the mighty Yakuza want in our little country, having it off with a cheap tart on his annual leave perhaps? No doubt the receptionist downstairs will be able to assist us with our inquiries, to some degree at least.'

'Anyway, I would have thought that you as a travel agent, born in these parts too, would have been able to find more suitable accommodation,' the Inspector said with a wink. 'If it were me I would be very embarrassed if my wife knew I had been staying at a place like this, but there you are, you see we are all different.'

The comment annoyed Rick. 'All the good places were booked out, it was an internet booking, sight unseen. Anyway, no doubt when you have been on rugby tours you have stayed at places like this, or visited them, if for no other reason than you don't want to be the wet blanket when the team wants to play up a bit and have some fun!'

'Touché. It's a fair observation but to be honest I don't think you would deliberately come to a place like this in ordinary circumstances.'

Rick realised the Inspector was making one final probe to see if Rick was really innocent, and he did not like the word 'ordinary' in that context. It left open the possibility in the inspector's mind that there could be something extraordinary, perhaps of a criminal nature, which had motivated Rick to use this dump.

'Websites don't tell you everything,' Rick said. 'I keep telling my travellers that. I found this place on a website when I was tired and anxious to check in somewhere. As a travel agent I frequently ignore the advice I give my clients and make quick decisions on travel arrangements, on the spot, because I don't like spending time on doing the research. Take this place, it looks good on a website and outside, but the receptionist, owner, whatever she is, is hard as nails, and the atmosphere is just plain sordid. There is nothing on the website to tell you about her disposition or her customer base, or the junk yard outside my window.'

'The only clue I got that it might be the local knocking shop was when the receptionist, madam, or owner, whatever she is, said 'if you want anything or anyone let me know. By then I had checked in and it took me a moment or two to work out what she meant.'

'But you did not want to have 'anybody?' the inspector probed.

'Of course not, my wife is over here in the UK with her family, while I visit mine, and it was only because of a sickness in the family that I could not stay with a cousin.' Rick was starting to fear this could be a preliminary to many long, probing interviews.

'OK fine I believe you, not just because you are a Welshman, at heart at least, but everything you have told me so far can be very quickly checked without your assistance.' Inspector Roberts gave him a grin.

'You know every time you say something there is always a word or two in your sentence that has a twist to it, like 'so far!' I really do not have anything more to add which would be of help to you, so I hope 'so far' will be enough.'

'Yes, I think it will, providing everything checks out as you have told me, but it is very possible that you might be needed as a witness so we would prefer that you did not talk about this to other parties. It is in a tender preliminary stage of investigation, you understand.'

The inspector indicated he wanted to press on with other things.

'You are going to have to move out of this hotel room of course, and I have more good news for you, the Mid-

Wales Constabulary will pay for a couple of nights accommodation for you elsewhere, and any incidental expenses incurred thereon. We will close this place down for a few days at least I would think.'

The inspector dug deep into one of his inside jacket pockets and pulled out a small notebook and pen, and then his business card.

'There is my card, call me at any time if anything comes to mind. I will take a collect international call if necessary, and I need a 24 hour 7 day email and mobile phone contact from you, as well as your permanent address, and passport details.

'We will need to take your rental car for forensic tests, but I am sure the rental car company will provide another one. I don't want to hold you up so if you can give us a bit of time now it may save having to call you back later on if something interesting comes up.'

Rick protested that the police would find nothing in the car as he had only just hired it and been the sole user and occupant.

'I am sure you are right but we have to be sure and it will help eliminate you from our inquiries. I want to look at your passport to see when you last visited Japan and ask you if you have any plans to visit Japan in the near future,' the inspector reeled off his demands politely but firmly.

'I was last in Japan about two years ago; you can see the entry date at Narita, Tokyo and exit from Kansai International at Osaka. It was travel agent's business, and no, I have no plans at all to visit Japan for the next 12 months or so,' he added.

'You will have to come to the station and make a formal statement, then we can fix up the accommodation allowance and rental car as well, and that could take us to about 8.30 pm and give us an hour for a glass of beer while my forensics boys are doing their work here.

'Don't talk about what we have found here, other than saying you found a dead body, do not mention anything about his race, or apparent Yakuza connections. We have a crim or two to catch here I suspect, and I don't want to advertise any punches to the opposition now.

'On that score the press boys will be along shortly and I don't want any doorstep interviews outside this place and I doubt you would want to appear on national TV lurking in the background, either.'

Rick groaned at the thought.

'The local media are ok, The County Times , it's a small place and we respect each other's roles but those national tabloid boys take no prisoners if it's a juicy story and this has the omens of one, murder in a brothel a great headline for a start.' The Inspector was positively gloating at the thought of being at the centre of a murder that would make the front pages of at least some papers.

'No, I will do the media interviews when I am ready after forensics has something positive for us to consider and in my own office. Let's go. You will join me for a beer so I can remind you that we still keep "A Welcome in the Hillsides in Wales" as the song says.'

He beamed a genial smile, patted Rick on the shoulder and indicated it was time to move on. They had just reached the ground floor when a middle-aged man tried to brush past and held his head low, obviously not wishing to show his face to strangers.

'Good afternoon Mr Morgan, how are the wife and kids?' the Inspector asked with glee. His head was still bowed as he mumbled 'ok', but Rick could just see him glaring in anger as he squeezed past them as fast as he could.

'You know him but you don't want to question him,' Rick asked, feeling somewhat victimised by being the subject of most of the police attention.

'Mr Morgan is a well known Rotarian in these parts. It's a bit of a surprise to see him here. Normally I would not 'recognise' anyone I knew here except Mr Morgan has been giving my boys a very hard time recently over a law and order issue at a local pub which could easily be solved if the publican observed the laws relating to serving drunks. It seems the publican may have thrown a couple of eggs at Mr Morgan's car one day.'

'Petty stuff really,' he added.

'I will talk to Mr Morgan later and any others my men will pick up as they check out of the rooms. I am sure Mr Morgan will be very eager to put the record straight about his presence at this place on the basis that his presence is not made public.'

Rick noticed that the sole police presence in the hotel yard, a constable, had swelled to four men who were setting up the usual incident tapes to keep the public out of areas of interest to the police. He decided then he would not accept the offer of a few beers with the Inspector after giving him a formal statement. It would either involve a discussion on the New Zealand All Blacks compared with the Welsh Rugby Team and/or subtle questions about the body in the bedroom or both. The whole bloody thing would probably drag on for months and the worst aspect was that if he were called as a witness his name and association with the brothel would be blazoned about the place, and it would not do his travel business any good at all.

CHAPTER 2

Janine dumped a pile of mail on the kitchen desk at Mereleigh-on-Thames and noted with including a letter from Japan addressed to her husband Andy.

'This is a puzzler, He usually tells me or drops a hint he is about to spend a lot of money in his softening up process. He has never shown any interest in Japan at any time in his life, but there you go, maybe it his weapons thing, Andy collects historic weapons. That is what it will be.' She smiled the smile of wife used to her husband's eccentricities. 'He must have brought a very expensive Samurai sword and this will be the invoice.'

She still could not figure it out. 'He doesn't know anybody there, and he has this Second World War thing about the He has never even owned a Japanese car in his life!' She turned over the letter and saw the postmark was Fukuoka; a place she never knew existed, let alone was in

Japan. It was addressed in clear type and he was given the title of 'President of the Cast of Mereleigh Record Club.'

The Mereleigh Record Club had been an informal organisation, no more than a gathering of late teenagers in the early sixties who met Friday nights and paid into a common kitty a few shillings to buy the then latest rock music LPs. Janine knew immediately this letter could not be about the club's happenings of three decades or so ago as few beyond themselves knew the club existed until about 12 months ago when a big film company made a movie about the group's eventful reunion tour to New Zealand. One of their members had been duped into bringing drugs into New Zealand, and what a merry chase it had led to. She smiled at the memory. They had run foul of drug smugglers, a member was kidnapped and they had assisted the New Zealand law enforcement authorities in a sting operation. It had made headlines in the international media.

It must be about the movie, as why else would her husband be addressed as President of the Cast? She laughed to herself as the thought of Andy being president of a cast. 'Pure Japlish,' she chuckled. 'Well it certainly made us all famous and a little rich,' she mused, 'but this was the first thing that looked like some new commercial opportunity to come out of the movie.'

Janine's husband Andy was the group leader then and had been among 30 or so teenagers who formed the Record Club. Members would meet at a vacant house on a large estate which his late father managed, play their vinyl records, drink coffee and hard liquor, and enjoy rock and roll together.

More than a few relationships were formed, broken and re-formed over that period and, like many teenage things, it had a finite life and ceased to exist when everyone entered their twenties and many moved on out of town. Only a chance visit by a member, Rick, from New Zealand two years ago had resulted in a group reunion for the first time in about three decades.

This week, actually, Andy was away from home meeting up with Rick and another old Record Club friend Peter, in Mid-Wales where Rick had been visiting his ancestral village. Rick's first wife had died earlier of cancer. He had remarried, his new wife being a member of the record club, so he had decided to take a break and see his old friends and places.

Janine regarded herself as a bit old-fashioned in some ways, like her husband Andy. As the letter was clearly addressed to him she felt she should not open it. Obviously it was not a bill, or something like that, which she would normally open and deal with.

The mail came at about 10 am, and she knew Andy would have his mobile phone turned off, probably until about lunch. Andy believed a mobile phone should only be switched on when you wanted to use it and he consequently made time schedules for Janine. He hated being interrupted by it. That was a hang-up from his final occupation as a buyer for a large retail outlet, where he was pestered almost every minute of the day by companies wanting to sell his company products.

It was a dull, boring day, and Janine could not put the letter out of her mind. The New Zealand trip had given them all a huge new interest in life and she dearly hoped this letter could in some way bring them all together again on some kind of venture. She made her scheduled lunch time call to Andy and, to her extreme annoyance; he had his mobile switched off. 'Oh bugger and blast, he is the very limit sometimes,' she said to herself. This was almost worse than being a kid at Christmas Eve having to wait hours to check the presents.

She was angry at herself for being so impatient, but her life had been so dull and routine recently. She plunged into the other letters, all bills or circulars and sorted them into several piles for Andy to deal with. 'When I write the cheques he bitches to me about the cost of everything. It's as though I create the bills by just writing out our cheques, but when he writes the cheques he says nothing. Weird really,' she muttered.

About 2 pm, an old friend, Fran, from the Record Club days popped around on a routine once a week visit for a bit of chat and a cup of tea. 'What's new?' she asked as Janine let her in. Fran could detect an aura of the unexpected about Janine who seemed to be quivering with excitement.,

'Well, you would never guess, a letter from Japan arrived, addressed to Andy as President of the Mereleigh Record Club tour, or cast or something,' she responded excitedly.

'What's it say?' Fran demanded without hesitation.

'Don't know, I haven't opened it yet and I have been trying to contact Andy who is in Wales most of the day just now as you know, to see if he will let me open it,' she said.

'Why don't you just open it for God's sake, you have been married for several decades and there should not be any secrets between you, unless Andy has had it off with some young Japanese English language student, and she is asking for money to support his kid!' Fran teased.

Janine pooh-poohed the idea, 'Can you really imagine Andy having it off with some young "foreign" girl?' she said with a grimace.

Fran nodded in agreement. Not that he was racist, she thought, he had just probably never had sex with anyone else in his life since he got married.

'Where exactly in Wales are Andy and the others now?' she asked.

'Well, the three of them, that is Andy, Peter and Rick, took off on one of those vintage steam trips, a re-run of the old "Cambrian Coast Express," except this one started at Birmingham and not Paddington because they have a job getting permission to bring old steam trains to Paddington these days.'

'Open the letter, Janine, it might require immediate attention!' Fran commanded.

After a bit of coyness, Janine agreed to open it. 'I can always say I opened it by mistake and then, when I ring Andy, hope he will ask me to open it, and read it to him. I am sure he will ask me to do that. Yes, that's the best way around it,' Janine stated, smiling at her own sub-terfuge. It was not the first time she had applied a bit of devious tactical thinking to overcome Andy's stiff for-mality about things

By this time Rick had completed calls on his Welsh

relations, and was grateful that only the local press seemed to have carried anything about the man found dead in his hotel room. They had restricted their coverage to a few paragraphs buried on inside pages. He decided not to tell anyone as they would wonder what the heck he was doing staying in such a seedy place.

He had mentioned it to his wife Maggie by phone the day after, in the briefest of terms, inferring that it was probably natural causes, like a heart attack. However, he had made the mistake of telling her that the body was under his bed, and immediately wished he had not. That could make it a talking point and Maggie would probably tell her friends! But he did not mention anything about the man being Japanese or a probable Yakuza member. Fortunately Maggie did not know Newtown that well so if she learnt the name of the guest house she would not know what a seedy joint it was.

After the family visits, Rick went to Shrewsbury to meet the Mereleigh Record Club male members who were to do a vintage steam train journey and some tramping in Wales. In British terms this was a 'chaps' tour' for old buddies whose conversation and plans would be unfettered by female interjections and demands. There would be wild boasts of past and secret loves, and daring exploits that mostly existed in the mind and had never quite been lived out in the manner boasted to others. Everyone revelled in the freelance fictional experiences. The story was more important than the truth, and the golden rule was that the truth should never be allowed to foul up a good story.

Rick arrived first and was waiting on the platform for

his friends when they arrived. There were warm hand-shakes, much back-slapping and wide grins. Andy, true to form, had gear that could be identified with what they were doing. He had bought himself a grease-top vintage British Railway engine driver's cap complete with a brown 'Western Region' Badge. Peter felt the cap was a bit over the top, but that was Andy.

Rick politely noted the cap and its appropriateness for the train trip and Andy was suitably flattered. Peter grunted something which ended in an observation that he expected a few others on the train trip would also be wearing that type of hat, which wiped the smug smile from Andy's face. Clearly Peter thought Andy was making a fool of himself by wearing it.

'Nearly bought one of those myself, but you know New Zealand engine drivers had a posher cap with a silver badge and they actually used to wear white ties over black shirts!' Rick said.

'If I was forced to wear one, which I certainly would not do voluntarily, it would be one of those American loco engineer's caps. The striped ones, blue and white like a baseball cap,' Peter said in rather superior tones.

'God you would look like a convict, or a concentration camp victim, if you did.' Andy joked.

'OK chaps, here is something. While I was staying at Newtown I found a dead man under my hotel bed,' Rick struck out, anxious to put an end to a petty squabble and introduce the topic he knew could embarrass him if he did not deliver the account of the dead body in his own words and before they heard about it from their wives.

'You what? That's a tall story!' Peter suggested with more than a touch of cynicism.

Rick kept his account succinct, sticking strictly to the basic facts with no mention of race, or a Yakuza connection, and strongly inferred it was probably just a heart attack. He made a point of not mentioning the name of the guest house as it would certainly bring to mind the Animals' hit song 'The House of the Rising Sun' and raise questions as to what he was doing staying in a place of that name.

'Don't remember reading anything about it or seeing it on TV,' Andy observed, adjusting his cap slightly at the same time to get exactly the right cant on it.

'Well, it is a bit hush-hush for some reason or not important enough for them, only the local papers carried a few lines.' Rick shrugged as if he was disappointed that the national dailies had not run the item

'The national dailies are only interested in chainsaw murderers now, the rest is small beer. Crime has got out of hand in this country,' Peter stated, on the verge of launching into a lecture on the moral decay of society.

The conversation was cut dead as their steam train made a sudden fast entry into the station at a sprint with the engine driver seemingly applying the brakes at the last minute to add some urgency and excitement to the scene.

It was pure theatre the engine driver probably imagining he was in charge of the Flying Scotsman and not the 'Bradley Manor' a far more modest branch line loco with the fireman posing on the left hand platform side of the footplate, hoping the large crowd of enthusiasts would mistake him for the engine driver.

A colourful headboard on the front of the boiler declared it was The Cambrian Coast Express. It might not be as impressive as the Flying Scotsman in full roar, but was pretty formidable all the same to younger genera-tions who only knew the silence of electric traction and the grumblings of diesel-hauled freight trains.

Hundreds of flash bulbs blasted the relative gloom of the station as the fans jostled for the best positions.

It was all hissing steam and screeching block brakes, metal on metal, slowing rapidly until coming to a rather sudden abrupt jolting halt when the brakes finally locked on to the carriage wheels. Old fashioned manual slam doors were opened and slammed shut.

Glad of this interruption, Rick was satisfied that he had delivered the news of the dead body to his friends in such a manner that it should not create any further ques-tions.

'Those of you who know anything of geography will see that the train is heading north, and we will exit Shrewsbury heading roughly south west to Wales so while we are boarding they will uncouple the loco and run her around a triangular track, and couple her up at the other end,' Rick explained

Scores of enthusiasts went to one end of the train to photograph the uncoupling, and then rushed to the other to photograph it being recoup led. It took about 15 min-utes at the least for the loco to go around the triangle and reverse up at the other end as if it were a delicate outer space operation where every second counted. The rail fans observed each operation with the same measure of concern and seriousness that space scientists apply when watching a satellite dock at a space station in deep outer space for a Mars probe.

Safe in the knowledge that their loco had been correctly and firmly attached to the rest of the train, the steam fundamentalists could then confidently board the train with an assurance that it was in good hands.

The carriages were all in the splendid chocolate and cream colours of the Great Western Railway complete with the GWR crests on each outside panel. They were traditional corridor and compartment jobs with each compartment providing a sort of Wild West stage coach intimacy within its confines to its occupants. A feature of vintage train rides is that everyone wants to stick their head out of the windows. There never is enough window space so the outside impression is of a mass of humanity trying to force an escape from some internal disaster on board.

The last few carriage doors slammed shut, there was a blast on the guard's whistle as he waved a green flag, an acknowledging toot from the loco, a jerk as the heavy carriage brakes reluctantly released their fierce grip on the wheels, and the first loud chuffs as the loco's twin cylinders exhausted spent steam up the chimney in distinct white puffs.

'We are off!' Andy stated the obvious with a huge grin, 'and the driver has managed to get her away with a full load and no driving wheel slip. These Great Western engines are very firm-footed. Excellent for the Welsh hills and Devon Banks where they used to operate on local expresses.'

'Andy, mastermind of the bleeding obvious,' Peter replied but with a smile clearly ending the little spat on the platform. Rick relaxed and stretched his legs. He noted about 30 percent of the adult male passengers sported various items of steam railway memorabilia from around the world. Giant American locos in brooch form, German wartime Kriegs loco badges, hats, T shirts, lapel badges from dozens of heritage railways and even an American husband and wife team in complete Union Pacific loco engineers' denims and striped hats.

Some of the most serious fans were busy with their watches, calculators and notebooks timing the train, and would periodically announce things like 'She is averaging 45.9 miles an hour and is 2.46 seconds ahead of schedule.'

Some had graphs which recorded the runs of previous steam-hauled Cambrian Coast expresses and were busy trying to establish if Bradley Manor was doing better or worse than other locos that had headed the train. Most of the passengers were there for pure, simple unashamed fun.

'It's a bit like being on a Royal Train really, that is what I like about these steam trains. Every one waves to you,' one fat woman said, Look at all the cars following us, stopping to take photos at bridges, and then racing ahead to get more shots down the line and all the kids and people at windows and doors giving us a wave. I really feel very important on this train! I just love the way the engine driver toots the whistle so frequently, but I just hope he is not a Toad of Toad Hall character. This is fast enough for me.'

'We shall be in Wales in about 15 minutes or so, this brings back so many memories,' Rick observed, reflecting on his school years when he would take a series of trains from Mereleigh where his family had lived to go on holiday in Wales with his Welsh relations.

The train had picked up a good rhythm and Peter shocked everyone by bursting into song:

'Taking a trip up to Abergavenny

Hoping the weather is fine

If you should see a red dog running free

Well, you know he's mine.

A chase in the hills up to Abergavenny

I've got to get there and fast

If you can't go

Then I promise to show you a photograph.

Ah, passing the time with paradise people

Paradise people are fine by me

Sunshine forever, lovely weather

Don't you wish you could be?'

'It's the 1960s pop song, well Marty Wilde made a better job of it than you,' Andy joked in an approving manner.

'Hey, how about 'Rock Island Line? Now that is a real railroad song and none better than Johnny Cash singing it,' Rick chimed in.

'Definitely not appropriate for a British train journey,

Peter has got it right for a change with his tune. Nice jingle but of course the only thing in common is Abergavenny being in Wales and travelling with paradise people. Abergavenny is well to the south of where we are going.' Andy started to hum the tune.

Everyone was in a good mood, and normally reserved English passengers who hardly acknowledge other people on trains chatted freely with their fellow travellers, swapped food and drink and God was in his railway heaven. Andy excused himself to go to the toilet, and came back a few moments later with a look of astonishment on his face.

'You would never guess it. There is a Japanese couple on this train!' He announced it as though he had discovered life on Mars.

'Unbelievable,' said Peter with sarcasm.

'We live in international times; from my perspective as a travel agent we see Japanese everywhere these days, they are not a rare species,' Rick added.

'Give me time to finish, I know all that. You don't get the point, its how they are dressed!' Andy started.

'At least they have their clothes on! I believe they still practice nude bathing at public baths in Japan,' Peter tapped the end of his nose as if he was the holder of state secrets.

'It's how they are dressed, they…,' Andy was cut short again as the Japanese couple entered their compartment doorway, politely bowing and seeking use of a couple of reserved seats.

'I see what you mean,' Peter whispered to Andy as

they shuffled around to make room for them.

The couple were in their mid 60s. The husband wore a complete British railway guard's uniform, including a guard's leather brief case, and adorned with a Great Western Railway badge and buttons. His wife wore the national costume of Welsh ladies and could only get away with wearing the tall black hat in the confines of a train because she was so tiny, almost doll-like, in stature.

Rick tactfully broke the ice and said he really liked the uniform and costume.

'I really admire the Great Western Railway,' said the Japanese man. 'It is what you say, quintessentially English. Engine names after Kings, Castles, Halls, Manors and Counties. Job for life and self improvement for employees at Swindon before Japan had same systems, stations with flower displays so nice and also joke. You know joke. It says GWR stands for 'The Great Way Round' because Great Western routes very long winded way to travel, not short cut route. Ha ha ha,' he laughed at his own joke.

And Rick, Andy and Peter roared in response, relieved that they had such a funny eccentric in their midst.

'I am Funakoshi and of course she,' he indicated his wife, 'is Mrs Funakoshi.' She smiled obediently and bowed slightly.

'Let me explain how you can remember my name, think of 'fun' and then 'a' and 'koshi'. You can call me Funny koshi if you like, but to be polite you should place 'san' at the end. Ha ha ha.'

The Mereleigh friends roared again, and said 'funny koshi san' several times to get the hang of it.'

Funakoshi continued, 'My first desire, or should I say ambition, was to buy uniform of famous Cambrian Railway Company. Well, I really want Cambrian Guard's uniform but impossible to find the buttons and cap badge so GWR guard's uniform next best thing.' He beamed a million watts at them. He had bought the uniform by mail order through a 'Steam Railway' heritage magazine advert, and selected this rail tour from the same source.

'My wife, she love Wales. She is very good singer, she can sing and speak Welsh, so when we decide to go on this trip to Wales she must wear Welsh national costume. She goes to Welsh National Eisteddfod to sing and has very good voice like nightingale.'

'You must know the famous Llangollen International Eisteddfod was established as a contribution to world peace, and now many musicians and dancers from all over the world perform there every summer,' Mr Funakoshi explained as though Rick, Peter and Andy were ignorant of that fact.

The trio nodded politely as if it were news to them. His wife smiled with modest pride noticing the approving glances from Rick and his friends. It appeared that she had been a minor office girl at Kitakyushu City Hall in south eastern Japan and had been in a local choir that had visited Cardiff under some sister city arrangement.

The Japanese choir had learnt many traditional songs in Welsh for this exchange and her interest in Wales and Welsh singing grew from that.

'She can sing now for you,' Mr Funakoshi said with enthusiasm as his wife prepared herself to burst into song.

Fearing the worst, Andy quickly said he would not want her to put herself to any trouble on their account. It was too late she stood up, adopted the classic singer's pose and gave a very tuneful and impressive rendition of 'Ar hyd y nos,' (All Through the Night), in Welsh.

Andy, Rick and Peter were stunned! It was so professional and even accounting for the background noise of the train and constant movement of the carriage here was a lady of opera star standards. Rick quickly brushed away a tear hoping the others would not see. Like many ex-pat Welshmen, traditional Welsh songs always brought tears to his eyes. He led a round of applause and Mrs Funakoshi sat down, her credentials now fully established with the group.

'How about you and steam trains?' Andy asked of her husband.

'I am from Shimonoseki, at bottom end of Honshu Island, just the other side of Kanmon Strait that divides Kyushu, southern island, from Honshu. You know where my wife comes from is Kitakyushu and is most closest city in Kyushu to my home town Shimonoseki, and we have Shinkansen, or bullet train tunnel beneath sea to link both places, just ten minutes or less by train.'

'So when I small boy, it was just after war and every town in Japan almost totally destroyed. At this time at Shiminoseki we have nothing, and New Zealand soldiers, so-called 'J Force' based there. One kiwi soldier, he young man and likes my elder sister very much and she tell him I have no toys and I like train. When he returns to New Zealand he sent me famous Hornby train set. Just his second hand set, but it begins my interest in big way and I begin to love British steam train. From then I become crazy steam train fan very much, especially British train and GWR!'

The trio of friends nodded in agreement. Andy pulled out from an inner jacket pocket a silver hip flask of single malt whisky, brandished a silver cupful and offered it to their newfound Japanese travel companions. It was accepted and downed with relish.

The hip flask cup did the rounds of the others and everything took on an extra rosy glow. It appeared the Funakoshis had met in Wales when one of them was visiting the narrow gauge railways of North Wales, and the other in the same area singing at a local festival.

After 15 minutes or so the long rolling hills of Shropshire were giving way to the more frequent steeper and higher hills of the Welsh country. Sheep and cattle farms became more common, the River Severn would run alongside the tracks then disappear only to reappear again several miles down the track, and Rick excitedly pointed out local 'Kerry Hill' sheep and 'Welsh Black' cattle.

'They are very nuggety small cattle. You don't have to winter the cows in calf in a barn. They will happily stay out on the hillsides to rear their calves.'

'Hey look,' he pointed to a far hillside. 'Over there you can see some typical Welsh ponies. They are apparently a very old breed. They used to be worked down the coal mines as pit ponies, before the mining companies put in rail lines and electric locos. Most spent most of their working lives down below, and became blind. These days there is quite an international demand for them as kids' ponies.

A Welsh farmer friend exports them to New Zealand.'

The lilting accents of Wales were first heard at a water stop at Welshpool when Bradley Manor's tender was filled from the large stainless steel tank of a large articulated truck.

'There are very few old water towers left for steam trains,' Andy pointed out apologetically, trying to explain why there should be this crass modern technical intrusion into the sacrosanct world of steam rail travel.

'It used to be fun watching the fireman swing a large leather hose from a tall water tower at the end of the platform, and then, while the tank was being filled, get to work shovelling the coal forward so he could more easily reach it from the footplate. Everything was simple and apparent then. We knew what was going on and why, but how many times have you been stuck on an airport taxiway waiting for a pilot to check his instruments, and never know if he has a faulty one and is about to make a decision to fly or not!'

Rick was mulling over whether he should mention his bullet train rides in Japan, and tell the Funakoshi couple about his Japanese connections, but decided against it. The atmosphere was just right now and the Funakoshis would probably want to talk of Japan and it would exclude Andy and Peter from the conversation.

He gave a fleeting thought to whether the Japanese couple might in some remote or sinister way be connected to the dead Yakuza but, priding himself on being a good judge of character, dismissed the possibility. They certainly did not look like a hit squad tracking him down, not that he knew anything incriminating. Rick decided to test Mr Funakoshi's train knowledge instead.

'So what do you know or have seen of the Cambrian Railway in its present form?'

'Very nearly everything there is to do and see. This trip I did before, by rail car, but not the same atmosphere, most passengers just read I Pad, talk on mobile phone or read. They do not see the outside world or talk to other passengers like we do. I sometimes I made overnight stops. For example I got out at Welshpool and visited Oswestry to see old Cambrian Headquarters, and existing heritage steam operation there. Then I did the narrow gauge line Welshpool to Llanfair and make visit to Powys Castle but no railway there of course.'

'Some time ago I got off at Newtown to see birthplace of famous socialist and starter of cooperative movement Robert Owen 1771-1858 I believe. He set up communities in Scotland and United States based on mutual co-operation. Also I saw the Royal Welsh Warehouse, so-called site of the world's first mail order company, set up by Pryce Jones. We can see this big brick building right next to the Newtown railway station on the right hand side.'

'I have not visited the Corris Railway at Machynlleth but they tell me the restoration is very good and they also have very interesting environmental technology centre there. I did not visit Towyn Railway yet. Famous mountain seat of King Arthur called Cader Idris is near so maybe one day I will see both.'

'This time I am going to do the Festiniog and Welsh Highland Railways. This is a must see especially with big restored ex-South African Beyer Garrett locos on the Highland Railway. Most unusual to see this large kind of loco on a narrow gauge. I visited the Aberystwyth Devil's Bridge Railway before, very nice scenery, and also before I did the Snowdonia Railway.'

'For us the coast section of this journey from Dovey Junction along the cliff and shore of Cardigan Bay is very, very nice with understated scenery,' he wound up with a look of obvious pleasure at the treats ahead.

'I heard from Rick that Japan has marvellous scenery and a magnificent rail system,' Andy said.

'Yes, I can say from my heart it is most excellent, so I hope one day you can enjoy that pleasure.' Mr Funakoshi gave a small bow to Andy.

The Cambrian Coast Express stopped at a few more stations, and after Dovey Junction the passengers soon spotted the open sea to the west and shortly afterwards the Cambrian Coast Express was tracking a very narrow man-made ledge between cliff face and a very rocky shore line down below.

At one point they could see the very battered rusty remains of an early steam loco which met its Waterloo and ended up on the rocky beach after hitting a landslide. It then ran around the Barmouth Estuary at almost sea level before heading north. The trip was a gem and the last 30 minutes or so of it a bit of a blur after their new Japanese friends produced a sake bottle which everyone had to help consume. At the end of the run there were lingering fond farewells to the Funakoshis, and the Mereleigh trio had a few problems getting into a taxi to take them to their hotel at Pwllheli.

Later that evening at the hotel Andy realised he had arranged to ring Janine on arrival and here he was in a semi-alcoholic blur. He glanced at his watch and was annoyed at his own forgetfulness. He had not switched on his mobile phone after charging it overnight. He immediately did so and noted a voicemail message from her saying she had received a letter for him from Japan.

He told the others, 'It ssheems, I mean to say seems, I have a letter from Japan which Janine sounds very excited about so I better ring her now.'

In their rather drunk state it appeared quite normal to Rick and Peter that Andy should receive a letter from Japan, nothing is really that surprising when you are pissed. As he rang Janine, he told Rick and Peter he knew no one in Japan and wondered what on earth it could be about.

'Possibly some devious way of getting me to buy a new Japanese car,' Andy said shrugging his shoulders in disgust at the thought.

'Andy, the world's car manufacturers don't, they don't I must repeat, quite realise what a huge mental transformation you had to make to buy German and French cars after British quality makes vanished a few decades ago, and if they did they would realise what a hopeless task it would be to get you to buy a Japanese car. How on earth could anyone so dedicated to things British ashely, sorry I mean actually, buy "continental" cars let alone Japanese!' Rick teased with a broad drunk smile.

'There is nothing wrong with BMWs and Mercedes,'

Andy snapped back in defence. Rick just smiled.

'Who said there was?' he then added. 'Maybe it's some Japanese geisha you met on that cruise ship you took to the United States about 18 months ago.'

Janine was now on the line and Andy too wrapped up with the call to reply to him. Andy quickly made his decision, 'Well you had better open it then, if it seems important, or urgent. I don't know anyone in Japan, but it might be important.'

At the other end of the line, Janine smiled and gave Fran a knowing look, upon which Fran rustled the envelope as though opening it for the first time. Janine then feigned surprise and interest as she delivered its contents to Andy.

'It's from a place in Japan called 'Fukioka' or something. I will spell it as it sounds a bit rude, F-u-k-u-o-k-a, and a person there called Nomura who is president of a record club group like ours and wants us to go there as his guests for some rock festival fundraising concert.' She paused to get Andy's response and winked at Fran.

'Well I am blowed … how strange ... no I have never heard of the place, it sounds rather rude … you sure this is not some prank by some of the other Record Club members, perhaps Perry or Dick?' Andy was suspicious.

'I don't really think it's a prank. It's so Asian, the Japanese stamp, letterhead etc and this man Nomura refers to the film company who did the movie on us and it looks as though the film company has been in touch with him about it. I would say they would be very disappointed if we did not go!' Janine was trying to lock Andy into this and the best way was always to play on his sense of decency and obligation. It worked most of the time.

He said, 'OK, look, let me think about it for a minute or so and I will ring back. If it is 'official' then of course we must go. It would be rude not to. The Japanese are very formal people. I know that.'

'Well, what's up, Japan about to declare war on us and they want to give you advance warning or something?' Peter said sarcastically.

Andy just gave Peter one of his superior school teacher-like looks. He knew the other two were bursting to hear the news so he would make them wait a moment or two, and thus enforce a touch of politeness out of them.

'Don't make this too long, we could all do with a bit of a rest after the sake,' Peter pleaded.

Andy explained the letter came from the 'Fukiyoka' or something record club on the southern Japanese island of Kyushu. 'It seems they were a club like Mereleigh in the same era and they saw the movie about our tour to New Zealand and it gave them an idea.

'Long story short, they want to invite us all to 'Fukiyoka' in cherry blossom time next year to take part in some fundraising type of event to support a drug and alcohol abuse charity of some kind and they will cover our travel costs,' he said.

'Phew, sounds too good to be true, as far as I can see. There must be a catch!' Peter was not convinced.

'Sounds legitimate to me, The Japanese do these things and when they do they don't do them by halves. Auckland has a successful sister city relationship with Fukuoka in Kyushu, this place could even be Fukuoka and Andy, if it is, it is pronounced Fuu Kuu Oh Ka and means a happy hill or something,' Rick added. Then a frown crossed his face as he wondered, 'Was this just another coincidence, a dead Japanese male from Fukuoka, a delightful Japanese couple on the train from cities close to Fukuoka and now an invite for the group to go to Fukuoka? Or was it something more sinister?'

'I know I am a bit pissed,' he admitted to himself, 'so perhaps it's best to leave it all to the clear sober light of day to mull over,' he decided.

The other two obviously did not see any likely connection between these things but they did not know the dead man was from Fukuoka. Rick suggested that Janine could either fax it or scan it to their hotel so they could all read it, and she agreed.

'Before we go any further, should this thing prove valid then we need to be prepared to give a firm commitment as soon as possible. I don't like hesitation in these matters, things go off the boil and I would hate to be blamed for any delays etc. So this is what I suggest.' Andy was back in charge making policy decisions.

'I rather assume it must also involve all our friends and that includes Chuck from Oklahoma who was on the tour to New Zealand with us and featured in the movie, so I will personally acquaint him of the situation by phone later tomorrow. We could not go without him!'

'No, no, of course not,' Peter and Rick said almost in unison, nodding to emphasise their agreement.

It was decided to take a shower and a coffee break to

sober up a bit before getting into the detail of things. They met in Andy's room where he had already received and copied the faxed letter from Japan, sent by Janine.

The guts of the letter was that a Mr Toshi Nomura, who was president of a Fukuoka Record Club, had seen the film about the Mereleigh Record Club Tour to New Zealand, and been very impressed. He wanted to invite everyone to Fukuoka for a special sponsored fundraiser which would raise a lot of money for a local anti-drug and alcohol society.

The letter had more than a touch of slightly incoherent Japlish in it like 'very enjoy so much' and plans for a rock and roll ball which would be 'a never go to sleep party.' Nomura-san spoke about his enthusiasm for 'Criff' Richard and the Shadows, the Beatles, and the Rolling Stones who had left 'an everlasting memory in my bosom.'

It requested Andy bring his 'full cast but no more than 40 members', saying there would also be a mayoral reception, some free sightseeing of Fukuoka provided by the Fukuoka Visitor and Convention Centre, and a chance to experience 'the real secrets of Japan.' The letter seemed to have found its way to Andy via Universal Studios at Osaka then via the UK film company which had forwarded it to Andy unopened.

'Seems genuine,' Andy pronounced, and Rick agreed. Peter was a bit suspicious. 'Nothing is free in this world except your own funeral if you don't leave enough money with your relations to pay for it.'

'Rick, you know Japan…,' Andy started.

'Like the back of his palm...,' Peter ventured.

'Yes Peter yes, he probably does, but let's keep away from the seamy side of life. This is serious. Rick, you said you have contacts there in the very same city we are talking about. Can you please make a few careful checks in the next day or two to suss it out for us?'

Andy did not want to be made a fool of, and Japan was a long way to go on some freebie tour which might have a sting in its tail.

'Will do, it might take a couple of days though. Fukuoka is a big place, population several million but it's a pretty intimate place and I have mates in rugby and city hall circles as well as travel, so between them all we should be able to get some perspective on this.'

'Fukuoka is a pretty flash city by any standards, it's a sort of political capital of the southern island of Kyushu. About 16 million people live in Kyushu and Fukuoka has a great history. The first rice cultivated by man was grown in Fukuoka several thousand years ago and of course this is the place the Mongol hordes twice tried to invade Japan. The first time Kublai Khan's men were driven off by the Japanese and, in a later invasion, a big armada of ships ran into a typhoon just before they tried to land. The storm destroyed their fleet and it was called kamikaze, or divine wind, by the Japanese. Even today you can find some relics of these ships on the harbour bed.'

'It has a great natural harbour called Hakata Bay, and a long sandspit leading to Shinkanoshima. About 70 years or so ago, some locals found a small official seal of the kind used to mark official documents. It was found to be an ancient Chinese seal belonging to a kingdom of sorts, Na I think, dated back thousands of years ago when this part of Japan was controlled, or under the influence of China.'

'If you take a look at Fukuoka today you will see a very sophisticated and modern waterfront , a fisherman's wharf and beaches etc but back inland, Daizaifu Shrine is the most important shrine in Fukuoka and relates to an early legend about a flying plum landing at Fukuoka in ancient times.'

'Sounds like a piss-take for naïve tourists to me,' Peter interjected.

'Not so, it's an important old legend and anyway the shrine is very picturesque, nestling at the bottom of some big hills and mountains and surrounded by 1,000-year-old camphor trees. There are also traditional houses and shops, a very swish art museum and a small old folk museum plus Fukuoka Tower for a scenic view of the city. In short, it's a great place,' Rick added

'If any travel arrangements have to be made, my company can do it at cost, and we can always find some cheap sauna capsule hotels and Love Hotels for Peter. If he behaves and does not make racist remarks we treat him to a love hotel, and if he misbehaves we send him to one of those tiny hole-in-the-wall capsule hotels.'

'Ho, ho, very funny, who said I am coming? I don't know that I can take a lot of raw seafood and all that karaoke singing stuff.' Peter's normal response to Rick's jokes was to play hard-to-get and inhabit higher, more distant territory.

'Well, Peter, if you don't come I know your good lady wife will be very disappointed, and coming on the trip would be a more pleasant option than having to endure her cold bum and tongue for years over missing the trip!'

Andy made his point well and knew at the end of the day if the trip went ahead Peter would be there. He knew it would not just be his wife's wrath he would have to endure, but also the sideways looks and collective scathing comments from all the other record club wives if he did her out of the trip.

'I am much obliged to you, Rick, if you can check out the Fukuoka end, and Peter I am not totally unsympathetic to some of your concerns about Japan but we have to admit it is new territory to us all and Britain would never have become the great country it once was if we all sat on our bums and refused to go abroad because we did not like foreigners. I understand the Japanese have a similar shared outlook to ours in some respects,' Andy added as Rick nodded furiously in agreement with the last statement.

Rick suggested the record club members be assembled to make a group decision. Though it was now late, Andy got on his mobile and rang Janine, and was pleased to discover Fran was still at his house. He figured correctly she had hung around waiting for a reply out of curiosity. With Janine on one domestic phone and Fran on the extension, Andy gave his orders.

'Fran, please get all the members together at my place for a meeting on this in seven days from now at 1pm, and say apologies not accepted. We want everyone there. In the meantime Rick, our own in-house travel agent, albeit New Zealand-based, can sort out some travel arrangements for us, and maybe we could do a week's tour of Japan first taking in Tokyo, Mount Fuji, Kyoto and Hiroshima before going to Fukuoka. Rick has an agent in Tokyo who can cost and arrange it at cheap rates.

'Also if I go, it will be by train all the way connecting to the Trans-Siberian express from Moscow to Vladivostok then ferry to Japan, and it would be great if Chuck could join me, and Janine, as you know I hate flying,' Andy finished.

He hung up and Rick burst into song, singing the old Japanese pop classic 'Sukiyaki'

'Ue o muite aruko

Ue o muite aruko

Namida ga kobore nai you ni

Omoidasu haru no hi

Hitoribotchi no yoru

Ue o muite arukou

Nijinda hoshi o kazoete

Omoidasu natsu no hi

Hitoribotchi no yoru

Shiawase wa....'

He was cut short by Peter.

'Ok, ok, so you know the Japanese words to Sukiyaki, no doubt a product of your decadent stays in Japan. We won't embarrass you and ask who taught you the words or what they mean. It's a great tune but not enough in itself to make going to Japan a great idea. After all, they haven't apologised for the Nanking Massacre or half the atrocities in Southeast Asia,' Peter exclaimed in total seriousness, shaking a finger as he spoke.

'If they were to apologise for all those things I take it you would come?' Andy added sarcastically.

'If it comes to that, have we apologised to the black population of America, the Caribbean and Africa for shipping about 4 million slaves across the North Atlantic over a period of several centuries?' Rick was getting tired of Peter's arguments.

'The chance of a free trip to Japan at someone else's expense is clearly a better proposition than being asked to buy a Japanese car in your view, Andy,' Peter teased.

'We have to keep an open mind on things, chaps. I don't buy Japanese cars because I believe European cars are better, that is all,' Andy protested.

Rick quickly intervened to keep the peace and reminded them that Maggie Moss was driving up to pick them up at the hotel in six days' time after their mountain walking. Maggie was a very old flame, in fact Rick's first love back in the Mereleigh Record Club days. After being out of contact for about three decades Maggie had turned up at the record club reunion and had also taken the trip to New Zealand where she had become attached to Rick as he coped with the death of his wife.

They had kept in contact since and Maggie, along with several other members of the record club, had been obliged to return to New Zealand as witnesses for the prosecution for a major drug boss's court case because of the role she had played in helping snare this international crime ring. They were now an item and Maggie would have been part of Rick's Welsh pilgrimage if it had not been for her own family and work commitments.

⌘⌘⌘

Fran called around at Janine's place two days after Janine had called Andy in North Wales about the Japan invitation. The two would set up a meeting for the Mereleigh group as Andy had requested.

'I have a tit bit for you,' Janine said as she opened the door to let Fran in.

'Oh yeah, a bit of sleazy gossip?'

'No, you know I never indulge in that sort of rubbish. Rick found a body under his bed at a Welsh hotel a few days before he met Andy and Peter at Shrewsbury,' Janine gushed with excitement.

'My God what next? How long had it been dead, did it pong and was it leaking out body fluids? Sounds very messy,' Fran commented.

'No, from the brief account Rick gave Andy and what Andy told me it seems it might have recently died. That really is all we know or what Rick is prepared to say. We are really not supposed to say much about this. Rick is apparently not allowed to talk about it because of police investigations.'

Fran shrugged in disgust.

'Sounds very sinister to me. Is Rick a suspect ?'

'I don't think so as he had only just checked in and apparently reported it himself to the police.'

'God, under his bed! That would be a shock. Imagine that you could be sleeping over a corpse for a few days without knowing it, until it started to stink.'

Fran was never one to hold back on life's realities, and continued, 'I would have never thought that Rick had any skeletons in his cupboard.'

Janine grimaced, 'that is not even funny, Fran.'

'It does not say much for the hotel's cleaning services if the cleaner can miss a corpse under the bed mouse or perhaps a rat, but a corpse!'

'Let's get off that subject, people die in the most inconvenient places at the most inconvenient times,' Janine did not want to dwell on the topic.

'I agree, but what the hell was this person doing under the bed to die there? Some sort of sex fetish wanting to hear others have sex, or was he hiding from someone at the time? You can be sure, Janine that I shall check under every hotel bed I use from now on.'

'OK, don't dwell on it with Rick, he is probably embarrassed by it. Anyway, they went through Mid-Wales past Welshpool and Newtown on the train and up the west coast of North Wales to Pwllheli. Very scenic, in old coaches, you know the ones that have individual compartments and corridors where you can open the windows manually and stick your head out. Of course it has everything to do with old steam trains as far as they are concerned. Nice countryside but I would get bored gazing at steam locomotives. Nice to be pulled by one and experience the thrill of it all, but not the museum parts, though I do like the Welsh castles and all the Italian architecture at Portmeirion. It was designed by Sir Clough Williams-Ellis apparently based on southern Italian styles. Then there are all those traditional beautiful half-timbered black and white houses. '

'OK, down to business Janine, let's fix the date and time now and split the list of members between us to phone and email. We can bowl this thing over by lunchtime.' Fran already had her laptop computer open and was flashing it up for use. Another call to Andy at his Welsh hotel that evening and the meeting date, time and agenda were fixed

Working independently Rick had already very discreetly sussed out the Fukuoka Record Club Group though his Japanese friends and, without speaking to them directly, his friends had found out enough information to be able to vouch for the Japanese group. They also confirmed that the group had been in contact with Fukuoka City Hall regarding a major rock music event to raise funds for a charity. Rick had therefore given Andy an assurance that everything looked kosher. Fran had got in touch with Rick and with his help had sorted out some flights and a draft itinerary for a Japan tour.

Andy phoned Fran to see if she had contacted Foggy Night and Helena. She replied in the affirmative and said they were now living together and seemed to spend half their life in Britain and half in New Zealand. Like Rick and Maggie, the couple had only met up again as a result of the Record Club's tour to New Zealand, where Helena had been living for many years and working as an artist. Andy and Fran expressed some doubts about Peter going to Japan with them. He liked to stay in Britain.

'He might not come voluntarily. Reluctantly, yes, but perhaps not with a smile on his face. You all know his feelings about the Second World War, he was very forthright in his views on Japan when the subject was first mentioned,' Fran said.

'He found the Funakoshis on the train great fun,' Andy said

'The who?' she asked.

'Oh sorry, a delightfully eccentric Japanese couple on our vintage steam train journey. They had Peter in fits,' Andy explained.

'Let's hope the joke has not worn off by decision time and he is still coming voluntarily. His wife will get him there one way or another anyway,' Fran added. 'He has been particularly moody recently, though Brenda, being the good wife she is, has made it clear she will travel whether he does or not!'

Fran said most members had indicated they would attend the meeting and the usual one or two had failed to reply but could be expected to turn up.

'Let me guess, Perry and Dick for starters,' Andy said.

'Right on the button,' Fran replied.

⌘⌘⌘

On the other side of the world at Fukuoka, Toshi Nomura, a short, stocky man with glasses, had, a few hours earlier, concluded a briefing with his members of the Fukuoka Record Club at their favourite karaoke bar in the nightlife district of Nakasu. He had briefed them on the progress so far. Universal Studios Japan, at Osaka, had passed on the request that the Mereleigh group come to Fukuoka for the fundraiser and had also passed their request to the British film maker.

Universal Japan decided on a very minor role, so Nomura-san had approached a large real estate development company in Kyushu to underwrite the hosting costs at Fukuoka by 50 per cent on the understanding they would have first rights to all publicity. Universal Japan was able to confirm a response from the associated UK studio, saying the proposal was being favourably looked at by those concerned and a reply could be expected in about 10 days.

Nomura-san said a very favourable meeting had been held at the Mayor's office and there would be some funding from City Hall as well as a civic reception.

'They indicated they can provide a banquet room at the New Otani Hotel free of charge for our main function,' he said with a glowing smile. 'It looks like the Fukuoka Tourist and Convention Office can get free-of-charge accommodation for the group at the Sea Hawk Hotel at Momochi, and we visited the Fukuoka Prefecture office and through them they can provide a top-market ryokan (Japanese traditional inn) in the country providing we have them visit the Prefectural Governor and provide opportunity for publicity.' Nomura-san was glowing with pride then.

Nishimura-san, who was always to the point, asked 'What is going to be left for the alcohol and drug charity we are doing this for?'

'Oh yes, of course, I should have added two of our

functions will involve pay ticket entry so everything from that except some food cost is for the charity and maybe we can get at least 500 to 1,000 people at both functions and possibly some other sponsors so the situation looks very good. We just now have to wait acceptance from the Mereleigh cast,' he explained. The Fukuoka group sank a few more sakes and whiskies, sang some of the old numbers of the 1960s and wended their merry way home.

Back at Mereleigh, Andy was impressed with the turnout, including, to his astonishment, Peter and Brenda's son Adam, a feature writer on a local newspaper. Peter greeted Andy defensively, 'This does not necessarily mean I am going to Japan with you,' and walked in. Perry with wife, Jean, and Dick, accompanied by his wife, Joan, arrived all smiles, ready for another bit of action.

Fran got them all seated and down to business quickly, gave them the guts of the proposal, copies of the letter from Japan, copies of a draft itinerary for the proposed Japan tour and a cost estimate. Andy spoke in glowing terms about how beneficial it could be to the Japanese charity if they went, and concluded it would be rude not to go under the circumstances. There was a loud cough from Peter which was silenced with a hard stare from Fran.

Andy quickly told Peter he was aware of his view so would take comment from others first. There was overwhelming support for the project and the itinerary. Peter's son, John, asked if he could join to do a feature on the trip and, as their total numbers were slightly fewer than the Japanese budget allowed he got the nod to go. Rick and

Maggie said that, as they planned to be in New Zealand for the southern summer, they would make their own way to Tokyo and join the group there.

Foggy and Helena were eager to be part of the tour from the very beginning and Foggy said being Jewish, he would not eat any shellfish on the trip but was pretty easy on other things except pork. Oswald said he would not eat any raw fish, and did not want to sing any karaoke, and the two unattached ladies, Frances Mold and Lindsay Love, said they did not want to be put in any compromising situations at dubious nightclubs.

Ewan Perth, the only gay member of the group jibbed, 'Blow you, I want some fun. The more compromising situations, and dubious nightclubs the better. You couple of killjoys can sit in your hotel rooms all night but don't expect me to do so!'

Fran, somewhat bored, noted this all down on her laptop but was polite enough to give an appropriate nod of understanding at every request. Andy said he had telephoned his American friend, Chuck, in Oklahoma and he would fly to the UK so he would spend a few days with Andy and join then on a train journey using the Trans-Siberian Express to Siberia.

Chuck had fallen overboard from a liner in the Atlantic and claimed Andy had saved his life by organising a chain of deck chairs and life belts to be thrown overboard to mark a course back to him before the liner could be turned around. Andy was sailing to New Zealand for the reunion tour at the time and two became such close friends that Andy invited Chuck to join the New Zealand tour.

Perry asked if two New Zealanders, Herewini the Customs officer and Chris the cop, with whom they had worked had also been invited. Andy peered over the top of his glasses at Fran and she in turn re-read the letter of invitation. 'The words say you, Andy, as the Director, are invited to bring the 'full cast', so I assume it means those two as well, through of course they were not members of the Record Club.'

'It's clear in my mind that Herewini and Chris should come but of course we are paying for the full tour from Tokyo to Fukuoka ourselves, so unless they wish to join us on that part they would only do the Fukuoka bit as guests of the Japanese club,' Andy added. Fran was accordingly instructed to get a letter off to Herewini and Chris.

Rick pointed out that, as he was the only member of the group to have visited Fukuoka, it was desirable that everyone boned up on Japanese culture. Derek Sloan, the ex-Royal Navy man, said he had been to Nagasaki on his ship.

'We had a week in port and it was unbelievable. The girls, phew, you would not believe it,' He caught the glances of his wife and a few other wives and changed tack. 'It was well before I met Ann, of course, and I was pretty young then but these girls would do anything for you, that is where the legend of the Nagasaki greyhound was born!'

Rick cut in, 'I don't suppose the Fukuoka Record Club has the same sort of entertainment in mind that you enjoyed then, Derek, so we'd better stick to the straight and narrow, so to speak.

'We should all have name cards and hundreds of them as everyone exchanges cards in Japan and ladies have cards with rounded edges as everyone is simply called 'san' in Japan so the only way that they can recollect if the card came from a male or female is if it has round edges,' he began.

Rick went on to explain many other things including the use of bathroom slippers, Japanese baths, food, green tea ceremonies, the importance of punctuality and politeness, and formalities concerning the exchange of business cards.

'It's very important that you bow slightly and exchange your card with both hands and, when you receive theirs, take a hard polite look at it and place it very gently in your wallet as if it were gold. A lot of human contact in Japan is about little ceremonies. It's a culture of presentation and gift exchange,' he explained.

'Sounds very Victorian to me,' Peter declared, a bit weary by all this and still undecided about going. He saw no reason why he should become a pretend Japanese person and bow and scrape to everyone in a servile manner. His comments drew an instant response from the rest of the group, so he retreated into his shell with hardly a murmur.

A timeline was set by Fran by which deposits and final payments should be paid, another two pre-trip meetings agreed to, and a draft letter of acceptance to the Japanese hosts drawn up for Andy to sign and post. The group stuffed themselves with tea and cakes and left for home in good humour. It was only a day later when Andy came to sign the letter to the Fukuoka club that he realised he had no address, only the sender's name. It was clearly a translation of a Japanese letter.

So after a bit of thinking he checked out the envelope it came in, to see it had been originally directed to the UK film company, and then redirected to him. Thinking about it for a minute he concluded the Fukuoka club would not know his address so trying to contact him via the film company was logical. He therefore addressed his reply to a casting director at the British film company with a request that he pass it on.

It was almost a month before Nomura-san received the reply and he was at the point of giving up hope. In reality the letter had lain on the desk of the British casting director for a couple of weeks before he found time to send it on to Universal Studios at Osaka, and they in turn took a week to find Nomura-san's address.

The first thing Nomura-san did was note the address of the British casting director, and vowed to send any future correspondence direct to him. He already had a young lady in his group who did all the translation from Japanese to English so had no need to rely on anyone outside the group for that service.

Thing were now well on track as far as he could see and his group had already had several meetings between the letters to set up the arrangements. They were elated at the news that the group would come and in the rather typical Japanese way began to worry about things.

'Our preparations must be perfect,' Nomura-san kept telling them. All members of his group already carried large individual folded paper files that opened out spreadsheet fashion. This could be the biggest moment in his life, a chance to stand tall before the Mayor of Fukuoka and the Prefectural Governor, and be interviewed by Japanese TV and newspapers as the man who brought the Mereleigh people to Japan and raised so much money for charity.

Nomura-san had told the group that if it went well they might have some administration money left to go towards a group trip to Britain to visit Mereleigh. Deep in their hearts his group knew they would all be working towards that end so all the effort could have another reward for them. Nomura-san could have had them at meetings almost every night of the week working to midnight if he wished but he decided to restrict the meeting to one a week and the odd Sunday afternoon get-together, supposed to be social but always involving more paperwork and discussion.

The Japanese have a love of meetings and planning that few other races can comprehend and the more important or interesting the topic, the more meetings should be held regardless of whether they were necessary. It was what people expected! The successive meetings and correspondence with Andy progressively raised Japanese enthusiasm to fever pitch. Members of Nomura-san's group had all been delegated off to handle different things, leaving Nomura-san to deal with the Mayor and Prefectural Governor personally, and his members their respective underlings.

This principal sponsors, a large Kyushu-based real estate development company and a few retail outlets including a large Fukuoka department store, sent their own representatives to Nomura's meetings so the meetings progressively grew in magnitude and importance and resulted in Nomura-san having to organise his own in-house meetings for his own members to plan for the meetings with the sponsors.

The only people who privately complained about the frequency and duration of the meetings were the sponsors' underlings who worked unpaid overtime to be there and the young lady in his group who did all the translation. Though her volunteer services were only needed for correspondence with Andy, she was required to attend all meetings so she would be totally conversant with everything. She had a regular boyfriend and that relationship was so strained by the demands of the meetings that only frequent brief sex at Love Hotels, where rooms were booked for an hour, would keep this relationship alive.

It was not enough to just attend meetings. Normura-san expected everyone to take notes and expected intelligent comments and observations, even if they were not necessary.

The meetings procedure created a sort of group comfort zone for Nomura-san as he could claim all matters were fully considered by everyone involved and all decisions were by consensus so if anything should go wrong, he personally would not have to take responsibility. In other words failure would be an orphan but he felt he could claim success for himself, as did about 30 other individuals from the Prefectural Governor and Mayor down to their sycophantic heads of department who were managing these affairs for them.

Nomura-san was now a man who had risen from

almost nothing as a middle level salary man to a person that the Prefectural Governor and Mayor would invite into their personal rooms for advice and consultation. He had bought several new suits and shoes and had a new set of upmarket name cards made which designated him as "The Director" of the Mereleigh Record Club Tour.

His wife did not particularly like the changes in him through this reinvention of his personality. He had become more arrogant and vain, took to spending more time at karaoke and nightclub 'Snack Bars' which had hostesses, but he was not earning anything from this as far as she could see, but clearly dining out on other people's expense accounts. It was obvious, he told her, that a lot of people wanted the Mereleigh people to visit their shops or clubs and some just wanted to meet them. Nomura-san had told his wife in the end there should be enough money for a good holiday in Britain and that might lead to bigger things.

At Fukuoka City Hall there was a realisation that this could be a major promotion for the city especially when one of the Mayor's aides discovered the British Ambassador was doing a swing through Kyushu at the time.

'We must invite him to Fukuoka for the event,' the Mayor said.

'It's a she,' his aide pointed out

'Ooooh soo desu ka,' which by his tone translated into English as 'Bugger, how do we entertain a female ambassador?'

His aide pointed out how 20 years ago a predecessor of his had hosted the lady Mayor from Auckland, Dame

Catherine Tizard, when the sister city relationship was formed. The aide said she was a good sport and would go almost anywhere! The Mayor still held a few reservations and requested his staff pull out the file on Dame Catherine's visit and use that as a model. He was then reminded that the current Mayor of Auckland might also like to be around then as the film promoted New Zealand a lot.

'We need a very big communications budget for this,' the Mayor stated, envisaging lavish entertainment at the ratepayers' expense which would give him a chance to invite all his major political supporters along.

Every country has a word or words to cover the cost of big business lunches and wining and dining clients. In Japan most organisations liked the term 'communications', for it sounded like phone bills and transport costs and not huge traditional dinners at upmarket Japanese restaurants followed by late night drinks and karaoke at exclusive clubs with glamorous hostesses.

Miss Winsome Alsop-Smith, the British Ambassador, was suitably impressed by the invitation and was vaguely aware some people connected with the film would be going to Fukuoka. She had seen the film and quite liked it as it was her era. Similarly, the Auckland Mayor's office also saw an opportunity too good to miss so decided to send the Mayor and Mayoress, plus a city promotions manager and a personal assistant for the Mayor.

Back at Mereleigh, Andy and his group had little idea of what they were letting themselves in for. He was still receiving letters via the UK film company from Nomura-san and, as time elapsed, the letters and questions became more demanding and frequent. It started with about one letter every 14 days then one every seven days and he and Fran would need to record the contents and respond.

At first it was just to confirm their arrival and departure times and arrangements at Fukuoka and how many twin and single rooms would be required plus any special meal requests. Then the inquiries became more detailed, listing a whole range of meetings and visits each day above and beyond the actual fundraising concert and official meetings with the Prefectural Governor and the Mayor.

Nomura-san had observed the Mereleigh group's request for sightseeing which would include the Arita pottery village, Nokonoshima Island with its traditional cherry orchards and magnificent harbour view, and a visit to Daizaifu Shrine with its thousand year old camphor trees, and beautiful wooded hills. They would go to the city's famed museum and see relics of Kublai Khan's failed invasion attempts of Japan which took place at Hakata Bay, and many other places.

Their sightseeing plus the official concert and two local government meetings seemed to create a rather full itinerary in itself, Andy and Fran thought, but more and more requests came in. Nomura-san would like them to have dinner with this sponsor and lunch with another and always stressed how important it was. Then there were the service clubs: Rotary, Lions etc who expected to see them.

After two months of correspondence Fran and Andy were at their limits both handling inquiries, which were now directed to Fran by email from the young female translator Nomura-san had set up, and also trying to accommodate still more requests for meetings and visits, all of which Nomura-san said were vital to the success of the visit.

'They must have an army of people organising this. I just can't imagine how a small outfit like ours in Japan could go to all this trouble on our behalf, or have the pull to arrange so much, but I have to say it's really well over the top and we must call a halt to any more requests, Fran,' Andy instructed firmly.

'My sentiments entirely, in fact I am sure most of our members will be aghast at how little free time we actually have for things like shopping,' she said.

'Thank God they have not discovered we will go to Tokyo first and have a week to ourselves before we get to Fukuoka,' Andy said.

'Err.. I am not so sure that they don't know,' Fran admitted.

'Why?' Andy snapped back.

'Well yesterday their young translator lady, Nishimura-san, asked for our arrival and departure flight details in Japan and I had to give the London Tokyo flight and date, and explain we would travel to Fukuoka by the bullet train after visiting a few places,' she explained with growing doubt about the consequences in her voice.

'For God's sake tell them we are absolutely totally committed during that period. You can make out it's associated with film company work of a hush-hush nature or something, anything to give us a breather and time to our-

~ The Mereleigh Record Club Tour of Japan

selves in Japan,' he advised vigorously.

'You know this has become a full time job for me,' Fran said in exasperation.

'What worries me is how our members will take all these new activities and visits at Fukuoka. It's best we don't give them the full itinerary yet and at the next meeting we will let drop verbally that Nomura-san has requested we include "a few" other items. It's grown like Topsy and we cannot dishonour the things we have already agreed to. Frankly, I must blame myself, I had no idea we had agreed to so many things until we put the itinerary together today,' Andy exclaimed.

'You know, Rick told us they will expect you to make speeches at every major meeting and function and at my rough count that will be about two dozen in the time we are there,' Fran pointed out. Andy groaned. 'I really don't mind one or two, let's spread this task around and get a couple of the others to do some of the talking,' he instructed her.

Jill and John Blount, the most athletic members of the group, had insisted everyone brush up on a few modest rock and roll steps and also learn a few songs to sing as a choir. They had learned the Japanese always sang and it would be expected of them. Andy tried desperately to resist this but fought a losing battle over the weeks. They decided on the Beatles' 'Yellow Submarine' as an opener as it was simple, and everyone could join in the chorus, Jim Reeves' 'Welcome to my World' and John Lennon's 'Imagine,' as it had peace and international connotations and there was the Yoko Ono connection.

Jill wanted them to sing the old Japanese classic 'Sukiyaki' but Andy hastily added he was sure the Japanese would sing that so they should not steal the thunder of their hosts. Andy had raised the subject of singing again with Fran in the hope he could change her mind and get Jill and John to drop the idea. He got a curt 'certainly not' from Fran and thereafter resigned himself to the inevitable.

It was about 6pm on a dark winter's night, and Janine came in with a large single malt whisky for Andy and a G and T for Fran. 'Here, you chaps look as though you need this. It can't be all that bad,' she said cheerfully.

CHAPTER 3

On a clear, crisp spring morning, members of the Mereleigh Record Club made their way to Andy and Janine's house for a final meeting and briefing before setting off to Japan. The members had not heard a lot from Andy, or Fran, in the last few weeks but had been posted dossiers a few centimetres thick with tour details and plenty of heavy ink at the beginning reminding them of the check-in time at London Airport for the Japan Airlines flight and the need to bring their passports etc. Fran had thought of waiting until they arrived before giving them the dossiers but felt it best they arrived fully briefed so any questions could be answered.

Andy greeted them and started the meeting by briefing them on the financial situation, saying all was in order. The group as such owed no money, the small working fund to cover postage, etc had been covered, the

Japanese had asked then to purchase their own airfares and pass the invoice to them, which had been done, and all the tickets were ready for distribution including vouchers and Japan rail passes for the seven-day tour.

The Fukuoka hosts had passed on to them discount vouchers to visit Space World at Kitakyushu before going to Fukuoka as it was en route and their hosts said it would take a bit of pressure off the crammed itinerary at Fukuoka. Andy actually used the word 'crammed' and that caused a minor uproar from the more diligent members who had actually read the Fukuoka section of the itinerary and realised how jam-packed it was.

Fran adroitly intervened, saying as this was being paid for they really had to go along with it, and stressed how much time and effort she and Andy had to put in to get everything sorted. Clearly she would not agree to any changes. Most of the group were well aware of her efforts, and quietened the others down. They said they were sure it would all be fine.

Rick, who had returned to New Zealand with Maggie, had e-mailed the group saying when and where they would join them, and said he had been in touch with Herewini and Chris. Chris, he said, was unable to make the tour because of other commitments. On the other hand Herewini was conveniently going to be on some Customs familiarisation in Japan at the time, and felt he might be able to get some leave. He said he would definitely be at Fukuoka and might be able to get to Tokyo earlier, but not to worry if he did not front up at Tokyo.

Fran read out a tit bit from Rick's email about the godwits which flew between his place at Mangawhai, New

Zealand, and Fukuoka en route to Siberia and Alaska each year.

'They leave Mangawhai about mid March each year which is autumn for Siberia and Alaska and return to Mangawhai about September. It seems they feed like crazy for a week or so before they depart, and their vital organs, kidneys, liver etc shrink to make space for more body fat which they burn off in flight. The amazing thing is they shut down half of their brains at a time to rest while still flying and when they arrive they sort of crash land because they have not used their legs for a while and they are so exhausted.

'Just imagine it, all that way in just a few days. We may be able to see some on the mud flats at Fukuoka, Rick says.'

The information drew a few amazed gasps from the group, and Peter cut in.

'I knew that. I actually saw them on the sand dunes at Mangawhai on our trip to New Zealand when I went for a walk with Rick.'

'Bet you didn't know they went to Fukuoka though!' Fran was not going to let him get away with this smug-ness. Peter just shrugged his shoulders and concentrated on his sushi, the rest of the afternoon having been given over for a late lunch at a Japanese restaurant. Foggy and Helena found the Japanese restaurant a bit of a trial, as once they eliminated shellfish and pork from the menu, it left just chicken and beef items to eat.

'I had an email from Rick and he mentioned the night life area of Fukuoka called Nakasu, sounds interesting. I reckon that Dick and I will have to make a few morality patrols there to make sure the good citizens of Fukuoka are behaving themselves,' Perry grinned.

'You and your morality patrols! All you want to do is ogle at those hostesses in split skirts,' his wife Jean chided.

'No, Jean, it's the Chinese girls that have the split skirts. They have geishas in Japan, you known, all bundled up in some sexless garb like a cracker on a Christmas tree. You can't even see what their faces are like because they are all plastered with white make up,' Dick pointed out.

'Japanese nightclub hostesses wear short skirts and when they bend over you can just about see their nameplates,' Derek the ex-sailor said with glee, obviously recalling some youthful memories.

'And he would know, he went to Japan when he was at sea and God knows what he got up to!' his wife Ann exclaimed with a toss of her head.

'I am sure most of us will be more interested in seeing fine arts like Arita pottery, traditional paintings and ladies' tea ceremonies, and learning how to wear a kimono,' Andy rather stuffily intervened to alleviate some concern among the ladies that their men folk would all be going on brothel cruises.

'Not to mention ikebana and bonsai,' Peter added sarcastically.

⌘⌘⌘

The same day in Japan, Nomura-san planned to drive through some parts of the itinerary with one or two members, to simulate some of the key coach transfers and make sure enough time was being allowed for. He was not totally convinced the coach company being used had things properly estimated even though it had umpteen coaches doing these transfers every week in varying traffic!

Nomura-san was on a high and he was out to squeeze every scrap of glamour and enjoyment out of this event. He even imagined people recognised him in the street as he had been photographed by the local Nishi Nippon Shimbun newspaper and a couple of others as well as local TV stations. He did not realise it was his strange, cheesy grin that attracted attention, and not himself as such.

He had tipped off the Nishi Nippon Newspaper about the group arriving early in Tokyo but had sworn them to secrecy so they could get a sneak advance preview. He had arranged to go to Tokyo with his interpreter Nishimura-san in advance to greet them and the newspaper said it would pay his and Nishimura-san's airfare and hotel bill for one night in return. It occurred to him Nishimura-san might be won over to his charms and he might get a one night stand out of it.

Nishimura-san feared Nomura-san might press his charms so was a very reluctant starter and it was only after her boyfriend said he could get a couple of days off so they could have two nights together in Tokyo that she agreed. But she decided not to tell Nomura-san of this as she did not want him blabbing about her love life.

Rick had decided to skip some of the one day excursions planned to take place at Tokyo, which he had done many times before and make contact with a few Japanese friends. One of those, Hiromitsu Tanaka, was an old rugby mate from Fukuoka who said he would be in Tokyo on business and would be glad to see him as he had seen the film. Rick had spoken to Tanaka-san by phone which was always dangerous as Tanaka's English and Rick's Japanese were both shocking.

Rick said afterwards to Maggie, 'He is always a funny bugger. He said he could not recognise me in the film. I looked much younger so the make-up must have been good. He must have thought we played ourselves in the movie or is just piss-taking!'

'You look younger by the year to me dear,' Maggie replied.

Rick got a phone call from the Mayor's office at the Auckland City Council where an official had word from Fukuoka City   its sister city   about the Mereleigh tour and as Auckland was sending its Mayor over for the occasion it could be a good tourist promotion for New Zealand as the film was set in New Zealand. The Auckland Mayor's official pumped Rick for information. Rick said the whole Japanese hosting arrangements seemed somewhat over the top but there was bound to be some benefit for New Zealand. On that note the official thanked Rick for his help and hung up.

Rick only received one further message before he and Maggie left for Japan and that was two days before the trip and from his Welsh cousin at Berriew. His cousin Geoff Watkins told him a neighbour's adult daughter Jenny had gone to work in Tokyo and they had not heard from her for nearly two weeks. No texts, emails or phone calls.

It was totally out of character and they wondered if Rick could possibly try to track her down while he was there. She used to ring or regularly text her parents on her mobile phone, so it was a bit strange, Geoff explained. Her parents did not feel it quite urgent enough to contact the police but were scared to their wits' end for her safety.

'She is from Welshpool, you see. Her Mum is Welsh, of course, a Jones related to our Uncle Thomas by marriage and her Dad from Kenya where you used to live. She is 23 and has had one or two bit parts in TV serials but was resting or something when she had this offer for a song and dance job in Japan, so she took it.

'Her Mum said it seemed okay and the money was good and airfare prepaid so it was hard for her to refuse. Well, that is it really,' Geoff apologised for troubling him, asked after Maggie and kidded him about his cracking new girl friend. Maggie said, 'Here we go again!' when Rick told her and added, 'Whatever way you look at it's going to be an inconvenience, either big or small, but knowing you, you will not rest until you find her.'

Rick's mind flashed back to the body under the bed incident and wondered if there was a connection. It was commonly known that many of the so-called show biz entrepreneurs who recruited foreign artists and models were front men for Yakuza-owned sleazy hostess bars and prostitution outlets. Should he tell Geoff this and thus perhaps cause the girl's parents to worry even more? He had not told Geoff about the dead body incident and thankfully his name had not been published in the one or two brief stories about the suspicious death.

First things first, he would make some inquiries in

Japan and if Jenny was safe and sound it would be the end. If not then maybe he should pass that on to the police, but in any case if Jenny ended up being listed missing then he assumed the Welshpool police would think of the dead Japanese Yakuza and check it out to see if there was a link between the two.

That is what he decided to do but it did not sit comfortably with his conscience and would lead to a few sleepless nights. The alternative could be even more embarrassing, as everyone would tend to think he had been mixing with undesirable elements. He promised himself that he would contact Inspector Roberts in Wales if he could not track Jenny down

'I can imagine if it were my daughter all too well. I would be worried out of my skin. You better do your best Rick,' Maggie insisted shaking her head with concern.

'I met her once briefly when she was just a young teenager at Geoff's place and she has a great personality. I can't imagine her turning into some sort of tart,' Rick added.

'There is a thing that also worries me a lot. I have not been that frank with Geoff, or you, and if I tell you this you must not mention a word to anyone until, or if, I give the OK as I promised to keep quiet about it.'

'Fire away, I suspected there may be something more. Were you having it off with another woman at the hotel at the time?' Maggie smiled as she asked.

'It was a Japanese Yakuza gangster. He had lost the tell-tale end of a little finger which is a punishment they dish out if a mob member fails to execute a job properly.

He also had a business card for a nightclub in Fukuoka's red light district Nakasu.'

'Now what the heck was he doing at Newtown? Even the cops felt it was very unusual and then Geoff rings about Jenny. Am I to break police silence and tell Geoff who would tell her parents? Maybe it has nothing to do with this man and if it does maybe it would stuff up the police investigations. I don't know. Should I ring the Welshpool police and tell them about Jenny being missing? She went to Tokyo which is hundreds of miles away and maybe she is just having a great time and forgot about Mum and Dad for a week or so.'

Maggie thought hard and long while Rick scratched the back of his head in anxiety.

'It's not for you to tell Geoff something you promised the cops to keep quiet about, so that part is right. At this time Jenny's correspondence or phone calls are a bit overdue. Nothing too unusual in that, we all have kids who forget to contact us and have no idea how much we worry.'

'If her parents were really concerned they would have gone to the Welshpool police immediately. I think you have some time to make a check in Tokyo when we arrive. So take it from there,' Maggie said, squeezing his arm in reassurance.

⌘⌘⌘

The first part of Andy, Janine and Chuck's journey started with the Eurostar from St Pancras, London, and an ICE train express to Berlin, went like clockwork. Andy and Janine still could not get over just taking a train to Europe, and Chuck, who had been a GI in post-war Germany, called the Eurostar 'the Peace Train.'

The next trains were from Berlin to Poland and Moscow with a track gauge change on the Russian border. The carriages were hoisted up so that the narrower standard gauge bogies of European railways could be removed and the broader Russian gauge bogies attached as the carriages were lowered on top of them

Andy busied himself taking numerous photos of the operation disturbing and annoying folk around him who preferred to sleep.

'It's amazing, do you know Hitler wanted to establish a massive seven foot gauge from Europe to Asia that could take massive trains. That would have been even bigger than Brunel's broad gauge in England in Victorian times!' he exclaimed.

Janine yawned, Chuck was impressed, 'Gee that would have been something else.'

Hours later as their train pulled into Moscow Chuck pulled out two pocket sized Berlitz foreign Language books.

'I got these to help me with the lingo. This here one is 'Japanese for Travellers' and the other 'Russian for Travellers'. All the sections are colour coded for food, medical help, travel directions and you don't have to speak the words as the text is in both languages and you ca just point to a phrase in English and the equivalent text is alongside in Russian or Japanese, as the case may be,' he said proudly.

'I guess I am going to try out the Russian one soon,' he added clearly looking forward to bridging the language gap al Berlitz.

'Well show him what you had Andy,' Janine smiled smugly.

'Oh it's a state of the art electronic voice activated translator, or EVAT. Do you see its about the size of the Berlitz pocket book you have there and it can take photos as well like a mobile phone,' he brandished a small box containing the EVAT around.

'Open it up Andy so we can see it. He just bought it at London before we left and we hav'n't used it yet,' Janine explained.

'Once we get off the train I will use it to ask directions to a taxi and then to instruct the taxi driver to our hotel,' Andy pocketed the unopened box contained EVAT.

They hauled off their luggage on to the station platform Chuck could see a sign which indicated where taxis and busses were parked.

'Say Andy no need for EVAT the taxis are over there somewhere,' Chuck pointed in the general direction of the taxi sign.

'No Chuck I insist I must try it out in safe territory, so to speak, to test its accuracy. I forgot to say it has a GPS capability as well,' Andy added proudly.

'But we know where we are,' Chuck protested.

'Let him have a go Chuck, we will not have any peace until he does,' Janine knew from experience that nothing would stop him from using his new toy now.

Andy painstakingly removed it from its box and from layers of plastic packing pulled out the instructions and spent at least five minutes reading them as the other train passengers rapidly dispersed.

'I have got it now its quite simple it a touch job so if I touch here and get English, and then there to get the subject and scroll down to the phrase I want, hey presto I am there. Look here this is the phrase "where are the taxis please?' Andy had the grin of a five year old on his face, opening a Christmas present.

Andy looked for a victim among the now almost people less platform, to practise EVAT on. He sighted a lone drunk slumped in a seat nursing a brown paper bag.

He strode up to the drunk in such a determined manner that it sobered him up for a moment thinking Andy might be the secret police coming to take him away. The drunk was on his feet ready to bolt for it when Andy who was at least a foot taller penning in against the wall and said in slow load tones to EVAT 'Please tell me where the taxis are?'

EVAT emitted a rather high pitched female voice making the request in Russian. Andy had a slightly smug smile on his face.

The drunk clearly shocked at being spoken to by a tiny electronic EVAT blethered out an incomprehensible drunken sort of pleading response, judging from his body language.

EVAT responded with a short Russian question, or what Andy took to be a question. There was another mangled reply from the drunk which prompted EVAT to ask the same question.

Andy, Janine and Chuck were now merely bystanders to a conversation between the drunk and EVAT. Chuck started shifting around with impatience.

'I would like to use a toilet fairly soon,' he told Andy.

Andy by now quite annoyed at being excluded from the conversation, '; Snapped back' Chuck, pal, just hang on a second and we will get the answer,'

'We know the answer, the taxis are` over there, "Janine pointed the sign out to Andy.

'OK leave it to me,' Andy braced himself to take command of his rogue EVAT. He switched it off.

Andy closed in on the drunk and shouted

'Where are the Taxis?'

The drunk crouched in fear of being hit, and pleadingly pointed to the taxi sign.

'Well why the hell didn't you tell EVAT that, for God's sake?' Andy shouted.

At that point a Russian who had quietly watched the proceedings stepped forward, and in faultless English said.

'Mr Englishman I think if you check you machine it may say it could not understand this man's reply because he is too drunk to speak properly. Even I can not understand him,' the Russian spectator explained as he started to walk away shrugging hi shoulders.

'But he understood me when I spoke to him in English,' Andy protested.

'No you are wrong you looked at the taxi sign when

you spoke and everyone in this world understands Taxi and he only pointed to the taxi sign when he replied to you,' the Russian spectator decided to quit and walked off in disgust at a brisk pace.

'Not bad for our first encounter with Russians on their home territory Andy. A ridiculous conversation with a drunk and then you upset a friendly Russian trying to help us,' Janine picked up her bags and headed to the taxi at a risk pace.

'Lets go I am bursting for a pee first,' Chuck was already at the gallop towards a public toilet.

'I have got it sussed now,' he told Janine at 11 pm on their first night at Moscow. You see I have the drunk's reply translated and I will just touch the screen here and EVART says, wait for it:- 'I can not understand you,' and repeats that several times because EVART could not comprehend the drunk's Russian.'

'Then EVART tells me his answer is incomprehensible. I should have hung on a moment or two and it would have all been explained quite logically by EVART,' Andy was satisfied now that his translator was not a dud.

'You should have had more sense than trying to make sense out of a conversation with a drunk. Now put the dammed thing away and get some sleep,'

The trio had elected to take the Rossiya train from Moscow's Yaroslavski station.

'It takes seven days to get to Vladivostok via Mongolia and Beijing and we travel 9,258 kilometers (or 6,152 miles) via half a dozen Russian cities including Omsk, Novosibirsk and Irkutsk, then into Mongolia, and over the border to China with another carriage bogie change on entering China on its standard `Chinese railway gauge track, and a stop at Erlian. A few nights in Beijing and then on to Vladivostok,' Andy beamed with enthusiasm.

'And we have a four berth compartment to ourselves.'

Chuck took an instant liking to the Trans Siberian.

'This is a real living train. It is a something else, more like the old long distant trains of yore back in the age of steam in the USA, more second class than first class but a great stuff,'

'Look as I said it's a corridor and compartment job, bunks, a bar a restaurant,' Andy glowed with excitement as they boarded their reserved compartment,

'I hope the toilets are clean. That is my main worry, and that we do not have to deal with any drunks, those are my concerns,' Janine cast a critical eye over her new surroundings.

'Andy could endure hell on wheels so long as the wheels ran on a railway line Chuck, so you and I are dealing with a person with impaired judgement on this train ride,'

'Well that is a great way of putting it and I admit I'm an addict too, but I am not impervious to the feelings of others so if we guys get carried away just give me the nod and we will settled down,' Chuck reassured her with a smile.

The big train clawed though the Moscow suburbs and then hit its pace in the open country maintaining a steady sedate speed of yesteryear rather than the breakneck speed of the French TVGV, and Japanese Shinkansen.

A walk through the train revealed the vast majority of travellers were ordinary Russians, and citizens of the former Soviet Union, a mix of rather Nordic Slavs, and dark featured folk who originated around the Black Sea revealing perhaps ancient Greek and Persian ancestry , Turks, and the blended features of Asia and Europe among those who came from the lands not too far west of Mongolia and China.

'There is a rhythm to life on board a trans-continental train.' Chuck explained, ' One of the tricks is to be able to identify folk who could become bores , the dishonest and others who were good company.'

'The folk on this train aren't your high powered business men or Government officials. Those guys jet around the place like our business guys do. I guess most of the passengers are poorer people relocating or taking a holiday to see relations and some like us tourists. See how they like to keep some of their own food and many are keen to share it out. Just watch the Vodka flow.'

'Chuck you are truly a keen observer,' Janine noted.

As the train rattled across Russia. They drank vodka almost every evening with a case-hardened old soldier called Boris who had been a brigadier in the Red Army during the Cold War years. He was a great huggy bear of a man whose permanent equipment in life was a large hip flask of vodka, and a much travelled battered guitar. Boris had been groomed for a military translation job because of his good English, in addition to being a fighting soldier in a missile battalion, in addition to his role as officer in a missile battalion.

'If we got something from the KGB on American missiles they could not understand I had to translate it. If they wanted a military voice to broadcast something to the west I was one of those voices. Nobody wants old soldiers in Russia any more but because I know a lot they have sentenced me to Siberia,' he quipped with a broad smile, just to keep me out of circulation while the ex KGB crooks cut the business deals for themselves,' he grinned.

'You mean you are under punishment and making your own way to some penal institution?' Chuck asked in amazement.

'Not quite like that, my friend. It's more subtle, a bit like the Mafia. They offer me a job I can't refuse, but it's not all bad. I will be working for some international trading organisation at Vladivostok as its export manager and I get a regular salary. You see I don't know any national secrets, only people, and as you say "where the bodies are buried" and how they became rich. Who cares about state secrets, nobody these days, but there are very many who care about their own histories because their past could kill them if the truth came out.'

'They told me I don't have to do much, mostly entertain overseas customers, drink vodka, talk nicely and make sure our customers have the best girls in town. If that is what they want.'

'Can they trust you on your own?' Chuck was intrigued.

'Of course not, even now there is some creep on this train in our carriage who watches me and he will have photographed all of us together. There will be a plant at the company in my office who will be there to see I do not disclose any personal secrets.' He roared with laughter as though it was the biggest joke in the world.

'You're joking!' Chuck felt he had been taken in.

Boris gave Chuck a stern glassy look of a kind he reserved for enemies and fools and it left no doubts that he was deadly serious. 'In the old days it was obvious, there was a Communist Commissar to make sure we all believed in the idealogy and did nothing to shake it. Now it's almost undercover with one ex KGB millionaire or another guarding their pot of gold and using their own spooks as protection.'

'Ok, ok, I believe you,' Chuck was on the retreat and beginning to understand some things had never changed in Russia.

'I am sorry, I did not want to offend you, Chuck. Compared to the West, Russia is still a very tough country for ordinary people and if we have been near the top in the military we have to be very careful. Why are you travelling via Beijing when you could go direct to Vladivostok, or fly?' Andy quizzed him.

'Like you I want to see a bit more of the world I have never been to Beijing and my travel allowance is sufficient for the diversion , and I want to se if the Chinese ladies live up to their reputations,' Boris winked at Janine, who did not appear that amused at the comment. Chuck and Andy laughed.

'That is easy enough to understand. Well I for one believe you, Boris, and I pride myself on being a very good judge of character,' Chuck said.

'And that goes for the rest of us. I can't imagine a KGB man carrying a guitar around unless it was a machine gun or something, why don't you strum a few cords for us?' Janine chimed in putting an end to that line of conversation.

'I would have expected you to have a balalaika, not a guitar,' she added.

'I play the balalaika too but for Russian music. The guitar is more international and the musical symbol of 'flower power' and the age of hippies and make love not war,' he explained. 'I think the guitar is much better for playing Bob Dylan protest songs, don't you?'

Boris knocked out Russian perennials like the 'Volga Boat Song' and 'Midnight in Moscow,' on his remarkably well-tuned guitar. 'Me, I really like the American pop songs.'

'What's your favourite? Chuck asked.

'It has to be "Hotel California".'

'Can you play it?' Chuck threw down a challenge he knew Boris would have to accept, and would probably accomplish with the prowess of a professional guitarist. The old battered guitar had rendered up those notes a thousand times before, and was played with such expertise you could close your eyes and imagine the Eagles' lead guitarist Joe Walsh was up there up on the big stage pumping it out to a fanatic horde of fans. Boris was no Glenn Frey though, but he made a workman-like job of the lyrics, enough not to mar the excellence of his guitar playing.

'Hell, that's good, really good Boris. Even accounting

for the damned train noise. In another age you could have been an American pop star,' Chuck tailed off misty-eyed.

'It's one of those tunes that really gets to me,' he apologised.

'Do you like the Beatles' 'Back in the USSR?' Janine asked.

'Oh yes, the Beatles were very popular here, they came to Moscow of course and were so irreverent about Western Governments. We adored them. Well, "Back in the USSR" was a bit funny to us as we already knew our society and Communism was not so adorable then.

'Boris that's enough, you probably need some sleep like us' Andy hinted.

Then she added. 'Keep you energy for tomorrow and the remaining week we will spend together on this train.

That is, unless you want to spend tonight and every other night of this journey entertaining us 'Janine hoped Boris would take her hint.'

'It's no problem to me I can sing and drink all night and every night. It's how we pass the time on long train journeys and dark winter nights at home.'

She whispered to Andy,' see what you have let us in for! Listening to drunken yodelling Russians, toasting every Russian train there ever was and all the girls they ever knew, in over-proof vodka.'

Boris caught the drift. 'Tonight you need rest after your journey to Russia but tomorrow it will be full on!' He roared at his own joke made a point of picking up the nearly totally s consumed vodka bottle and went to his cabin.

'The biggest worry I have is Andy getting proposi-tioned by a Russian tart when he goes to the toilet at night' Janine joked trying to break the ice as the two men were clearly disappointed at having the evenings drink-ing cut short.

'Yeah, he seems to need to go more frequently than before,' Chuck replied with a grin.

The comments were met with stony silence from Andy.

Boris returned every night with a fresh bottle of vodka to be consumed and his guitar at the ready.

The days, conversations, and impressions, shared Russian meals, forests, tundra, lakes, mountains and the changing faces of the east as oriental features became more common at stations, all rolled in the accompani-ment, accompanied by much Russian singing, drinking and story telling. For much of the journey Janine was con-tent to window-gaze at the passing scenery while read-ing her book and listening to her I Pod and the conversation of others.

A day before the train left Russia and entered Mongo-lia Boris appeared at their cabin door looking anxious and distant and sat down quietly. He left after about ten min-utes saying he had to get his papers ready.

'I hope we have not offended him Chuck,'

'I don't think so Andy, but like you I note a change in his demeanour,' Chuck responded scratching his balding head.

'I can't leave on unfriendly terms I will ask him what's up but let me choose the moment, and I will do it by myself,' Andy insisted.

The opportunity presented itself when Andy went off to the toilet that evening and bumped into Boris. They came together as though Boris was also very anxious to talk to Andy so Andy let him take the lead.

'I need your help, in fact a group of people need your help right now Andy but promise me you will do nothing until you get home or into a safe Country.'

'Yes of course, you can depend on me 100 per cent,' the moment he said it Andy had some misgivings. This was a very rash commitment God knows what Boris was involved in. Andy took a deep breath knowing he would go through with what ever Boris wanted.

'First up I want to borrow your EVART until I leave the train and I want you to take a sealed letter and documents to a British Diplomatic Post. What ever you do, do not let either items out of your sight as in the wrong hands it will mean the death of about 50 people. Don't tell the others about this until you have safely delivered the items.'

Andy could feel the hairs on the back of his head rise and his heart started to race, but he nodded instantly in agreement and looked furtively up and down the train corridor.

Andy probed the deep pocket of his photographers jacket and hauled out EVART and slipped it onto Boris' hands, 'I will tell the others it was stolen if they ask me where it is.'

Boris slapped him on the back and in a theatrical whisper announced that he would share his vodka with them that night and then confided that he may have to leave the train before it crossed into Mongolia.

Andy returned to the shared compartment and told the other two, it seems he has been a bit off colour but will be with us tonight for drinks.

'That is hardly unexpected considering the amount of Vodka he drinks. Don't think you are getting into bad habits Andy. You're bad enough to deal when sober yet alone drunk!'

Chuck winked at Andy who to Chuck's surprise winked back.

The evening's drinking was serious and desperate on Boris' part, everyone could see Boris was under some sort of pressure, and Janine told a very drunk Andy when she had at last got him into his bunk at about 3 am, that in her view Boris was very worried about something, not sick!

The train started to slow as it approached the Russian frontier station of Naushiki and a very ashen and hung over Andy wended his way to the toilet,

'You look like a vulture's breakfast my friend, the Russian accented voice right in his left ear was accompanied by an overpowering wiff of Vodka and cigars.

'Boris you old bastard don't give me a heart attack,' Andy responded.

'This is important EVART is back in your pocket and also a package. You are unlikely to be searched by the border police today. I have to leave the train at this stop do not wave to me and if the others do I shall ignore them. If all goes well I will see you in London in six months time,'

Boris was gone before Andy could turn around and

face him and the EVART was in his pocket along with a long envelope.

The magnitude of what he was doing frightened him. He had been bloody reckless in agreeing to this. Boris may be a Russian mafia man. This could be an international drug transfer or part of a plan.

He felt compelled to tell, Janine and Chuck but a sixth sense prevented him from doing so.

Janine said he looked dreadful, when he came back from the toilet.

'I chucked up in the toilet and have a huge headache so just talk to me in dulcet tones today and don't let anything fall over or go bang,' he pleaded

Chuck smiled tolerantly. 'We will handle you with kid gloves. I guess Boris is also pretty sick too. He drank like a condemned man!'

The train started to coast under its own momentum and then driver gently applied apply the big express's brakes as the trio prepared themselves for a passport and general immigration check at the border station as it clattered over the station's complex points system of interconnecting rails .

Andy decided he would hold EVART and place the package among some travel books in his large suitcase. He hoped like hell there was no LSD or other chemical for making drugs in deliberately soaked into the package. Boris had hand written Andy's his name in full on the package.

As the train ground to a halt there was the usual exchange of passengers but those getting off were handled first and then the documents of those remaining on board checked as a team of immigration officials went through the carriages.

To his relief they were only interested in their passports and making sure the holders of the passports were the persons depicted inside them. They answered a couple of questions about where they were from, and going, to satisfied the officials that the trio were tourists.

'You're sweating like a stuck pig Andy, what's up got a fever?'

'No Chuck, may be it's a bit warmer,' Andy noticed his hands were sweaty and there were beads of perspiration on his brow and he was slightly shaking at the knees with nervous tension.'

'He's ok Chuck, he gets these panic attacks at the sight of a mouse in the kitchen,' Janine gave Andy a studied look and wondered if he was working up for a heart attack.

'Hey I thought I saw Boris out on the platform with a group of men and they were pretty ugly customers.' Chuck was visibly concerned, and the others rushed to the window to see the small group with the back of a person of Boris's build being ushered away.

They were bunched together but the bunching itself was the give away. No one walks that close to someone unless they wanted to force the captive to go where they wanted him to go and from a glance at the food word Andy caught sight of Boris' familiar winter boots and they were almost off the ground.

'The bastards are carrying him off. Christ what shall

we do,' Andy implored them.

'For God's sake don't get out of the train Andy, or you may be next!' Janine was clearly traumatised by it all

'My God I hope it's not him. It does not look good at all,' Andy struggled for a better view from the carriage window.

'Shit it is, how long is the stop at this station?' Andy pleaded with the others.

'Its probably going to be at least 15 to 30 minutes as we are a bit ahead of schedule, but don't even thing about it Andy! Those toughs would smash us up in a few seconds and then we would probably find ourselves in the local jail on an assault charge,' Chuck said calmly.

'I have been through a war and I can tell you there are times you can help and times when you darned well can't. This is the saddest thing I have seen for a long while' Chuck was rock solid with his advice, ' We like the guy, we had great fun and enjoyed his company but what the hell do we really know about him and what's more we could end up in strife with the Russian police or whoever they are, mafia etc,'

'I agree and…..' a large loco shunting railway stock on another line drowned her out as it passed their carriage. 'I was going to say this is not our country we know absolutely nothing about it so leave sleeping dogs lie,' Janine was visibly distressed

Andy had mixed feelings of guilt and power knowing he probably held the key to Boris' problems in the packet but he was not going to let Boris down now.

It was now even more important that he god the package through to the British Embassy at Beijing.

The fact that he could do something calmed him down and he knew the last thing Boris would have wanted was for him to join the fray and then get caught with the package on him. That is why Boris did not want them to fuss over his departure and why he did not turn back to wave to them he guessed what might have been in store for him

'He is a professional,' Andy said with clear admiration.

'What do you mean professional. Professional what? He has got himself into a huge mess and that is not very professional,' Janine stated the obvious.

'How do you mean professional Andy?' Chuck was surprised at the quick change in Andy's attitude.

Without wanting to give anything away Andy said.

'He told us not to farewell him and he did not look back once at us, when he could have, when those toughs first approached him. I am sure he wanted to protect us and keep us from suspicion. We must all have been photographed drinking with him by what ever spooks were on the train watching him.'

Janine shivered at the though. 'We have done nothing wrong we only talked, drank and sang songs.'

'I tell you what. I did not want to mention it before, but I am reasonable sure someone has been through my suitcase. There is nothing missing but it is not as I packed it. I am sure you guys have not touched it but it must have happened in the last 12 hours,' Chuck said.

'Better check your cases to,' Chuck added.

'There is no point in Andy doing it, his is always a mess and I am sure he could not tell one mess from another.' She added.

Mine is locked and…. my goodness look at this, some bugger has had a go at the lock but it still closed.

Andy felt a temptation to tell them about the package but managed to hold out.

'This is very serious stuff we must all be very careful.' He knew he would give to find a temporary hiding place for the package in the cabin in case the Russian Mafia did their bags over again. He had a better idea and decided he would tape the package to his inside left thigh with a roll of first aid sticking plaster they had brought with them.

'Come let's have a nip of whiskey to wish Boris luck, and calm ourselves down. Regard it as being for medicinal purposes.' He managed a thin smile, and started to pour out three generous tots.

The great train tooted and started to roll forward as the carriage bogies started up a progressively escalating clatter running over the complex points system beneath their wheels.

'We are going to miss him,' Janine sobbed.

'Yes the hell we are, but he is a tough buzzard and let's not give up hope.' Chuck added.

'I wonder if he has a wife and kids.' Janine asked.

'I would wager he has a lady some where and maybe a few others in his life and most likely some adult kids.' Chuck added.

Well I am going to make out a full account of this now

while my mind is fresh,' Janine said.

'That would be about the worst thing you could do if someone finds it on you we will become witnesses and that could place us at risk,' Andy was beginning to fell exasperated by it all

'Well I shall write it up in Pitman Shorthand and they will not understand it,' Janine said determined that she would not be over ruled.

'For Christ's sakes the Russians have the best code breakers in the bloody world they would sort out Pitman's Shorthand in a couple of flaming minutes," Andy shouted.

'Calm down Andy this cabin may be bugged,' Chuck warned them.

They were all silent for a minute or two contemplating their own situation if it was.

Janine wrote a note on a sheet of paper and passed it around. It read 'What shall we do?'

Andy wrote down ' If it were not so serious it would be as funny as ' Faulty Towers' and added 'We should stop talking about the matter until we get off the train at Beijing and as a foot note added ' If we make it.'

Chuck picked up the note and added 'Agreed but who is going to eat this note?'

Janine smiled as she wrote, 'I will screw it up and throw it out the window, or flush it down the toilet. I have to go to the loo now.'

Andy was thinking thank God I did not mention the package to anyone and trying to convince himself that even if they had bugged the cabin they may leaved them alone knowing they could risk international attention if any harm came to them and they probably could not influence the course of events planned for Boris.

Having disposed of the note Janine came back looking more relaxed and proceeded to write up her Pitman Shorthand account of the happenings.

The train rolled relentlessly through the huge rather monotonous scenery of Mongolia, and several stops could not dispel the gloom shared by Andy, Janine and Chuck. Andy continued to fight a huge urge to tell the others about the secret package. He placated his urge by telling them he was absolutely sure the three of them would be able to see some sort of justice was done.

Janine and Chuck looked at him in total disbelief.

'He lives in fantasy land much of the time," Janine smiled at Chuck in a patronising fashion.

'With due respect what happened is well out of our depth, and influence, do you think those bandits who did this to Boris could be forced to take note of what little we saw and knew about Boris?' Chuck said looking at Andy in disbelief and a degree of despair.

The more varied scenery of China raised their spirits, and the outgoing Chinese passengers welcomed a chance to speak English to them, and eagerly exchanged some tasty Chinese food.

As they neared Beijing the full extent of the modernisation of China's railways became apparent as high speed 'Bullet' trains became common. The first glimpse of Beijing's railway station was of its massive mushroom shaped super dome top with a maze of rail lines entering it from below.

'Of course they got the technology for these 'bullet' trains from Germany. They are based on its Ice Trains,' Andy could not resist imparting his knowledge on all things to do with railways, 'but I must admit the sheer size of the station takes your breath away. You could accommodate about 20 St Pancras Stations under that huge dome.'

'We sure will have to get our platforms right when we leave here for Vladisvtok. They must have a hundred of them,' Chuck shook his head in astonishment.

Andy reached in his clothes to reassure himself that he still had Boris's package His next problem would be to find a reason to visit the British Embassy by himself as per Boris's instruction and not let any one know about it.

That had to be his first assignment at Beijing.

"I shall also need your shorthand notes Janine.'

'What on earth for?' Janine demanded

'I think your shorthand notes would be of interest to the British Embassy and I feel I have to make a statement to them.

'He mad, he has gone completely mad Chuck. He has these moments of self delusion.

'You now it may help a bit,' added Chuck, 'so let's all go together.'

Andy realised he had to be careful how he responded.

'Chuck old pal why should you and Janine give up half a day of our very brief time here at Beijing to do a small thing I can do by myself. I insist that you and Janine stick to the tour plan and I will link up later. If they want to see us all then I will let you know.' His tone indicated and end to the discussion and Janine

'Now this is getting plain daft but if you insist you can take my note book while Chuck and I find a local market near this hotel, and do some sightseeing.'

Andy did not use his EVART to call for a taxi knowing that Boris would have left an important message on it and anyway there were always taxis outside the hotel and a hotel doorman told the driver where to go.

He arrived at the Embassy unannounced and it took about 15 minutes to see some one of reasonable importance, he had second secretary status and introduced himself in a slightly bored way as John Russel.

'Nice to meet you Jack…..,' John Russel cut in, 'No its John. Jack Russel is the dog.'

'Oh sorry no offence meant I am tired and I have a very important package for you from a former Russian Army Officer I met on the train and he left a message on my EVART. They killed him almost in front of our eyes,' Sandy's voice was torn with anger and emotion and he was visibly shaking.

John Russel noted his emotional state. 'I can see you are very concerned about this but I warn you there are very sever limitations as to what we at the Foreign Office can do about domestic injustices in Russia and unfortunately murder or what ever it was is rather common in Russia now…'

'Yes yes I know that but to cut to the chase please open

and read this package and then lets see what is on my EVART,' Andy emplored him.

John Russel opened the fat package in a slightly disdainful manner but as he started to read his interest and excitement rapidly increased.

'Have you read this and do you know what it's about?'

'No, all that Boris told us was that he knew the secret histories of many KGB men who were now part of the Russian mafia. His very words were 'I know where the bodies are buried' and they keep an eye on me. He was supposed to be going to Vladivostok to take up a new job and then suddenly decided to leave the train at Naushikji and was taken by force on the platform by some thugs.

Andy passed on Janine's shorthand note book.

'Well I don't read shorthand but I believe we have a senior lady in our Library who does so we can get her to translate it.'

'Now can I look at your VERT thing? The package has a note saying there should be an info chip hidden in it.'

'I am not sure there is any room in it for any foreign article like a chip. '

Andy carefully opened it and immediately spotted a chip delicately inserted.

'Can you leave the whole thing with us for the night and we will get an expert to check it all out?'

'Yes, but please ignore the recording of a conversation with a drunken Russian at Moscow. It has nothing to do with Boris I can assure you,'

'Of course we will respect your privacy. Please do not mention this to anyone else.'

'No even my wife and friend Chuck?'

"If you can trust them to keep silent it's probably ok but we don't want to put you in the Russian mafia spotlight. They have long tentacles. I don't suppose you know if you were followed here or to your hotel from the train?'

Andy suddenly felt like a hunted animal. 'No I don't think so but we did spend a lot of time drinking with Boris on the train and that would not have escaped notice by anyone plotting to get him. We are sure someone went through some of our luggage and they may have bugged our cabin.' He added.

'Well we have someone here who can keep an eye on you and hire a few locals for surveillance if necessary, but keep it under your hat,'

'Don't come back here again unless it's necessary I will have your VERT thing delivered to your hotel by hand and as they say in the theatre world, 'don't call us we will call you.'

'How do you define 'necessary' Jack?'

'The name is John! Well you could take an Oxford Dictionary definition of necessary but I think you are an intelligent man and would not bother us unless it was vital!'

"Yes and sorry about Jack, John,' Sandy was flattered at being able to use his own judgement on what was vital or not.

Suddenly he found himself on the street and wandered down the road to hail a taxi. In his hurry to get to the Embassy he had forgotten to get any directions for the return journey and to his annoyance found he had virtually no Yuan left for the fare.

He boarded the taxi dumb struck for words, with a taxi driver talking nineteen to the dozen and the meter ticking over.

He could really have done with the EVART right now. 'Blast and damnation..'

To go back to the Embassy would be a loss of face especially with a local taxi driver in pursuit.

He dug deep into his pockets in desperation and pulled out a Laundry receipt from the Hotel.

Gleaming at the driver, like a man who has been saved from drowning, he presented the laundry receipt, 'Take me there.'

Chuck and Janine were sitting in the reception area when Andy arrived back.

Without hesitation Andy said, 'I delivered the goods,'

'And?' asked Janine

'We will take a walk and talk outside,'

'Don't be so melodramatic, you are not 007 Andy.'

Andy got his way and said, I have no idea of the contents of the letter and stuff in the package but the Embassy chap I saw took it away along with a chip that Boris had planted in the EVART. I didn't mention that before, and they still have the EVART and will return it later. Getting a taxi back here was a real hassle trying to deal with a driver who can't speak English; any way that is another story.'

'So that is it then?' Chuck's disappointment that the episode may have come to an end was clear.

Andy told them he rather hoped the Foreign Office would contact him in due course with some sort of explanation and how John Russel was pleased to have Janine's shorthand notes.

'I have to stress John Russel emphasised we should not discuss this with anyone else as it is serious stuff, and we could put ourselves in grave danger,' Andy was quietly revelling in the drama of it all.

'I don't want you holding out on a single detail. Chuck and I expect to be informed of everything,' Janine knew Andy liked to be a control freak where information was concerned, and she would have nothing of it.

'We have a couple of days to sightsee here so lets get back on track and enjoy ourselves and try to get some fun out it,' Chuck was ready to move on.

The next two days passed quickly and Andy had almost forgotten about his EVART when just an hour before check out time he had a message to go to the hotel lobby.

"Ahh Andy, I have something for you,' John Russel handed Andy a small parcel containing the EVART and added,' Lets take a short walk.'

'It has to be short as our transfer will be here in about 20 minutes.'

'It will take about five minutes,' John Russel assured him as they hit the pavement at a brisk pace.'

'You acted wisely in passing the letter to us though its

not quite in our street, but there are others at London who are eager to have it..'

'MI5 or MI6?' Andy interjected.

'Something like that, anyway we need a copy of your itinerary and home addresses. By the way we are really interested in the conversation with the drunk at the Moscow railway station,' John Russel smiled.

'Oh I am sorry it's embarrassing to me.'

'Its no joke, like you, at first we through it was all drunken rambling but we put a Russian linguist on to it, and guess what? It seems the drunk is a well known Russian poet who vanished from the scene a few years ago, presumed dead because he offended the regime with his pro democracy prose. His drunken gibberish contained a few phrases, sufficient to give pretty positive identification.

He has been picked up by friends and is now in a safe house pending an arranged exit to a safe country.' John Russel shook Andy's hand.

'Don't forget the itinerary and addresses. Nice meeting you bon voyage.' and he was gone.

Janine and Chuck had already check out of the hotel by the time Andy returned and Janine quickly prodded Andy into a waiting taxi,

'Don't tell us anything until we get in the train, we are cutting this a bit tight the man at the Hotel said we should have left ten minutes earlier! Janine was rattled.

Their final train to Vladivostok was already embarking passengers. There would be one stop in between at Khabarovsk and the border crossing back into Russia.

'Vladivostok or bust!' yelled Chuck.

'What a trip so far, talk about the Orient express. What next can we expect?' Janine was scribbling another entry in her travel dairy.

As the train rattled though Beijing's outer suburbs Andy brought them up to date on the John Russel meeting.

'Without EVART we would never have discovered him. You guys can laugh and joke but a Berlitz phrase book would never have done the trick.'

Chuck nodded in agreement, but you have to say something for old technology, without Janine's Pitman Shorthand your guys at the Embassy would not have had such a comprehensive and detailed account of Boris' abduction.

Andy told them it was truly a team effort, 'Let's toast Boris!'

The journey came to an all-too-quick close as they entered the Pacific part of Russia, and imagined they could sniff salt air as they drew close to Vladivostok. The express reduced speed to a semi-crawl and rattled its way through a rather bizarre mix of suburban buildings, tall state apartments, old wooden residences and factories. Then over a mangled maze of railway points, which at times seemed to be a touch indeterminate over which way they were actually supposed to point, causing the train to rock and roll a bit more than the passengers liked. However, it glided into its platform and the engine driver expertly brought it to a final halt without a jolt.

Chuck, Andy and Janine grabbed their suitcases

'Was he really an ex KGB man?' Janine asked.

'No dear, he was ex Red Army. A soldier who did not like the spooks who tried to manipulate things for their own ends,' Andy explained.

'Boris is like the enigma of modern Russia. Boris is a tough guy with a good ear for music, brought up in tough times, He is a pragmatist. I think he will survive' Chuck gave Janine a reassuring look.

'He never spoke about his family and we never asked him,' Janine said with regret.

'Now for our transport,' Andy looked anxiously up and down the pavement for a taxi.

He saw a cab that seemed to fit the bill, hailed it and moved in at speed. It was not his taxi it was already on a course to other customers. Andy commandeered it and pushed the other two in before its driver could complain. The driver, quickly realising his luck in getting foreigners whom he could over-charge, instantly ditched the Russian customers who were left shouting and shaking his fist on the pavement.

'I never in my life believed I would ever travel across Russia in a train. The Iron Curtain and Cold War looked so permanent not so very long ago, and even if we had got visas the US Government suspected we were communists for wanting to do the trip!' Chuck had achieved an ambition of a life time

The cab heaved up outside their hotel after what Andy suspected was a rather circuitous route, and twice as long as the 'Lonely Planet' guide said it should take from the station to the hotel

'What an experience! Even though there are a lot of adjustments and crap going on in Russia just now, how great for the world,' Chuck generously, ignored the hassles en route in his brief summary.

'Oh for a breath of salt air after all that land.' Andy was clearly delighted at having a hotel with a sea view.' This is more my kind of place than Ulan Bator and all those places on the Steps of Russia we passed through.'

There would be one night and a full day to check out Vladivostok before taking the ferry to Japan.

'Its amazing that here we are in the Far East, east of China, in a European City!' Janine was impressed.' You have to travel across Russia by rail to really understand just how huge it is.'

'Yeah and remember Russia once owned Alaska and sold it to the USA to a President called Seaward. Everyone thought Seaward was dumb and called Alaska 'Seaward's mistake.' Some mistake!' Chuck shook his head in wonder.

⌘⌘⌘

Two days later in London, Fran arrived at the Japan Airlines check-in area 30 minutes before the deadline time given to the group. Jill and John Blount had offered to help her and turned up spot on time. They noted the JL flight was on schedule and Fran designated a couple of minor tasks to them.

She checked her name list and mused over the events which had brought them together again after 30 years and where everyone was at now. Jill and John Blount loved ballroom dancing. They were reliable, predictable, and helpful.

Rick Foster, a widower since the last trip to New Zealand, had now teamed up with Maggie Moss. She was rather self-effacing still but had recovered very well from the kidnapping attempt in New Zealand, and the associated trauma, and was really looking forward to a fun trip now. She and Rick lived in New Zealand and would travel direct from there to Tokyo.

Derek and Ann Sloan, good all rounders, always cheerful and happy, especially Derek with his old nautical quips and anecdotes. Dick and Joan Round, Dick the eternal dry wit and his quiet wife were fun people to be with.

Fran Wallace, myself, the one who does all the organising and sorts out the detail that the men are too stupid, or lazy, to get on to, she observed. Mat and Vickey Tenby, your average Mr and Mrs suburban Smith, I suppose, with a keen interest in the 1960's music and middlebrow concerts.

Ewan Perth, a nice chap, gay of course but really sociable and a good help in an emergency, always able to bring something unexpected out of the hat so to speak. Perry and Jean Fowler, well, Perry was another joker in the pack but always a bright spark, the cheerful ex-Bucks cop.

Peter Green, the old cynic, and Brenda, was a practical, down-to-earth person with a love of dressmaking. Adam Green, their 25-year-old journalist son, was a new chum to the group, a nice bright chap interested in most things and people.

Andy and Janine Cole, well, Andy the father figure of the group, a little pompous at times but took his responsibilities well and something of a rock for them all as he had started the Record Club decades ago. Lindsay Love, another single lady like Frances, also quiet but loved antiques and porcelain so was excited at the chance of seeing Arita pottery and other Japanese knick-knacks.

Who else? She thought. Chuck of course, the American who was travelling with Andy and Janine and not with the group by plane. Chuck, a new great friend of the group, who fitted in so well and was so kind and generous. She liked Chuck a lot. He never asked for anything and was always ready to help.

That was it really except for Jock MacTavish, the missing member who had yet to be traced and, of course, Foggy Night and Helena, who met on the trip to New Zealand for the first time in 30 years. They were now a couple. Foggy was a successful merchant banker, and Helena a painter of some ability. They were both Jewish and great company in that intellectual and artistic liberal way.

Fran really hope that Herewini, a New Zealand Customs officer, would make it to Fukuoka at least. There was still some doubt about that in her mind despite his expectation of being there. He was very popular with the group, a fun person to have along and at the same time intelligent and protective as well.

The group was leaving behind fresh, clear spring weather for something they hoped might be a bit warmer in Japan. Fran was a bit concerned about overweight luggage. Everyone had been advised late in the piece, that they should take one gift each for their individual hosts, as there would be a buddy hosting system, and contribute towards three group gifts, one for the Mayor, another for the Governor of the Prefecture and also one for Nomura san's group.

They arrived in the usual fashion, being tipped somewhat unceremoniously out of sons' and daughters' cars or taxis, then searching frantically for passports and other documents as they tugged their suitcases towards Fran. Remarkably, there were no stuff-ups and they were at the gate lounge boarding in no time, each passenger being politely bowed to in almost military fashion by the Japanese cabin staff. Some felt obliged to bow or at least nod their heads back.

Peter's journalist son, Adam, had been in journalism to become a cynic and when he saw the final itinerary for Fukuoka he was astonished at the lengths the Japanese were going to on their behalf. He kept telling Peter it was unbelievable. He had checked out Fukuoka's various websites and taken a look at Google Earth and could see it was a very smart modern-looking place of some size, but he just did not feel comfortable and could not put his finger on it. His father being an archetypal cynic had more or less inferred he would not be surprised if the whole group was bait for some huge international plot but everyone else in the group laughed that idea off.

At Fukuoka the Nishi Nippon Shimbun had designated two journalists to travel up to Tokyo to meet them on arrival and in normal Japanese newspaper style both journalists would take photographs and also produce a single story between them for publication. The journalists had generous expenses and knew they could afford a night at a moderately priced night spot from that allowance.

It looked like a pleasant assignment and they would meet Nomura-san and his young interpreter Nishimura-san at their hotel and go to the airport with them. The journalists had already met Nishimura-san and joked between themselves about her being Nomura's 'night secretary', not realising she had her own agenda planned with her boyfriend.

Miss Alsop-Smith, the British Ambassador, had toyed with the idea of sending a Cultural Affairs secretary to Narita Airport to meet the group but decided against it as a sort of show biz thing, and the main action would be in Kyushu. She had also decided against a cocktail party at the Embassy for them as the Embassy's entertainment budget was low and she wanted to have ample expenses at Kyushu.

Rick and Maggie arrived at Tokyo a day before the group and checked in at the Shiba Park Hotel, which specialised in rugby groups, had a rugby theme and was popular with general New Zealand travellers and rugby groups worldwide. He thought Mr Hiromitsu Tanaka would be there to meet him and he was exactly right.

In typical brisk Japanese fashion Tanaka-san hardly gave Rick and Maggie time to wash their hands and check their room before dragging them down to the bar. He spoke in deep booming samurai tones and apologised for his broken English. It was a standing joke that when he first met Rick he had said, 'My English is not so good but my Germany is much better.'

They exchanged pleasantries and Tanaka-san was genuinely impressed with Rick's second 'okusan.' Maggie was not quite sure what that meant and looked a trifle disturbed until Rick explained it translated as wife. Rick told Tanaka-san about his cousin's request to hunt down Jenny Jones and gave him a copy of her last known address. He volunteered that they could probably sort it in about 10 minutes if they could get a phone number for her at that address.

'OK, we check now,' Tanaka said and pulled out his mobile phone.

He rang the number which turned out to be a nightclub and was told by some at the end of the line that they knew no one of that name, and then hung up. Tanaka-san was a bit miffed by what he called rudeness at the other end and told Rick the result.

'You see, this is the only address and lead we have on her and she must have had some sort of connection with the address to give to her parents. She does not speak Japanese and I doubt she could or would make up this address. Perhaps she was deliberately given a wrong address for some reason?' Rick suggested.

'Hai, hai, soo desu,' Tanaka-san agreed with Rick's logic and looked concerned.

'How long you stay Tokyo, and do you have some time?' Tanaka-san asked.

Rick explained they had three days and he would not participate in all of the itinerary with the group, but had to meet them tomorrow on arrival.

'Can you keep some nights free and make one free

morning?' he asked Rick.

Rick feared a massive drinking session was being lined up and gave a very guarded yes, depending on the circumstances.

'OK, we will make some check on this place and might try to find a place where she might stay. Yakuza, Japanese mafia controls these places and usually provides accommodation for foreign girls so they can control their free time as well. You have to be..., what is the word, silent or secret?'

'I think you mean discreet,' Rick corrected.

'Hai, hai ,' he thundered back.

'Tonight, please excuse me from big drinking night with you. I can see you are tired and new okusan might get angry if I take you out. I will go and talk to my friends here to see if they can help me a bit. I am member of Japanese rugby mafia!' He roared with laughter and continued, 'and we are very strong men and have big face in many places.'

Rick felt very reassured by his confidence and told Maggie if there was one man who could find Jenny it was Tanaka-san.

'A Japanese agent once owed me about $40,000 for a Japanese group that I made arrangements for in New Zealand. The agent was going belly up and trying to renege on payment. Mr T here made one phone call to him and one visit. He waited for the agent outside his office at 8.30am and told him you MUST, you MUST pay Rick-san today, and so he did.'

Rick loved telling the story for it demonstrated one of

the great strengths of Japan in group loyalty and Tanaka's acceptance of him as part of his clan. Tanaka san bowed modestly and said it was nothing, 'just a Rick-san very tall story.' Then he left, bowing his way out the door. As soon as he stepped out the door he rang a Tokyo rugby friend who knew the Ginza night life scene as well as anyone, explained the situation and they agreed to meet in about 40 minutes time on a corner near the address given by Rick.

His friend Yoshi, a front row forward with crew-cropped, bull-shaped head grinned all over his face on seeing Tanaka-san and they both bowed deeply to each other for a few moments like some automated puppets controlled by a stuck record. Yoshi knew the gist of things and their strategy was simple. They would sink a few sakes to look drunk and try and gain entry to the club. Most were technically membership only but if a stranger turned up and looked as though he could be a big spender or had an impressive business card he would often get entry at the cost of a large unofficial cover charge.

They found the building and in the foyer found the club marked on the sixth floor. There were several other clubs in the same building and scantily-clad girls and overdressed bellboys were poncing around outside to encourage punters to come in and see a floor show or two at the clubs in the building.

Tanaka san and his mate Yoshi did not really have to act. It was familiar territory and they knew the style. Super-confident Tanaka-san breezed up to the club, pretended to find a membership card and deliberately let slip a name card which impressed the doorman who said he would get the mama-san to see if they could come in.

Tanaka-san could see it was a flashy, swank place by the occupants. At a glance they looked well representative of the gangster side of Tokyo life, with spivvy dyed hair and excessively dazzling cuff links and male jewellery, and they spoke in the harsh direct tones of the arrogant nouveau rich. Few, if any, had any company or organisational lapel badges to indicate their association with any reputable company.

The mama-san, a hard and careworn-faced person in her sixties, gave them the benefit of a long stony gaze before she put on one of her many false smiles and said they could enter but would have to pay an exorbitant cover fee. She was well-practised in fleecing men and complimented herself on being able to extract a huge sum out of them before they had even begun to drink.

Tanaka-san guessed she was the rude lady on the phone. Tanaka-san and Yoshi quickly moved into raucous banter with the other guests, flattering them and gaining their confidence. They admitted to being rugby men on a night out and made coarse groping gestures at the hostesses. Their behaviour was exactly right for this sort of expensive dive and it earned them a few free drinks from some of the other customers who clearly believed women were nothing more than men's playthings.

At an appropriate moment Tanaka admitted to the drunken mob his preference for mixed-race European and African women and Yoshi, to make it seem less obvious, said Tanaka was dumb and the best-looking women in the world were Thai girls. It had the desired effect of enticing talk about girls and where the best ones could be found in Tokyo and, from a corner, one of the drunken customers said he had seen a part-African British girl at that place about a week ago and that was confirmed by another customer who asked the mama-san where she was that night. The mama-san gave him a cold stare and said she had other appointments.

Tanaka quickly dropped the topic and started chatting up a hostess, apologising secretively to her for his earlier bad behaviour. He started to draw her out about their lives and the work at this place, which was named the Otani Bar. She told him the money was okay but the master who owned the place was very tough and he had demanding friends. Tanaka asked for more drinks and shouted her each time knowing she was only drinking a cheap whisky-lookalike cordial, and taking a cut from each drink he bought her.

It had the desired effect. She appreciated his generosity and concern. Tanaka-san caught the mama-san's gimlet cold eyes checking him out a few times so he was careful not to seem overly inquisitive but just a benign good-natured drunk. He noted her name was Emi, almost certainly a professional adopted name. Tanaka-san needed to know if the British African girl worked there regularly and where she stayed. The latter information was not normally given to any customers.

Emi was a somewhat shop-soiled thirty-eight year old who could look about twenty-two to half drunk punters in dark lights when made up, but first thing in the morning after a hard night might even pass muster as a fifty year old. Tanaka-san knew the type and had occasionally in the past availed himself of their services, half out of pity and half from a feeling of being in a fairly non-demanding comfort zone.

Emi had sussed Tanaka out and started to think he might become a new paying boyfriend, so told him she had a free night after 2 am. Tanaka-san said he would like to see her. She suggested a hotel, one he would have to pay for. He agreed thinking of how he could find Emi's home address which could be part of some shared apartments used by a number of the Otani Bar hostesses. Tanaka-san rightly figured out his liaison with Emi would not arouse any suspicion as Emi probably only had another year or so of working life left in her at an upmarket bar of this kind.

When it came to chuck-out time, the mama san and all the hostesses came to the lift, bowed their customers into it, joined them in the lift and then bowed then off into the early morning chilliness of a Ginza street. Tanaka-san knew the form. He and Yoshi had a ten minute drink at a yatai street stand where he explained his moves and fixed a meeting time and place for the next day, then he got a call from Emi on his mobile with directions of where he should meet her.

He and Yoshi parted, whereupon he picked up a taxi, collected Emi and made for his hotel, tipping the man at the front desk not to observe his female partner for the night. The night with Emi was predictable. She looked less sexy and youthful stripped down and was clearly tired out of her skin. Both took baths, him first and she scrubbed his back and showered him off before he entered the freshwater tub. She took care of herself.

Tanaka-san could see she was very tired and told her to get some sleep and if she felt up to sex they would have sex in the morning. He set his watch mobile phone on silent vibration alarm and both slept soundly until about 7am. As he turned over he could feel her pressing her body against him and her hands started to fondle his penis.

'You were so considerate last night. It has made me very happy and grateful,' she murmured sexily in his ear.

Tanaka-san knew what was expected of him and obliged her. He was pleased to note she did not seem to have faked an orgasm like most of her kind on a business arrangement but had genuinely enjoyed it. She was clearly used to one night stands and was ready to leave at his command, but was pleasantly surprised when he said he would take her to breakfast and see her safely back to her place in a taxi. She accepted, flattered that this could be more than a one night stand.

Her rather bawdy nightclub type clothes did not look too good in the cold light of day and from the glances of other patrons at the hotel's restaurant he knew what everyone was thinking but it was of no concern to him. Tokyo was huge and anonymous and he hated treating any human beings with disrespect.

As they left the hotel, he could see a pleading look of expectation in her eyes, hopeful that he would fix another date sometime. He hated raising false expectations and found it hard to be cold and brisk and said with sincerity that he would like to see her again in a day or two. She squeezed his hand with genuine pleasure. She wanted to ask him if he had a wife and family and also to say she had a grown up daughter of twenty-two, but Japanese politeness does not permit such directness and even if she were brave enough to ask the questions she guessed it might cool off his ardour.

She gave the taxi driver directions to a street which was noted for the number of apartments that were used by nightclub hostesses and 'dancers.' Tanaka could not ask her directly if the British girl stayed in the same group of apartments without arousing suspicion so as they entered the narrow street he pulled a ruse.

'Hey, look there is a black girl there like the British one you were talking about last night, look she is walking just behind the van on the right,' he lied. It was more than enough to catch her interest she looked in vain and asked, 'where, where?'

He told her she must have gone down a side street. Emi asked what she looked like and Tanaka-san described Jenny from the description given him by Rick. Emi said it sounded like the British girl they knew as Jen but she was surprised if it was her as she had been restricted to her apartment by the owner of the Otani Club. Tanaka-san asked Emi where Jenny lived and Emi said in the next door apartment to hers with two other girls.

'You know, these foreign girls are a big investment for the boss. He pays their fares to Japan and the accommodation so he does not want them running away before he gets his money back, and he makes them do certain jobs for preferred customers,' Emi added.

Tanaka-san nodded in understanding and asked who protected the girls at their apartment. She said the Yakuza.

'Does the boss keep their passports in a safe place?' Tanaka asked.

Emi smelt a rat and shot him a glance. 'Are you a policeman?'

'No, no.' He roared with laughter. His denial was perfectly true but he had worried all along she might suspect he was.

'Your boss does not treat you like this?' he suggested.

'Because I am now a bit old and soon he will want me to quit. He knows I depend on the Otani and customers' money so my situation has become different, might be he would be glad if I quit.' She looked hard and hopefully at Tanaka-san in expectation.

'Who knows what the future will bring?' he replied philosophically, remembering he had not paid her. She was genuinely reluctant to take his money as she wanted a deeper relationship and told him she would like to see him again soon for friendship not professionally. Tanaka-san agreed, noting they were nearing her address so he guided the conversation back to the British girl and how quickly she had vanished. Emi said she was not permitted out alone at any time so perhaps she had escaped and, if so, all hell would break loose.

'What kind of guard does your boss keep on her?' he asked

'The usual, you know, foreigners who don't speak Japanese are like children in his hands. He takes their passports, only gives them a little bit of their money at a time, and has a trusted lady to watch over them and the Yakuza guard who lives next door.'

She said it generally broke the spirit of the foreign girls after a time and they would then agree to sex and do what the boss told them. If not then the boss would try some drug and alcohol to make them dependent, possibly a bit of physical hard treatment. This British girl had spirit and was resisting, and she seemed to be a genuine song and dance person, not just a money grabber with a good body, Emi added.

Tanaka-san dropped Emi off, promised he would call her on her mobile soon and headed back for the hotel, taking the taxi to the nearest subway station. As soon as he was out of the taxi he called Rick at the Shiba Park Hotel and was glad that he was still there. Today was the day the Record Club group would arrive and he needed Rick's assistance.

Rick and Maggie had risen early and taken a stroll to Tokyo Tower, which was about 20 minutes away, and then had just returned when Tanaka-san rang. He told Rick very briefly what had transpired, asked him to stay and said he would be at the hotel in about 30 minutes.

Rick explained this to Maggie and asked her if she wanted to go to Narita Airport to meet the group or hang about with him. She decided to go to the airport, so Rick got her a seat on an airport shuttle and told her the arrival gate number and to look out for a JTB Tour guide who would have an English language sign on display for the group to see on arrival.

Tanaka-san had also made contact with Yoshi, so he

turned up at the hotel almost the same time as Tanaka-san. Rick took them both to the hotel's coffee room and thanked Tanaka-san profusely for his quick detective work. Tanaka-san said it was nothing. He was happy to help but they could not be certain it was Jenny until they saw her and that is why he believed Rick now needed to join the hunt.

'How about the Japanese police?' Rick asked.

Tanaka-san said at some stage they might need to involve them but they must be sure she is the person they are now looking at and also that she is or has been held against her will.

'You know Japanese police get a lot of inquiries like this and very often the girl is willing and the person who complains is a boyfriend or a parent. You know the most usual kind of girl that does this never wants to tell parents!' he explained.

'If we need help my friend Inspector Yamoto will help. He is old rugby friend and also plain-clothes man based here in Tokyo. We will use rugby mafia to beat Yakuza', he said, letting out a deep belly chuckle.

Tanaka's plan for the day was to discreetly stake out the lodgings and have Rick at hand to identify the British girl. Rick had already received a recent photo on his mobile phone from his cousin Geoff in Wales. If it was her, then Yoshi and he would tail her and, providing there were not too many muscle men around, stop and question her in Rick's presence to ascertain if she was willingly working for this group or not.

It seemed simple and straightforward to Rick so he

agreed and then phoned Maggie to tell her of his plans and apologised to Andy and the group. He instructed her not to mention this business as it might soon be solved. He also rang his Tokyo agent to make apologies for not being at the airport. They were not worried and assured him that JTB who were doing the coach transfer from Narita to the Shiba Park Hotel would have a person there. Rick already knew this, but in Japan it was polite sometimes to directly report and state the obvious to let others know you also were aware of things.

As the Japan Airlines airliner began its descent to Narita forty-five minutes ahead of schedule, the group grew excited at the prospect of landing in Japan for the first time. Fran checked the arrival notes and re-emphasised to the group a need for them to stick together during the arrival procedures.

Nomura-san and Nishimura-san were about to arrive at Narita by the Japan Railways Narita Express from Tokyo. He had made a crude approach to Nishimura to share his room for the night but got a firm rebuff. He was miffed, but the excitement of the big tour now commanded his thoughts. This would be one of his finest moments, he thought, as he was the man who would bring this fame to Fukuoka and receive the primary gratitude from the drug and alcoholics group who would be the main financial beneficiaries.

'After this, I might be able to get many girls,' he thought, so Nishimura-san is unimportant. Unknown to Nomura-san, Nishimura-san had had an excellent night with her boyfriend and was still not quite of this world, though it was her initiative to check flight arrivals and she had got them both on an earlier train to Narita.

The two journalists from the Nishi Nippon Shimbun had been out on the town spending part of their expense account at some karaoke bars and a dimly-lit back street jazz bar. They were hung over and woke up late so did not bother to check the flight arrivals but made their way to Narita on a later train.

Nomura-san had his own welcome banner for the Mereleigh Record Club group and was aware they we being transferred by JTB so he scouted around and soon found the immaculately-clad young JTB Tour Guide in a form-fitting, almost military, navy blue suit and white blouse. He noted her perfect legs and short skirt, and the little gold JTB badge and Mereleigh Group sign.

He bowed very deeply to her because he was impressed by her beauty. She was impressed by his politeness rather than his looks and Nishimura-san bowed a lady-to-lady bow as if to say, 'you know what he is after, men are all the same.'

They exchanged notes about the group's arrival procedures and Nomura-san assured the JTB lady he and Nishimura would make their own way to the Shiba Park Hotel as they knew they had not been costed in for travel on the coach. The JTB lady was relieved as she did not want to have to deal with any unexpected things.

It took the group less than an hour to clear customs and they were led out by Jill and John Blount and Fran, with Perry and his wife offering to take up the rear to keep the group together. John Blount had donned a jacket and tie as he understood the Japanese were very formal and, of course, he was British and would do what was right. He had some brand new name cards in his wallet ready for instant use.

He gazed at the waiting crowd for a split second or so before he saw the JTB sign and Nomura-san's sign. The JTB lady bobbed over to him in that distinctive rabbit-hopping style of Japanese ladies who wish to convey the impression of speed yet do not wish to take unladylike big fast strides.

At first glance Nomura-san's face was radiating a huge sun-like smile at the Blounts and Fran and waving wildly. Nishimura-san was also smiling and waving but as more of the group members emerged and became visible to Nomura-san, he suddenly seemed to have been gripped by a severe heart attack or stroke.

He went deathly white while almost crumpling to the ground and it was all he could do to bow and shake John Blount's hand. He almost needed propping up by Nishimura-san as she was distracted by him while greeting all the members individually. At the end of the ritual Nishimura-san appeared as stricken as he. It was as though some instant plague had smitten them both but the JTB lady remained bright, cheerful and super-efficient. She told them they should follow her to their coach and that Nomura-san and Nishimura-san had said they would proceed by train and meet them at the Shiba Park Hotel.

The Blounts and Fran, like the rest of the group, were by now totally bemused by Nomura and Nishimura's sudden affliction. Fran asked if they were okay and if what the JTB lady said was correct. Nishimura-san weakly reassured them and with that they both bowed lamely to the group and made a hasty retreat for the railway station.

They disappeared down the escalator just as the Nishi Nippon journalists arrived at the arrival gate. The noted the early arrival of the flight and cursed looking frantically around for the group. Both journalists had seen the Mereleigh movie but they could not even find the coach, let alone the group. They knew the editor would not wear an excuse that the flight was early as a reason for not getting some pics and an arrival story. They were in deep trouble.

Once the group had entered the coach they all expressed surprise and concern over Nomura and Nishimura's behaviour. It seemed extraordinary, even unusual, for Japanese they agreed. The asked the JTB guide's opinion, but she was not paid to give opinions and sensed there was something very unusual in which she did not want to get involved. She simply reported that Nomura-san had said there was some kind of difference, but was not sure if he meant that as a problem or a compliment.

The group was heartened to hear from the JTB guide that Rick had been in touch but she was concerned about Maggie as Rick's wife was supposed to meet them. Almost on cue Maggie rushed along the pavement to the front of the coach waving madly. She too had been caught out by the early flight arrival. The excitement of seeing Maggie and catching up on New Zealand overtook the group's interest for a while.

The sheer efficiency and cleanliness of things at Narita

greatly impressed them. At the rear of the coach a big V12 diesel engine only occasionally gave indication of its massive power with a well-silenced whine and rumble which produced a massive extra thrust forward when necessary.

The coach hissed silently as brakes were applied and it swung gracefully into corners like a huge liner nudging aside trifling seas. All the windows were curtained and spotless antimacassar were placed on the headrest of every seat. The driver sat immaculately in a dark blue uniform, spotless white shirt and tie, and a smart cap, and gripped the wheel by way of white gloves which would have done a royal butler credit.

The JTB guide made appropriate announcements, with polite restraint and apologetic tinkling tones. The coach was soon coasting on the motorway to Tokyo and the group was able to take in odd patches of remnant rural Narita interspersed by houses, warehouses, some small hotels and cafes.

The tinkling-toned JTB guide pointed out they would pass by Tokyo Disneyland and could see in the distance the high-rise towers of downtown Tokyo. Everything looked so new compared with European cities and very compact. It was almost impossible for them to see any dirty or battered vehicles on the motorway and they were amazed to see all the private cars and minibuses had curtained windows and mostly crisp white seat covers.

Though the motorway was rather congested the traffic moved in an orderly, disciplined manner with motorists seemingly going out of their way to be polite to other vehicles as though many points and rewards could be gathered by those who were the most polite. Perry was moved by it all to tell the group, 'This looks like a very couth country. They even have the sense to drive on the same sides of the road as us!'

⌘⌘⌘

Andy, Janine and Chuck had enjoyed the salt air, after the dust and expanse of Russia, and a good crossing by ferry from Siberia to Japan, and were soon Tokyo bound on a fast Hankinson bullet train to Tokyo. The transformation from the more than casual Russian style of doing things and the rather well-used and battered nature of Russian transportation to an immaculate bullet train and super-efficient and polite Japanese railway staff amazed them.

'The Japanese make a tourist feel like royalty,' Andy observed and Janine and Chuck nodded in agreement as they sampled the railways' bentos.

'I can't say the chow is entirely to my liking, too many tiny bits of things and strange spices and tastes,' Chuck observed.

'You got Budweiser beer, so what more can you ask for?' Janine pointed out.

He nodded back in contentment and they wondered at the grandeur of the Japanese Alps and great feats of civil engineering as the bullet train raced over high viaducts and bridges and dived into solid mountainsides. It whooshed past tiny traditional hamlets with tiled-roof wooden farm houses and paddy fields crammed in on odd pieces of man-made flat land between the hills and mountains.

Roy Vaughan ~

The Japanese scooted around in tiny, narrow cars on roads hardly wider than the vehicles. Between the rice paddies, old ladies rode bicycles and the occasional farmer could be seen tending the land, guiding large, two-wheeled walk-behind type cultivators. They passed a high school during a lunch break and commented on the students' rather dated military-style uniforms. The boys in dark blue old Prussian-style midshipmen-type uniforms, and girls in what looked like enlarged gym slips with sleeves, and large naval collars.

'God, they are still militaristic!' Andy exclaimed in horror.

'Aw, I wouldn't put too much store in the uniforms, from what I read and hear the Japs these days aren't too keen on the military, but they like to live a smart orderly life,' Chuck explained.

Janine was taken by the performances of the bento girls as they came through each carriage, first of all bowing and announcing their trolley loads of goodies and then, before exiting at the other end, stopping, turning around and bowing to everyone before departing.

'It's like an Elizabethan court ritual!' she said, and asked if the Japanese all behaved like this.

'Of course,' Andy answered in rather superior tones.

'How would you know, you have never been here before!' she responded.

'The difference between you and me is that I tend to read a bit more about these things,' he replied in even more superior tones.

'How come you did not know about the school uniforms, then?' she replied with spirit.

'That's the spirit, girl,' chuckled Chuck, grinning at a rather annoyed Andy who decided to terminate the conversation.

They alternately dozed and conversed and were surprised to find the bullet train entering the dormitory suburbs of Tokyo and were amazed at the sheer mass of organised humanity piled up at various levels above or beneath one another in large blocks of apartments, offices and department stores.

'When you run out of flat space for folk you got to put them in layers to fit everyone in. Ain't that what the Chinese are doing now, building all those big modern cities? If we keep breeding like this we will all end up in human layer cakes,' Chuck joked.

'Either that or we shall send people off to sea in eternal floating cities,' Andy suggested.

'It's already happening! Remember all the rich dudes on the cruise we took from Britain to the USA, you already got folk who pre-bought, or have long-term suite rentals and who spend most of their life just cruising the world,' Chuck observed.

The bullet train began to slow to a crawl and then came a couple of tinkling announcements, first in Japanese and then in American-accented English, advising passengers that the train would be at Tokyo in a few minutes or so and not to forget to take all their luggage with them and also thanking them for travelling by train.

They grabbed a taxi at Tokyo station and Chuck

144

squeezed his lanky frame in the front next to the driver while Andy and Janine took the more spacious back seat. The super-smartly dressed cab driver was all smiles and efficiency as he tried to squeeze their suitcases in the boot which was already about 20 per cent occupied by a large LPG fuel cylinder.

Then Chuck discovered the driver had much shorter legs than he and had the front bench seat, which he was obliged to share, drawn right forward so he could reach the pedals. The problem was the tops of Chuck's knees scraped against a taxi fare meter which intruded into his area.

'This is excruciatingly painful, I hope the journey is not too long!' he exclaimed in pain.

'You can now understand why in Japan the important people sit at the back and the mere lackeys sit in the front next to the driver,' Andy stated in a know-all style. 'It actually pays to bone up on foreign countries before you arrive!' he stressed.

Andy, Janine and Chuck arrived at the Shiba Park Hotel about two hours before the group, cleaned up, found Rick and relaxed over coffee, awaiting the group to arrive from Narita. They were pleasantly surprised when the coach turned up an hour earlier than scheduled, but Andy was shocked to hear about Nomura-san and Nishimura-san's behaviour. It was inexplicable but, as Nomura-san had said he would come to the hotel, he felt it would all be sorted before nightfall. He did not have a phone number for either Nomura-san or Nishimura-san, only their Fukuoka address, so when they had still failed to make contact by 9pm he began to realise something serious might have happened and he had a restless night worrying about it.

Back at Narita airport, as he had got out of sight of the group, Nomura-san had searched for something to lean on and stopped.

'This is nuclear disaster, worst nightmare known to man, and someone must be responsible for very big mistake,' he burbled to Nishimura-san.

Up to now she had been more concerned about Nomura's health than individual members of the record club group, but now she was getting an inkling of the problem but was too fearful to mention it in case it was another problem and not what Nomura-san was thinking of.

'This is NOT the cast of the Mereleigh movie. There is no Judy French, no Helen Bitten, no Geoffrey Farmer, no Anthony Watkins, no big name actors that were in the cast. The people we invited. These people are just *ordinary* people. Who made this big mistake?' He sunk to his knees, hands over his eyes, and started to sob, his shoulders shaking with fear.

Nishimura froze with fear too, all too aware of her vital communications role. She tried to recollect every letter and every e-mail she had translated or written and could not find a single instance of a misinterpretation on her side. She had meticulously filed all outgoing and incoming correspondence so she desperately hoped she could clear her name. She tried to reassure Nomura-san but he would have none of it.

'It is world disaster for me, I am going to be the person

to blame and every newspaper and TV and radio will have big story and I will be most hated person in Fukuoka and my family treated worst than Japanese untouchables,' he exclaimed.

Nishimura-san could not get rid of her own shakes as she knew how small people like them would be held responsible. She contemplated eloping with her boyfriend but was made of more stoical stuff and decided she would try to get to the bottom of it.

Nomura-san said he had to go to the toilet and Nishimura said she also. While in the toilet she rang her boyfriend to say there was a very big problem and he must get to their hotel as soon as possible so she could discuss it. He at first thought she might be pregnant but she curtly dismissed that suggestion and, in a manner which upset him a bit, said it was much worse than that.

She tried to calm down, but her heart was racing with fear and trepidation at being accused as the one responsible for this huge mistake. She fought away tears but they poured forth, and one or two Japanese ladies asked her if she was okay. She just grunted replies through the sobs and she overheard one lady say to another, 'She probably has a foreign boyfriend going back home leaving her pregnant. You can see this sort of thing at Narita any day of the week.'

It made her angry so she dried the tears and stormed out to find Nomura-san. There was no sight of him. She hung around and around and even rang him on her mobile but his phone was switched off. That made her more concerned. Perhaps he had collapsed in the toilet, she though, and asked a kindly looking old gent to check out the cubicles. After a thorough search and quizzing all Japanese males, he gave up and told her there was no one answering to that name or description.

She started to panic again and rang her boyfriend fearing Nomura-san might do himself in. A lot of things flashed through her mind. She was suddenly hugely depressed at the thought that all the voluntary work she had done for the group for a good cause could end up totally damaging her career possibilities and reputation. She told her boyfriend that both she and Nomura-san had no idea it was the club members and not the stars in the film who were coming.

Her boyfriend checked to see who the first communication was sent to. She said Universal Studios, Japan and they then forwarded it to the UK film company that made the film and the letter was addressed to the director and the cast, and this person Andy who she had assumed was the casting director had taken over all correspondence.

Her boyfriend said surely she should have seen the error when they bought airline tickets for the group. She said they did not buy the tickets, they were bought by the group in Britain, and the Fukuoka group simply paid out the invoiced sum sent by the group to them.

'Actually we did not make rooming arrangements for them in Fukuoka either, we just asked them how many double and single rooms they needed at each place, and they booked their own private tour of Japan from Tokyo to Fukuoka themselves,' she explained.

'I can see how this happened now, but have you told

Fukuoka City Hall and everyone else it is the real club members and not the cast?' he asked

'Of course, we said the cast, for if we invited the club members I don't think we could have got all the sponsorship,' she replied.

'What do you plan to do?' her boyfriend asked.

'I have no idea. I thought you might be able to help. Just now I am worried sick about Nomura-san and fear he might do something bad and kill himself. He has a wife and kids and if he does not turn up soon his wife and kids will be worried sick. It's a shocking nightmare and I am alone in the centre of it. I just don't know how to handle it!' she burst into tears again.

Her boyfriend told her he would wait at the hotel lobby. She should get back to the hotel as soon as possible then check out and they would go to another hotel for the night where they could think of the best thing to do.

'Don't tell anyone and only answer phone calls from me in the meantime,' he advised.

The Nishi Nippon Shimbun journalists were getting frantic. They could not get either Nomura-san or Nishimura-san on their mobile phones nor raise them at the hotel. They did not have details of where the Mereleigh group would be staying as Nomura-san had kept that and the group's private itinerary confidential. Rick, appreciating that the group wanted to do the 'own arrangements' part of the tour confidentially, had booked them through his Japan agents as the Cole Group, using Andy's surname.

The Nishi Nippon men rang Nomura-san's wife and

also Nishimura-san's parents to see if they had word. This caused worry for the families and also much added frustration for the two journalists. They conferred and tried Japan Airlines but were told curtly by JAL that for security reasons they could not divulge passenger information.

The journalists decided the only way would be to go through all the inbound tour companies in Tokyo to track the group down. They agreed it was needle in a haystack stuff, but decided they should at least make a start so they could honestly tell their editor they made every effort. At 10pm they received a call from the newspapers news editor asking when the interview with the Mereleigh stars was coming. They had to humbly admit their failure to meet the group on arrival and emphasised their efforts in trying to track them down. By 5am the next day at their hotel they were still at it and had got nowhere.

CHAPTER 4

The Mereleigh Record Club Group were presented with a rather chilly windy morn at the start of their first full day in Japan, and a "Sunrise Tour" of Tokyo arranged by JTB via Rick. Andy woke up still puzzled and worried about Nomura-san's reportedly strange behaviour on arrival and his failure to front up to the hotel yesterday as he had promised. When he and Janine went down to breakfast they grabbed seats at Fran's table and she also agreed it was weird and very contrary to what she believed was normal.

'If nothing else, the Japanese are certainly noted for their politeness and reliability, so let's grab Rick before he goes out on this search for a missing girl and see what he makes of it,' Fran suggested.

Rick was more familiar with Japan than any of the others, having made numerous visits to that country. He arrived at the restaurant almost as though he had been summonsed and, after the usual morning pleasantries, asked them if Nomura-san had turned up or left any messages.

'Zilch,' Andy told him, and Rick agreed it was very strange and out of character. He told them he would make some inquiries and not to worry as there was probably a simple explanation. He added that his rugby friend Tanaka-san had told him of big arrangements being made at Fukuoka for their arrival and advance publicity. That reassured Andy and Fran, and they were more than happy to focus on the day tour ahead of them.

The two haggard Nishi Nippon Shimbun journalists greeted the day unshaven in a sleep-deprived state. They had left voice mail messages with a few dozen travel companies at Tokyo on their after-hours message systems and expected to receive a few dozen calls from about 9 am onwards once the offices opened up for the day. They decided to snatch a couple of hours sleep before then.

Rick took his breakfast seat next to Adam, the journalist son of Peter and Brenda Green. Adam's instincts had been raised by the strangeness of Nomura-san's behaviour, and he decided to pump Rick about it and also ask a few questions about this missing girl that Rick had been asked to find. Rick asked Adam to keep everything under his hat at this stage on both subjects. On the former subject he repeated what he had told Andy and Fran, and on the latter said he had asked his Japanese rugby friend Tanaka-san to check out her last known address.

'And the result?' Andy asked.

'Inconclusive and disturbing.' Tanaka-san said he found the address which is a bar-cum-nightclub place that seems to specialise in gangster boss customers and bent politicians, and he made contact with one of the hostesses — discreetly, you understand — who took a shine to him and mentioned they had a British girl there of mixed race who had recently arrived and was working several bars owned by her boss,' Rick explained.

'So did you case the joint yesterday and check it out?' Adam interrogated him with customary media directness.

'No, no, you can't do that here. These clubs are exclusive, you have to have membership or some conniving way of getting in as Tanaka did — bullshitting them he was a drunk, rich rugby man out for a good time. The rugby men in Japan are often professionals from rich backgrounds, a kind of respected élite.

'He suggested that he and I try discreetly to check out the flat which she is supposed to stay at, which we did for half the bloody afternoon and got nowhere, apart from drinking a lot of coffee at several coffee bars in the vicinity. I asked him to contact the bar hostess who had taken a shine to him but he said these things were very delicate, especially if funny business was involved, and that would advertise our punches,' Rick added.

'Why not go straight to the cops or tell the media and get a media thing going?' Adam asked.

'Because in the first instance she might be willingly and legally working for these jokers and would be mightily pissed off if we did this, and secondly every day the Japanese police get scores of these inquiries in Tokyo and would want something positive, certainly more than no communications with her parents for a couple of weeks.' Rick drew a breath. He sympathised with Adam's approach, it was a western way of handling things, but this was Japan so he reassured Adam that Tanaka-san knew best and was a person who would get results one way or another.

'But he is not a policeman or a trained detective!' John said in exasperation.

'True, and that is the strength of it. In a big society like Japan you can only really survive by belonging to some formal or informal group. That is why you see all these Japanese salary men with corporate lapel badges. If they don't have a badge they are nobody. Even the artists can be distinguished here: have you noticed all these chaps wearing French berets with long hair? That is the gear that places them somewhere in society,' Rick explained

'A bit like the old school tie brigade, and the redundant Spitfire pilots Dad used to talk about with their walrus moustaches and ex-RAF ties,' John volunteered.

'Precisely, you have the drift. Plus, of course, their business cards, which every Japanese man of status must have, and membership of very pricey clubs for the upper-echelon chaps, and gigantic expense accounts for communications expenses. Communications expenses cover anything from buying piss for customers or potential customers, shouting then tarts and indulging yourself in these things at the same time so you don't appear a wet blanket and deter them from having fun at your company's expense,' Rick said.

Ever to the point, Adam asked,' So how much is it costing you or the girl's parents to pay Tanaka-san for his costs, which I presume involve a lot of drinking and perhaps some entertainment of this friendly hostess at the bar?'

'Nix. In Japan there is a word 'giri.' It means kind of return favours. In New Zealand I do things for Tanaka-san, certainly not fixing women etc, but organising some golf, providing some free accommodation and helping him with any business inquiries. Up here he will do what I ask him to do for nothing. Get the picture?' Rick relaxed and drew heavily on his morning coffee.

'OK, I understand now. Wow you really know this society well; having had an Asian wife must have helped a lot,' John added.

Rick was tempted to give Adam verbally a kick up the arse for the last comment, but realised he was still genuinely ignorant of Asia, so he restricted himself to a few comments that his first wife was an Iranian born in East Africa, so her culture was as much British Colonial as Middle Eastern, and she had indeed spent most of her life in New Zealand with him raising his kids before she died a year or so ago.

Adam continued to press Rick for information. 'This missing girl, Jenny Jones, she is part Welsh and part African but essentially Welsh born and bred. But what is she like, and can you determine if she is likely to be playing up a bit now she is away from home?'

Rick replied that, in a nutshell it seemed she was level-headed and organised. She had won some sort of scholarship to RADA and she was essentially a song and dance act with good potential acting possibilities, according to her parents. She had enjoyed several bit parts in regular UK TV drama serials and was between jobs or 'resting' as they say in the theatre, when this job in Japan came up. It was apparently referred to her by someone she had been an art student with and they wanted someone for song and dance.

Rick told Adam that Jenny was reported to have fashioned herself on Eartha Kitt, the black American singer who started as a dancer and ended up a singer based in France and Britain. Eartha was around in the 1950s, had a very sexy voice and looks to go with it and sung great songs like 'Let's Do It,' 'Under the Bridges of Paris,' ' Just an Old-fashioned Girl,' and 'I Want to be Evil.'

'It appears she did a few Eartha numbers at an audition for a couple of Japanese guys at London who hired her on the spot and promised her a fantastic sum. They said they would get her gigs at all the best Tokyo nightspots. She is only 22 and has no experience of Japan so could be putty in the hands of crooks,' Rick added looking concerned.

Adam's eyes were bright with enthusiasm and anticipation.

'This is great. I tagged along on the trip only expecting to get a run-of-the-mill type tourism-cum-international social intercourse thing, now I could have two cracker stories on my hands: this Jenny, and a huge question mark over Nomura-san,' he beamed with excitement.

Rick glowered at him. 'You will not write a fucking

word about anything until we have got to the bottom of both things, you promised that. It is not a story for these folk. Its life and it might be some kind of disaster they are facing.'

As Rick began to rise from the breakfast table a waiter told him there was a phone call for him and brought a phone to his table. It was the Nishi Nippon Shimbun men. They had tracked him down as Rick was known in Fukuoka both for his travel business and his connection to the Mereleigh Record Club group.

The Nishi Nippon men wanted to come and see Rick immediately and were hugely disappointed that he did not know the whereabouts of Nomura-san and Nishimura-san. They had started to believe that Nomura and Nishimura had gone off together as neither could be reached on their mobile phones nor at the hotel they were supposed to stay at. Rick reluctantly agreed to see them within an hour. Adam asked who it was and Rick let slip it was the Japanese media before he realised he would have preferred to keep Adam out of the loop for the time being. John insisted in staying for the meeting rather than joining the tour.

By this time Nishimura-san and her boyfriend had worked out what they would do. Nishimura insisted they reach some conclusion for an action plan before having sex otherwise her mind would be elsewhere. The boyfriend reluctantly agreed though he said they might think a lot more clearly after sex!

Nishimura-san had repeatedly tried Nomura-san's mobile phone without luck, and she was very aware of an impending meeting of her group at Fukuoka in two days' time. It had been agreed with her boyfriend that she would ring Nomura's wife, swear her to secrecy for a day, and tell her everything. Nishimura and boyfriend would return to Fukuoka today as planned, and she would go through all the paperwork to see if any fault lay on their side. If so, she was game enough to accept her responsibility but she felt concerned about being blamed for any misunderstanding.

They rang Nomura's wife and found she was beside herself with worry with still no word from her husband.

'Perhaps he went to some capsule hotel last night after getting drunk,' Nishimura-san said.

His wife said this could be in character as he had slept at those tiny bed-in-a wall type places before after late nights out, but she was so worried he might have taken his life.

'Look, your husband is a good man, he knows he has you and your two kids, he must be feeling a lot of shame and responsibility like me and be beside himself with worry. Probably he just wants time to try to find a solution or reason for this before he comes back.' Nishimura-san was trying tried to soothe her concerns.

Nomura-san's wife said the Nishi Nippon Shimbun had been phoning her almost every 15 minutes and she wanted to know what to say to them.

'Tell them nothing until I get to your place and we will work it out from there. I should be there about 2pm so please, please hang on and don't answer any phone calls or answer your door. When I come I will tap four times and then open if for me,' Nishimura-san instructed her. She glanced at her boyfriend and squeezed his hand as if to say, don't worry, I am a tough, organised modern Japanese lady. I can handle it.

Back at the hotel, Tanaka-san turned up to check out the next moves in the hunt for Jenny. Rick told him about the Nishi Nippon Shimbun journalists and Nomura-san still being unreachable. Tanaka-san responded with concerned 'oohs' and 'aahs' and a sympathetic 'aah soo desu ka.' Rick then invited him to sit in on the meeting.

Everyone turned up on time and met at the hotel's coffee shop. Rick invited the two Japanese journalists to open the discussion. At first the two journalists in their broken English complimented Rick on his youthful appearance in the film. Rick being a bit puzzled just put it down to their poor English. They told him how Nomura-san had tipped them off about their arrival at Narita so they could get an exclusive preview of their visit, and how disappointed they were that they missed the group.

Rick was annoyed that Nomura-san had breached the arrangement for privacy at the first part of the tour and told the Japanese journalists Nomura-san has exceeded his responsibility and they must respect the group's right to some privacy. The two Japanese journalists felt chastised and bowed acceptance of the conditions but asked if they could file a short piece on Rick and his assurance that everyone had arrived safely. Rick agreed and they took many photographs of him.

Then they told Rick they were very concerned about Nomura and Nishimura's absence and wondered if the two had eloped or something. They also asked about the whereabouts of the group.

Adam cut in announcing his credentials as a journalist and saying he did not think Nomura and Nishimura were having an affair as Nomura looked as though he had suddenly been taken ill and Nishimura also seemed very shocked by something. He said it was a very sudden transformation as they had been smiling until they saw the group.

Rick tried to joke about the sight of the group being enough to turn anyone sick but it fell flat and the journalists said everyone in the film looked very good to them, and that further bemused Rick. Tanaka-san pondered very deeply, trying to think of a reason why two people should suddenly have this problem illness at the same time. Tanaka-san asked if they had contacted the homes of Nomura-san and Nishimura-san. He was told the Nishi Nippon Shimbun had been ringing constantly but his wife had heard nothing, and Nishimura-san's parents had also heard nothing from her since she left for Tokyo, and were very concerned.

Tanaka-san asked the journalists what they proposed to do next. They just explained it was very difficult, meaning they had no idea and felt it might be premature to write a story about missing persons as they could turn up before the paper's next edition went to press.

'There is a secret here somewhere which I think just Nomura-san and Nishimura-san know about, or else they experienced food poisoning and might be in a hospital. That is all I can think of at this moment. Might be you could do a check of hospital accident and emergency departments,' he suggested.

They agreed, and it was decided they would check back with Rick and Tanaka-san at the hotel about 6 pm. Before they left the Japanese journalists said if they had time they would like to take Adam out to some media drinking places at Tokyo or certainly at Fukuoka when he got there. Adam said it would be great. They exchanged name cards and then they left wearily knowing that had some hours phoning to do and would also have to explain to their editor what they were doing.

At least they had some pics and a story from Rick confirming things were on track and that was a huge relief, but as they walked out of the hotel they were a bit confused. Was this Rick-san the real travel agent or the Rick in the film? As far as they knew all the parts were played by famous British and New Zealand actors. After some debate between them they assumed this Rick was the travel agent and Watkins-san who played Rick in the film was out on the tour with the other actors. They held off telephoning their editor about Nomura-san and Nishimura-san for a while as they felt it would be better to phone when they had covered all bases or else found Nomura and Nishimura.

After they left, Rick, Adam and Tanaka-san rEvarted to the search for Jenny and what to do next. Yesterday had been a total failure so Tanaka-san suggested they start late with a watch on the apartment she was supposed to stay at and he would get Yoshi to pose as some sort of salesman making a call to see if she was in.

'My idea is Yoshi is some sort of magazine sales rep who is checking Jenny's address for a UK magazine her family has subscribed to for her as a birthday present. We have to move fast and make a business card. You must tell me the name of a ladies' magazine,' Tanaka told the others. Rick and Adam agreed it was a good idea to get business cards and pick some magazine agent address from the Tokyo yellow pages. 'It can take just 30 minutes to one hour to get cards made,' he explained.

As soon as the All Nippon Airways flight had landed at Fukuoka, Nishimura-san and her boyfriend took the subway to Nomura-san's house to meet his wife. As the meeting with this desperate woman drew closer Nishimura-san felt less confident about her theory on Nomura-san's absence, and started to feel empty in the pit of her stomach.

She made the appropriate raps on the steel door of Nomura's seventh floor apartment at Hirao and they were answered quickly by his wife whose face lit up with expectation. Nishimura-san was hoping his wife might have heard good news by now but it was clear she had heard nothing.

Nomura-san's wife said she had thought of everything and had rung everyone she knew in Tokyo and also some places her husband was likely to frequent but received no leads. To make matters worse she was receiving more phone calls but had taken Nishimura-san's advice and was not answering them.

'I am sure they must be from our record club members and other people wanting to check some things regarding the Mereleigh visit. It's terrible!' She burst into tears. At this point Nishimura-san knew they had to inform the police about his absence as it was sheer torture for his wife.

'Look, we will report him missing to the police. I am sure they will track him down soon.' Nishimura's decision brought some relief to Nomura's wife.

She had done as Nishimura-san had requested and kept her phone off the hook and not answered any mobile calls to save herself the trouble of having to repeatedly tell people that her husband had not returned from Tokyo, but she regularly checked her voice mail and did so as Nishimura-san stopped talking. Amid the many messages was a strange call from Tokyo along these lines:

'Konnichi-wa, sumimasen, Tokyo wa Nishi ku Capsule Hotel desu, last night a Nomura-san stayed with us and left small problem with laundry and cleaning. He also forgot his name card holder, thus we could get your phone number. After he left, we noticed some dry cleaning and washing matter in the hallway near his capsule which he did not pay for so please telephone me as soon as you can. I am Watanabe.' The call trailed off with apologies and thanks in the normal polite manner of Japan.

Nomura-san's wife told Nishimura-san to grab the spare phone and explained what the call was about. She reached Watanabe-san who had the deep, cancerous, throaty voice of a chain smoker. Watanabe explained in the most apologetic and politest terms that Nomura-san had arrived at the capsule hotel very late, very drunk and in a dishevelled state, and had just turned in without properly changing, or even bathing!

Nomura-san's wife was aghast at this, particularly him not taking a bath. She apologised profusely and told Watanabe-san that her husband was sick and had had a terrible day. Watanabe-san sympathised and said that, while Nomura-san had prepaid for his capsule, he had not apparently paid for the cost of cleaning up vomit inside the tiny sleeping capsule and more vomit in the hallway before he left. His wife was embarrassed to the core and made hasty profuse offers to cover the damage as soon as possible, and then asked if Watanabe-san had any idea where he was going as she was afraid he had lost his mind.

'No, unfortunately I do not, but he left very early, about 6.15am, and the night staff said he looked quite sick,' she added.

The two ladies sat down after the call to consider what to do next. Clearly he was still alive wandering around Tokyo. Should they still inform the police or not? Nomura-san's wife was not as worried as before and even somewhat angry that he had not bothered to call so she tried his mobile again. Again she got a voicemail reply and then angrily told her husband to sober up as soon as possible and ring her. Nishimura-san and her boyfriend allowed themselves a small smile at her tone.

It was then decided that Nomura-san's wife check his voice mail and tell anyone asking about the Mereleigh group arrangements that her husband had been delayed in Tokyo and would be back either later in the day or tomorrow. Meanwhile Nishimura-san requested access to all the correspondence and files on the Mereleigh visit in an attempt to try and exonerate herself from any blame and try to establish how the shocking misunderstanding had happened.

She had explained to Nomura-san's wife about the mistake and huge embarrassment of finding the wrong people at Narita and if she could clear her and Nomura-san's names it would encourage Nomura-san to return home as soon as possible.

Nishimura-san and her boyfriend got Nomura-san's wife to unlock the filing cabinet with all the correspondence and details of arrangements. After four hours of detailed searching, she managed to assure herself she had accurately translated and communicated the invitation request to the UK group and that there was nothing specifically in the inward correspondence and emails which stated the group was the Mereleigh Record Club and not the cast of the movie.

'So you see, as far as I can see, the mistake has been made by the UK film company which forwarded the invitation to the Mereleigh Record Club rather than to the casting director of the studios who hired all the actors for the film,' she said, relieved. 'Both sides kept communicating without realising that we wanted the film cast, and the Mereleigh group thought they had been invited,' she said.

'But what do we do now, should I call Fukuoka City Hall and all the others and tell them of this mistake and also how Nomura-san is missing? But you know we banked a lot of money from sponsors and some might become suspicious that your husband has taken off with the money!' she added.

'That's impossible, he is not a crook and I am sure we can check our record club bank account now to verify it's all here,' Nomura-san's wife protested.

They found all the bank books and statements and it appeared there had been no withdrawals, and nor had Nomura-san taken any card or cheque book belonging to the record club with him. It was a huge relief to all of them, though they never doubted his honesty, and another potential problem out of the way.

'I don't want to contact the police yet. He might be sick but might be just very sick with worry and you know he is not a traditional type of Japanese man who would commit suicide. I am sure as he sobers up he will try to think of a way out of this problem and we should give him time,' his wife pleaded with Nishimura-san.

'OK, but we have little time. This is a ticking bomb and the sooner we can defuse it some way the better,' Nishimura-san argued.

⌘⌘⌘

At Tokyo, Rick, Adam, Tanaka-san and Yoshi took a taxi to the street where Jenny was supposed to be staying. Yoshi had managed to get a very realistic set of business cards printed out and had bought a copy or two of the English women's magazine that he was supposed to represent in Japan. Adam had coached him a bit on the publications business and even suggested that Yoshi should infer that the magazine would be interested in a story on Jenny's show biz success in Tokyo.

'Very good idea John-san, very good clear thinking.

Rick-san you were right in bringing this young man along,' Tanaka stated.

The taxi dropped them off at a little yakitori place a hundred yards from the residence and Yoshi strode forth confidently. He was a large, simple, amiable person who was really enjoying this bit of detective work. In his early 20s, he came from a wealthy family who had hoped he would become a lawyer but he dropped out of law school and went to catering college to become a chef instead. He loved food of all kinds and was also just overcoming a natural shyness of females which had rather held back his practical experience with the opposite sex.

If Jenny was there and it looked like trouble, he had set his mobile phone with Tanaka-san's number and would simply press call. On that cue the other three would race over to lend any physical assistance that might be necessary, so they sat tentatively on the edge of their bar stools, and had some cash handy to leave on the bar to pay for the food should they have to exit quickly.

Yoshi found the building and took the small lift up to the appropriate floor in a confident manner. He had rehearsed his lines and he noted just one or two other people, a sallow, sickly-looking man probably in his early fifties but who looked a cancerous 60 year old, and a couple of tarts in short-skirted sparkling dresses of the kind worn by hostesses, who were on their way out. They spoke in common rasping tones and not the tinkling high pitched tones they would have to use at their place of employment to induce male customers to part with their money.

He found the door, pressed the bell, and a rather hard mama-san type voice demanded to know who was there. He explained and the door opened a few feet so he could see a reasonable apartment, and the backs of two women who were making their faces up for the night. The mama-san did not invite him in but seemed convinced by his line and did not deny Jenny resided there or any knowledge of her. She just kept her comments to an ambiguous 'Maybe someone here can get in touch and let her know about this magazine and the story.'

It was all she would concede even when pressed by Yoshi for a specific address or phone number, or detail of where she worked. He felt if he pressed any more he might give himself away and had to remember he was posing just as a kind of modest sales-type rep. who would not be that interested in doing a lot of follow-up work. He took care to leave his name card for Jenny to contact him and also had the presence of mind to suggest that there was a deadline of a couple of days by which she was supposed to respond to the offer of free publicity, which he said the publishers would actually pay her for.

The mama-san gave him a hard look as he left and he noted a Yakuza type had come out on the landing from another apartment and took the lift to the ground floor with him. Yoshi did not want that clown following him so he made pretence of anger that his taxi had not waited and asked the Yakuza if he knew a local taxi company. The Yakuza gave him a number, he rang it and waited, and the Yakuza pretended to cross to a nearby convenience store ostensibly to make a purchase, but in fact kept Yoshi under surveillance the whole time.

The taxi came and Yoshi boarded it. He took a five minute ride to the driver's annoyance and then walked back to the other two at the yakitori bar by a different route; certain he was not being followed. He gave his account to the others and it generated a lot of excitement. Tanaka-san, a restrained man by temperament, said it seemed clear to him that Jenny was at least associated with the people in that apartment, and he would try and see his Otani Club lady friend that night if he could, and dig out some more information.

'Lucky you,' said Rick.

Yoshi said he would be happy to swap roles with Tanaka-san as there was no sex in his role. John was revelling in this jocular repartee in broken Japlish, and said as an aside to Rick, 'The Japanese have a great sense of humour, don't they!'

Tanaka-san rang Emi on his mobile phone and got a firm indication that she would be available after 2am, so he made a date and went back to the Shiba Park Hotel with the other three.

⌘⌘⌘

Nomura-san was beginning to come to his senses when he woke on a park bench near the Imperial Palace. He had a crashing headache and was uncertain where he was or of the events of the past 24 hours, except he had a huge headache, his clothes were like a tramp's and there was this massive problem. No-one paid too much attention to him. He appeared like just another alcoholic, drop-out middle-aged man who slept rough in the park in the summer and at subway station entrances between cardboard sheets in the winter or wet weather.

He was desperate for a drink and a little food and began to stumble his way out of the park when he came upon a parking spot for big tour buses. It was a place where they disgorged their passengers to walk around part of the ground for 30 minutes or so, and then picked them up again.

He though he was hallucinating at first as one of the big red tour buses had passengers on board that looked like the Mereleigh group. This was probably a nightmare as he had spent most of the night dreaming about this horrific cock-up. His feet took him towards the coach and in his still-alcoholic state a brainwave came over him. He must stop the tour and send them home and that way everyone's face could be saved, except that of the Mereleigh group. Perhaps he could offer them some money not to go to Fukuoka!

Most of the group had already just got on the coach when he came to the coach's door and burbled to a JTB tour escort that the tour must stop. It was a different young lady to the one who had met them at the airport and to her he just looked like some loony tramp. The Mereleigh group showed mild interest in this encounter, not recognising Nomura-san.

He persisted and the JTB tour escort knew she had a very persistent drunk on her hands and asked the driver for help in Japanese. The driver stepped down and barked off some sharp words to Nomura, basically saying, 'Piss off, or we will call a policeman.'

Nomura pleaded to be allowed to, speak to the leader

of the group. That was the last thing the driver and JTB lady wanted. This was a very ugly side of Japan from which they must protect the British tourists. A couple of Japanese policemen rode past on bicycles and seeing the disturbance, took over and man-handled Nomura-san out of the way. By then he was shouting in English.

'Please go home, so sorry tour cancelled, please go home.'

Andy and Fran sitting up front caught the words and were trying to make out what he was about when the JTB lady stepped back in and the driver resumed his seat behind the wheel. The door was closed and the JTB lady rEvarted to the tinkling apologetic talk required of her role.

'So, very sorry for the disturbance. I think he is a little mad; unfortunately we have a few of these men who sleep in the parks. Mostly they are no problem at all.'

'It's sad really, but why would he want us to go home?' Fran asked the tour escort.

'I don't really know, might be he thinks you are Americans as sometimes these old Japanese men are a bit right wing and anti-American,' she explained.

Peter made a predictable comment about the Second World War and how the Japanese should be very grateful for what the Americans did under General MacArthur. He was reminded by Perry that he was never that complimentary about the Americans and the war in Britain, to which Peter said it was an entirely different situation.

'The Americans came into the war only after Pearl Harbour and fleeced Britain for everything it had during those years when Britain stood alone against the evil Axis fascists. They did not do Britain any favours but they let most of Japanese war criminals off the hook,' he concluded. The JTB tour guide waited patiently until Peter had finished and pretended not to have heard anything.

'Now we are going to drive past the Diet, which is Japan's Parliament, and this is where our democratically-elected governments have sat since the end of the war.'

As they drove past they noted the Japanese riot police always had a number of strategically-placed riot vehicles around. She explained most Japanese people were very peaceful but there were a few extreme right wing and extreme left wing groups who like to set up street protests so Japanese police were always ready to stop any problems.

'Almost every day of the year it is fine but sometimes there may be some discussion in the Diet, or some commemoration day that might bring out some protestors. It's very unusual for anyone to get hurt or killed. Usually just a lot of pushing and shouting through megaphones and the riot police put up some temporary barriers and have the water cannon to disperse them. We have never had terrorist bombs like the IRA or fanatical Muslim groups yet,' she added.

'The next stop and building we will see, I think you will recognise as something very familiar even if you have never been to Japan before,' she continued, waving in the general direction of the building.

'My God, it's Buck House or else a king-sized cardboard replica,' Oswald exclaimed to the group.

'Yes, yes, you are right but not cardboard or king-size, but exact scale and design as Buckingham Palace,' the JTB guide explained.

'Akasaka Palace was built by the Japanese Royal family because they wanted to mould the image of a modern royalty on the British Royal Family. These days they don't use it themselves, it's just kept for visiting foreign dignitaries and the Japanese Royal Family stay at the Imperial Palace which is traditional Japanese,' she added.

'During the Meiji period more than a hundred years ago it was decided that Japan must catch up with Europe as fast as possible, so Japanese experts were sent to many countries in Europe and the United States. The navy, for instance, was based on the British navy and the army developed along the lines of the Prussian, and so on,' she said.

The record club group noted that Japan had retained a lot of its original culture, including its own distinctive food, tatami mats in houses, and religions. The tour had taken in both Shinto shrines and Buddhist temples and left the Mereleigh group confused over how someone could have two religions at the same time.

'To the Japanese there is no clash between the Shinto and Buddhist beliefs and we might find many Japanese who have a traditional birth ceremony at a Shinto shrine then like to dress up and have a Christian church-style wedding and a Buddhist funeral,' she told them.

None of them could be unimpressed with what they had seen of central Tokyo which was modern, wide, spacious, clean and well-organised. It was, the group were told, the dubious benefit of having the central city razed by fire-bombing during the Second World War. Almost everything had to be rebuilt.

Nomura-san had been abandoned to his own fate by the two policemen after the coach left, with a stern warning that any further crazy behaviour would see him locked up. The encounter had sobered Nomura-san up a fraction but he had become enslaved to the idea of getting the Mereleigh group to end their tour short of Fukuoka. It would, he thought, be the best solution, and any kind of excuse could be dreamed up like sudden illness, or an urgent need for film-making. He decided to head for the Shiba Park Hotel via one or two sake outlets.

The group had already returned to the hotel about ten minutes earlier and most had gone to their rooms when he attempted to enter the hotel. He had gained a few yards inside the main entrance before a doorman saw him and blocked his passage, believing he was dealing with a drunken tramp.

'Stop, you can't come in here, please turn around and go out,' the doorman instructed, but Nomura-san protested in loud tones.

'I have come to tell them that they must cancel their tour. They must go home. We do not want them in Fukuoka, it's all a big mistake,' Nomura-san shouted.

The doorman eased him outside, having no idea who or what this apparent drunk was referring to, and he stayed outside until he was certain Nomura-san had gone away.

The encounter was spotted by Frances Mold and Lindsay Love, the two single ladies in the group, who told some of the others there had been a repeat performance of the earlier encounter by another drunk, demanding people cancel their tours. They saw Rick and Adam taking coffee and mentioned it to them.

'Most likely just crazy old drunks. You still find a few of the old folk who are really anti-foreigner. I once had a young mate who wore an old British army battledress jacket around the place, and he was hounded several times by cranks,' Rick said.

Nomura-san then had another idea as he wandered down to Hamamatsu Cho railway station to find a small bento meal. He would ring Fukuoka City Hall and the Prefecture office and tell them the tour had been cancelled. Then if the British group contacted those places they might realise they were not wanted.

It was all crazily illogical panic stuff, and Nomura-san was clutching at straws. He made his calls to the two civic organisations but never mentioned his name or a valid reason why the tour should be cancelled, and was thus treated as some idiot with a weird agenda.

The Mereleigh group, including Rick and Adam, went out to dinner and exchanged notes on the day's happenings. They wanted to know how Rick and Adam had got on with the missing person hunt and were pleased some progress had been made, and they laughed off the two apparent cranks. Oswald was very impressed with the number of restored Minis he had seen. His first car was one of the first on the road.

'It looks like the Japanese have cornered the second-hand Mini Minor market and brought them all here,' he noted. Derek Sloan said Japan had changed a lot since his visit a few decades ago to Nagasaki, when he was in the Navy.

'Things were very cheap then and there was a lot of rebuilding going on, but now, phew, it's pretty pricey,' he told them.

Ewan, the gay member of the group, told them he had been speaking to one of the barmen and there was a good bar uptown which had been recommended so he would lunge forth on his own to check it out.

'Good luck, mate,' Perry shouted.

John got a surprise call from the two Nishi Nippon Shimbun journalists who said they would be round in 30 minutes to pick him up and take him out for the night.

'You know they mentioned it but I just thought they were trying to be polite so

Did n't take it seriously. Anyway, I will see them in the lobby then,' he added.

Maggie said she had missed Rick on the tour and asked him to make a point of joining her tomorrow. The rest of the group strolled back to the hotel and were glad to have a reasonably early night. Tanaka-san had managed to get a bit of sleep, knowing he was up for a physically active night with Emi. Apart from having it off, he wanted to keep reasonably alert so he could dig up a bit more about Jenny.

At Fukuoka, Nomura-san's wife was keeping a vigil next to her phone, accompanied by Nishimura-san and her boyfriend, in case her husband rang. She was beginning to get very worried again. Earlier in the day Nishimura-san had received a call from a Fukuoka City official asking her if she knew anything about the Mereleigh tour being called off. She told him, in surprise and total honesty, she did not and she asked who had suggested it. When told it seemed to be a drunk or crank she guessed immediately that it was Nomura-san.

About 9.15 pm, Nomura-san rang home and blathered out in a drunken manner that he was ending the Mereleigh tour and it might take a day or two but not to worry, then hung up. Nishimura-san instantly tried to get him on his mobile but it was switched off and they had no idea where he was. She cursed and wondered how on earth she could stop it happening and also what would be the disastrous consequences of doing so.

'You know, I still believe he holds himself personally responsible for this misunderstanding, and believes he can cover it up if the trip is cancelled.' She shook her hands in the air in exasperation. Nomura-san had found a convenient capsule hotel to sleep in and a huge bottle of sake to keep him company.

CHAPTER 5

The Nishi Nippon Shimbun journalists still had some expense account money in their pockets when they picked up Adam, and their first stop was a traditional journalists' watering hole not far from the Mainichi Shimbun, one of Japan's largest daily news papers. It was crammed with extroverted journos all exclaiming over their scoops of the day or some huge frustrations at having stories spiked or held over by news editors, or the usual frustrations of trying to get people in key places to speak.

Though Adam hardly knew a word of what was being spoken, it was a familiar atmosphere. He was instantly made welcome and everyone, it seemed, wanted to shake his hand and try out their Japlish on him. There was a constant flow of sake, and small dishes of food and skewered yakitori were placed in abundance in front of him.

His Nishi Nippon Shimbun hosts told him a young lady from their Tokyo office would soon join them as she was good at English and also, nudge, nudge, good looking. John was very impressed and when she walked in and he first saw her he knew he was in love. It was one of those occasions where a look into her face was a look right deep into her soul and she responded. She stood about five foot four, which was a bit tall for most Japanese girls, had a great figure and well-shaped legs, and her face was the picture of Asian beauty, high cheek bones, nicely slanted eyes that were quite large, and full lips.

'This is a girl to die for,' he told himself, and the way she was looking at him made him weak at the knees. Her eyes were boring into his soul and they both knew they would get on. She had a short skirt on that swirled provocatively about her knees. She was as intelligent as she was good looking, and her near-perfect English had a slight American twang about it. He guessed she was in her early to mid-twenties.

They talked as if they had just met on some desert island and no one else existed in their world. Within 30 minutes they knew each other's history, interests and ambitions and everything between them seemed totally compatible. Adam knew they would sleep together soon and blessed his luck in finding such a girl so soon. He also knew she could well be his life's companion. As they talked she frequently touched him and each touch sent a shiver of sexual desire through him.

The two Nishi Nippon Shimbun journalists were astounded at how quickly the two had chummed up and said to Michiko, their female colleague from Tokyo, more in jest than seriousness, that perhaps she had now found her husband. To their surprise she looked back at them in total seriousness and said, 'Yes, I think so!'

Michiko Hirai was one of her newspaper's Tokyo writers. She came from Fukuoka and would do a year or so in Tokyo before going back to Fukuoka as a normal step up the promotional ladder. Adam was content to stay at this place and just talk to her but the two journalists said they were off to the next place, a slightly risqué nightclub that provided free entry for Nishi Nippon Shimbun journalists in return for the occasional favourable write up.

Adam was concerned that Michiko might not be included or the place a bit unsuitable for a well brought-up girl, but to his relief he found she was coming too. In fact, she had decided to stick to his side like glue, as he was the best looking foreigner she had ever met and also he was intelligent and kind. He could be a very good father and husband she had decided, and this was one big fish she planned to land.

They crammed into a taxi and headed off toward Ginza and the bright neon night lights of clubs and bars. The place was located about six floors up and was quite spacious. Everyone was dressed up to the nines, the furnishings were plush and some acts were performed on a smallish cabaret-type stage. The show seemed to be an almost non-stop affair with people coming and going as they felt fit.

Adam and Michiko found themselves jammed together on a smallish bench seat against a wall. The warmth and intimacy of her body next to his and the delicate whiff of her perfume were overpowering. He apologised to her, 'I am sorry we are so squeezed up, you almost have to be married to sit this close,'

'Well might be we will have to get married after this!' she said with a grin. They both laughed and he felt compelled to squeeze her hand. To his pleasure it was returned in kind.

It was impossible to hold any kind of intelligent conversation. The stage microphone was almost on full volume and most of the customers seemed as intent on making their own jokes and conversations as on watching the show. Added to this was the constant attention of the waitresses plying drinks and finger food. The Master who owned the place spotted the Nishi Nippon Shimbun journalists and came over to greet them. He knew they were up from Kyushu and made a couple of jokes in Hakata-ben, the local dialect as he was from there originally.

He was introduced to Adam and bowed deeply and presented Adam with his business card, and said it was an honour to have someone connected with the Mereleigh film project. He also acknowledged Michiko and thanked her for coming to the club though both he and she knew she had no say in the matter, and told Adam he was lucky to have her as a companion.

He then went to the stage and interrupted the next act and told the audience they were privileged to have some famous British journalist with them who had a connection with the well known Mereleigh Record Club film and beckoned for Adam and Michiko to come up to the stage. Adam was red with embarrassment, both at having to go on the stage and the gaff that he was connected with the film. Michiko detected his reluctance and said to him,

'Please come up, it is expected and he will be hurt if we do not go.'

'But it is not right, I have no real direct connection with the movie,' he explained.

'You and I know you are not a film star but in Japan it's sometimes an honour just to have a foreign visitor as we are still not very international in some respects,' she explained. For the first time in his life Adam knew what it was like to be a minority race person and he realised instantly that middle-class Europeans seemed to be a desired minority by many Japanese people. It was very flattering.

Adam and Michiko joined the Master on the stage and he bowed and gushed at them in a very theatrical manner and asked Michiko to translate. She paraphrased his address just saying he was so honoured to have Adam there tonight as so many Japanese people had seen the movie of the Mereleigh tour to New Zealand and admired the sentiments of the film. It was stated as though Adam had personally written the script and acted out the main role.

He just thanked the Master for his hospitality and said how great the club was and how impressive Tokyo was. He did not mention that he had missed the first full day tour to look for Jenny! He ended praising his father and mother who were original members of the Mereleigh Record Club.

Michiko looked at him quizzically not quite understanding the last part but was not given time to ask him to explain as the Master wanted to get on with the show, so she said Adam was the son of the famous actor who took the part of Peter Green in the movie and was a journalist.

They were loudly applauded as they left the stage and returned to their seat. Adam was a bit puzzled by the use of the name of the actor who had played his father in the film and Michiko was puzzled by Adam's statement that his father was a member of the original Record Club.

'I did not know your father was also an original member of the Record Club, the movie publicity did not make it clear,' she said.

Adam was a bit bemused. 'Did you say my father was an actor in the movie?'

'Yes, because that is what they,' she pointed at the two Nishi Nippon Shimbun journalists, 'told me,' she explained.

Suddenly Adam was very worried. Perhaps she had just been making a fuss over him because she thought he was the son of the famous actor.

'Look, there seems to be a terrible misunderstanding, my Dad is an ordinary person and was a member of the group, not an actor. The events portrayed in the film happened to him,' he explained.

She patted him on the shoulder affectionately and said, 'don't worry, I still think you are a very nice person and honest, too, but someone has made a mistake and I have to tell my two colleagues.'

Adam's mind raced ahead as she began to explain how Adam fitted into things. Adam suddenly realised perhaps there was a very big misunderstanding and they thought the whole group consisted of the film stars and not the original club members. He was not given a chance to speak his fears. The conversation between Michiko and her colleagues was very intense and the two journalists started to look very worried. Michiko calmed them down and took charge.

'OK, it's kinda complicated. Our newspaper was told at the beginning by a Mr Nomura that it was the cast of the movie who had been invited to come to Fukuoka for the fundraising affair, and they still think the members of your group are the movie's stars !' she explained.

Adam felt weak at the knees and sick in the stomach. 'Oh dear, what a stuff up, it's a shocker. Does everyone in Fukuoka think we are the stars and not ordinary people?' he asked.

Michiko politely referred the question to the journalists. They nodded profusely indicating there was no doubt that, from the Mayor down, they were all expecting the stars of the movie.

'Shit, shit, what a fuck up!' Adam immediately apologised to her for use of the f-word. She immediately said that she would use it herself in the circumstances. The two journalists explained their own predicament: the story written the other day proclaiming the group had arrived was based on the interview with Rick.

'We never met the group. Your flight arrived early so we missed you at the airport and, when we went to the Shiba Park Hotel, we only saw Rick-san who we knew was the real person and not the actor. He did not make clear if was just the club and not the actors on the trip,' they explained.

Adam jumped to Rick's defence, saying 'He had no reason to give an explanation as he was always organising a trip for the club members and there was never any question of the stars of the movie being invited to go, as far as I know.'

The two journalists whistled in astonishment at the magnitude of the stuff-up. They argued over who might be to blame and who would take responsibility and also reflected miserably that they had failed to see the group in person at Tokyo and could thus be held responsible for not uncovering the facts.

Michiko asked, 'Do your group know or suspect anything is wrong?'

'No, not really, apart from Nomura-san's and Nishimura-san's strange behaviour on arrival at Narita, and some weirdo who came to the hotel to say the tour had to be stopped,' he said. 'We would have expected Nomura-san to welcome us with open arms but instead he sort of collapsed as if suddenly stricken ill and Nishimura-san also became very withdrawn and they both disappeared very quickly. We expected to see Nomura at the Shiba Park Hotel that evening but he failed to show up and we have not heard anything from them.'

The journalists said it explained a lot. They too had tried to contact Nomura-san and Nishimura-san. No-one knew where he was and now, perhaps, he had committed suicide or was thinking of it, they suggested. Michiko said she thought Nomura-san would not go to those lengths. 'Maybe there is another reason for this mistake, but first someone must tell the Mayor at Fukuoka and the others and also your group must know.'

Adam wilted. 'This is a huge disaster. Our group will be so disappointed and hurt by it all, and ashamed and angry that they have been misled some way, and I can see the problems in Fukuoka.'

The journalists reminded Adam that the Mayor had invited the British Ambassador to some functions and also the Mayor of Auckland because the movie was located in New Zealand and Auckland was the sister city. There would be many other very big-noters and sponsors.

The noise and interruptions by nightclub customers wanting to meet Adam and exchange name cards was so disruptive that they decided to go elsewhere to sort out the problem. They were on the point of leaving when the show compére announced a new act from Britain.

Adam was almost though the door when he heard the name Jenny Jones and her famous Eartha Kitt repertoire. He had just time to glance over his shoulder and see a very glamorous Afro-Briton walk on to much applause, before he was guided and pushed out the door by his friends.

'I think I know who that is…,' Adam protested as his friends almost thrust him into a waiting taxi. 'Sorry, this is another subject but very important. Has anyone got a mobile phone?'

Three mobiles were thrust at him. 'Well, can someone dial Shiba Park Hotel so I can talk to Rick?'

The call was made and Rick was told that Adam had

almost certainly sighted the missing girl. The journalists gave Rick the club's address.

'Why in the hell didn't you stay there and approach her?' Rick asked.

He replied that there was another huge problem they had to deal with that would involve everyone in the group. Adam said they were en route to the Foreign Correspondents' Club and he appreciated Rick needed to know about the new problem as soon as possible.

'So you want me at two different places at the same time! Look, I think I can get Tanaka-san to check out the club and see if he can contact Jenny, and I will join you at the Foreign Correspondents' Club, if they will let me in.' Rick was exasperated by it all. Adam assured Rick the Nishi Nippon Shimbun journalists would fix his entry okay and gave him the address.

'It should take about 30 minutes from the Shiba Park Hotel at this time of night, I am told,' he added.

Rick managed to get Tanaka-san before he left for his early morning assignment with Emi, and he agreed to check out the possible sighting of Jenny. He then bumped into Andy at the lobby on his way out and in answer to Andy's question as to where he was going at that time of night he said there was a possible sighting of Jenny that needed checking out. Andy sent him on his way with a cheery 'best of luck,' then retired to his bed oblivious to the impending disaster over the tour.

Adam was treated to a quick look around the Foreign Correspondents' Club on arrival and was greatly impressed at its commanding position and fantastic views of Tokyo.

'My word, I would not mind being a foreign correspondent here,' he said, and got an unexpected glow of
approval from Michiko, who was already thinking a year
or two ahead of Adam as far as this new relationship was
concerned. They found a table, ordered drinks and got
straight into the serious business at hand. Adam sum-
marised a possible course of action.

'Right, we have confirmed there is a serious mistake,
but we don't know who made it or under what circumstances it arose. Let's give Nomura-san and Nishimura-
san the benefit of the doubt for now even though their
behaviour is very strange. It seems only us here, and
Nomura and Nishimura, are aware of the problem.'

'What are our responsibilities as journalists?' he asked.
'We should check the facts with Nomura-san and his
team, and also Andy and Rick on my side, before we file
stories,' Adam told them.

The three journalists listened intently and nodded frequently. Just to be sure they understood Michiko translated everything Adam had said. After a pause, the two
Nishi Nippon Shimbun men agreed with Adam and
again pointed out that finding Nomura-san and
Nishimura-san was the problem on their side whereas
Rick might be able to throw light on how the preparations
were made and what understandings were taken and
given by the Mereleigh Group.

Adam told them he was a stringer (part-time correspondent) for the Guardian and this was a major story
now, so he had to balance his journalist's instincts against
doing a hard-nosed story that could possibly throw the
book at whoever was responsible. The Nishi Nippon

Shimbun journalists pointed out the intent of the visit was to raise funds for charity and it really involved dedicated, unpaid volunteers on the Japan side so they wanted to be as kind and considerate as possible. Everyone agreed with that point, and they were just getting into what they should do next when Rick walked in.

Adam briefed him quickly and earnestly about the cock up. Rick went distinctly pale and pointed out he was not in the communications loop between Andy's team and Nomura-san's and, being based at Auckland, he had simply booked travel arrangements for Andy and liaised a bit with his agent in Japan over the Fukuoka hospitality they were getting.

'You have to inform Andy as soon as possible and let him decide, but not tonight. Let him sleep and let us try to think a bit more about this,' Rick told them.

Adam asked the Nishi Nippon journalists if they were filing a story on it tonight for the morning edition. They conferred for a long time between themselves and Michiko whispered to Adam,

'They are both reluctant to do so until we have found Nomura-san and got Andy's reaction to this'.

They stopped and spoke to Michiko in Japanese.

'Are you going to file for the Guardian now?' her eyes pleaded with him suggesting that perhaps he should not.

He got the drift. 'If you don't file, I will not either but perhaps we should inform our respective editors of this dilemma confidentially, and ask them to hold off for at least twenty-four hours to give us time to get more on it,' he suggested.

Rick said he thought that fair enough, although he would prefer they gave it a couple of days as the Mereleigh group deserved to know what sort of reaction the news would have on the Fukuoka part of the tour. There was more discussion between the journalists. It was obviously going to be a very big story in Fukuoka, and they did not think their editor would agree to hold it off for as much as forty-eight hours but might agree to a twenty-four hour delay.

Rick interjected and said he did not want anyone telling the Mayor of Fukuoka about this until his group had been properly briefed, and he asked the Nishi Nippon Shimbun to keep it in house. He noted that Nomura-san and Nishimura-san were still missing and if the news hit the headlines they both might do something very stupid. For their sakes, perhaps, they should all try to find them first so that collectively both sides could discover how the misunderstanding occurred and prepare for a possible change of plans.

So they decided that Adam and Rick would let the Mereleigh group know of the problem and try to track down where a misunderstanding occurred, and the two Nishi Nippon Shimbun journalists would concentrate on their hunt for Nomura and Nishimura. It was decided that Michiko would make herself available to help Adam and do whatever translation work he needed.

'Could not be better,' Adam thought to himself, and he smiled a nod of approval to her.

The group treated themselves to a round of stiff drinks to gain a bit of Dutch courage before breaking the news to the various parties. Rick insisted that he tell Andy first in confidence and asked Adam to keep quiet about things and not even tell his parents until something had been sorted out.

'If you have a problem in the travel industry, you try to find a solution for your customers before breaking the bad news, so just give me some space and time,' he told Adam.

With work to do they set off on their various ways but Michiko insisted on accompanying Adam and Rick back to the Shiba Park and used a taxi chit on the company account. It was near midnight when they got back. Rick quickly excused himself and said he would tell Andy. Adam asked Michiko if she would like a coffee. She accepted and began to walk towards the lift. Adam hesitated for a moment, about to tell her the coffee shop was on the same floor, when he rightly guessed she was prepared to take coffee in his room.

'What a night, what a night,' he kept telling himself. 'You meet the most beautiful girl in the world; you catch a glimpse of a lost person at a club then learn about a huge disaster.'

Michiko stood close to him in the lift, not like some cheap tart but in the manner of a long-time girlfriend or new wife. He smiled bashfully at her, she blushed and smiled back. He just could not believe it. 'Is she prepared to go to bed on the first date or is she just here for coffee?' he asked himself. 'How do you tell with the Japanese? If she were British it would be more than the coffee, I guess.'

He decided to play it cool and polite out of fear of destroying what looked likely to become a great relationship. She liked the way he let her in and out of the lift door first, so British and so different from a lot of vain Japanese men.

When they got to his room he offered her one of the two comfortable arm chairs and he took the other, a respectable distance away, so she did not feel crowded. They both started to talk at the same time about the events of the night, and then they stopped and laughed in unison.

'Are you going to call the Guardian news editor now?' she asked him.

'No, there is no point. No one else knows about this story, so why bother him until we are ready to file a story,' he replied. There was a pause; both had the same things on their minds. She looked delicious sitting relaxed, legs crossed, skirt just on top of the knee, top coat off displaying a form fitting sweater and hair almost to her shoulders.

She laughed and smiled easily, and always waited from him to say his piece. Every time he looked into her eyes it brought a kind of shuddering nervousness. He felt her gazing deeply into his soul and that this could be one of the most decisive moments of his life. He was not going to stuff up with some sort of cheap shot approach to lay her tonight, but he felt that was what she wanted.

She broke a silence and said, 'You know, I have an idea for a story which maybe you can help me with?'

'What is it?' he asked.

'Whatever happens about the Mereleigh tour there is going to be a big story and if we take a negative view that it might have to be cancelled, or at least temporarily can-

Roy Vaughan ~

celled, then I want to interview and write up the story of your members and their huge disappointment at the loss of a chance to help with some worthwhile fundraising.' she explained.

'That's terrific. It could shame everyone into making this thing happen if the sponsors at Fukuoka pull the plug on the event, but I want to do a story on Nomura-san and Nishimura-san as it seems they have done most of the work and must be recognised for their great efforts and intentions. Can you help me with that?' he asked.

'Certainly, but first we have to find Nomura-san and Nishimura-san and get their confidence, and I think we have to let this thing take its course for a few days. If the problem is sorted and the event goes ahead, we still have a story, I think, but it might not be so dramatic,' she added.

'You are not just a pretty face, you're a very smart lady,' Adam added enthusiastically.

'Who said I was a pretty face? I am just ordinary really,' she said in the typical Japanese self-effacing manner, but blushing as she said it.

'You're a cracker. A girl a man would die for,' he said unashamedly 'I am so glad I met you.'

'Me too, but what are we going to do, sit here and make our plans for the story or go to bed?' she asked, guessing he would suggest the latter. Adam was taken with a sudden touch of embarrassment, thinking he might have been a bit presumptuous.

'Oh, I am sorry. It is late and perhaps you have a way to go,'

193

'No I was just thinking of the bed here.' She smiled broadly.

'Err, yes, of course,' he added bashfully, genuinely taken aback by her frankness. She came over and they passionately hugged and kissed. Suddenly she broke off.

'In Japan we always take a bath before we go to bed, so please take a bath first,' she instructed.

Adam thought perhaps he ponged a bit after all the rushing around and apologised. She assured him he did not, it was just a customary thing to do in Japan, and she explained how in Japan everyone soaps and showers first and then immerses themselves in a tub of clean water.

She noted the hotel bathroom was a western-style one with a shower and bathtub, so she said, 'I have no need to show you how to do it, but when we stay at a traditional Japanese ryokan, I will demonstrate as there will be room for me to rub your back.'

Hell, it gets better; Adam thought to himself, I can't wait. She gently removed her clothes and then his, and it was all he could do not to have it off with her there and then. She then neatly folded his clothes while he took his shower and a bath. By the time he heaved himself out of the bath; she had undressed and was wearing only a dressing gown but had a towel ready for him. He was embarrassed by his own huge erection as he caught sight of her perfectly-formed, brown-tipped breasts and shiny, close-cropped black pubic hair.

'God, you're beautiful!' He clutched her and gave her a kiss.

'Wait, wait, you have not seen all of me yet, and I must

take a bath,' She gently pushed him aside and threw off her dressing gown, displaying a beautiful smoky-white torso as she stepped into the shower.

'My God, this is agony,' Adam thought. 'I feel I might blow my top like some over-excited teenager at the first touch of her naked body,' he worried.

He tried to read a book for the few minutes she took to bathe, but it was just pretence. Shortly she slipped naked into bed and told him apologetically that she did not make a habit of this but her instinct told her they were right for each other. He agreed profusely. They kissed tenderly. He felt her breasts and remarked that the nipples were brown.

'Can you imagine a Japanese girl with pink nipples and a yellow skin colour?' she laughed.

'No, I never thought of it before,' he said in naïve honesty.

'It's like us. We see you with light brown hair and I find your pubic hair is almost blond. How come?' She laughed provocatively and threw back the covers so they lay together totally naked on the bed.

They romped like kids, touching each other's parts until the passion overcame them and he entered her compliant, writhing body. She groaned with ecstasy at his thrusts deep inside her and threw back her head. Then suddenly it was over, and they relaxed in total satisfaction.

Adam glanced sleepily at the clock. It was 2 am and the group was expected to move out on the next tour at 8.30am. He was also conscious that he had finished inside her without using a condom and apologised for not with-drawing or using protection.

'It's okay, it's a safe time for sex with my cycle,' she explained, 'and with you I took a chance that you don't have any disease.'

She nestled close to him with one leg over the lower part of his thigh and breasts against him. They dropped off to sleep and at about 4.30 am he was very aware she was sharing his bed. They felt for each other almost in their sleep and coupled up for another round of passion.

⌘⌘⌘

Tanaka-san, who had taken up the task of checking out Jenny Jones at the nightclub, arrived towards the end of the club's cabaret act and was only there in time to see a small cast of performers taking a final bow together. Jenny, the Euro-African girl, fitted the bill age and race-wise, and was very like the photo Rick had received on his mobile phone.

It had to be her, he concluded, but at the time he was still in an entry tangle at the door waiting for other cus-tomers to move in. He knew the master of the establish-ment vaguely as both he and the master were from Fukuoka, and he remembered this master also has a bar at Nakasu, the Fukuoka nightlife area, which he had visited years ago.

He spoke in Hakata-ben to the doorman and was given entry for a tidy sum just when he would have pre-ferred to have been refused so he could apprehend Jenny leaving the establishment. He thought quickly. It would look strange if he left suddenly and he guessed Jenny might be heading for another gig, perhaps for a more select audience where an encore of a different sort would be expected!

He was shown a table by a super-attentive, brain-dead hostess who tittered at his every word. He looked at her; she was probably little more than eighteen and looked as though she might have been one of those high school girls who rolled up their skirts at the waist to show off their upper thighs to the world in order to invite sex into their lives. She had probably had it off with a few paying salary men in dark corners before some Yakuza got on to her and put her on the game and into one of these dives, he reflected.

There were various levels of prostitution in Japan, ranging from semi-nude provocative photos on name cards that were plastered around public phone boxes to the hostesses at bars who made themselves available after hours to special paying boyfriends. Then there were the dancers and singers at seedy joints who earned more from their paying boyfriends, and the 'nieces' who were paid retainers to be available to go out with their 'uncles' or bosses and perform the task of 'night secretaries.' Compared with this lot geishas were very respectable.

Tanaka-san allowed himself a couple of very diluted and grossly over-priced whiskies and probed a bit about the night's entertainment that he had missed. He asked some of the hostesses about the black girl. They said she was new to this place and did not work for the master but was just part of a small group of performers he hired from time to time.

'The master thinks entertainers are too much work, so he just hires what he wants from several different people,' one of the hostesses explained.

Tanaka-san decided to make a move. He delicately extracted himself from two super-attentive hostesses, more interested in his wallet than his body, showered them with compliments, pinched one of them on the bum and told the other her breasts were like twin Mount Fujiyamas. It was expected chauvinistic behaviour and he did not want to create any suspicion about his intent. Once outside, he flagged a taxi, rang Emi and agreed to pick her up at 2am at a prearranged place.

Now in his early sixties, Tanaka-san was still a burly, virile man, a qualified civil engineer from Wasada University who had worked long and hard for a Kyushu-based construction company. Rugby was his real passion in life, especially after losing his wife to breast cancer a few years ago.

He knew the rough side of business life in Japan where deals were cut ostensibly on a friendship basis, and the friendships secured with appropriate gifts at the right time and sometimes a number of additional profit margins had to be cut into a deal. He had in latter years been more of a quantity surveyor working ostensibly for a small independent company as its MD, but in fact the company was owned totally by the big construction company he had worked for all his life.

There was nothing sweet or innocent about Japanese business life. The politeness and bowing was part of what went on above the clean tablecloth as were the super polite meetings with prospective customers. It was at the late night drinking sessions and clubs that the customers expressed what they really wanted, and then only after they had been well-oiled with liquor and women, and with the promise of undeclared expenses.

There was more honesty and directness in rugby circles than among some slime-balled developers with their Yakuza connections ready to lean on local government politicians and Dietmen to get what they wanted. He hated to think just how many Dietmen depended on Yakuza money for their election campaigns and what they had to do in return. Tanaka-san found himself looking forward to meeting Emi. She was a world weary, rather battered person like himself and a lot more honest than many of those in Japanese society who set themselves up as paragons of virtue.

She was waiting by an all night café when he arrived by taxi and was clearly pleased to see him. She saw in Tanaka-san a worthy person and a possible soul mate for a while. They greeted each other with such warmth that the taxi driver wondered if this was just a cash relationship for the night or perhaps something deeper.

The taxi dropped them off at Tanaka's place; he gave the driver a chit and they disappeared quickly inside. Emi went straight away to the kitchen to make something to drink and play the okusan role. Tanaka-san really appreciated it. It was a genuine, natural gesture and not the act of some ingratiating late-night tart.

'Okusan wa, doomo arigatoo gozaimasu,' he thanked her as his wife.

She smiled with deep, warm pleasure knowing that

maybe she could have a long relationship with him. After some refreshments and a bath they tumbled into bed. He looked at her 50 year-old body which was in pretty good nick. She had smallish breasts but they did not sag and a somewhat careworn face, but her smile was always ready and that made up for a few wrinkles.

She knew exactly what he wanted and pressed the right buttons to help him on his way. He was surprised at the extent of his sexual attraction for her but he detected a deep need in her and pulled every trick in his repertoire to make sure she had a real orgasm. They both needed a bit of recovery time afterwards, and then she cleaned them both up and brought in a hot drink.

'Well Otosan, what do you want to know about this black British girl?' Emi decided to cut to the chase, confident that Tanaka-san would come clean with her about this. She had rightly guessed he was a man on a mission and the affair was a side-show. Tanaka-san was not surprised. In fact he was grateful that Emi had worked things out for herself. She was smart and likely to be more cooperative and honest if he squared with her.

'Emi-chan, I trust you, and even with my life, but helping me might put you in some danger too, so before I ask or say anything just reflect on it for a moment,' he said.

'I made a decision to trust this rough rugby man after our first night together, so don't worry.' She poked him in the ribs and laughed. 'But if I tell you too much and they find out, at best I could lose my job and at worst they could physically harm me or kill me. So you must consider if you are prepared to help and protect me, tough guy-san!' she said. Tanaka-san knew and expected her to react that way and was prepared.

'Since I lost my wife my rugby friends have been constantly introducing me to lots of ladies, most of whom I have nothing in common with. You know some middle-aged divorced misfits, some single crackpots, some selfish types, and I have to say a few nice ones who would be far too good for me.'

She cut him short. 'So this old tart is just what you want, a person who knows how to give you good and regular fucks, can stay up late and care for you when you come home depressed, and get up early to see you leave on time in a smart suit and clean shirt,' she joked.

'You probably never ever played that role in your life, so how do you know you can do it?' he asked.

'Because it is exactly what I and most women want, a man of their own who can love them, not 10 men a day in different body positions and fetishes, not false charm and ugly soulless bosses, and spewing drunks in the club's toilets. My only child, my grown-up daughter had a good education and is now 26, and she wants to have a mother that she can introduce to her husband-to-be, not some old worn out nightclub cat!' she explained.

Tanaka-san roared with laughter. 'You will do me, but we have to play out our existing roles for a week or so yet, I think, and then you and I will disappear to Fukuoka. To put it simply, my good friend, Rick-san, who is originally from Britain, asked me if I could find this girl Jenny. Her parents in Britain are very afraid something might have happened to her as they have not heard from her for more than two weeks, and that is right out of character. It is her first visit to Japan and she is a genuine entertainer and not a tart.'

He told her the Euro-African girl had been at another club entertaining earlier that evening and he was sure she was the missing person. He also mentioned Yoshi's call at her accommodation ostensibly with an offer from a magazine for free publicity and a story about her life.

'The mama-san at that accommodation next door to you did not deny she was there but did not confirm it either, so we basically know she is there. We now have to see if her boss will take the bait and allow her to be interviewed. If he does, then he will have her totally under his control one way or another, and if not, he will be scared she might try to do a runner,' he explained.

'He is getting her under control progressively by the usual means,' Emi said. 'They put sedatives in her food and drink when they want her quiet and add something else to make her excited for performances. As you can understand, the main effect is that she is becoming confused and disorientated, not quite knowing what is happening, and there are always the sex demands for her to satisfy the boss's main customers. She has resisted so far but her mental state is getting worse and, as with these things, it can only be time before she does. Or else commit suicide. I have seen that before with stubborn girls.'

Tanaka-san told her that he had set a timeframe. If Yoshi did not get an answer within two days, they would act to get her out of the place as it would be a clear indication that she was not able to control her life.

'If she comes forward for an interview then Yoshi can organise a fake interview and we can pass her a note or something to ask her if she is being controlled against her will. We can get Rick-san to do that interview. She will recognise him as she met him in Britain with her parents a few years ago but the Yakuza will not know him,' he explained.

She asked if he would use the police. Tanaka said, 'Probably yes,' once they were sure she was being held against her will. Emi nodded and said she would help by trying to keep track of Jenny's movements and also if she could try to talk to her privately. Tanaka-san responded by saying emphatically he did not want Emi to take any risks at all.

'You know very well if the Yakuza finds out you and I got her released they will be after us!' he added.

⌘⌘⌘

Back at the Shiba Park Hotel, Rick woke early with a dull headache, not from booze or necessarily the late night but worrying about the future of the tour and how to handle things with the group. They would be utterly disappointed and hugely embarrassed at the stuff-up. He had been racking his brain for options as it seemed likely to him that either the Fukuoka side or they would want to terminate the tour. His only relief was that he had not booked any part of the Fukuoka section. As that had been arranged and paid for by the hosts at Fukuoka, in a sense what was going to happen or not happen there would depend on Nomura-san's group and all the sponsors.

He needed to keep Adam back from the day tour today and confer with him as he and the Nishi Nippon Shimbun journalists were key parties to this secret. His gut instinct told him they could be either totally damaging or else a huge asset. It would depend on how they read things and in that regard, the view of the Nishi Nippon Shimbun's editor would be the key.

Upstairs, Michiko was woken by her own watch alarm. She jumped out of bed, gave Adam a wake-up kiss on her way out and told him, 'Adam-san, we have very big day today, please get up.'

Adam woke in a pleasant daze recollecting the erotic events of the night. Then he had a reality check when he realised they would have to make some tough decisions about the Mereleigh tour disaster. Michiko had a quick shower and told Adam she would slip out to the hotel shop to pick up a few essentials, then meet him as if it were prearranged at the hotel lobby. Then she could join him for breakfast but avoid hotel staff and parental suspicion.

'We do not want to shock your parents too much,' she said with a smile. 'Also the other two journalists might contact me soon and we must all meet and talk,' she added.

She left just as Rick rang to say he wanted a word. Rick did not want to break the news until he had word from the Nishi Nippon Shimbun journalists. Adam agreed and said that Michiko had contacted him 'this morning' and would meet them for breakfast. Adam agreed with Rick that it was best for him to miss the tour, but he said Michiko was keen to do a human interest story on the group so it might be a good idea if she took his place and went on the tour and began her interviews. She would simply tell them she wanted their story and leave it at that, then when the storm burst she would get a true measure of their disappointment.

Rick had a few reservations. 'Is she a person of integrity and will she write something favourable, not some cheap mass media crap, and not let the cat out of the bag before time?' he asked. Adam said she seemed a very nice, honest person to him and Rick could stipulate a few conditions if he wished. Rick agreed and noted Adam seemed to have got on well with her last night!

Adam nipped down to meet Rick, and also greeted Michiko as though he had not seen her for about six hours. They sat in a corner of the hotel lobby to mutually work out the details of things to do for the day. Rick got his undertaking from Michiko, and she was eager to have the chance to go with them but also understood that Adam was eager to help Rick find Jenny, and Tanaka-san might have something to report.

Dick and Joan Round were the first into breakfast, Dick was his normal cheerful self and the first to notice that Adam seemed to have acquired a nice young Japanese lady from somewhere. Adam's parents, Peter and Brenda, were the next to appear, Peter taking a lot in at a glance when he saw Adam sitting next to Michiko and asking what Adam got up to last night.

Adam blushed and stuttered that he had been out with the Nishi Nippon Shimbun journalists, and Michiko was one of that number who was going to do a human interest story on the group. Brenda said that was nice but

Peter glowered, and Adam explained in a side whisper to Michiko that he was always grumpy in the morning.

Brenda made a point of sitting with Adam and Michiko for breakfast and immediately took a shine to her, asking heaps of questions about Japan and Japanese culture. Peter pretended to be bored and faked an interest in the international news in the English language edition of the Japan Times. He was amazed to find an English cricket test report with the current end of day's play test match score in the game against Australia.

'How many people in Japan play cricket?' he asked Michiko and was told by her there were no regular teams she knew of.

'Amazing,' he muttered to himself.

The rest of the group turned up, all in good humour, excited at having a full-day trip by coach to Hakone and Kamakura. They were all pleased that Michiko was joining them and a little surprised that Adam was bailing out. Perry poked Adam in the ribs and said, glancing at Michiko, 'You're a bloody fool to miss out on a girl like that. What a honey! I can't think of anything that would make me give up a chance to sit next to her on the bus all day!'

His wife Jean said, 'Come on, I have no doubt Adam has things sussed in that department.' Jean gave Adam a wink, and he smiled back a little shyly, thinking that women were bloody perceptive, they seemed able to sniff things out without actually seeing or being told about it.

The resplendently polished red coach was already purring at the hotel entrance with a smart young female bus attendant, coach driver and JTB guide standing by at attention like the crew of a royal barge, ready to welcome their royal highnesses on board. The JTB guide felt privileged to have a journalist on board and bowed very deeply to Michiko and she bowed deeply back. The JTB guide knew she would have to be spot-on with all her information today and was a little nervous, not that she had ever faltered before, but she could have her name in the newspaper and possibly be photographed, and the slightest mistake could see her in trouble with her bosses.

The tinkling-voiced JTB guide welcomed them all back on board and then she began to tell them about Hakone and Kamakura, saying she hoped everyone would really enjoy the beautiful Japanese country and mountain scenery. They would travel a bit on a lake, take a ropeway (cable car) to a mountain top, see Tyrolean-like inns and buildings, and have a very delicious lunch. They would also go through a park that was full of famous sculptures, statues and works of art.

It was a beautiful, clear day and Michiko's heart felt heavy with the knowledge that within about 24 hours their dreams of a great time at Fukuoka might be shattered. She had contacted her office just before they left to leave word of her plan to do this story and, of course, the Tokyo office of her newspaper did not know of the bad news.

She had set herself a few topics for this story. First and foremost she wanted to find out what sort of people the group consisted of: their backgrounds, professions, family life and how it was back in a small Thames Valley town in the late 1960s going to rock and roll parties every

Friday night. Was it really sex, drugs and rock and roll? When she looked at their faces, she could imagine a few of them being tearaways and living a bit recklessly for a few years, but most looked somewhat contented, middle-class people caring about children and families.

She wanted to find out how many had married child-hood sweethearts and how many were meeting up with ex-childhood sweethearts who had married others. She realised that most had not met for 30 years before they did their famed trip to New Zealand and wondered if there had been any illicit bedroom swaps in the small hours of the night. She had seen the film and knew that Foggy Night had met his old girlfriend, Helena, in New Zealand and they were together, and how Rick had lost his wife to cancer and was now back with Maggie Moss, his old childhood sweetheart.

Most of all she wanted to find out how much the real people differed from the film stars who portrayed them and what they were really like. Michiko was a good listener and quick on the uptake, a few years learning English in the USA had taught her a lot though she had to admit the British were a bit more restrained and more like the Japanese in many ways, enjoying an older culture.

She sat next to Fran, and Fran told her about her married life in South Africa and the difficult decision she had made to return to the UK when her marriage broke up. She still loved South Africa in many ways but had not regretted moving back to Britain. Fran told her about the invitation to come to Japan and the letters and e-mails between her and Nishimura-san and Nomura-san. She also said how strange it was that Nomura-san and

Nishimura-san did not call them since their arrival, and how they thought Nomura-san had been taken ill suddenly.

Michiko tried to look shocked and surprised, and she began to realise that the record club group had not even sensed that something might be radically wrong. Andy and Janine took Michiko under their wing and gave her an expansive overview of all the personalities and the high and low points of their youth back at Mereleigh. Michiko said she would have loved to be there then in that small Thames-side town.

'There must have been a kind of innocence about it all, no one had a mobile phone, no computers, and how on earth did you communicate?' she asked.

Andy told her people planned ahead a bit more because a lot of people then did not even have telephones in their homes, so when they met they made plans for the next day, or next week, and had to keep them.

'You have to remember that at best most of us only had motorcycles or bikes. Only one or two could afford cars. Oswald had one of the Mark I Mini Minors that we all used to cram into, and Rick a very ancient Vespa motor scooter,' Andy explained.

'You probably noticed the Mini is so popular in Japan. Japanese people probably bought a hundred thousand or so of them second hand from Britain. It's a kind of a cult car for us,' Michiko explained.

'Yes, and Oswald was a bit of a one-man cult in his youth too. Who else would buy a car with horizontal sliding windows, a manual choke and push-button starter on the floor, and drive along at an altitude lower than that of a snake sleeping under a railway line,' Dick joked.

'You and several other members of this group were very glad of a ride home on cold, dark rainy winter nights!' Oswald reminded them.

'We younger people don't have cars so much in Japan because of the cost and difficulty of parking in crowded cities, and the expensive highway tolls,' Michiko said. She added that everyone had a mobile phone and public transport was very good so there was no problem communicating or getting around.

Michio really liked talking to them. They all had different takes on life but you could see a common origin and heritage behind it. She moved around between the seats quite a bit and made a point of talking to Peter, Adam's dad. He had a kind of gruff reserve that a lot of Japanese men had, men who had been a bit disappointed with life and maybe had had some bad experience when young. It took a moment or two for her to tease any conversation out of Peter. He professed to be very impressed with many things in Japan but said astutely, 'Perhaps you keep the dirt under the table!'

She agreed and said how essential it was to keep everything nice and sweet above the table but ordinary people complained and worried about the same sort of things as westerners and a lot of traditional Japan was changing. She told him how the old generation was blaming the young people for not working hard enough and adopting the superficial values of Americans.

Peter was frank and said that, in Britain, many of his

generation, and particularly his father's generation, could never properly forgive the Germans and Japanese for the Second World War. She asked if his father had hang-ups and was a bit surprised and shocked when Peter told her that he had never seen his dad as he was an RAF pilot and was killed before he was born.

Peter took the lead and said he believed one of the problems was that Japanese people had never been educated about Second World War atrocities whereas the Germans had. Michiko confessed it was true but she was a liberal and had had many arguments with old right-wing males who could never forgive America for defeating Japan.

Peter found himself liking Michiko for she was refreshingly well-informed and frank and so polite. Michiko could understand Peter's lifelong bitterness and when he went on to talk of the bombing of London and all major British cities the civilian deaths, the food shortages and rationing that lasted until the 1950s, she began to understand that Britain had had some very bad times, like Japan.

⌘⌘⌘

As their coach ambled its way to Hakone and Kamakura, Rick and Adam were left drinking coffee in the hotel coffee shop, waiting anxiously for news from the two Nishi Nippon Shimbun journalists and also Tanaka-san. The Nishi Nippon Shimbun journalists rang to say they would be at the hotel within 30 minutes and, shortly after they arrived, Tanaka-san turned up unannounced.

Rick invited the journalists to start first. The Nishi Nippon Shimbun editor had agreed to the 24-hour news embargo on the Mereleigh problem but told his two journalists they must pull out all stops to find Nomura-san and he would get one of the more senior lady journalists to call on Nomura-san's wife and also Nishimura-san today.

The editor had agreed to Michiko doing a story on the group and was very pleased with her initiative. He welcomed Adam's co-operation and said, when the time came to tell the Mereleigh group of this problem, it was important to convey his deep sincere personal sympathy with them. The editor had also set a time for informing the various parties. He and a senior journalist would make an appointment to see the Mayor at about 7 pm, if possible, and tell him or a senior aide of the problem and he suggested that Rick tell the group at the end of the day's tour, after they had had dinner.

Rick groaned at the thought and said he wished there was someone from Nomura-san's group or Fukuoka City Hall to break the news as the group would ask heaps of questions that he could not answer and they were likely to make all sorts of demands for inquiries to get to the bottom of it. The Nishi Nippon Shimbun journalists felt confident that their journalist colleagues who would interview Nomura-san's wife and Nishimura-san would find out why it had happened and would let them and Rick know as soon as possible.

'The next vital question is does this tour to Fukuoka go ahead?' Rick asked.

Tanaka-san intervened, 'You know, maybe the people in Fukuoka cannot answer that for at least 24 hours as they have to digest the implications of this, and then perhaps because the Japanese decision-making process is slow, everyone has to come to a big meeting, perhaps, and make a collective decision. In Japan one man cannot say yes or no,' he added.

The Nishi Nippon Shimbun journalists said it was vital they found Nomura as soon as possible for two reasons. Firstly, he was theoretically more informed than anyone else on the Japan side about the events leading up to this big misunderstanding. In addition there was also the question of his mental health. They warned his condition could be getting worse and they wanted to find him before he did something stupid.

'How about the police?' Rick asked, and was told they had been informed that morning that Nomura-san was missing but he was just one of a few thousand missing people in Tokyo. Tanaka-san cleared his throat, reminding everyone of his presence, and Rick looked blankly at him then remembered why he was there.

'Sorry, Tanaka-san, how are things going with Jenny?' he asked.

Tanaka-san filled him in and told him of the deadline they were setting for a response to the magazine interview ploy and said Rick would have to front at that interview if it took place as he was the only person she knew and could trust in Japan. Adam said he also would like to be there and could pose as a journalist as he was one and Rick could assume the role of a camera man.

Rick winced at the thought. 'But I don't know the slightest thing about modern cameras,' he said in protest.

The Nishi Nippon Shimbun journalists told Adam they had a possible lead on Nomura-san and should be off on the hunt as soon as possible. Adam asked if he could come along and the journalists welcomed his presence. The trio took their leave and headed for the Mita subway station to pick up a train. The journalists explained that Nomura-san had phoned a few places recently and through a friend of a friend who worked at the British Embassy, they heard he planned to make a visit there, possibly today, to ask the British Ambassador to call the Mereleigh tour off.

'The man is crazy, what the hell has it to do with the Embassy!' Adam demanded.

They explained to him that Miss Alsop-Smith, the Ambassador, was invited to the fundraising function as she would be visiting Kyushu at the time.

'Jesus, that is helpful!' Adam responded sarcastically.

They made a few subway changes and were soon within walking distance of the Embassy.

'Might be you can introduce us to the Ambassador?' one of the two journalists asked hopefully.

Adam volunteered that without an appointment none of them probably had a snowball's chance in hell of getting an interview even if she were in, but he agreed to give it a go.

'Let's get your names straight. I have your cards but pronounce them for me please as I am totally confused by Japanese names,' he said.

'Funny, Adam-san can remember Michiko-chan's name very well,' one of the journalists joked.

One journalist said he was Takanori Kinoshita but he should be called Kenny for short as it was like English; the other said he was Osamu Funakoshi but please call him Sam. So Kenny and Sam it became. It took them about five minutes to be admitted through a security gate and a door to an inquiry desk after being frisked and producing journalists' identity cards.

They had to wait another five minutes or so before a rather officious-looking third secretary for something interviewed them. This official, a youngish man in his late twenties, looked at them in a rather bored, superior way with glances at his wristwatch while they spun their tale. He thanked them in a rather insincere manner after taking a few notes and jotting down names and address, and said it was most unlikely the Ambassador would be able to see them but he would try.

They sat and waited about 15 minutes until he returned and said in tones that indicated they were being granted a very rare privilege, that the Ambassador's time was very limited, and she would see them for about five minutes. He ushered them along a corridor past a few offices where Embassy staff shifted piles of papers and answered phones, then to large double doors where they knocked twice and were told to enter.

The Ambassador barely glanced up at them from some paperwork as they entered and greeted them as she raised her head. They could see a professional, bureaucratic woman in her late fifties wearing a trim black suit. She had steely eyes, a pale face and thin lips. Kenny and

Sam insisted on bowing very deeply as the proffered their name cards and apologised profusely for the interruption. Adam felt a bit clumsy heaving his business card out of his well-used wallet and offering his hand which she accepted and shook with almost manly firmness.

She waved them all to some chairs and came around the other side of her massive desk to sit near them. There was a slight pause, and Sam and Kenny looked at Adam and he realised he was to act as the speaking chief. Adam outlined the situation succinctly, saying that they had a tip-off that Noumura-san might be heading to the Embassy with a request that the Ambassador call the Mereleigh visit off. Noticing her concern, he quickly added Nomura-san was harmless but somewhat out of his mind with worry.

Miss Alsop-Smith informed them she was completely aware of the visit by the group and was very distressed to hear about this problem but could not see what she could do about it. Her first concern was whether Fukuoka City Hall had been informed and what its reaction was. She was less relaxed when she heard they had yet to be told officially in the evening.

'I hope you are not thinking that I will somehow call off this tour and solve the problem!' she said pointedly.

They quickly assured her they were not as they were just journalists and had no authority. They were on a hunt for Nomura-san and wanted to find out what was happening. Miss Alsop-Smith relaxed a little. 'What you have said solves one problem slightly. Yesterday one of the staff received an anonymous phone call from a rather excited Japanese man asking that we call off the Mereleigh tour for some incoherent reason my staff member could not work out. We took it to be a wild call from some anti-foreigner rightist, but on reflection it might have been your Mr Nomura.'

Adam did not like the way she attributed the problem man Nomura to him and said politely but firmly that Mr Nomura was his own person and not in his employ or that of the group. It served its purpose. Miss Alsop-Smith realised Adam was not a pushover to be sent out to do the Embassy's dirty work, as her next line would otherwise have been a few suggestions as to what Adam and his team could do to help the Embassy.

Kenny and Sam sensed it was time to leave and Adam, still a trifle miffed at the Ambassador's style, was happy to go. As they were on their way out, Miss Alsop-Smith's parting gesture was to the effect that it might possibly serve diplomatic ends best if the Mereleigh group quickly decided to call off the trip and indicated it was due to a technical hitch of some kind, and she would appreciate being told of their decision one way or the other. Adam was too taken aback to respond and just glared in reply.

As soon they had left, Miss Alsop-Smith summoned one of the undersecretaries and drafted a signal to be sent directly to the Foreign Office, London. The draft went something like:

'Regret the official attendance and call at Fukuoka might have to be cancelled due to a major misunderstanding between the Japanese hosts and British Mereleigh Record Club Group. Fukuoka was expecting the cast of the movie not the members of the actual group and all sponsorship arranged in Japan was on that basis.

Have advised Mereleigh group best interests of British diplomacy might be served if they offer to cancel the tour. This post stresses it has had no part in the planning, preparation or implementation of this totally private tour by the Mereleigh group and has recommended that UK posts and staff in Japan distance themselves from it.'

Her next instruction was to draft a signal to the UK consulates in Japan and all staff to the same effect and a request to the Osaka consulate to try to ascertain as soon as possible what Fukuoka City's reaction would be once it heard the news later in the day. She felt it wise not to place her recommendation for cancelling the tour on paper, nor make it a formal verbal request. She was certain Adam, while clearly not co-operative, would nEvartheless convey her sentiments to the group and that might do the trick.

Miss Alsop-Smith had got where she was today by avoiding blame and adroitly side stepping any kind of responsibility or association which could possibly put her in a poor light. With that done once again, she looked at her appointments book to see what else she could do in Fukuoka to replace the two or three days that she would have been there if the tour went ahead.

Once outside Kenny and Sam could see Adam was very pissed off and asked why, saying they thought the Ambassador spoke very politely and carefully. Adam tried to explain the nuance of the term 'your man' and how it was an insultingly superior way of trying to cast some blame on his group and get them to react in the manner expected by the Ambassador and to take responsibility for the problem. They saw this immediately and spoke in Japanese to each other for a moment or two, then addressed Adam saying it was totally wrong for the Ambassador to think that way.

Kenny and Sam decided to make a couple of phone calls. Kenny rang the newspaper's Fukuoka office and Sam tried for the millionth time in a few days to get Nomura-san's wife. Adam was left brooding over the group's likely reaction to the bad news. Kenny's and Sam's calls were long-winded and involved excited ups and downs, long pauses and ended with the usual string of 'thank you's'.

Kenny was the first to talk. He reported the senior female staff member at Fukuoka had contacted Nomura-san's wife and Nishimura-san, and Nishimura-san had spilt the beans on how the mistake had been made at the British film company's office which should not have passed the invite to Andy. Nishimura-san was happy to hand over copies of the correspondence to the Nishi Nippon Shimbun and said she must bring her group together as soon as possible to discuss the possible implications that day before the Mayor of Fukuoka was informed. She had no idea where Nomura-san was, and she and his wife were out of their minds with worry.

Adam was relieved to hear who had made the mistake and said it was a small relief that neither side had been responsible but rather an intermediary. Sam was able to confirm Kenny's report and said he had actually talked to Nomura-san's wife direct and promised to do his best to find him. She had mentioned one or two places where he had friends, and bars that should be checked. Adam looked at his watch, it was 11 am.

'Well, we have about six and a half hours before the shit hits the fan,' Adam exclaimed. The two Japanese journalists did not quite understand the English but got the general meaning.

'What is our priority?' Kenny asked.

Sam said that based on both humanitarian and news values it would have to be trying to track down Nomura-san. Kenny produced a notebook with some places and numbers Nomura-san's wife had given him including a small business hotel he had often stayed at in Tokyo. Kenny and Sam split the phone calls and after about 45 minutes, Sam struck gold at the business hotel. A man of the same name and fitting the description had stayed there last night, and he had not formally checked out. The hotel was in the Shibua district of central Tokyo, a kind of super king-sized Piccadilly Circus. Trying to find small business hotels in side streets of Shibua could be a nightmare even for locals.

With grim-faced determination they headed off with Adam trying to keep up with them as they dodged through large throngs of humanity at the various subway stations and trains necessary to get them to Shibua. He was scared stiff he might become separated, every station seemed to have about 30 different exits and trains arrived and departed every few moments. The two journalists laughed at his fears and helped bustle him in and out of subway carriages at the appropriate times.

Eventually they reached Shibua, and the two journalists debated for about five minutes what exit to take to get to the right street. They had about two dozen to choose from! Adam was glad to see daylight again and somewhat staggered by the mass of humanity and traffic at Shibua. The two journalists went to a street directory and carefully tried to plot a course to the hotel from where they were stood.

'Might be 15-minutes walk, and if we take a taxi might be 20 minutes because of the traffic,' Kenny explained.

Adam said a walk suited him so they charged off at some pace under railway bridges, over large pedestrian crossings, avoiding bicycles being ridden on the pavements, and eventually deviated from a main road into a much smaller side street. Adam looked around and thought if they abandoned him there he would have no chance of finding his way back to the subway station they had started from. Most of the streets looked the same; most of the buildings were so similar to many others that he could not even find the sun in the dull grey skies.

They eventually found the right street and the trio stopped while they checked street numbers. They quickly spotted a tall, thin maroon building, named 'Welcome Delight Hotel,' and they made for it. Sam went straight to the reception desk to ask if Nomura-san was in. After a bit of checking it was confirmed and he was then paged. The Nishi Nippon Shimbun journalists could not believe their luck and, so as not to frighten him away, they just gave their family names and not their occupations when the clerk asked who wanted Nomura-san.

Shortly, a short stocky bespectacled man in his mid 30s appeared, and he looked about furtively. He appeared as though he had showered and had his suit and shirt recently laundered and dry cleaned, but he was clearly nervous and defensive in manner. Sam bowed very

deeply and respectfully and introduced himself, present-
ing his business card. Kenny followed and then introduced Adam. Nomura-san had accepted the first two
introductions in a dazed and world-weary manner but
was genuinely surprised to be introduced to a European
and a journalist travelling with the group at that.

Sam and Kenny spoke gently in Japanese to him for a
long while, trying to assure him they wanted to help him
and not exploit the situation. They told him they knew
the full story from Nishimura-san and that his wife was so
anxious to hear from him. They insisted he call his wife on
Sam's mobile right now. Nomura-san unwound a bit and
agreed. His conversation with her was shy and apologetic, and he seemed relieved when it ended. Everyone
had stood back while he talked to her to give him some
privacy.

Sam and Kenny encouraged him to take coffee. He
agreed, and then they explained he should have nothing
to fear for the mistake was made by the British film company and everyone would realise he had acted in good
faith. Nomura-san then burst forth telling the journalists
with great passion how much effort everyone in his group
had put into this project and the massive sponsorship and
publicity it had engendered.

'Even though it might not be my fault, it is a very big
disaster and you know even though we in Japan like to
blame foreigners for mistakes, many people will also look
at us to blame,' he said. He admitted he had been drinking very heavily and living a bit rough and had tried to
get the tour stopped.

'I just contact the tour bus at Imperial Palace to tell Mereleigh group to cancel but JTB guide call policeman to chase me away. Then I telephone Fukuoka City Hall and make same request but they just hung up and think I am crazy. So I contact British Embassy and again no one listened,' he explained in broken English.

They told him they would be telling the Mereleigh Group the bad news that evening, and also the Nishi Nippon Shimbun editor was making an appointment to see the Mayor that evening as well.

'So nobody but us and a few at Fukuoka knows yet?' he asked.

He told them that he had become paranoid that the police would arrest him for fraud or something and it would be a huge embarrassment for his family. He broke down and sobbed, covering his face, 'I just not know what to do, and when I see faces of real people at Narita, and it almost kills me with shock. Then after I think I am as sorry for Mereleigh group as they are just like my group, just ordinary people.'

The three journalists said they wanted to run his story to help him and explain what a shocking position he was placed in, and they would not dwell overly about what he had been doing the past few days, except to say he had been trying to find a solution and had worried himself sick. He looked pleadingly into their eyes. 'My life is in your hands. This was the biggest thing in my life, now it becomes my worst disaster. Everything changes in just a few hours.'

Adam said he would like Nomura-san to meet the

Mereleigh group that night after they had been fully briefed on the situation. Sam and Kenny agreed it was the best way and told him that the tour might still go ahead if Fukuoka City and the main sponsors agreed, so best not to look just on the bad side. He brightened at that but was clearly totally mentally exhausted by the events of the past few days.

Sam and Kenny said they had some expense money which would cover the cost of putting him into the Shiba Park Hotel for the night. It would also cover the cost of a couple of new shirts, and tie, plus meals. They could not help noticing Nomura's rather worn gear which he had cleaned overnight. There were some stains on the suit that would not come out. Sam said they would buy him a new suit regardless of whether their newspaper would cover the cost.

They checked him out of the hotel and set off on a shopping spree, but only after Sam had rung the Nishi Nippon Shimbun with the news and Adam had contacted Rick to bring him up to date. They all agreed Nomura-san's whereabouts should be kept confidential for a while to protect him, and also to give them the first news break on the story that evening.

Rick was greatly relieved to hear Nomura-san had been found and had set up a briefing session with the Nishi Nippon Shimbun journalists, Adam and Nomura-san for 4 pm before the group returned from Hakone and Kamakura. He agreed it would be wrong to bring Nomura-san to a meeting before the Mereleigh group had been fully briefed.

There were far too many balls in the air for his liking

and the Jenny thing was beginning to have shades of the same kind of problems he had encountered with the Mereleigh tour to New Zealand when Frances was kidnapped. Rick had phoned his cousin in Wales to update him about Jenny and tried to sound upbeat about things, but in his heart he felt there might be complications.

Tanaka-san had left at lunch time to tend to his business but said he would like to attend the meeting in the evening to hear the latest news about the Mereleigh tour. Rick welcomed his interest and support. At Fukuoka the editor of the Nishi Nippon Shimbun was delighted with the news that Nomura-san had been found and was very pleased that Michiko had had the bright idea of doing a human interest story on the group.

News-wise, his paper was well ahead of its rivals and he could see an excellent front page human interest story arising. The big question would be how Fukuoka City hall reacted to this and, just as importantly, how the major commercial sponsors did. He had decided to try to see the Mayor himself with his senior City Hall reporter. The newspaper had the reputation of being a bit of a kingmaker where city mayors were concerned, but the editor tended to think it had less influence on who was elected but more on the demise of inefficient or corrupt mayors.

A mid-afternoon note from City Hall informed the editor the Mayor would be delighted to see him at about 6pm at City Hall. He summoned the senior City Hall reporter to his office and told him he wanted a succinct two-page briefing paper to give the Mayor outlining where the error seemed to have been made and the events to date. It should not advertise any punches to other media, and should be marked for the Mayor's eyes only.

⌘⌘⌘

Michiko felt like she was comforting the dying towards the end of her day out with the group. She totally enjoyed their company and began to realise their happy times in Japan could come to a drastic end in an hour or so. Hakone and Kamakura had worked their mountain magic on the group. It was parkland Japan at its best and so unexpected by the group who were beginning to think Japan only consisted of very large, rather grey cities. They were fascinated by the many hot springs resorts and the fact that they nestled within the crater of a 40-kilometre extinct volcano, and by the numerous temples and shrines at Kamakura and its old artistic treasures.

Helena the artist was very impressed with traditional Japanese art and Foggy more so with sculptures and out-door modern art they had seen in a park. They all admitted Japan had some of the best temperate climate alpine scenery in the world, and they just loved the little traditional houses and farms tucked into valleys. By the end of the day Michiko had made herself known to everyone and she liked talking to Maggie Moss, who was bright, cheerful and full of fun but clearly had had a rather tempestuous life that only sorted itself out after she parted from her crooked car dealer husband and took up with Rick.

Perry, the ex British cop, and his wife Jean were fun. Perry seemed to have a joke a minute and exchanged a lot of banter with Dick Round and Fran Wallace. She could see Perry and Dick were long-time friends. Perry was impressed by the Japanese police system and the proliferation of community police boxes throughout the towns and suburbs. He said it was like old-time policing to have a constable permanently in the district. He noted that they carried pistols but Japan's crime rate was very low by world standards and wondered if they ever used them except for firearms practice.

Jill and Adam Blount were impressed by the high turnout standards of ordinary Japanese people. 'They always seem to wear good clothing and as so fastidious about dirt,' Jill had said. She was impressed by the farmers and gardeners. The women always wore hats and covered their arms against the sun and the men did the same. In Western countries, outdoor workers liked to strip off in hot sunny weather and get a tan, she told Michiko. Michiko already knew this but pretended surprise at this statement to try to draw out a few more observations.

Lindsay Love was very interested in flowers and flower arrangements, and was jealous of the hot climate plants that could be grown in parts of Japan. Ewan Perth said he would like to take up bonsai and had met a chap at Tokyo with whom he had struck up a friendship and who was an expert in the subject and had promised to visit Britain to show him the techniques. Michiko read more into this than just a bonsai friendship and was glad most of them had found something interesting in Japan. She reflected that, if they had all been film stars, she doubted if their lives would have been as interesting and wondered if it would be possible for a coach-load of film stars to live together on a tour like this for a week or so without a few egos getting in the way.

Her thoughts turned to Adam. He was so English but nice and polite and considerate, and she wondered how best to develop their new relationship. Would he stay on if the Fukuoka tour collapsed and if not, when would they meet again, if ever? She would love to visit Britain but could she work there as a journalist and get a work permit? She began to get a deep lonely feeing in her stomach at the thought of having to part so soon after meeting him. She had not held back because of an instinct that this was the right man and the right time and time was very short.

Did he feel the same way or was it just a one night stand for him? Certainly he seemed very moved and impressed with her but was it because she was the first Asian girl in his life? She dismissed that for she had found a lot in common, and temperamentally they seemed compatible. She told herself that she knew in her bones he was the right person and just prayed his feeling were as deep.

Now she had to find a reason to stick with the group for the rest of their Japan tour regardless of whether the Fukuoka visit took place, and she would have to convince her editor that there was a continuing news story in it. Given another four days or so with Adam she felt she could work her magic a bit more and ensure they stayed together somehow.

The trip had now reached a stage where there was not too much to see or talk about on the return journey to Tokyo so the JTB guide pulled the regular sing-along trick, asking if anyone knew tunes. She knew from experience that British groups tended to be reserved unless they were Welsh or Irish, and they only needed stopping once they had started! Michiko got into it, and she and the tour guide sang Sukiyaki as a duet and got resounding applause from the group.

'There is one song you will all know so I only want you to put up your hands if you do not know it,' the JTB guide said. 'How about Slim Whitman's 'You are my Sunshine?'

'Slim?' Perry asked in mock confusion.

'Slim, you stupid bugger,' Dick corrected, 'of course he knows it, we all do as it's one of the songs our parents used to sing to us.'

They all entered into the swing of things then and had a go at 'She'll be coming round the mountain when she comes' and a few other hoary old chestnuts like 'Over the mountains, over the hills.'

Michiko smiled. 'These English just need a bit of encouragement at times and they are good fun.' This made her feel more at home. She could be part of this group and it would be great to meet their kids who would be her age group. She looked at Peter, and he was singing with great gusto and had requested they sing 'It's a long way to Tipperary.'

The coach drive back to Tokyo was too fast, she wanted to cling on to the moment and the anticipation of seeing Adam again, and not suddenly find they would soon be parting. She knew most foreigners tended to think the Japanese were unemotional people but the truth was quite different.

Adam was dealing with his own fears and feeling as he, Sam, Kenny and Nomura-san made a slow progress back to the Shiba Park Hotel. Nomura-san had been kit-ted out in a new smart suit, shirt and underwear and, apart from some nervousness and tiredness in his eyes, looked fine.

Adam realised what a nightmare he must have been through and felt very protective of him. He also realised his time with Michiko was also looking very limited and he might have to make some quick big decisions. She was so perfect physically and mentally. No-one could walk away from a girl like that, he told himself, but perhaps Japanese girls could do these things and walk away as if last night never happened.

Someone had told him 'In Japan it's rules before feelings.' He would be so pissed off and depressed if that were the case. In his heart he felt they were made for each other, and when they looked into each other's eyes they could almost see each other's hearts beating in unison.

'You look worried Adam-san,' Kenny said.

Before he could reply, Kenny added, 'Maybe a bit lovesick?'

Adam nodded sheepishly. 'Michiko is a fantastic girl!'

The two Japanese journalists had figured out that something had happened last night. They could see Michiko walking on air and noticed the warm knowing glances between the two of them.

'We think you Adam-san and Michiko-chan are man and wife possibilities,' Sam joked half-seriously. Adam said that, given a half chance, they might be, but their time together in Japan would be so short and it could be hard to develop a long term relationship.

'You know it's not true that Japanese are slow to make

a decision, might be as far as business and money is concerned, but Japanese woman can make decision very super quickly, and she is tough. She can be stoical and wait as long as it takes if the man loves her,' Kenny said encouragingly.

'That is very good news,' Adam said, and he allowed himself a smile.

'Just don't treat her like Madam Butterfly,' Kenny joked back at him.

'Oh no, I couldn't. I would take her with me now to England if I could,' he said.

'This after one day,' Sam said to Kenny. 'He is really love-sick person. Adam-san you know this joke. One man says to another, "Do you know this girl?" He replies, "I only just met her but I have seen a lot of her." Might be same applies to you?' Sam said, as both he and Kenny roared with laughter. Adam's deep blush clearly indicated he understood exactly what they meant. They got off the subway and walked from Mita station to the Shiba Park Hotel where Rick and Tanaka-san whisked them upstairs to Rick's room for a pre-meeting briefing.

CHAPTER 6

The Mereleigh Record Club coach pulled in to the Shiba Park Hotel about thirty minutes late because of heavy traffic on the Tokyo motorway system, but everyone was in good humour except Michiko, who began to get the shakes. She had also just realised that her being a party to the secret might make the group think she took advantage of them by doing the interview in the knowledge of the impending disaster. She quickly found Adam and dived into a corner of the hotel's coffee shop with him.

'I am so glad to see you, today was fantastic but I am very scared about tonight when everyone gets the bad news.' She grasped his hand beneath the table as she expressed her concerns. Adam found he was quite relaxed and in control, perhaps because he was able to say they had found Nomura-san and Tanaka-san was taking care of him for an hour or so before the meeting.

He told her where they found him, and about his general condition. She expressed relief and surprise that he had been found okay, and rightly assumed the other two journalists were covering his story and felt it might be some consolation for the group that Nomura-san had been found and might be able to throw a bit more light on the situation.

There were a lot of things to think of and do in a very short space of time, Adam told her. Story-wise he assumed she would put her piece about the group together fairly early in the evening and file it for the morning edition. She agreed saying she would file a backgrounder on the group as soon as possible and put an updated head on it after the meeting when they heard the bad news, and with whatever developments Nomura-san had to add. Adam said he was doing exactly the same.

'So with our work commitments scheduled, let's get stuck into that and make sure we have some time together afterwards,' he said.

'Adam, I've been thinking a lot about us, this is so sudden....'

Adam cut her off. 'I understand, maybe it's all been too fast and we should try to pace ourselves a bit if you like, but I thought a lot about us almost all day and I want this to last.'

'It's okay, last night was fantastic, but I have been so worried that today might be our last day, and I don't want it to be.' Her eyes began to fill with tears.

'It's the same with me. We have to find a way to keep

seeing each other for the rest of this tour. Can you stay with us until we finish it, whether it is at Fukuoka or at Hiroshima?' he pleaded.

'That is what I worry about most of all. I don't think my newspaper will let me as I already got the story today, and when you leave tomorrow by shinkansen to Kyoto that might be it!' she said in despair.

'No, there has to be a way, maybe I can do something, stay behind at Tokyo and miss the rest of the tour,' he suggested.

'But you have some contract with your own newspaper, and the Guardian will also expect more from you, so it's stupid for you to risk your job,' she pointed out.

He clutched her hand and said there was time for them to take a walk and eat some yakitori by themselves before the meeting. They went out quietly, and as they walked down the street he felt like a king.

'What a girl to have next to you,' he thought, and she looked up every so often to make sure he was still there.

'You know many people in this world get married and they never really know what true love is, but now I really know what it is,' she told him. 'It means you can't help yourself, being with your lover is everything!' she said.

As she guided him into a smoky yakitori bar he had a brain wave.

'Look, I want to do a story on Nomura-san and his group at Fukuoka, and I must do it in the next day or so. Do you think your editor will let you come to Fukuoka with me ahead of the group to do this as we helped you here?' he asked expectantly.

'It's a fantastic idea, and I'm going to call my boss now. We can take the same shinkansen as the group tomorrow and continue on to Hakata,' she said.

'No, Fukuoka,' he corrected.

'Yes, Fukuoka,' she added, 'Hakata is the old name and the name of the shinkansen station at Fukuoka.'

'Can you arrange the meeting with Nishumura-san? We could take Nomura-san back with us on the shinkansen too,' Adam suggested.

They received the usual rousing welcome when they entered the yakitori bar and she quickly produced her mobile phone to call her boss. She spoke in very careful, very polite Japanese, first outlining the events of the day and the interviews she had conducted with the group, and then the impending meeting which Kenny and Sam would also attend. He boss had already heard most of it from the other two journalists but was genuinely impressed with her efforts.

She then delicately inserted Adam's idea as a request from Adam and asked him to explain in simple, short English what he had in mind. It was all Adam could do to hear the Japanese boss on the other end of the line there was so much noise. He explained as simply and emphatically as he could, received many 'hai's at the end of each sentence and then 'doomo arigatoo gozaimasu' which he understood to be thank you. He then passed the phone back to a very hopeful Michiko.

Her boss had sussed out another agenda between the two of them and smiled to himself. He was inclined to say no. He could get someone at Fukuoka to help Adam but he appreciated two things, Michiko had worked very hard and was a good journalist and he detected a pleading note in her voice, and being a father of daughters, he recognised she was starting a new important relationship. He paused for a moment and he heard an urgent whisper from Michiko to Adam in a tone that could only be described as intimate.

'Well Michiko-chan, I think I can say yes, it's a good idea to bring Nomura-san by train as it will keep him away from all the other newspapers who will be after him by tomorrow morning, but please try to do the best story you can so my staff down here don't complain that I am favouring you, and look after your English friend as best you can.'

He could almost hear her leap for joy and smiled to himself, thinking she might end up being their stringer in Britain some day! He was a cynic   the world was a shit place all too often   but it was great to help someone occasionally. Adam and Michiko were so elated they almost forgot to get back to the hotel in time for the meeting. The sight of a very worried Rick and serious Kenny and Sam was a reality check and they felt guilty for being so happy.

Rick said the meeting would be on time and that had sent a few ripples of concern through the group because he would not say why it was necessary. He told them Tanaka-san was taking care of Nomura-san and would bring him in when they gave the signal after they had had time to discuss things. Peter spotted Adam with Michiko and noted neither had had dinner at the hotel. He seemed quite delighted when he heard they had taken a meal together elsewhere. Brenda pulled Peter aside out of earshot of Adam and Michiko and said,

'I thought you did not like the Japanese, but you seem delighted that your son is getting friendly with Michiko!'

'Oh, she is very different, very special, a very nice girl and of course partly educated in the west. That makes all the difference,' he said in slightly racist terms. Rick had arranged a mini-conference room and after-dinner coffee and cheese for the group meeting. Most were still chattering about the day's trip. Adam, Michiko and the two Japanese journalists were also invited in.

Rick went straight to the point and told them about the stuff-up and how they meant to invite the stars of the movie. He also asked the Nishi Nippon Shimbun journalists to produce copies of letters and e-mails which indicated the slip made by the UK film company. He also thanked Kenny. Sam and Michiko profusely for their help and consideration for being able to embargo the news until the group and the Mayor of Fukuoka had been told.

He then gave an account of what had happened to Nomura-san, his breakdown and his later discovery today and what hell he had been through. Rick added he would bring him in later after everyone had ample time to digest things. He sat down drained, waiting for the bomb to burst. The group sat like stunned mullets for a moment or two. They were clearly very embarrassed and had no idea what to do. Peter managed to mutter, 'It was all too good to be true.'

Andy said it was shocking, but Fran seized the moment and said she had her laptop with her so could do a quick check of the e-mails and also had scanned the first few letters and filed them on the laptop. The group remained stony silent while she set things up. After a moment or two she was able to confirm the ambiguous first letter sent to the UK Film Company and non-specific reference to actors or film cast in all the rest of the correspondence.

'It's quite right, there has been one hell of a stuff-up, so what do we do now?' she asked Rick.

'I think we are in the hands of Fukuoka City Hall and whatever decision they make this evening, and also how Nomura-san's group feel about things. If they want to end the tour to Fukuoka, we can't stop them as they were paying for everything.'

He pointed out Nomura-san was in no fit state to make any decision as he had experienced a severe mental breakdown, and it would be appreciated if members of the group would respect that. He also told them he and Michiko had arranged to go to Fukuoka tomorrow to see Nomura-san's group and to take him with them so they would be able to get the lie of the land. Peter mumbled to Brenda, 'God, he is a fast worker, never misses an opportunity!'

During a general discussion it was agreed they should not go to Fukuoka even if they paid their own way if no one wanted to see them, but they definitely wanted to finish their own tour as far as Hiroshima and Miyajima. One or two of the women had a sniff. Lindsay Love cried and said she could not believe such a dreadful thing could happen after such a wonderful day. Her comments summed up the feeling of most members of the group.

Perry said they would look like fools when they returned to Britain empty-handed so to speak, given some of the pre-trip publicity they had received in local Thames Valley newspapers. Adam intervened and said he would be filing some sympathetic reports on their behalf. 'It will not be exactly what my own editor or the Guardian thought of, but at least we can put our own view across before some rat bag members of the press corps try to whip up a storm and cause an international incident,' he added. Most people in Britain, he thought, would be sympathetic.

The group still felt very uncomfortable. They had read up a lot about Fukuoka and were looking forward to meeting Nomura-san's group before all this happened. Rick pointed out the trip might still be on and, until word came from Fukuoka City Hall and the sponsors, they had to be prepared to go. On that note he called Tanaka-san and asked him to bring Nomura-san down to the meeting.

The group clapped Nomura-san when he entered. He looked a broken man, despite his new suit, and their hearts went out to him. Andy took over the meeting and told Nomura-san not to worry about this problem as they had been thoroughly briefed and knew it was not his fault.

'We, too, must take some responsibility, for when I received the first letter addressed to 'the Casting Director' I should have twigged, but we thought it must have been some typo or mistake in the translation,' he explained. 'We have had a magnificent time in Japan thus far and plan to continue our own schedule to Hiroshima at least, but clearly we should steer away from Fukuoka if we are not wanted,' he finalised.

Several other members felt compelled to make similar comments and thanked Nomura-san for everything. They pointed out they would never have visited Japan if it were not for him and that in itself was very rewarding.

Nomura-san's spirits were greatly lifted by these sentiments and he said: 'I really made the biggest mistake of all. It was not the UK film company so much but me. I was looking at the big time, commercialism, my name in headlines as the person who could raise a lot of money for this drug charity. I forgot ordinary people and more so as this project grew and the big boys came in as sponsors. I was starting to lose sight of what the objective was and developing a big ego at the expense of my family and friends because the Mayor of Fukuoka would invite me to his office and I was taken to parties by the big companies.'

'I am a small person, just an ordinary salary man with a wife and two kids and a mortgage, but I have this love for the 1960s music as do my friends. We are not as old as you perhaps as most of my group were not alive in the 1960s, so we can learn from you about the real scene then and that is what we should have been thinking of.

'When we saw the movie about you in New Zealand we loved it because it displayed good humanity against the evil and always accompanied by very nice rock and roll music. The actors were so good, like the real people we thought.

'You know now we live in a virtual reality world and sometimes in our subconscious we mistake virtual reality for real thing and that was my very big mistake right at the beginning. Tonight I can sincerely see my mistake. We should have invited you right at the beginning because you are the real people who did these things, not the actors who get paid a lot of money to act them out. That was my mistake and everything else was subsequent to that, so I must accept full responsibility.' He bowed deeply, apologised many times in Japanese and stepped back. There was a brief silence as the magnitude of what he said sank in, and Tanaka-san filled the gap.

'I am an older person like you, I play Golden Oldies rugby in New Zealand and Britain, and Nomura-san is a bit younger than us, but as you can see he is a very well-intentioned person. Most of us do not think he should accept responsibility at his end. His objective was to raise funds for charity and of course like most of us he looked at the best way. I do not wish to be offensive to you as you have given your time to help him and the people of Fukuoka to do this. I am from Fukuoka and speak from the heart.'

'When we think of it with the benefit of backsight — is that right, oh, I hear Rick-san say hindsight, sorry, back-sight might be rude — we can see what Nomura-san said is true. It should be you that come to Fukuoka, but it's so easy for us humans to be sidelined — that is right I think Rick-san, like rugby — that we can miss the point and for-get the people who made the difference in the first place.

'Whatever situation we face now, Nomura-san and his team have done a very big and good job and we know you are most sincere, well-meaning group. The kind of people we should have at Fukuoka, so I want to end by saying I am going to do my best to see you do come to Fukuoka, and I have many rugby friends in Fukuoka who will help. Thank you, doomo arigatoo gozaimasu.' He concluded with a smile to Nomura-san. Andy leapt to his feet saying Nomura-san was a very worthy person and should not assume it was his fault, and Tanaka-san's sentiments were most welcome.

'I think I can speak for everyone here, if we are welcome to visit Fukuoka, and there are no funds, then we can pay for ourselves and meet the real people in Fukuoka like you who matter,' Andy stepped back to a round of hearty applause.

The Nishi Nippon Shimbun journalists were overjoyed at the tone of the speeches, as was Adam. It was fantastic copy and so spontaneous and sincere. Adam smiled at Kenny and Sam, and they grinned back unabashed. Michiko, who was standing with Nomura-san on the other side of the room, gave Adam the V for victory sign with a big smile.

Rick told everyone it would be prudent to await the outcome of the meeting with the Mayor of Fukuoka as there might be bigger implications involved. He also said he had a fact he did not want to mention at first but felt he should, in the interests of complete transparency, and that was that the UK Ambassador Miss Alsop-Smith had asked Adam to convey to them her opinion that they should consider cancelling the Fukuoka visit on diplomatic grounds to save face and embarrassment.

That drew an outcry of displeasure from the group with Dick and Perry both demanding to know who the heck she thought she was. Peter added, 'Perhaps she is pissed off because she has now lost her meal ticket for Fukuoka and wants to take it out on us!' Adam told them he did not want to mention it as he knew it would be upsetting and maybe he had things in the wrong context.

Just then the meeting room door opened and hotel staff came in with some complimentary cocktails. Tanaka-san said the owner was a rugby man and a friend of his and when he had told him of the situation he insisted on shouting them the drinks. Nomura-san was feted by all and sundry and began to enjoy himself, swapping yarns about favourite 1960s numbers and what his club did.

At Fukuoka, the editor of the Nishi Nippon Shimbun, accompanied by his senior City Hall reporter, was walking into the Town Hall, a huge new building near new Tenjin, for his appointment with the Mayor. He always felt uncomfortable visiting the City Hall. Although he did not dislike the Mayor or his senior aides, it was just that he would have preferred to have met him on neutral territory. In short, he felt like a lobbyist for some cause and that was inappropriate for an editor of his status.

A smart young lady ushered him from the reception desk to a waiting room outside the Mayor's office and a senior male aide of the Mayors came to chat with him as they supped green tea. It was the old story, the editor would give the aide a few words about the subject he wanted to discuss so the male aide could prime the Mayor a bit before the meeting.

The aide looked at his watch, strode a few yards to the Mayor's door, knocked and entered and in about five minutes, returned to usher in the editor and his staff member. The Mayor seemed genuinely pleased to see the editor, and had risen and walked to the door to greet him. They talked for a couple of minutes about their shared interest in sumo wrestling and who the next champions might be and then the editor came to the point.

The Mayor's aide had only mentioned there was a problem concerning the Mereleigh Record Club Tour but not what it was. The Mayor guessed it would be a major problem to warrant the editor's visit. The editor explained it in clear, simple terms, pointed out Nomura-san had been missing but had just been found this day by his staff at Tokyo, and that he had been aware of this situation for the last 24 hours but sat on it in the hope that something might be reconciled. The Mayor sucked his teeth with many 'oohs' and 'aahs' of depressing exclamation at how bad the situation was. At the end the Mayor let out a long 'hoooo' like a steam locomotive blowing off a safety valve.

He paused, and then commanded his senior aide to bring in several other senior staff members as quickly as possible. While they waited for their attendance, he told the editor it was a huge diplomatic and political nightmare. The British Ambassador had been invited, the Mayor of Auckland was on his way, most of the top companies in Fukuoka had put a lot of money into it, receptions rooms, restaurants etc., had all been booked to fete the stars of the movie, invitations sent out to local dignitaries and now   nothing!

'What to do, what to do?' the Mayor kept repeating.

'How can anyone make a mistake like this, the sponsors will be furious, the general public will want blood and even if it was a mistake made by a minor clerical clerk at a UK film company office, I am sure people here will look for someone in Japan to blame. Some are going to ask why we entrusted this man, Nomura-san, with so much without checking everything, but we did check everything except the actual names of those travelling who we had assumed were the names of the stars he first mentioned were coming!' he concluded.

The editor's mobile phone jangled. He excused himself and went to a corner of the Mayor's capacious office to answer it. It was from the two journalists Sam and Kenny saying the Mereleigh Group had decided not to visit Fukuoka if they were unwanted because it would cause embarrassment, and that Nomura-san was still trying to accept total responsibility for the mix-up although it was not principally his fault.

Half a dozen city hall officials bustled in, some carrying huge files. The Mayor looked daunted by it all. He could see a meeting being started that could go to the wee small hours of the next day.

'Right, we face a disaster here, but because many companies and organisations at Fukuoka are involved, we must bring all of them together at an emergency meeting and put all the cards on the table so that whatever decision or decisions are taken will involve everyone. Fukuoka City Hall cannot stand alone and make a decision, we are the servant of this city. We responded to a call for support for this project and we did it in good faith. It was not our initiative but we will do our best to help clear up this terrible mess,' he said.

He looked at the editor and asked, 'What is your newspaper's official position?'

'Before this evening, my personal view was the whole thing should be called off but the phone call I just received from my staff at Tokyo who attended the Mereleigh meeting with Nomura-san has changed things, and I think we as a newspaper must encourage this visit to happen. It might be on a smaller scale if sponsors go but I think my company will put some money in, though of course nowhere near all the money that the other sponsors are collectively providing,' he said.

'Why did you change your mind?' the Mayor asked.

'Tonight Nomura-san told the Mereleigh Group he took primary responsibility because he should have invited the real people and not the film stars in the first place and they were dazzled by the tinsel and glamour of things,' the editor stated.

'But if he had done that they would never had got the sponsorship and publicity that was needed to raise the funds for events and the charity!' the Mayor observed.

'Nomura-san's point, with which I have much sympathy, is that we as a society have difficulty in telling the difference between virtual reality and reality itself,' the editor concluded.

'When are you going to press?' the Mayor asked.

'Tonight with our morning edition, and my colleagues at Nishi Nippon TV might do a brief late night news item as they will not have a chance to do any on-camera interviews until tomorrow,' the editor pointed out.

'You can't embargo until noon tomorrow?' the Mayor asked.

'It's too risky for us; too many other newspapers are

trying to find Nomura-san as the word had been out for 24 hours or so that he is missing. Now we have found him we want to be the first to present his personal problem and the major problem the city faces. Of course I can only speak for myself, but it would be possibly a bigger loss of face if we turned the Mereleigh people away,' he said.

'Are you going to say that in your editorial?' the Mayor asked.

'I think so, but I would also appreciate your personal view if possible,' the editor said.

'My heart is with your sentiments but I am afraid the city might have to be guided by the reaction of the sponsors and the people of this city and also the cost. That is all I can say for the moment. My staff here will burn the midnight lights to get to the bottom of this and arrange sponsors' meetings tomorrow morning,' the Mayor stated.

The Mayor dismissed his staff and invited the editor to stay on a moment. He told the editor everything was off the record now and only for background. It appeared many sponsors were the Mayor's own personal backers and he could not risk offending them, also the British Ambassador would have to be consulted and the Mayor of Auckland advised.

'I think both of us have a shared responsibility to do our best for Fukuoka and protect the image of this city.' The Mayor beckoned to a female assistant to bring in a sake bottle and small cups.

They supped a few cups before the editor left, promising to tread gently on other peoples' dreams and see if they could make the visit possible. He knew exactly how he wanted to present the stories from Sam and Kenny, and also Michiko's piece, and almost word for word what he would say in his editorial.

'You know when you have troubled waters it is very nice to know you have a good crew on board and our staff at Tokyo have done an excellent job portraying the very human aspects of the situation. Tomorrow the voice of big business and local government will speak, and that might be a very different story, but at least we can get our piece in first,' he smiled at his senior City Hall Reporter who nodded in silent agreement.

At Nomura-san's house, his wife and children relaxed for the first time in days. She could not care less about the problems of the visit, she was just thankful Nomura-san had been found and was coming home the next day. Nishimura-san and her boyfriend came around to join in this personal celebration, and they rang around all other members of their group to let them know Nomura-san would be back and he could explain everything the next evening.

Adam and Michiko had drunk a few cocktails before Michiko told Adam she needed to go back to her flat for the night to get things ready for tomorrow morning's departure to Fukuoka.

'Will you come back here afterwards?' he pleaded.

'It might be too late because of public transport, but you can come and stay at my place with your suitcase and we can join the group at Tokyo station tomorrow morning?' she suggested. He leaped at the idea, saying he had never been inside a Japanese apartment before.

'It's so small, just one DK,' she told him.

He had no idea what a DK was, so she explained all Japanese houses were built according to the size of standard tatami mats so that each room was in proportion to the dimensions of the number of tatami mats it could contain over the floor. Her place was one tatami room for eating and sleeping, plus a small dining room and kitchen and a small bathroom.

'So we also have two DKs and three DKs etc,' she explained.

Adam briefed Rick on his plans and asked him to let his parents know that he would see them at the railway station with Michiko. He did not want to go through a whole preamble about it with his parents. Rick said he had more or less decided to stay behind in Tokyo for a couple of days to help Tanaka-san find Jenny. He felt he owed that to his cousin's friends in Wales.

Adam's bag was packed in a thrice, and he and Michiko boarded a shared taxi with the other two Nishi Nippon Shimbun journalists for most for the journey to central Tokyo, where he and Michiko bailed out and took a subway train to Setegaya-ku. The dormitory suburb was close to the old 1960s Tokyo Olympics stadium.

Michiko's apartment was a 15 minute walk from the subway station along a busy main road with a motorway built on top of it. Numerous smaller streets branched off it in a grid-like pattern and unlike central Tokyo, which was modern, spacious airy and grand in the style of many modern capital cities, the suburban streets were narrow and cluttered with webs of power and telephone lines above ground. The pavements were crammed with various forms of humanity all dashing one way or another, their passage only interrupted by numerous cyclists tinkling their bike bells as they wove through the pedestrians on the pavements.

There was a kind of order to all this, quite different to the pushing and shoving that goes on in most major overcrowded Asian cities. The Japanese politely observed the passage of others, and always where possible, gave way to provide space and the occasional physical encounter was always followed up with a nod or word of apology. Adam's initial reaction of irritation to the crowded streets gave way to the style of things and he decided he should behave in the most gentle way possible as he was very noticeably a foreigner and the slightest impatience or ill humour on his part would make him stand out as an uncouth person. Michiko noted he was handling it well.

'So many Europeans get angry and impatient with the crowds but you are an English gentleman. You always insist I enter a door first and open it for me and I notice you always stand on the kerb side of the pavement to protect me from the traffic. Japanese men would never ever consider those things,' she said proudly.

Adam noticed all the shops were still open and Michiko said she wanted to pop into a convenience store to buy a few things so she could make him dinner. She asked him what he would like and he said sukiyaki, because it was the only thing he could think of at the time. She smiled, relishing the chance of playing wife to him that night. He could almost see her glow and it made him feel very protective towards her.

He was surprised at the wide range of foodstuffs available and the way everything was so neatly packaged and presented. The checkout staff were bright and cheery, they obviously recognised her and joked about the gaijin (foreigner) with her. She blushed and they smiled back at them both with broad, friendly grins. Her apartment was just a block away, a smallish grey building with only three levels. Her place was on the second floor and accessed by a lift and an open alleyway. He noticed all the doors were steel but everything was neat and tidy, no graffiti and no litter anywhere.

She opened up and they immediately took off their shoes. Michiko apologised and said she did not have man-sized slippers so he could either use a pair of hers that were several sizes too small for his stockinged feet. He opted for the latter. The steel entry door opened to a tiny hallway with lino type floor and natty places to hang raincoats and umbrellas and store outside shoes. Everything was fitted in a large caravan style way to maximise storage space and living room.

The tiny hallway led into a small kitchen with cooker and sink bench on one side and a pantry and storage area on the other. That in turn led a multi-purpose tatami room with shoji blind sliding doors and next to it a small bathroom and toilet cubicle.

It was all so neat and well thought-out that Adam overlooked its tiny proportions. Michiko apologised for its size and told him to take a bath and use one of the yukata dressing gowns folded in a small airing cupboard. He took a look at the square bath tub and a hand shower hanging over an adjacent tiled showering area and realised he had no idea of how to turn it on and select hot water. Michiko had begun to prepare get some food and suddenly became aware of his confusion.

'Of course you do not read Japanese, and you have never taken a bath in a Japanese house before!' She laughed and showed him how it all worked, and then started to help him off with his clothes when he grabbed her in a passionate embrace.

'Wait, wait, we've got all night and the food will burn,' she said, pushing him away gently and making sure he had the shower at the right temperature. She got the main dishes underway, and then came in to scrub Adam's back before he got into the tub of hot clear water to soak.

With the food nearly cooked and simmering to keep warm, it was her turn to take a shower. They were suddenly naked in the shower, she ready for a plunge and Adam dried off. They embraced and Adam almost penetrated her then but she laughed and said, 'It must be better later, after I have bathed and we have eaten.'

Adam thought, 'Stuff the eating, how can anyone hold off with her around stark naked', but he decided this was the way she wanted it and that was good enough for him. It seemed to take an age before she emerged clean and shining in her own gown next to him with absolutely nothing on underneath. She quickly placed a small, low table in the centre of the room, covered it with a table-cloth, produced some place mats and chopsticks, and then whisked in several pots of steaming food.

It smelt delicious, and Adam suddenly felt ravenous.

Between them they demolished the sukiyaki feast in a few minutes with not a scrap left over. She produced a few bottles of Kirin beer from her fridge and a small bottle of sake. While he drank a beer, she whisked the dishes away, slid open a wardrobe door in the tatami room and produced a large futon and duvet and two small hard pillows.

The tatami room was now a bedroom. He slipped out of his yukata and into bed. She did the same after dimming the room light, but he could see every curve and shadow on her smooth body. His eyes feasted on every inch of her before she nestled down beside him, touching his hair, his face, his chest and then his penis.

Adam knew the biggest challenge would be to hold on for a decent length of time and not fire off a couple of barrels before she was ready, but as soon as she touched his cock he had to get into her as soon as possible. She was very moist and ready when he rolled over on top of her. They reached climaxes almost together, rested and slept for 30 minutes, took a tumbler of sake each, watched a bit of late night TV, all in incomprehensible Japanese for Adam, and then rolled over for another romp.

⌘⌘⌘

At the hotel, Tanaka-san had left Nomura-san in the safe company of Andy and other members of the group, chatting about their various group activities and pop music of the 1960s, while he sought out Rick to try to fathom out the next moves to help Jenny. They adjourned to Rick's room and were shortly joined by Yoshi. Rick produced a bottle of Johnnie Walker black label and, after sculling a few drams, they got into stride, trying to sort out the next moves to help Jenny. Tanaka-san said they should wait until tomorrow evening to see if there was any response to the magazine interview offer made by Yoshi posing as a an agent for the UK magazine.

'I would like to visit the club tonight but it could be a disaster as it is not usual for a Japanese businessman to spend so many nights one after another at such places, especially because I am a new face there and if Yoshi makes an approach before the deadline they could suspect his motives,' Tanaka explained. Yoshi, carefully nursing his double whisky, nodded in silent agreement.

'To use an analogy, we have baited the fish hook but we don't even know if they are interested in the bait let alone are going to take a bite at it,' Rick said. 'I feel in my bones we have found her, and I am scared they might move her on if they get at all suspicious,' he added.

'That is very true", Tanaka-san agreed, 'so we have to keep watch on this part of the river, so to speak, to see if the fish are interested in taking a bite,' he added.

'Yes, but how?' Rick pushed for ideas.

'Well, I do have a new friend who is already helping a bit, but I am concerned about her safety and do not wish to push too hard,' Tanaka-san told them.

Yoshi shot him a glance, guessing it was Emi, one of the ladies at the club, and Tanaka-san's bashful looked more or less confirmed it. Yoshi broke into Japanese to confirm this with Tanaka-san and in a well-meaning protective way, asked if Tanaka-san was going out of his mind, or genuinely knew what he was doing.

Tanaka-san told his younger friend he was quite sane and knew perfectly what was involved and, as an old campaigner, knew better than younger people how to tread carefully through the minefields of life. Yoshi looked Rick straight in the eyes and exclaimed, 'He is in love with a lady at the club!'

Rick shot Tanaka-san a glance and Tanaka drew a deep sigh and said, 'At a certain age love might be difficult but friendship, affection and a comfortable relationship is still necessary, with a bit of sex too.'

Rick laughed and called him an old rogue but then advised to tread very carefully.

'Tonight I shall see this lady again after she finishes work, and if anything needs immediate attention I will call you both, otherwise relax until tomorrow morning,' he advised them.

Rick said he had elected to stay on at the Shiba Park Hotel for an extra two nights but would have to square it off with Maggie as she was already a bit niggly about the time he was spending helping find Jenny rather than accompanying her on the day trips.

'Let me talk to her. You know I have a certain charm, and your lady Maggie is intelligent and, I believe, has a good heart, so when she learns fully from me what we are doing, I think she will understand better,' Tanaka-san offered.

'You are more than welcome to try Tanaka-san, more than welcome,' a relieved Rick sighed in appreciation.

Yoshi glanced at his watch, made mention of another appointment and begged to be excused, saying he would make contact with Tanaka-san next morning.

'He is off to a pump up a buxom waitress at the Shibua Hofbrau House. I met the girl; she drinks very big steins of beer and could drink Yoshi under the table. What you say, suck in and blow out the bubbles of Yoshi? That is what she can do to Yoshi,' Tanaka-san teased, and punched Yoshi on the arm as he good-humouredly made his exit.

Rick and Tanaka-san decided they had best make their peace with Maggie before getting too pissed, and Tanaka-san asked Rick to keep an eye on Nomura-san as he would stay at the Shiba Park with them and then, of course, the Nishi Nippon Shimbun journalists would take him back to Fukuoka tomorrow. Rick suddenly thought about the huge media-fest which could erupt once the cat got out of the bag regarding the Mereleigh Group stuff-up.

'If this thing is made public tomorrow by the Nishi Nippon Shimbun, as they plan, we could have every newspaper and TV station in Japan chasing us, and I am not sure we want excessive publicity and being forced to adopt positions until we know how Fukuoka City Hall and the sponsors at Fukuoka feel about things,' Rick told Tanaka-san.

The idea of keeping the first and private part of the tour confidential would help but in reality the media could probably track them down to the Shiba Park if it really tried, he felt. The group was due to check out at eight o'clock by coach to Tokyo railway station and then take a Hikari express as far as Kyoto for a couple of nights there with sightseeing before proceeding further south to

Hiroshima and possibly Fukuoka.

It was decided that the hotel phone operator should not accept any calls to members of the group from now on, and refer anything that might be an emergency call to Tanaka-san's mobile so he could filter out anything that would expose them to publicity. Rick would brief all members of the group before he turned in. He was sure most, if not all, would agree. They could still phone out but not accept any incoming calls.

Once she heard the full story and the problems Rick and Tanaka-san faced in trying to get to Jenny, Maggie agreed Rick should stay but jokingly told Tanaka-san she did not want Rick running off with any Tokyo hostesses!

'Actually I have really enjoyed catching up with Fran, and she is glad of the company as she still has no man in her life and was eager to hear how you and I were making out Rick,' Maggie said.

'I can find her a big Japanese rugby man very easily,' Tanaka-san offered.

'I don't think she is up to the physical and cultural challenges that might involve at her time of life,' Maggie joked. Tanaka-san made his apologies, and Rick thanked him and told him to make sure he took care.

Tanaka-san was quite enjoying the situation. It was new kind of challenge to be a sort of private investigator and he realised he could probably have made a career in the police as a detective. He gave Emi a ring and arranged to meet her after hours at the usual pick-up place at 2 am. He was at a bit of a loose end with about three hours to fill in, and he did not want to go to some club. Instead he found one of those all night café-type places in Ginza, ate a bit of food, watched TV, and chatted to a few other customers until the time came to pick up Emi.

He hailed a taxi, gave directions and set off for the pick-up point, but as the taxi drew nearer a kind of an instinct told him to be a bit careful, so he stopped the taxi a bit short of the street around a corner on the pretext of wanting to buy cigarettes from a street vending machine although he had long ago given up smoking.

It was 2.04am. He bought the cigarettes and acting as if a bit confused, walked 30 feet or so to the street corner to glance down the street. He saw Emi at the usual spot and in the shadows hidden from her view but on his side of the street corner a large American car of the kind favoured by Yakuza. He decided he would pay off the taxi and make some other approach. The taxi driver thought he was pissed, took the money and seemed to be glad to be rid of him.

Tanaka thought about ringing Emi on her mobile but if the Yakuza types were watching her they would guess there might be a change in plans and follow her. He figured she might ring him or else get tired of waiting and start to go home which was no more than a 15-minute walk away.

He desperately wanted to ring her and hoped the Yakuza were not connected with her but he did not want to take chances. He saw her walk to the kerbside to look down the street to see if his taxi was coming, or if he was walking, and she must have spotted the Yakuza saloon. The sight of the American car clearly had an impact on her as she looked at her watch and decided to walk home.

That was good. It was what Tanaka was hoping for as the route she took home down some narrow, one-way streets would make it impossible for the Yakuza car to follow her all the time. Tanaka rushed to one of the narrow one-way streets on her route and waited in a doorway until she passed by. He grabbed her arm quickly and gave her a note that said to see him later as per the note's instructions.

She immediately caught on and was on her way before she sighted the Yakuza car cruising along a T-junction at the end of the street. She arrived at and entered her apartment as instructed by Tanaka-san. She had seen the Yakuza Yank-tank cruise off into the night, leaving just the normal Yakuza night watchman to keep an eye on the hostesses' apartments in the building.

Tanaka-san had suggested she come out to meet him at about 3.30 am and take a taxi to his place, figuring the Yakuza would have dropped off to sleep after he was sure all the hostesses were back. He was correct and Emi, thinking smart, decided to wear some day clothes. She easily slipped past the night watchman without being seen, not that he would have done her any harm or prevented her, but if asked he would have told his bosses that she had gone out and for some reason they were watching her.

Tanaka-san was almost asleep when she arrived; he quickly let her in after having been assured by her that she had not been followed. She told him quickly that she had heard some of the bosses discussing the interview offer for Jenny and they were very worried and concerned about it as either way it would create problems for them.

They, the Yakuza, knew how to fix publicity with Japan-ese magazines and control things but knew they could not control a foreign interview especially if it had a western journalist who could see things were wrong with Jenny.

Tanaka said that conversation confirmed it was Jenny and to his mind they were controlling her in some way, perhaps against her will. But which way would they jump? That was the question now. He asked Emi if they suspected she might have overheard that conversation or otherwise have an interest in Jenny. Emi told him she believed they did not until tonight, when she was sure she was followed by the Yank tank.

Tanaka-san said he feared for her safety and maybe she should stop helping him, or else quit the establish-ment. She said she wanted to keep helping him, and also wanted to quit the establishment, and she was glad she could help as it kept her close to Tanaka-san. He told her about the deadline for a reply to the interview offer by 6 pm. He scratched his head, asked her to make herself at home, commenting on her day clothes. She said she planned to spend most of the day with him.

'Those people will not notice I am missing as they sleep from 3 am to lunchtime at least, and will think I got up early to go shopping, not stayed out the night as they saw me return to my apartment,' she explained.

Tanaka-san was realizing he had just passed a point of no return with Emi. Even if they could both get through this tricky patch okay, she would have to quit her job and she clearly saw her life from here on with him. He remem-bered Yoshi's advice. His young friend was clearly more perceptive and caring than he thought. He also recalled

Rick's look of concern, but here he was in his early 60s, a widower who had a lot of experience of life and women, and he certainly was not going to spend the rest of his life in a house without a woman.

He made a decision. 'After all this you will come and live with me at Fukuoka, so don't get yourself killed or something stupid. This might be your last night at the club.'

They both turned in an hour or so before the first glimmer of dawn when the morning editions of the Nishi Nippon Shimbun and national daily newspapers were being delivered to newsagents throughout Japan.

⌘⌘⌘

Michiko, still in a deep sleep after a torrid night of sex, was woken by her home phone. She leaned over Adam to reach it, draping her breasts somewhat across his face in the process. The call was from the newspaper's Fukuoka office from a night duty journalist with an impassioned account of the newspaper's coverage of the Mereleigh affair, and then to her shock and surprise, news that several national daily papers had got on to the story and were telling a far less sympathetic account of the events.

Adam was vaguely aware of a nicely scented set of boobs being dangled across his face and put an arm out to clutch the naked torso to which they belonged to his body. He was somewhat miffed to be brushed aside as Michiko engaged in heated conversation with the journalist at the other end of the line. He knew instantly something bad had gone wrong.

CHAPTER 7

Jenny Jones' first memories of life were of a small village in the rolling hills of Mid-Wales about ten miles west of Welshpool. She realised from an early age she was different from other kids, being of Afro-Welsh descent and the only non-European at the tiny school. It was no handicap, the reverse in fact, as she was an outgoing fun-loving kid, bright and intelligent and a natural leader who loved centre stage. Her father was from Kenya and Mum from Wales. She and her brother had taken her mother's family name as it was easier, and seemed more appropriate after the family made its life in Wales.

Her path into the world of show biz was almost preordained. It was initiated by taking part in Sunday school religious plays and school plays then some local rep. work in her mid teens with minor bit parts and then a few holiday gigs at holiday camps. It was at the holiday camps she learned of Eartha Kitt and soon discovered she could strut Eartha's stuff with great conviction and acclaim, and it in turn got her a few nightclub gigs as well, which her mum and dad did not totally approve of for someone so young.

It did, however, help her get a place at RADA and some bit parts in a couple of BBC TV serials. She was also offered casting couch positions at seedy places with big money for unstated, but obvious, extra services for selected audience members. She turned them down, being confident that she could make it without having to sell her body as well.

A former RADA acquaintance just back from Japan gushed to her about the lucrative nightclub and entertainment scene there and pressed her to try her luck, saying there was a promoter in town looking for upmarket club acts and he had heard about her Eartha Kitt stuff. Jenny was resting between jobs so decided she would give it a go, as a couple of months in Japan could fit in before another possible TV serial part.

She was required to meet the Japanese promoter at a swank London hotel and do a short audition along with half a dozen or so other girls. It was an easy to find place, the hotel had been briefed about her arrival and all seemed very kosher and organised. The Japanese promoter, a man in his early 50s and very tidily dressed, was impressed, made a good offer with a contract and was prepared to sign her up on the spot. He mentioned a number of Tokyo and Osaka clubs and variety places. She decided to give it some thought, checked out the places on the internet and talked to the friend about them.

Her friend was enthusiastic so she decided to take the job. There was no serious boyfriend in the background and, apart from Mum and Dad and brother and the usual local friends, nothing really to keep her at home. Things happened like clockwork. Her visa came through okay from the Japanese Embassy, a sheaf of airline tickets and hotel vouchers arrived plus some yen cash for incidental spending until her first wages came through.

The flight went ahead without incident. The first night was spent at the New Otani Hotel, near the Akasaka Hotel in Tokyo, and she was taken out to dinner the second night by one of the two Japanese men who had interviewed her in London, accompanied by a sophisticated-looking Japanese woman who had little English.

She was not aware of when things started to change, or rather when she noticed a change in herself. The entertainer accommodation was no great shakes but a lot better than some of the gaffs she had stayed at in London, but she noticed the few non-Japanese entertainers seemed a bit uncommunicative or wrapped up in their own worlds and none seemed to have a lot of brain.

The boss had taken her passport on the first day, using an excuse that he had to get an arrival stamp in her work visa to prove she was now in his employ. The boss said the first week would involve meetings with potential customers who would hire her for gigs, and she began to realise that he was not a show manager but rather an agent or promoter and would take a cut on whatever pay she got.

Her wage was guaranteed so she was not unduly worried but felt like some slave at the meetings as all business was conducted in Japanese, and the only thing she could understand was her name and 'yen' when money was being discussed. She did not like the way that she was not consulted and treated like someone else's property, nor did she like the look of some of her boss's customers who were licentious to say the least.

After being there about 10 days, she realised she had received no time to herself for shopping or simple local sightseeing and that, as she could not speak a word of Japanese, she was a bit afraid of going anywhere herself in case she got lost. All the other girls seemed too tired or too busy to have any free time They came in during the early hours of the morning, slept until noon, and took half the afternoon to get ready for the next evening's shows.

She did not see or have chance to mix with the normal range of show biz characters as she had done in London or New York. And then, after the round of meetings, she was asked to do some clothes modelling, 'as it would take a week or two for her show biz engagements to come through.' She had told her boss she did not do negligée modelling at her London interview for the job, though she had agreed to do some occasional modelling between jobs in Japan.

She was taken to a Ginza address with an upstairs studio where she found a variety of gowns and garments hanging up and a stern faced mama-san there ostensibly to assist her, while a skinny, animated Japanese photographer took photographs as he openly leered at her bust and crutch.

After a photo shoot of various gowns, she was told to put on some skimpy underwear so translucent her pubic hairs would show through. She declined, the photographer threw a tantrum, the mama-san got heavy and there was no one there that understood her English. After a lot of hissing and snorting she was taken back to her boss's office for a dressing down. She was fired up by then but to her surprise the boss soothed the situation and said it was a misunderstanding.

After that she had a few days of performing at select parties with a few other girls and a Japanese transvestite before what she believed were high-powered businessmen and politicians. She knew she was much talked about at these men only affairs and was far from impressed as they all seemed to be seedy, leering deals, and she noticed most of the girls seemed to peel off with the customers afterwards. After the third show her boss put a lot of pressure on her to entertain one of the customers afterwards, promising her lots of money if she was nice to him. The customer was totally abhorrent, being fat with triple chins, a slobbering mouth and fat paws for hands.

It was about that time she began to get concerned about things. The mama-san gave her a stern dressing down, the guaranteed weekly payment of wages did not come through and worse still they had not returned her passport. She was not sure if it was the hours or food but she always felt sleepy and seemed to lack the drive to do anything about her situation, but would strangely spark up an hour or so before she was due to entertain people.

She got a few legitimate gigs at large nightclubs where she was well received but was greatly dismayed when her boss said there was no money to be made at these gigs, just peanuts. She was annoyed that some people had tried to approach her directly with offers of work but had all been turned away by her boss, except those who were his cronies.

After a couple of weeks or so, she noted she was not receiving any mail. Only one letter from her mum and another from her drunken ex-boyfriend had come through. Worst of all, she did not know how to use the phone and no one would tell her. The mama-san said all international calls had to be approved by the boss. As her mood swings increased, she blearily realised she was sick or suffering a kind of mental illness and asked to see a doctor. It was arranged but the doctor simply prescribed pills which made her care even less about her life.

Stubbornly she refused to have sex with any of her boss's customers and everyone at the establishment, except one older Japanese hostess, treated her like scum. One Filipina asked why she thought she was better than the rest of them.

'In Asia you do what Asians do and, if that means sex, you do it with a smile,' she said.

She seemed to be becoming a zombie and losing control of her life completely, so chucked out all the doctor's pills and started to watch her food, but the latter was impossible as others prepared it and she could not tell if this was how Japanese food should taste or if something had been added. She felt she had only one friend in this place, the lady called Emi with sad lines to an otherwise pleasant face. Emi's English was terrible but she would say from time to time,

'It's bad place, no good place,' and then a few days ago Emi had said, 'A friend want help you escape.'

Jenny was heartened by this but apprehensive of where she might be expected to escape to. Things had got so bad the boss was threatening her that she had destroyed so much business she would have to start repaying her airfare and full accommodation costs as he could not make any money out of her. She was scared of him and this violent side to his character. It made her realise just how alone she was. She thought of running away and going to the Japanese police, but her boss must have read her mind and said,

'My friends the police have very firm policy for girls who break their work visa contract and you might get jail here for some months until they discover how you tried to break law with false visa application and fine you.'

She had no idea how true it was but felt it would be safer to try and contact the British Embassy somehow. She mentioned this to the Filipina girl who told her the boss was Yakuza and they were capable of murdering people who owed them money, or making them work as prostitutes for the rest of their working life. It sent a shudder down her spine; she had guessed as much and knew for certain she was in at the deep end up to her neck. The Filipina told her she had been working as a prostitute in Manila before she came to Japan, so she realised what she was getting into.

'You have to know the Japanese don't like to show any dirt so they dress things up to cover it. You see covers on toilet rolls, covers on car seats, covers over the entrances to Love Hotels so young lovers cannot be seen going to, or coming from these places, and of course no one in Japan really talks about, or claims to know anything about their untouchable class or the bad things their grandparents did in Asia during the Second World War. They only become direct when things are not going their way and then it's like the end of the road. That is their national weakness,' the girl told her.

Jenny was getting a fast track education on the shady side of Japanese life and she did not like what she was hearing. She asked the girl about the other hostesses and was told they all did as they were told and most of the foreign girls knew what they were getting into and had problems or were in debt and needed the money.

'They are not all bad; some of the Japanese girls are okay. Emi she is honest, and has a good heart,' she said.

'You cannot win against these gangsters, they have been operating for centuries and have contacts through society from the yatai roadside stall holders who they mostly control, up to selected politicians. You cannot win and even if they don't hurt you, it will cost you a lot of money to break from them,' she warned. It seemed they held all the foreign girls' passports and withheld wages if jobs were not done to their satisfaction, and they kept a close eye on everyone to make sure their girls were not poached by rival gangs or tried to do a runner to escape the gang's obligations.

It made Jenny think long and hard. She drank water to try to clear her forever muzzy mind and found it helped a bit. That convinced her they were messing around with her food and drink to keep her drugged. She realised it would be foolish to try to beat them with an obvious frontal attack. It would be best for her seemingly to play along with their game, but she would need to avoid the foods and drink they gave her, but how was the question as she never had money to buy anything. She decided to feign a stomach bug for 24 hours and stick just to water in the hope it might help clear her mind so she could find a way out of the mess.

The girl told her she had overheard her boss in a conversation about her with another Japanese businessman and there was some talk of moving her to another place because some British magazine was trying to contact her. Jenny told her Emi had hinted at something like this but her English was terrible so she had no real idea what it was about.

'You really want to get away, don't you? If you do, you must have some money, you must have some plan and your Embassy might be the best place. In this district where the shops depend on the night life, club owners and their customers, they don't want to offend Yakuza by being too helpful to a runaway girl but if you go to another suburb away then they can help you if they speak English. But you will lose everything, your pay, your clothes, your passport, and if you go to the Embassy, it's likely the boss will guess that is where you are going and try to head you off by having someone watching and waiting for you to turn up there,' she added.

Jenny thought a lot of this far-fetched and perhaps the style in Manila, but it did make her think harder and more urgently about an escape bid. The girl told her she could sustain herself on food samples at the food sections at large Japanese department stores, providing she looked respectable and not like a tramp.

'It's quite easy. All you do is go to the food section and they are always offering sample bits of fish, meat, cheese and some drinks. You cannot get enough for one meal at one place, so you must visit several and it is enough to keep you going. It's what some Japanese students do,' she said.

Several hours later the mama-san came with her dinner, saying the boss was taking her out early to some engagement with the Filipina girl. Jenny clutched her stomach and said she was sick and went to the toilet after pushing the food aside. The mama-san was angry, and said in Japanese the boss would be very angry if she did not front up. Jenny guessed what she was driving at and indicated she would go out; it suited her as she was getting the grains of an idea of an escape attempt.

The Filipina girl saw her refuse her food and explained to the mama-san that Jenny had been feeling ill all day, to give her excuse some authenticity. The mama-san told the girl she had better not cause trouble and if Jenny started to act up in any way she, the girl, must help the boss to keep her under control. The girl stated emphatically that that was exactly what she would do.

Jenny and the girl were picked up by two burly, crew-cut headed Yakuza in dark suits in a large white Yank tank which cruised around several blocks for about 20 minutes and took a short motorway trip of about 20 minutes to another suburb where the two girls were met by more mobsters and taken to a flashy select club inhabited by moronic, ever-smiling and tittering hostesses, and middle-aged swaggering males whose vanity dictated that at least two girls should attend their needs at all times.

Jenny asked for the toilet on arrival to convince her boss, who she had seen seated with a fat, rough but rich-looking dude, that she genuinely had a stomach problem. She took her time and drank lots of water and started to feel better for it. In crude, broken English her boss told her Yamada-san next to him was a very important and influential show biz entrepreneur. He offered his name card to Jenny and she gracefully accepted it the Japanese way with a low bow and clutching it in both hands as if it were gold.

Yamada-san and her boss were impressed and he told Yamada-san she was learning fast how to do things the Japanese way and would be a good girl in a week or so. Her boss had organised an Eartha Kitt karaoke disc and told Jenny to sing it. She obliged with three items and drew big applause from the club's patrons. Her boss asked her to try Ella Fitzgerald. Jenny protested and said she had only occasionally tried her numbers, adding that she sang differently, but she gave two Ella numbers a go and impressing the boss.

Drinks were thrust at Jenny. She protested about her stomach, but the boss was angered saying it was rude not to accept. The Filipina girl vouched for Jenny's illness and her boss reluctantly let the matter drop but then tried to press some finger food on her, which she noticed no one else had touched. Even though she refused, he kept saying it was medicine but gave up when he realised Jenny was co-operating in every other way and seemed good-humoured.

Jenny had a brain wave. Some years ago she had seen

a documentary about Japanese night life and it covered among other things a mini-theatre where ordinary people could go and be part of a traditional comedy act, where everyone dressed up in old Japanese costumes, and they played out parts with a small full-time cast who prompted and teased them to the point of humorous ridicule.

She told the girl to tell them she would like to visit a place like that tonight with the boss and his business friend. They looked surprised at first and wondered how she knew about such places but because she was so apparently happy and enthusiastic, they decided it could be a bit of a riot and lead to other things. In the normal fashion, Jenny's boss snapped his fingers and several minions sprang into action. One phoned up a mini-theatre to arrange a booking while the others organised cars and sorted out the bill with the staff.

When the boss and his business friend started to move they had about half a dozen retainers each, a fairly normal situation for Japanese men who believe they have status. Some retainers are friends of a lower status, glad of a free ride on their friend's expense account, and one or two are gofers to sort out cars, parking, bills and other menial tasks. The mama-san of the establishment and half of her hostesses lined the exit, followed in the lifts to the ground floor and bowed the group off the premises as valued customers.

Two white Yank tanks had been lined up for the VIPs in the group and a few gofers took taxis. Jenny was impressed by the turnout though she had become accustomed to Japanese bosses never moving anywhere without at least two gofers. She got a seat in the boss's car along with the Filipina girl and the boss's business friend had his own floozy tucked away besides him in his car.

They drove for about 30 minutes before reaching the mini-theatre. It was several floors above ground level in a large building with a few other clubs and some boutique clothing shops. The master of the establishment was at the entrance to greet them along with his permanent cast of about half a dozen, mostly ladies, and a few gays. The Yakuza boss and his retinue did an immediate return to their childhood, behaving like pre-teen kids out on a Sunday treat at the thought of cross dressing and playing the fool. Although she was in a deadly serious mood, Jenny could see how this sort of thing could be fun.

The master of the house offered her boss a selection of skits from traditional Japanese plays for him to select. After some discussion he chose one and then they had to do the casting. The trick was to cast each customer as an opposite personality to themselves, so the fat Yakuza boss became a skinny housewife and the Filipina girl became a tough samurai etc. The roles were familiar to all except Jenny and the Filipina girl although she seemed to have had some previous knowledge of what was expected.

The master guessed correctly that the bosses would like to see Jenny in some very revealing skimpy thing, playing a damsel in distress, so she ended up in a very theatrical kimono which seemed to fall apart and demanded full time attention to retain any semblance of modesty. She was given of pair of high platform wooden Japanese sandals to wear which she handled with extreme difficulty as they were a size or two smaller than her feet.

She got the gist of it. There were several acts to this play and proceedings would stop every so often for brief photo sessions. Jenny was careful to pick up a few mementos of the place, in the form of matches and a name card. She also managed to pick up a pen on the bar and went to the toilet during a short break and wrote on one of the cards, 'Please help me, I am Jenny Jones from Britain being held against my will.' He plan was to escape, and at the first place that looked safe to give some-one this card hoping they could understand English.

Back on stage the things were becoming ribald, drink had been flowing like a river in torrent, and all but a few gofers were out of their skins including the Filipina girl who had been almost force-fed hard liquor. During odd moments, Jenny had been searching for exits to see if there was a fire exit so that she could avoid being held up at the lift or at the ground floor entrance.

She had spotted a green 'running man' exit sign in the landing outside the entrance to the club and thought if she choose the right moment to go to the toilet when a gofer was nowhere near, she could slip from the toilet to the entrance of the club which was just feet away and be out and onto an emergency exit. With luck they might not twig to her absence for a few minutes.

She got her moment between her own appearances on stage when no one was near the exit and excused herself to the toilet. They hardly noticed they were having so much fun. After a moment, she peered out the toilet door to see the entrance was still unmanned and quickly slipped out, certain no-one had actually seen her go. Once outside she followed several other exit signs, took an exit though a large steel emergency door and found herself on an external steel stairway. She took off the large wooden sandals to run faster, gathered bits of the kimono in her other hand and raced down the stairway as fast as she could go.

The cool night air was superbly refreshing after the smoky atmosphere of the small theatre. The emergency stairway was unlit and it emptied out into a narrow street which was mostly a service lane for large buildings. There was a small group of drunken Japanese businessmen wending their merry way through the narrow, short road. She raced past and they roared with laughter at the sight of her.

'Jesus,' she thought, 'do I look that bad?' She found a discarded and partly broken Japanese umbrella lying next to a rubbish bin and grabbed it. It still opened but with bent spokes and it would help to cover her face so people might not see she was a foreigner. She felt it best to appear like a drunken Japanese woman rather than a mad foreigner until she had put a lot of space between the Yakuza and herself. She had gone a fair distance before she realised she was still running without the slippers and the street was widening and there were more lights.

'God, what a nightmare,' she thought, 'this is just like a very bad dream but it's true.' She had a terrifying feeling of mental detachment from her own body as if she was watching dispassionately at someone else doing a frantic bunk and had to keep telling herself this was a real, 'get a grip, don't get a panic attack' situation.

The road she was in curved, crescent-like, so that she had a feeling she had been running part of a circle and was in danger of reaching another part of the circumference which would bring her back near the ground floor entrance of the small theatre. Her fears were realised when she got to an intersection and rounded a corner to see she was barely a hundred yards away from the main entrance.

'Oh, dear God, help me,' she kept saying, and then a large, white Yank tank pulled up alongside her and she had barely time to press the name card she had written on into a surprised stranger's hands before a couple of Yakuza forcibly took her arm as she kicked and struggled, and explained to the male pedestrian she had given a card to that she was a foreigner and needed their help. Her kimono had all but fallen apart, revealing only her pants and bra, and she was sobbing in dismay and anger as they forced her back into the car.

CHAPTER 8

Rick woke early to get his show on the road, he wanted to see them off, and go with the group on the transfer from the Shiba Park Hotel to Tokyo Station to assist with the validation of their seven-day Japan rail passes. It was not a difficult job, just a matter of rounding up everyone's passports and their rail pass vouchers and finding the right cubicle to present them and get the passes in return.

Everyone came down to breakfast on time with hotel staff wheeling away their suitcases ready for loading on their coach. There were the usual telephone and minibar accounts to be sorted and breakfast time chit chat. Most were nearly through their breakfasts when the coach drew up and a lady tour escort introduced herself to him. She was not a qualified guide but just an assistant who helped with directions and getting people on and off the right transport.

He judged the group's mood as optimistic after their meeting with Nomura-san and knew in their heart of hearts they would be terribly disappointed if the Fukuoka deal fell through. He was silently counting heads when he realised that Nomura-san had not shown up so asked the front desk to call him on the phone. They received no answer but one of the bellhops had seen him go out earlier so Rick thought he might just be taking a bit of exercise.

Michiko was pulling her hair out with fury at rival newspaper coverage of the Mereleigh affair after getting the early morning call from Nishi Nippon overnight newsroom staff at Fukuoka. She told Adam the other newspapers had the wrong end of the stick and were blaming Nomura-san totally for the stuff-up.

'No one but us really knows anything about it. I have no idea who gave them their information. They say he misled the City Hall and sponsors, and was not responsible enough in checking the facts,' she said. 'The reports say the major sponsors cannot go through with this as it would be a total flop. Where on earth did they get this opinion from? It seems to me they just invented it, as they only talk of sources, not anyone or any organisation!' she protested.

Adam was dismayed. 'You can guarantee that a lot of this stuff would have been wired to the UK by Kyodo news agency and others, and my boss, plus the Guardian, will soon be on my back wondering why my account is so different to the mainstream cable reports. Jesus, what a mess, but we are right. We have the facts, the rest of them are just publishing crap.'

'This could destroy Nomura-san. The poor guy has only started to recover from the trauma of it all. I think we should ring Rick straight away and get him to keep an eye on him. I don't think Tanaka-san is going to be there this morning so we can't rely on him to help. Maybe you should talk to Nomura-san?' he suggested.

'Come Adam, we have no time now. We can ring on your mobile. Get dressed, we can pick up some Japanese newspapers at the railway station but we have to get to Tokyo railway station in time to meet the group and get the train. I am very glad you got Rick to bring your big suitcase with him, it would have been a nightmare to take it on the subway in rush hour!' she said. Rick was marshalling the group on to the coach and becoming increasingly concerned about Nomura-san's whereabouts. He decided to give Tanaka-san a ring.

Tanaka-san had had a latish night after sending Emi off to her place. He paid for her taxi rather than risk her being seen by any of the Yakuza minders. He woke with a jolt when told Nomura-san was missing and told Rick he had not seen him since leaving the hotel yesterday.

'This is bad Rick-san, but why?' He went to bed, you say, in a good mood after the meeting. I don't know, I don't know. He knew he was going to Fukuoka with the Nishi Nippon journalists by the shinkansen and agreed with that when I explained it in Japanese with him. Maybe we can telephone his wife, but on second thoughts perhaps it's best if I can call the Nishi Nippon Shimbun journalists first in case they changed the plan and did not

Roy Vaughan ~

tell anyone,' he suggested, and Rick agreed.

Rick then got a call from Adam saying the rival papers had published some very damaging stories for Nomura-san, and they were concerned about his wellbeing if he read them. Rick told Adam he was missing and it all added to the concern.

'In these circumstances I will get the hotel staff to open his room in case he has done something stupid,' he told Adam and said he would ring back.

The hotel was happy to send one of its junior managers with Rick to Nomura-san's room and opened the door with the electronic key. The bed had been slept in, some clothes were hanging in the wardrobe, and a copy of a Japanese national daily paper left strewn on the bed. The under-manager spotted it and immediately noticed a story about the Mereleigh group which mentioned Nomura-san. It was all in Japanese and he read the very damning account to Rick. Rick sat down in shock and told the under manager he really feared for Nomura-san's sanity and safety.

They searched the room for any clues, careful not to disturb things too much in case the police had to be called in. They found a hand-written letter addressed to Andy propped up next to the room telephone.

'We better get Andy to open it,' Rick told the under-manager.

The under-manager carefully shut the room door and when they got to the lobby Rick saw that everyone was on board the bus except Nomura-san. He then asked Andy to step off for a moment and took him into the hotel lobby

281

out of sight of the rest of the group before producing the letter and saying Nomura-san was missing. Andy ripped it open and his jaw dropped.

'It says: "Dear Andy-san, it was so good meeting you and the real Mereleigh Group after all these months. I never realised how wrong I was to consider the actors before the real people until I met you all and found what good people you are and how wrong it was of me to consider the actors ahead of you. I am so sorry for the big mess I made of everything, and especially insulting and inconveniencing you. I have failed you; I have failed Fukuoka City and the sponsors and my group and also my family. When I read the newspaper this morning I realised how badly I have behaved. Please forgive me. I must make the sacrifice for this shame to save my family's face."'

Andy put the letter down and then exclaimed, 'What the bloody hell does that mean?'

Rick was white with shock and felt stunned by it all. He had this group to get to the railway station without the key figure responsible for them being in Japan. He was apparently intent on doing himself in, or perhaps had already done so. Then there was Jenny the missing girl. Christ, where did it all end?

'I don't know, I don't know, I just don't know, let me think. God, what a mess. Shit, it's all we need,' he spluttered.

Maggie Moss had left the bus and come into the lobby to find out what the delay was. Rick quickly briefed her and no sooner had he done so than a rather impatient

Fran joined them, pointing at her watch and saying the driver and escort were worried they might not make the train on time. Rick pulled himself together and instructed Maggie to brief Fran and board the bus with her but not to say anything about Nomura-san at that point. He would phone Tanaka-san and sort out the hotel, and be on the bus in two minutes.

He went straight to the under-manager, who had guessed the worst, and said he would come straight back to the hotel after seeing the group off at the station. Meanwhile, if there were any signs of Nomura-san or calls from him to let him and also Tanaka-san (he gave the hotel Tanaka-san's number) know immediately. He then rang Tanaka-san, who said he would come over to the hotel within the hour to keep watch and check developments with Rick once he returned from the station.

Andy was still waiting for Rick at the hotel entrance. 'What do you think, Andy?' Rick asked

'Like you, I suppose the worst but what the heck was in the Japanese newspaper you mentioned?' Andy asked

'I have no idea, I don't read Japanese, but I imagine it was pretty dreadful as far as Nomura-san was concerned. I am sure Michiko will know and we will see her shortly at the station,' Rick replied.

'I think I must bring the group up to date, they will never forgive me if I don't,' Andy stated.

They boarded the bus and a relieved tour escort and driver got their show going. The driver slipped the big coach into gear, it slid gently out of the hotel forecourt, and the escort tinkled a polite welcome on board to everyone and reminded them to fasten their seat belts, She told them how long it would take to get to Tokyo Station, traffic permitting, and hoped everyone would have a nice day.

Rick asked for the microphone and said he and Andy had some rather bad news then handed it over to Andy. Andy gave them a succinct account of the morning's developments. Apart from a few shocked 'oh's and 'my God's', the group listened in total silence.

'Has anyone told the police?' Perry the ex-British cop asked.

Rick smarted with embarrassment and said, 'No, but maybe we should. I will get Tanaka-san right now on his mobile and ask him to do it. He knows the background.'

'How on earth will this affect things at Fukuoka? Maybe we should cancel our tour out of respect and not go on from here,' Peter suggested. The group broke into many individual discussions before Fran took over:

'What might have happened or be about to happen to poor Nomura-san does not bear thinking about, and I have total sympathy with him and his family. He is not to blame for anything in my book. He did his best and was trying to do good for society. I for one would like to face those who have put him under so much pressure. Just who the hell do they think they are, some cheap-shot journalists and some lily-livered sponsors putting cash before human considerations,' she told them.

'We even have our own ambassador trying to tell us we might cause some kind of international embarrassment if we show up at Fukuoka. Oh dear, how terrible.

My God, let's get real. We came on this trip for a purpose in good faith. It's gone totally sour but not of our making, nor Nomura-san's.'

'I for one would like to go to Fukuoka to pay my respects to Mrs Nomura and the others in that group, and be a major embarrassment to those who have driven Nomura-san to this,' she told them.

Derek Sloan, the ex-sailor, took over, 'I totally support Fran. If we scuttle this trip now we will abdicate our responsibilities and hand over power to the detractors who might end up having blood on their hands if Nomura-san does anything to himself. Nomura-san was the man with the good idea who put things together, and his family must be told directly by us how much we admired him and what he was trying to achieve. That alone will help give his family and friends back some pride and dignity. If we turn this ship around and head home, it will just tell his family and friends he was wrong and everything is too embarrassing for us.'

The group gave Fran and Derek a solid round of applause, leaving only Lindsay Love to say, 'I think I agree with your sentiments but maybe we should also ask the advice of the two Nishi Nippon journalists, Sam and Kenny, and Michiko, of course, who have done so much for us, and also perhaps the Mayor of Fukuoka.'

Oswald cut in, 'That is a fair point. Certainly the journalists who have been with us, but I am not so sure we need contact the Mayor and make a decision based on his advice. After all, we are not really thinking of making a call at Fukuoka City

Hall now! We are just going to make a private visit now and we must pay to see our friends at Fukuoka'.

'That is a good compromise. Shall we leave it at that, with Oswald's amendment so to speak?' Andy suggested. 'We shall see Michiko and Adam at the station. Also I think we should thank Rick for being our anchorman in all this. He has, of course, another assignment at Tokyo, trying to find Jenny Jones, as well as waiting for news of Nomura-san.'

'Also Rick, on the practical side can you please sort out the cost and a suitable hotel at Fukuoka for us if we decide to spend the last two nights of the tour there, plus some transfers etc. I don't think I or anyone should commit the whole group to this until we know the costs as some might find it a bit much. Our original arrangements at Fukuoka were going to be paid for by Nomura-san's sponsors, and by the sound of the newspaper reports this morning that support might have vanished, not that we would want to have support from folk who might have sent Nomura-san to his death — heaven forbid!' Andy concluded.

As the coach drew into Tokyo station they spotted Adam and Michiko standing near the stopping bay. Michiko smiled and waved furiously.

'Hell, I would not mind her as a daughter in law,' Derek teased Peter, who in turn allowed himself a slight smug smile.

'You know, Peter, I heard the three best things in life are: Chinese food, a European house and a Japanese wife!' Derek roared.

'Had any experience of the latter?' Peter threw back and Derek decided to drop the subject, having been to Nagasaki as a sailor in his youth.

As the group disembarked and picked up their suitcases, Rick quickly briefed Adam and Michiko. She nodded furiously throughout; totally shocked that Nomura-san had disappeared again. They continued discussing the situation and future arrangements as they entered the large booking hall and queued up to exchange their vouchers for rail passes. Michiko took over the tour escort job at the railway counter and thanked the real escort for her help. They bowed to each other in that very correct Japanese way recognising the efforts of each other to make things work properly.

Andy explained the plan to go to Fukuoka for a couple of days to thank the family and friends and Michiko was delighted with their consideration. She said she was sure the Nishi Nippon Shimbun would give moral support to them, but the idea would have to be referred to the editor. She had no idea how Fukuoka City Hall would react. She told Andy and Adam she wanted to ring Sam and Kenny, the two other Nishi Nippon journalists, to break the news about Nomura-san.

San and Kenny were shocked to the core. They decided they should stay on at Tokyo and help Tanaka-san and Rick find him and also cover that aspect of the story. They agreed totally with Michiko that the group would do the right thing by going to Fukuoka. Michiko felt a crusading fire in her belly. There was going to be a big punch-up at Fukuoka over the rights and wrongs of this, and she was mightily pissed off with the treatment the other national dailies had given Nomura-san. She wanted to equal the score on Nomura-san's behalf.

Rick saw them off on the platform. The Hikari was, as usual, precisely on time, and the carriages stopped at the exact marked points on the platform that they should have done. Despite the major upset and uncertainties, the group was in reasonable spirits. Next stop for them would be Kyoto, about three hours away, with some nice coastal views and a glimpse of Mount Fujiyama en route, if the weather was clear.

Adam and Michiko were snuggled into a corner window seat behind the rest of the group, something Michiko had tactfully arranged so no one could see them holding hands if they wished to. Public displays of affection were not considered to be very polite in Japan, and she was a well brought-up person. She had picked up a few copies of the national dailies and pored over their coverage of the Mereleigh affair. Adam even noticed the English editions of two national dailies had given some space to it as well, and though perhaps watered down a bit, the stories put the blame squarely at Nomura-san's door.

Michiko looked sadly at Adam and reminded him of the empty seat next to them that should have been Nomura-san's, and the relief and joy he felt about going back home to see his wife and kids.

'My God, I wonder if anyone has told his wife he is missing!' she exclaimed in shock.

'Well, she certainly should not have to hear that from the police first and Tanaka-san will be phoning them about now, so what can we do?' Adam responded.

Michiko rang Nishimura-san immediately, saying he was missing and the police had been asked to assist. Nishimura-san was greatly disturbed by the latest publicity and said she felt like going into hiding. She had been overjoyed at the Nishi Nippon Shimbun's coverage but devastated by the other stuff. She spoke about how happy Nomura-san had been on the phone yesterday after meeting the Mereleigh group and now, well, 'how could anyone do this to another human being without even getting his side of the story?' she asked.

Nishimura-san said she would go and see his wife as soon as possible and help her through any disaster. Michiko confirmed that both she and Adam would be at Fukuoka in about six hours, and after checking in to a hotel would go around to see her.

Rick had meanwhile returned to the Shiba Park Hotel at Tokyo, where he was met by an impatient and worried Tanaka-san. He had no sooner arrived than the under manager asked him to go to his office with Tanaka-san.

'I have some bad news I think. When you were out we received a phone call from the police. It seems a male answering Nomura-san's description threw himself in front of a train at Hamamatsu Cho Station this morning. He had this hotel's electronic room key in his pocket and as we are near that station, they called us first just after you left and then they traced him by some stuff in his wallet to Fukuoka, so I guess they will tell his wife. The police would like someone to identify him as soon as possible.' The under-manager looked sympathetically at them both.

Tanaka-san groaned and told the under-manager he would do it, and Rick guessed what he said and added he could go along as well to support Tanaka-san. The under-manager left and rang a police number and said they would send a car for them in about 15 minutes. Rick and Tanaka-san decided a strong coffee was in order.

'This might not be very pleasant picture,' Tanaka-san advised.

'It's okay. I have seen a few dead bodies and accident victims in my time, but I just feel so sad if it's him and guilty. Maybe we did not do enough,' Rick said. Tanaka-san's feelings were the same but how could anyone guess the other media would be so harsh on him and not even wait to get his point of view before going to print?

'Yes, why foul up a good story by sticking too closely to the facts? Or else it's a case of we have three facts here which make a cracker of a story, but if we take our investigation one step further and pick up a fourth fact, it will put everything in context and destroys the angle we thought we had at the beginning!' Rick added.

The police car arrived all too soon and a courteous young officer invited them (Rick winced at the English expression) to visit the morgue. He began to think of the famous 'Invitation to the waltz' and a macabre version called 'An invitation to the morgue', with dismembered bodies and skeletons waltzing about some medieval torture chamber.

He tried to purge the thought of it from his mind as the police car made its way through the morning's heavy traffic to the morgue. A police sergeant was there to meet them when they arrived. For politeness' sake he tried out his very broken English on Rick.

'So sorry, so sorry, for trouble you. This man not so nice to look at,' the sergeant glanced at Tanaka-san and was reassured that he was a tough looking middle-aged person. He continued, 'I think you understand'. Tanaka-san assured him in Japanese that he did, and that Rick was not a novice at this sort of thing.

They were taken down stairs to a large, sparse room that stank of formaldehyde and had several layers of square doors like a railway station's left luggage locker. Everything was highly polished and super hygienic and the lights were fiercely bright like spotlights lighting up an international soccer match.

A couple of morgue officials met them and ushered them towards a mobile stretcher carrier, unclipped a locker door and drew out a shrouded body. One of the mortuary officials explained he had some head damage and the body had been very badly mangled by the train but they did clean up most of the blood and replaced his guts, which had spewed out, back into his stomach.

It was more information than Rick needed but to his relief they only exposed the head. It was enough for both Tanaka-san and Rick to know it was Nomura-san. They acknowledged his identity individually to the sergeant so he was sure they both agreed who it was. The shroud was replaced and Nomura san's remains placed back in their chilled cubicle. The sergeant said he needed some brief statement and asked the two to come back upstairs, where he took details on Nomura-san's movements during the last twenty-four hours and how they came to know him.

The sergeant said, 'then he was the man that has been written about in connection with the Mereleigh affair,' and they both agreed. He asked if they felt there might have been any foul play to which both said not as far as they knew. Both Rick and Tanaka-san were taken aback by that suggestion, and told the sergeant Nomura-san had gone missing for a few days before, and was in a very low mental state when they met him. The sergeant nodded, and said he wished the journalists who wrote about him were there to see what they had done.

'That is off record, you understand, just personal view-point not official,' he clarified. He told them they could now approach Nomura-san's wife at Fukuoka with some certainty. It would be a terrible shock but not the delayed agony that would have ensued if they had not helped identify him.

Tanaka-san bowed deeply to the sergeant and thanked him profusely in Japanese for his sympathy. Rick caught the mood and felt the same, and he shook the sergeant's hand vigorously. Not being accustomed to handshakes, the sergeant started uncertainly but got into the swing of it and would hardly let Rick's hand go at the end.

As they were walking out with the sergeant who was determined to bow them out of the main door, Tanaka-san mentioned how they had been searching for Jenny Jones. The sergeant listened intently and told Takana-san they should contact the Tokyo vice squad immediately and a certain Inspector Mori who was his good friend.

'He is ichi ban, not most senior officer, but ichi ban

person,' he told them.

Tanaka-san and Rick entered the police car sadly, reflecting on how devastated Nomura-san's wife and family would be by it all. Rick explained to Tanaka-san the group's idea of going to Fukuoka regardless to pay their respects to his wife and family.

Tanaka-san nodded in agreement, then thought for a few moments and said, 'I have a big face in Fukuoka rugby world and I can get my rugby friends to take care of you if you come. You know in Japan rugby is often played by gentlemen with money like architect, dentist, lawyer, businessman, like old boys' club. We are going to welcome you and we will stand up for the memory of Nomura-san,' he promised.

They were dropped off at the Shiba Park hotel. Rick said he would phone Michiko and Andy and pass the sad news on to them. They were shocked and saddened, but it was not a totally unexpected outcome. Many of the women in the group were moved to tears and the men got angrier at the turn of events. Andy and Fran had a brief chat and decided there was now even more reason why they should go to Fukuoka, and the empty seat next to Michiko and Adam on the train which should have been Nomura-san's looked even more lonely. Janine said if she had flowers she would have put them on that seat as a gesture.

At Tokyo, Rick and Tanaka-san went straight to the bar to sink a few single malt whiskies in memory of Nomura-san. Tanaka-san then excused himself to phone a few friends at Fukuoka and also to contact Yoshi.

'Yoshi will come here in about fifty minutes. We have to plan for tonight and I will contact Inspector Mori as the sergeant explained I should do,' Tanaka-san said, reminding him of the deadline in the hunt for Jenny that evening. Rick mentioned he had to find a hotel at Fukuoka for the group and a bus to do some transfers. Tanaka-san offered the services of a rugby friend who owned a pleasant hotel in the Tenjin area of Fukuoka.

'He always has good price for rugby groups and I know he will do his best for you. I will make contact later today and let you know. So relax, Fukuoka is my home town,' he assured Rick.

Tanaka-san then got a call from Sam and Kenny, the journalists, wishing to see him. Tanaka-san was able to confirm with them the bad news about Nomura-san but pointed out his wife and family had not been told so they better confer with the police first. Sam and Kenny insisted on coming over to see them and Tanaka-san was pleased, although he had at first requested politely that they not put themselves out on his account.

The journalists invited them all, including Yoshi, to take lunch on their expense account at a nearby restaurant while they discussed things. Sam and Kenny felt there was probably no need for them to hang around Tokyo much longer but when they heard that Rick and Tanaka-san were hunting for Jenny Jones their ears pricked up and said they would like to help in any way they could.

Tanaka-san said they did not want any publicity at this stage as it could have an opposite effect and make it hard to find her, but tonight they had to pose as journalists who wanted to interview Jenny for a UK magazine and, of course, none of them were journalists! He told them how Yoshi had posed as an agent for the UK magazine and Rick was going to pretend to be the journalist.

Sam and Kenny had a brief discussion in Japanese and the upshot was that Sam would go along as well and pretend to be a photographer and he waved his camera as proof he could take photos. He would help prompt Rick about the ways of journalists.

'Kenny can come as the interpreter as his English is quite good and we can pretend that Yoshi and I do not speak English, or at least not good English, and that way Kenny can take a lead in the interview,' Sam said.

'I like it, it's a well thought-out plan,' Rick said, glad that he had some good backup.

Tanaka-san and the two journalists looked at each other simultaneously and said, 'business cards.' It was vital to have the right cards so Kenny drew the short straw and went off with Yoshi get some printed to indicate who they were and what company they represented.

Tanaka-san excused himself and said he wanted to track down Inspector Mori and also call Emi. They fixed a time of 4 pm and the Shiba Park as their next meeting point to finalise the arrangements for the night.

CHAPTER 9

The shinkansen journey to Kyoto is a pleasant one once the suburbs of Tokyo are left behind. The bullet train dashed through tunnels, over viaducts and tracked the coastline at intervals, and on-board waitresses provided a constant supply of trolley-borne bentos and other food and drink.

After the call from Rick about Nomura-san's death, Michiko had received a call from Tanaka-san saying he would arrange accommodation for the group at Fukuoka in a few days time, and had spoken to Rick about it. He asked her to let Andy know. He updated her on the official identification of Nomura-san and the fact that the police would notify his wife. The only relief to the bad news and depressing follow-ups that had to be made was the magnificent sight of Mount Fujiyama, seen in its spectacular cone-shaped, snow-capped form at a distance in clear blue skies.

Shortly before their arrival at Kyoto, Andy joined Adam and Michiko in Nomura-san's vacant seat, and they briefed each other on their movements over the next few days and promised to keep in contact, with Michiko and Adam going straight on to Fukuoka. At Kyoto the group was met on the platform by another smartly-uniformed tour guide. She took a deep bow and expressed a hope that they had had a pleasant journey, then helped organise their luggage. She then ticked them all off her list before marching them to a waiting coach.

It was a magnificent clear day and it was easy to see why Kyoto was described as the Paris of Japan. Spring blossom and the new flush of leaves gave a scented air of newness. Everywhere the streets were huge tree-lined boulevards and the number of temples and shrines was overwhelming. Fran had done some research and before the tour guide got her stuff under way, she told everyone it had 200 Shinto shrines and about 1,500 Buddhist temples, and many of them were headquarters for various sects in Japan.

The tour guide, not to be upstaged, politely cut in and explained Kyoto had a population of about 1.5 million and was both the capital city and centre of Japanese civilisation for more than 10 centuries from 794 to 1868. Most of the temples and shrines had traditional gardens of various sizes around them, creating a park-like atmosphere. They saw the old walled Imperial Palace that had been superseded by the Tokyo one and visited the Golden Temple set in an ornamental lake. For a number of hours they almost forgot about the tragedy of Nomura-san.

Rick had advised them to try to experience traditional Japanese things at Kyoto so all their meals were Japanese in traditional Japanese restaurants and they stayed two nights in a ryokan and slept on futons placed over tatami mat floors. It was their first experience of using a Japanese bathroom and wearing yukatas and slippers around the place. They got a lot of fun out of it all and Dick, one of the tour's jokers, could not help pointing out how Japanese toilets ranged from the sublime to the ridiculous.

'Some places have this high-tech head seat jobs where if you push a button, a powerful jet of water squirts up your bum, and then we find a lot of other places have little more than a pipe in the ground. I soon learned not to keep my wallet in my back pocket when using the latter. It nearly fell out and dropped down the hole when I had my pants round my ankles!' he said. Helena told them she heard the Japanese were very fastidious about blowing their noses.

'I heard, and if you look, they don't use a handkerchief, only paper tissues, and they consider it rude to blow their noses in front of you so will often go to a toilet to blow their nose,' she explained.

'Most of them seem to have handkerchiefs, so what do they use them for?' Perry asked.

'To dry their hands after they go to the toilet as most public toilets do not have towels or paper to dry hands on,' Foggy, Helena's partner explained.

'When you come to think of it, hoiking a big green oyster into a handkerchief and then wrapping it up and putting it into your pocket or handbag is a bit unhygienic,'

Maggie Moss added.

'True, but a lot of them seem to suck in the snot and swallow the contents of their nasal passages and make a horrible noise at the same time,' Peter pointed out.

'What a delightful conversation! Perhaps we could move on to another less basic topic,' Andy said sarcastically.

'Do you wanna know how the old cowpokes managed these things out West in the old days?' Chuck, Andy's American friend, volunteered.

'Yes, tell us Chuck,' Dick said, knowing he would get a wind-up.

'Don't Chuck, I am sure a lot of it will have to do with a diet of baked beans,' Fran interjected.

Chuck raised his hands to the air and said, 'Sorry girls,' and let the matter rest.

The young tour guide had given them a brief talk about the Japanese, and their customs and make-up. The group was intrigued to learn that Japanese and Mongolian race group ear wax was different from Europeans', one having a wax-like substance, and the other a more liquid substance, and she explained that as members of the larger Mongolian race group, Japanese were born with a dark, bluish birthmark on their buttocks.

'Can we see yours, please?' Dick asked. The young tour guide was caught a bit off balance and for a split second did not know what to say and was saved by Joan's comment that her husband was just a dirty old man.

The young guide relaxed and smiled. She went on to

explain that the greater Mongolian race included American Indians, Polynesians, Chinese, many South-East Asians and of course the Mongols themselves. She said she envied European women in one respect because until the baby was born they could never be sure what their eye and hair colour would be.

'In Japan, of course, it's always black hair and dark brown eyes,' she added.

The group enjoyed their first day at Kyoto immensely, and the next day they would do some more sightseeing around the old capital and then go to Nara. Some of the ladies were particularly interested in seeing the silk weaving and dyeing industry and Kyoto lacquer-ware and porcelain-ware.

The many cultural dimensions to Japan were impressive and Peter was beginning to think what an uncouth attitude he had had about Japan before visiting the place. He had mentioned the Second World War to Tanaka-san at Tokyo and when Tanaka-san explained that Japan had lived under a feudalistic samurai- type government for almost 400 years it was not surprising when militarists tried to create an empire.

'It is not an excuse for bad things but perhaps a reason why these people took over the country and got us into the war,' Tanaka-san had explained to Peter.

They had only been in Japan a few days but everyone felt they had received an enlightening introduction into a lot of aspects of Japanese life. No-one had felt at all at risk, it was clearly one of the most orderly crime-free societies in the world but they were beginning to appreciate the subtle social pressures and expectations of this old Asian culture.

As Andy had observed, Nomura-san's reaction to the problem seemed very Japanese and most newspapers' reactions, like most Western mass media, was to find someone to blame and stick it all on him, the Nishi Nippon Shimbun standing out above all others in its thoroughness and fairness. The group had a quiet night at Kyoto at a traditional Japanese restaurant with some koto players and old-style Japanese musicians playing. It gave them the peace and tranquillity they needed to sort things out in their minds.

While whistling along down the line at breakneck speed in the shinkansen, Adam and Michiko did not have quite so much time to reflect on things. The latest development would widen their assignments at Fukuoka, particularly by having to interview Nomura-san's wife and see his kids. They knew that one of the newspaper's more senior journalists would probably see her first but they felt a strong obligation to pass on their commiserations personally because they saw him in the last days of his life.

Also when they came to write about it, they wanted nothing less than a first-hand expression. Michiko found Nishimura-san quite straightforward to deal with, a modern no-fuss young Japanese lady, so when she got a call from her and Nishimura-san said she had heard about Nomura-san's absence, she had no difficulty in saying he had been found dead and pleaded with her to let the police inform the family first.

Once Nishimura-san was aware that Michiko and

Adam planned to call on Nomura-san's wife, she said she and her boyfriend would meet them at Hakata station and taken them there in her car. Trying to brighten up, Michiko asked Adam where they should stay that night. He was a bit bemused as he had not given a thought to it and left that sort of thing to her.

'I can get expenses for this and perhaps you can too?' she said and then added that, if so, they should stay five star at the Sea Hawk Hotel.

'If we share a room, it is probably the same cost as two singles, so our companies cannot complain,' she said.

Adam could find absolutely no reason to disagree, so she phoned the Sea Hawk and got a room organised for a couple of nights at least.

'It will be our honeymoon suite!' She clutched his arm beneath the table so no-one could see. Adam desperately wanted to put his arm around her and give her a big hug but did not want to embarrass her by doing something un-Japanese in public.

'After we have had a few hours with Nomura-san's wife and family, plus their friends, I think we shall need the honeymoon,' he said.

'Before or after the wedding?' she replied.

'Whaaat....' he started

'Just joking,' she laughed with a twinkle in her eyes.

'Just a few days in Japan and marriage is being mentioned, I thought the Japanese were very slow decision-makers?' he asked her.

'We can make a personal decision as fast as anyone but

sometimes it takes a long time to find a way to get the right answer. Most of the time is spent in finding a way to do something, not in deciding to do it,' she explained.

'So you have decided and are now finding a way to get a positive answer?' he joked.

'Hey, hey, that is unfair, and too fast an assumption about me, even though I am a fast thinker,' she laughed back at his teasing.

The shinkansen stopped at Hiroshima, and Michiko pointed out where the A-bomb epicentre was. Everything looked very much like any other Japanese city to Adam with no signs of any lasting devastation and plenty of modern buildings. Michiko could read his frustration at not having time to explore Kyoto or Hiroshima, and promised him they would visit both places together sometime soon.

The journey to Fukuoka's Hakata station was barely an hour and Adam felt they were really getting to south-western Japan when it took a dive into the Kanmon Tunnel beneath the Kanmon Straits which divide the larger island of Honshu from the southern island of Kyushu. The shinkansen emerged in bright but somewhat smoky sunlight amidst the industrial sprawl of Kitakyushu and the port of Moji. The sheer magnitude of industrial production was impressive: chemical companies, steel companies, a car manufacturer, a major toilet manufacturer and thousands of smaller associated industries.

'Before all this there were just big coal mines and a steel industry at Kitakyushu, and many thousands of coal miners were made redundant when the mines closed but were eventually employed in the newer industries,' Michiko explained.

Clearly, cities like Kitakyushu were the power houses of Japan where muck and money rubbed shoulders. Adam thought whatever Birmingham and Manchester might have been to the old British Empire, Kitakyushu, Osaka and others were to the world, and a much bigger and more populous world at that.

'Of course China is now competing very strongly, and Japan has moved from heavy industries like shipbuilding to more high-tech computer and electronic industries, and we feel strong competition in that area too!' she exclaimed.

The shinkansen stopped briefly at Kokura, Kitakushu's main station. It was a major junction for lines heading on the northwest coast of Kyushu to Fukuoka, Karume and Nagasaki and others to Beppu, the main holiday resort area and its national park on the east coast of Kyushu, and lines right down to Kagoshima, the southernmost city of Kyushu which nestles uncomfortably close to a massive rather active volcano that spews out huge volumes of ash over the city from time to time.

Shortly after the shinkansen pulled out of Kokura, Michiko pointed out Space World, a modern theme funfair, and Kokura Castle which stood proudly on a promontory displaying the classic lines of a traditional samurai castle. She explained that many of Japan's castles had been destroyed by bombing during the war or by one thing or another, and most had been completely rebuilt since.

The shinkansen sprinted through small valleys neatly occupied by rice fields and old style hamlets, and into tunnels and past bamboo and Japanese cedar-clad hillsides and over one or two broad but shallow rivers to Fukuoka. In no time at all, the shinkansen was slowing down for arrival at Hakata Station and Adam could see that Fukuoka was a large, modern city with multiple level motorways threading their way, octopus-like, around large blocks of offices and flats.

Shortly before arrival Michiko received a call from Nishimura-san who asked what carriage they were in, so when the train stopped there she was with her boyfriend exactly at the marked stopping place for carriage 12. Michiko had never met her before, but each couple was easily recognisable to the other by the quizzical looks exchanged.

In rather typical Japanese male fashion, Nishimura-san's boyfriend grabbed Adam's suitcase to relieve the foreign guest of his burden and Michiko was left struggling with hers. Adam came to the rescue and Nishimura-san and Michiko joked in Japanese about Japanese males always ignoring women. Adam caught the drift and saw Nishimura-san's boyfriend smarting a bit with embarrassment at his gaffe.

'His was a traditional Japanese male upbringing, very chauvinistic by western standards' Nishimura-san joked, and he nodded apologetically in good humour.

As Nishimura-san led them to the car park and her car, she quickly briefed Michiko about Nomura-san's wife and family and the Fukuoka Record Club group. Michiko nodded vigorously at the end of each statement accompanied by a 'hai' or some encouraging or sympathetic sound, and she quickly translated the salient points for Adam's benefit.

As far as Adam could make out Nomura-san's wife and family had been devastated by the news of his death, particularly after their hopes had been raised when he was found. It seemed Nomura-san's mother and an aunt were consoling her and helping out with the two children. The Fukuoka Record Club group had planned to meet later that day once he arrived with them on the shinkansen. Nishimura-san said that meeting would still go ahead as they had a huge disaster to discuss now and that Adam and Michiko were expected to attend.

Adam winced a bit at the daunting thought of meeting all these folks in such shocking circumstances. He tried to say he was the son of a Mereleigh Record Club member but not an actual member when Nishimura-san cut him off by saying they really expected him to be there and knew what his position was. She also explained this in Japanese to Michiko so she too could gain the full import of his presence at the meeting.

Michiko pressed Adam's arm and said, 'We cannot lose face by not being there,' and Adam then knew absolutely what his responsibility was. Nishimura-san and her boyfriend worked wonders getting their large suitcases into the boot of their small car and said Nomura-san's wife was expecting them so they should go there first. Adam groaned inwardly and said to Michiko, 'Are you sure it's right for us to see her so soon after she got the news. Can't we give her a few more hours or so to get used to it?' he pleaded.

'No Adam, she can never get used to losing her husband like this but she must be given some understanding of what has driven him to this and a reassurance from you and me that he was not a bad man, but a good man put under huge pressure which he could not handle. If she hears that from you and me it might help her a little,' she said.

Adam always hated this side of journalism, having to interview the bereaved immediately after an accident and ask the blatant, obvious question of how they felt about things, only to receive the usual painful answers from those still in shock. Sometimes the immediacy of journalistic needs transgressed the bounds of common decency.

Nishimura-san assured Michiko and Adam that Nomura-san's wife would not be offended by their arrival, in fact she would welcome it as it would bring to her a last little bit more of the life of a husband who was fast becoming a memory. Adam struggled with what to say and his looks alone told Michiko what he was thinking.

'You don't have to worry so much. I have to do the speaking, because I don't think she will understand much English, and I am Japanese so I know how I should handle this politely,' she reassured him.

Nishimura-san told Michiko she felt sure there was something very malicious about the other news reports that slated Nomura-san and as far she knew, no one from the other media had approached any members of the

Fukuoka record group for any statements, nor Nomura-san himself. To Nishimura-san and Michiko it seemed as through the other media reports had come from one source and that source had some axe to grind.

'Do you think it was someone in the Mayor's office who wanted to make sure that no blame or mud stuck to the Mayor over this mistake?' Nishimura-san asked Michiko.

Michiko said no, it would be too obvious, everyone would think he was to blame so if it ever occurred to him to leak something like this, the risks of a blow-back to his reputation would be too great. She told Nishimura-san possibly an opponent of the Mayor or someone or some organisation with a different agenda was more probable. She decided to call the other two Nishi Nippon Shimbun journalists Sam and Kenny to bring them up to date. They told her that when they got back to Fukuoka they would try to hunt down the lead and see who was responsible for it and why they were so malicious.

The small car drew into the Nomuras' small driveway and before they could get out an elderly lady came to the door, announced she was Nomura-san's mother in law and invited them in. They removed their shoes, bowed very deeply and expressed repeatedly their sincere con-dolences. They were ushered into a small lounge where Nomura-san's wife sat in semi-darkness with her sister beside her. She had clearly been weeping a lot but had the steely look in her eyes of a woman who wanted to seek justice, and that was keeping her going in the meantime.

She bowed and they bowed back, and she welcomed them warmly to her house, and then thanked Michiko and her colleagues at the Nishi Nippon Shimbun for their excellent story on the Mereleigh situation. She told Michiko she would be in her debt eternally. She acknowledged Adam and again apologised to him for all the inconvenience. Adam brushed it aside, and said his group was really indebted to Nomura-san and his family and friends for the chance to visit Japan, and he was there to do what he could to help.

It was much easier than Adam expected. Nomura-san's wife was a strong, stoical person. She would get through this, he calculated, and woe betides the person who wrote all that crap about her husband. Nomura-san's wife was aware of her responsibilities to the Fukuoka Record Club group and had things to do that would help her get through this for the moment at least.

Michiko talked and took some notes as Nishimura-san and Nomura-san's wife gave her copious background on the formation of their group many years ago and the lead-up to this tragic event. Nishimura-san looked at Michiko in that polite way of saying 'Time, please,' and Michiko nodded and apologised for taking Mrs Nomura-san's time. She was reassured many times by Nomura-san's wife that she and Adam were friends and always welcome at her house.

They left after many thank-yous and a lot of bowing, got into Nishimura-san's car and headed for a small coffee house on the lakeside, near Ohori Park, to regroup their thoughts before going on to the meeting with the full Fukuoka Record Club group. At the coffee house Michiko translated the guts of her interview for Adam's benefit. He noted it all down and said he would definitely file a very sympathetic piece on Nomura-san.

Nishimura-san looked very pleased about it but said, 'the question we all face now is do we do something for the Mereleigh group or not? In my heart I think we must, but you know I am just an interpreter for this group, a volunteer who wanted that job to practise my English and get to know some English people. It follows that my opinion is not important to this group, and the group might think I made a big mistake in my translations so I am quite worried about that!'

Adam assured her he would stand up for her, and that relaxed her a little. He also stated his intention to contact Rick later that day and let him know what they had been doing so far. Nishimura-san told them the meeting with the Fukuoka Record Club group would be at 7 pm at a community hall.

'If we have time, I would love to take a walk around this lake. This is fantastic, so much open space, people walking, jogging, hiring boats, it's perfect. Ohori Park must be the most spacious city park in Japan,' Adam exclaimed.

After a brief tête-à-tête, Michiko and Nishimura-san worked out that Nishimura-san and her boyfriend would have some time to sort things out for the meeting before coming back in about 60 minutes to pick up Michiko and Adam, take them to the Sea Hawk Hotel to check in, and then go to the meeting afterwards.

'Sounds perfect,' said Adam, relieved to get a bit of time and space alone for himself and Michiko.

⌘⌘⌘

The day had begun badly for the Mayor of Fukuoka. After his meeting with the editor of the Nishi Nippon Shimbun newspaper the preceding evening, he had decided to organise two meetings, one being a meeting of the city council's sub-committee dealing with the Mereleigh Record Club visit, the second to bring together a meeting of all the sponsors and the Fukuoka Record Club with a view to deciding what to do.

He had observed the request not to go public on the problem. He advised all his staff that all matters relating to the visit should remain confidential and 'in committee'. So when he woke to find one of the local radio stations carrying a story, and several national dailies all with a similar account heavily blaming Nomura-san for this and by implication himself and the council, he was furious.

The Nishi Nippon Shimbun's write up placated him to some extent. It reflected the truth, as he saw it, and the problems to be sorted out urgently. Within a few minutes, he began to get calls from some of his senior staff about the publicity, so he decided to advise them to draft a simple press release saying the council had just been made aware of the situation and would consult all parties involved in the Mereleigh visit before deciding on a course of action.

He had an early morning meeting with his council and key staff planned within the hour at which he hoped the city could form some course of recommended action with which the major sponsors would agree. The sponsors' meeting would take place almost immediately afterwards, just after lunch time.

A little over half way through the council meeting, he

was advised that Nomura-san had apparently committed suicide. The news came just as it seemed the council would favour going ahead with the tour despite the visitors being club members and not the stars of the movie. To some members of the council, Nomura-san's suicide was a clear example of his guilt and a reason why Fukuoka City Hall should distance itself as soon as possible from this 'fiasco.'

The various newspaper accounts were quoted and debated, there was almost an equal balance of others who felt the council was obliged to go ahead, and they felt some guilt over Nomura-san's suicide, recognising him as a good man with a good idea who failed perhaps through insufficient support from his community in the project's early stages. The debate swung one way and another but with no clear majority view, so the Mayor decided the council should go to the meeting with the major sponsors with an open mind and make a decision on the subject once the views of the sponsors were known.

Privately the Mayor was very angry and frustrated, especially after he noted that the majority of those against the tour going ahead were his political opponents, so his political antenna told him that if the tour was cancelled it might well be more damaging to his political reputation than if it went ahead. But to go ahead with barely a majority of councillors backing it and perhaps only a handful of sponsors could also be a disaster!

He checked his watch and noted he had about 45 minutes before his next official appointment. He then summoned one of his senior aides and told him to get the mayoral car ready and, without saying what he planned, he got in the car with his senior assistant and headed for Nomura-san's house, telling his aide to notify the Nishi Nippon Shimbun where he was going and why he was going there.

His senior assistant looked at him, surprised somewhat at this bold political move by his boss, and told him in the most polite terms it was a very courageous move, meaning it was a bloody dangerous thing to do politically, particularly without the support of his own political faction at city hall. The assistant made his call to the local newspaper and told the Mayor they would send two journalists, and that they hoped to get something in the evening edition of the Nishi Nippon Shimbun about his visit.

The Mayor smiled quietly to himself. That is exactly what he hoped for. If some political animals had set up the national dailies against him with a poisonous account about Nomura-san, he felt obliged to steal a march on then and truly nail his colours to the mast and leave the public of Fukuoka to decide who was right and who was wrong.

Back at City Hall the officials were handling scores of calls from sponsors, members of the public, the media and the British and New Zealand embassies. The British wanted to know if their ambassador should still attend, and the New Zealanders to see if the Mayor of Auckland should attend. The embassy officials were furious that Fukuoka City Hall was unable to give a decision when the event and official visits were only days away.

Miss Alsop-Smith, the UK Ambassador, for once had

no clear idea which would be the safer course for her to follow. She was extremely annoyed that the Mereleigh Record Club group had not taken her advice to cancel the tour nor bothered to contact her or any of the Embassy staff.

'It really is not good enough, who do these people think they are? It's totally clear the Japanese did not want to invite them and expected the stars of the movie, and if the Japanese feel obliged to go ahead, they will be seething beneath all the politeness and smiles, and we can expect an approach from them for some sort of outrageous favour in return for their help over this matter,' she stormed at her cultural attaché.

The cultural attaché, was a rather tall, thin, intellectual man who had gained entry to the Foreign Service because of his very detailed knowledge of ancient Greek culture and a rather close personal friendship with a man of influence within the Foreign Service who, like himself, was also an ex-Cambridge man. He was by inclination a liberal and a person of fine principle who preferred to state his views and support that viewpoint if he felt it a right one morally. Couched in the delicate terms of an advisor, he suggested to Miss Alsop-Smith that some might see inviting the real people rather than film stars as a more worthy thing to do.

It cut no ice. Things got worse for Miss Alsop-Smith, who was reading a basic commercial and publicity reaction to it all that told her doors would start to close and shutters be slammed shut as the more cautious sponsors in Fukuoka distanced themselves from this disaster. What the cultural attaché did not say was that he had been at the gay bar the night Ewan had peeled off from the group to go there, and he had met Ewan but not revealed that he worked at the embassy.

It was a chance but useful meeting that he planned to put to good effect with the door about to be slammed shut on the British Embassy's involvement in the Mereleigh visit. He decided he would phone Ewan, if he could, outside the embassy during his lunch break. By the time he got through to the Shiba Park Hotel, Ewan and the group had checked out and were in transit to Kyoto in the Shinkansen, but he managed to get hold of Rick and again did not disclose his identity, but was able to get Rick to give him the phone number of the ryokan at Kyoto where they would stay that night.

Being a good civil servant, the cultural attaché knew two things were paramount, one being the good reputation and best interests of Britain, the other being making your boss look good even when she was acting stupidly. He would ring Ewan in the evening and pump him to see how the Mereleigh group read the situation and their obligations. He had been through the English language editions of the morning newspapers and was dismayed at the tone of most of the stories which he felt were negative and destructive.

Later in the day, when Japanese Embassy staff told him about Nomura-san's suicide, it came as no real shock, but he was nEvartheless greatly saddened for this man was, in many ways, an anglophile who was determined to bring a bit of British culture to Japan.

'Success has many fathers, disaster is inevitably a bastard,' he mused to himself.

As the mayoral car drew up outside Nomura-san's house, the Mayor got butterflies. What if the dead man's wife and relations came out screaming abuse at him just as the Nishi Nippon Shimbun journalists arrived? It was madness to go there without sussing out the lie of the land but there was no backing down now. There was no sign of the journalists but he decided to proceed without them. If the meeting went okay, and then someone could tip them off afterwards and if not, well, they would not know so there would be no bad publicity.

He tapped at the door as his aide stood well behind. Nomura-san's mother-in-law answered the door and recognised the Mayor instantly. Her reaction was typical of her generation. She totally supplicated her body with politeness, apologising profusely about the humbleness of the house and family not being worthy of him. He insisted, and was led to the darkened sitting room where Nomura-san's wife sat. She was also taken aback and started to smooth out her dress and look presentable.

The Mayor knew how to react. He became the most humble thing possible, craving forgiveness for not supporting Nomura-san adequately in his hour of need, telling the family as far as he was concerned personally; Nomura-san was not to blame. He told them about the Nishi Nippon Shimbun story which they had seen and the Nomuras told the Mayor what a truly great person he was, so understanding and considerate. Then the Mayor asked the question to which he really wanted an answer.

'What do you think we should do in these circumstances? Please speak to me very frankly. Should we go ahead and host the Mereleigh group, or should we cancel everything?' he asked.

The Nomuras told him it was up to him. They would be happy for him to decide what was best for the city. The Mayor knew that was just politeness on their part, and caution as they did not want to be out of tune with the Mayor's wishes. They played around at this politeness game for nearly ten minutes before Nomura-san's wife said she really liked the sound of the real Mereleigh people and would hate to disappoint then.

'It would be terrible if we Japanese people turned them around and sent them home,' she told him. The Mayor said he agreed totally, and added he could not make a decision himself but would have to put this view to his councillors, and also to the sponsors' meeting that afternoon. Just at that moment there was a tap on the door and the two Nishi Nippon journalists were let in. As if by magic they had arrived on time as far as the Nomuras were concerned. They got their story, and the exact angle the Mayor wanted.

The forces of darkness were building up. A large Kyushu real estate development company that had backed a different candidate at the last mayoral elections had lost a lot of money. They had invested in the rival's election campaign and made a huge purchase of land on the basis their man would win and they would get permission for the development of a very large department store.

Its boss, Suzuki-san, had been a very reluctant starter in the sponsorship arrangements to raise funds for charity through the Mereleigh visit. He was not a charitable person by nature; he disliked the Mayor to the point where he would oppose anything the Mayor supported simply because the election of this Mayor had cost him heaps of money.

One of the first things the Mayor and new council had done was to block a major housing and industrial development in the harbour area on environmental grounds. Suzuki-san felt compelled to sponsor the Mereleigh group as not to do so would be more damaging to his company's reputation than to be part of the project. When he heard about the case of mistaken identity through a secret source in the Mayor's office the previous day, he had no hesitation in calling in a few favours from Kyushu-based journalists who worked for several large Japanese national daily newspapers. Suzuki and his cohorts knew how to bend malleable journalists to do his media dirty work.

It was just a matter of periodically investing in some suitable nightlife entertainment at Nakasu, Fukuoka's night life area, and seeing they were well-fed had plenty to drink and some girls were made available to them. The gifts were always up front and the favours called in later when needed.

Suzuki had called in his own media expert and drafted a set of facts which they would release to the corrupted journalists. The line would be the same for them all and it would give them a chance of getting into the Mereleigh story close on the heels of the smaller Nishi Nippon Shimbun newspaper with an update on a story that would go national and not be restricted to the Nishi Nippon's mostly Kyushu-restricted circulation.

The objective would be to unravel the whole Mereleigh thing and show up the Mayor and his administration as being incompetent and the authors of a serious PR and organisational disaster. Suzuki-san was well pleased with the results. All the national dailies contacted by him were singing the same tune and local radio talkback stations had also got into the act with the majority of talkback hosts putting the boot into City Hall and Nomura-san.

His next move was to be the first company to pull the rug out on sponsorship, so he organised a very public announcement to that effect which was carried on local radio stations at midday. The press release he organised was firmly targeted against the Mayor. He was more than pleased that several other companies followed suit before going to the emergency meeting organised by City Hall. Everything was going his way and by the evening he firmly believed the Mereleigh visit would be history.

News of Nomura-san's death was of no consequence to him. Nomura-san was just an unimportant fool of a salary man with some naïve warm and fuzzy agenda. The only good thing that he had done, in Suzuki-san's mind, was thus accept responsibility for his own incompetence, and commit suicide! It remained only for Suzuki-san to decide if he should attend the emergency meeting. He elected to do so out of spite, and also to stir up as much muck as possible against the Mayor.

CHAPTER 10

Rick had little respite after the record group left for Kyoto, what with Nomura-san's death and the formal identification, and then lots of phone calls and decisions to be made about Jenny. Tonight was the night that he and Yoshi, with Tanaka-san backing up in the shadows, would try out their ruse as journalists. He could not help thinking what a shame it was that Adam had to go to Fukuoka with Michiko, as he was actually a journalist. Tanaka-san had contacted the sergeant's friend Inspector Mori and he had taken note of the venue (the Otani Club) and the rendezvous time and assured then the police would provide discreet backup.

Rick found himself dining alone at the Shiba Park; he missed not having Maggie around, she had become very much part of his life since his wife had died and Maggie had moved to join him in New Zealand. Amazing to think he could have married her a few decades ago and maybe he would have stayed in the UK and led a completely different life. He wondered many a time why he had not done this.

At the time he remembered she was his female idol, the most desirable thing in the world, yet he dated her a few times and let the relationship slip. He knew in his heart it was out of fear of being rejected. To live in hope was better than pushing your luck and being rejected at the tender age of 15. He had rather hoped she would come running to him and he was so clumsy at relationships with girls he really fancied that he never got around to saying and doing the things he wanted to for fear of stuffing it all up.

You read of these long-lost childhood love affairs coming about decades after the event, and it always seemed such crap when written up in saccharine terms in the mass media, but things were really working for Maggie and him in a way he would never have believed possible. His first marriage had been passionate and satisfying and her sudden death from cancer shocking, and it was an incredible piece of good fortune that he had met Maggie again a few months before she died. It was exactly the right time for both of them to meet, with Maggie still getting over a disastrous marriage to a wide boy used car dealer and him coping with his wife's terminal illness and death.

He was just getting stuck into his dessert when a waiter said there was a gentleman waiting for him at the lobby. Yoshi, he must have arrived very early, Rick thought, and told the waiter to tell the man he would be

there within a few minutes. Rick went to the lobby looking for Yoshi and was taken off balance when a Kiwi voice
said, 'G'day mate.' He spun around to see Herewini, the
Maori Customs officer who featured so prominently in
the tour of the group to New Zealand, standing behind
him.

'What the hell…?' Rick was cut short.

'I got the invite to Fukuoka like you guys via Andy. I
told Andy it was doubtful that I could attend and then, to
my amazement, the department sent me up here for some
familiarisation course on Japanese tourists, and said I
could have a few days off at the end of it. So I have just
finished the course. But I thought I had missed you lot as
the itinerary I had from Andy had you going to Kyoto
today?' he said.

'What an infernal circuitous way to learn things! You
know I live in New Zealand and drafted the itinerary, so
why didn't you contact me before you left?' Rick asked.

'Too long to explain, in short I didn't think I could
make it and just replied to Andy who gave me the invite,'
Herewini said.

'It's great to see you and, by God, we have another
bloody problem and that is why I am still here, trying to
release a Welsh girl who was duped into coming to Japan
and is being held against her will.' Rick went on to detail
the situation and the evening's operations.

'Deal me in, this is great stuff! Rescuing a poor damsel
in distress, its just my cup of tea. Is she good looking?'

Rick answered his question by showing him his phone
photo of Jenny.

'She's a stunner, mate, and a touch of the old tar, eh, to add to the flavour!' Herewini exclaimed.

'If you were not a Maori I would bollock you for a racist remark but, knowing your lust for the females recognises no racial boundaries, I realise this is just a crude casual throwaway remark,' Rick lectured him with a smile. They went to the bar and Rick also briefed him on the Nomura problem and the headache that was causing. Herewini said he would move in to the Shiba Park Hotel for the night and for Rick to consider him part of the team on both projects from here on.

Yoshi turned up a couple of hours later with Tanaka-san just five minutes behind. The two Japanese rugby men were delighted to meet Herewini and spent the first 15 minutes asking how the All Blacks were going. They were delighted to learn that Herewini played club rugby for Ponsonby in Auckland as first five-eight. Tanaka-san suddenly looked at his watch and got very serious.

'You know I have been talking to my friend Miss Emi today and she has become very worried that the boss of the Otani might be shifting Jenny to some other place as she tried to make a break for it from some small theatre. The result is her boss thinks she is a liability here so tonight might be our only chance to grab her unless we can find out where she is being sent.

'Inspector Mori has a finger on things but had no idea about Jenny as she is just one of thousands of foreigners in clubs in Tokyo. He does know the Yakuza and which group operates the Otani. He said they are both very bad and very smart. To be honest, I am worried about Emi, as she has got close to Jenny and if the Otani boss finds out she might have a fatal accident of some kind!' Tanaka-san added.

Herewini asked what role he could play. They thought for a while. Herewini's strengths were both his physicality and his ability to quickly gauge a situation and master it. Tanaka-san suggested Herewini could enter the club as a rather drunk New Zealand rugby player and just keep an eye on things. He would ask Inspector Mori if he could provide a detective to go in with him so they could have someone behind the lines as it were.

Tanaka-san rang Inspector Mori, and he agreed. They set the times and places they would start and finish from with Tanaka-san liaising with Inspector Mori and giving him the plan. The Inspector approved of it and warned that this Yakuza group was known to have fire arms though preferred other, more subtle, ways of human disposal.

Rick could see the adrenaline rush coursing through Herewini's body in anticipation of some real action after a few weeks of paper work no doubt. Herewini said he could not leave without alcohol on his breath. Tanaka-san agreed and bought Herewini a couple of doubles.

'I see you have not lost your habit of bludging free grog off others!' Rick quipped.

'All in the course of duty,' Herewini smiled back.

Tanaka-san rang Emi before she arrived at work, timing the call so she received it on her mobile in transit from her apartment to the Otani Bar. She said she had not seen Jenny all day and the Filipina girl who had been with Jenny last night was pretty upset at the events. She said

Jenny had made a bold attempt at a getaway and was rough-handled afterwards. Tanaka-san told Emi they would have someone inside the bar but he deliberately made no mention of the police involvement.

A burly young detective turned up at the hotel to meet Herewini and Tanaka-san and Herewini was happy to learn he also was a rugby player which made up for his limited broken English.

'That's good so if I say, 'ruck' we fight, 'pass the ball' means I want a drink, and 'line out' means time out for a piss,' Herewini told the rather bemused Japanese detective.

The Japanese detective told Herewini he was a 'franker' and Herewini started to wonder what sort of documents the detective had to frank when it dawned on him that he meant 'flanker'.

'OK I will call you Flanker. Is that OK?' Herewini asked

'Hai hai, its privilege to be called this, it means I must be very good franker,' the detective replied.

Rick laughed, 'In the travel industry we have to get used to 'fright numbers' and 'looming wrists' for flight numbers and rooming lists.'

'Oh yes, and we Japanese have to keep polite face when you say you are a name card instead of, this is my name card. Many times foreigner say, watashi *wa* meishi desu, I am a name card, instead of, watashi *no* meishi desu, this is my name card, and then you say other man's wife belongs to you because you don't realise that oku-san only applies to other person's wife and not your wife.

How many times do you say, watashi no okusan desu, instead of, watashi no kanai desu. You forget your own wife is kanai not okusan!' Tanaka-san roared back.

Rick, Yoshi and Tanaka-san set off across town to the accommodation block used by the female staff of the Otani Bar, and left Herewini and Flanker at the bar assuming the identity of drunk rugby mates. Tanaka-san noted as the three of them boarded their taxi that Herewini and Flanker would be so well-disguised as rugby drunks it might take a few days for the disguise to wear off, particularly after their surveillance later on at the Otani Bar.

'I just hope they remember to go to the Otani,' Tanaka-san added.

'You can relax, where a pretty female face is involved, Herewini is never far away. I could see he was very impressed with Jenny's photo!' Rick replied. Tanaka-san decided he would exit from the taxi at a point roughly midway between the accommodation block and the Otani Bar, and meet Rick and Yoshi at a small yakitori place after they had finished their assignment.

It was decided that, if Jenny was allowed to have the interview, Rick would either ask her directly or slip her a note asking her if she was OK or being held against her will. If it was the latter they would call in Tanaka-san, Herewini and Flanker and try to get her out of there as soon as possible after the interview. Tanaka-san said he would contact Inspector Mori on a hot line as well so full police back up could be brought to bear.

Rick said he would have to play things by ear as a

direct question to Jenny about her freedom could obviously give the game away, so he might have to react on instinct. Rick clutched a near new large digital camera and notebook as Yoshi pressed the doorbell. They had observed a large Yakuza type lingering on the lift landing making a call on his mobile phone. Yoshi had bowed to him and smiled, but the smile was not returned, just a curt half-pie nod of politeness.

The door was opened by the same mama-san that had given Yoshi some pretty frigid treatment when he first called. She reluctantly remembered Yoshi, though her eyes, when she first stopped him at the door, were a give-away; they displayed surprise and irritation that he had returned without any appointment being agreed to for an interview with Jenny.

Yoshi ate humble pie in a most convincing apologetic manner explaining the English journalist, Rick, was only briefly in Tokyo and his boss at the publishing agency had insisted that Yoshi bring him over to try and get the interview. He pointed out how well-known Rick was and asked Rick to present his meishi which Rick did with aplomb, accompanied by the right apologies for the inconvenience and, in simple slow English for the mama-san's benefit, how famous Jenny had become in Britain and how missed she was on that entertainment scene.

He could see the mama-san caught most of what he was saying and was turning things over in her mind. Rick then asked Yoshi in slow English if he could ask the mama-san how Jenny was getting on. Yoshi did so, realising that Rick was playing a game to entice the mama-san's interest and enthusiasm before requesting an interview. The mama-san was temporarily flattered by what she believed was a foreign journalist at her doorstep and lied and said Jenny was doing very well and becoming famous in Japan too.

Rick talked a little about her home in Wales, hoping to evoke some sympathy from the mama-san, and explained how her parents missed her. The mama-san responded in obvious false sincerity and concern but was again flattered that she was part of this conversation with the journalist. Rick then slipped the question asking if Jenny was there now and could give an interview. The mama-san replied that Jenny was going to move on to another city for some other engagements and she was not sure she would be available.

Just then the Yakuza, who had kept almost within earshot spoke in deep heavy tones to the mama-san telling her, 'it is time!' but did not say for what. The mama-san was brought back to reality and lost whatever bit of artificially-cultivated charm and interest she had and returned to her cold hard frigid self, indicating she really had no idea where Jenny was and she had to go. Rick felt things spinning away from his grasp and could only request the Mama-san please find Jenny and let her know he wished to interview her.

'Hai, hai, hai,' was all he got from her, spoken in the manner of someone who had not the least intention of helping or passing on any messages.

Even the normally good-natured Yoshi was taken aback and muttered 'bitch' in English to Rick, while giving the Yakuza a look which said, 'just give me the slightest excuse and I will smash your bloody head against the fucking wall.' Rick decided on one last parting shot and said to Yoshi in a stage whisper,

'What a shame I shall have to write a report saying this place was so unco-operative. And then this lady's boss (he nodded toward the mama-san) will be so angry to see his business mentioned in such poor light!' Yoshi added in Japanese for the mama-san and Yakuza's benefit,

'Yes, I understand your predicament. If you can't get the story or any co-operation then you can do nothing else but say this person and company failed to help with Jenny's career and we must all wonder why!'

The mama-san and the Yakuza both looked daggers, and knew that Rick had racked up some pressure on them, and if indeed there was a story in this magazine about Jenny and her boss then the boss would be furious, but what could they do? They were only responding to orders not to let Jenny do the interview and to keep her out of sight.

Excessive media attention on Jenny could be worse than police interest. The police always had so much on their hands it was hard to know where to start where missing foreign entertainers were concerned, particularly because the vast majority were only overstaying work permits and were perfectly safe and there was no way of knowing if Jenny was planning a similar game with the object of going bush. However, a missing entertainer, who had some sort of name, was a red rag to a bull where the media were concerned, particularly if she was young and pretty.

Yoshi and Rick left, hailed a taxi went round the block and met Tanaka-san. They relayed the story to him and he immediately phoned Inspector Mori. Inspector Mori again pressed them to find out if the mama-san had either admitted or denied Jenny was there and both Yoshi and Rick were able to state she had implied she was, because she said she was going to move on which meant she had knowledge of her whereabouts. He asked if any particular reason had been given why Jenny was unavailable for an interview and was told that Rick and Yoshi had been given no reason other than that she was going to move on.

He was not overly impressed with Rick's threat about writing a damaging article because it was impossible for Rick to carry out unless he was able to alert other media and get them to do a write up. It would also give the boss of the Otani Club notice that a hunting pack of media men might soon descend on him so he would have a day or so to stow Jenny away somewhere and play the Mr Innocent act.

Rick said he felt it was a good idea at the time and, if they could get this story out to a UK magazine, perhaps it would help. He told the inspector they had a journalist, Adam, in the group who, while now in Fukuoka, would probably play ball and do a missing person type article. He could hear Inspector Mori groan a little at the thought of a British media pack bothering him. Inspector Mori decided to look for middle ground and requested Rick hold off on any media story for a couple of days to give him and his men a chance to track her down. Rick agreed and the call ended amicably.

Meanwhile Herewini and Flanker had gained entry to the Otani bar looking every inch drunken rugby mates and been spotted by Emi as cohorts of Tanaka-san's. He had not told her Flanker was a policeman and just mentioned two friends would be there. Herewini was not very impressed with the exorbitant cost of liquor and highly diluted spots of whisky that were dished up.

'This is not even enough to get a goldfish pissed!' he exclaimed in horror to Flanker, who agreed. 'It's just as well we had a few drinks at the Shiba Park Hotel, otherwise we would be as sober as a judge now.'

Herewini's swarthy Polynesian looks caught the eye of the hostesses who told him adoringly how strong he must be and was he some sort of film star as they had seen someone like him in Lord of the Rings or some other New Zealand movie. Flanker, guessing no one in this bar knew the slightest thing about rugby, told them Herewini was a famous All Black rugby player in Japan temporarily to assist in coaching Japan's national rugby team. The hostesses all nodded in a somewhat vacant pretence of admiration and flattery.

Herewini looked at the girls somewhat sadly, none of them really had any fire. They were not the sort of girls you would find in an Auckland or Wellington bar or in London or Dublin for that matter. They lacked spirit and appeared to be downtrodden and somewhat defeated people. Tanaka-san had told him about Emi and he picked her as the older woman. She was different, she had perceptive eyes and seemed more kindly and sincere though a rather sad figure. Herewini could see how easy it would be to take the rise out of the girls and also how the girls could, beneath all the obsequious smiles and tittering, invent stupid nicknames for the vain Japanese business-men who inhabited these places.

'Do you like these places?' he asked Flanker.

'Not so much, Herewini-san, too expensive and not real girlfriends. I like German beer house drinking; we have some of these places in Tokyo and other cities. Also I like karaoke and yakitori, but most I like rugby drinking too much!' he laughed.

The evening seemed to go slowly for them with small groups of businessmen coming and going, with all of them being ushered in and out with high ceremony and much bowing by the club staff. It was like some Royal Palace ceremony. Many of the businessmen tried to involve Herewini and Flanker in their conversations as having a foreigner there was a bit of a novelty. When Flanker went to the toilet, one of the businessmen men-tioned a dark foreign girl who had sung there like a 1950s black American singer, but she was British.

'Very good singer like Ella Fitzgerald, I think,' he had told Herewini.

Herewini pressed him for more information and was told she was not a regular at this place and he heard she was going to Nakasu. Before he could press the business-man for more information, the group the latter had come with suddenly upped sticks and left for another nightclub joint with some of their drinks hardly touched.

When Flanker returned Herewini told him about the conversation and said the place sounded like 'Knacker Sue.' Flanker had no idea of any such place, but said it was interesting as it sounded just like Jenny.

'You know what else mate. When those jokers left, they left most of their drinks half drunk and shot through as though they were startled rabbits,' Herewini said.

Flanker could not understand half of his conversation except about the drinks and leaving quickly. He laughed, and said 'In Japan businessman on expenses is always very wasteful, and like greedy pig, they want to see so many places so quickly they always leave drinks behind so it is not so unusual.'

They were thinking of calling it a night when Emi came to clean their table. She whispered to Herewini that she knew Jenny would not be there tonight because of an overheard telephone conversation with the master of the bar and some comment that she was definitely being moved on to another city.

At that advice they decided to call it a night and rendezvous with Tanaka-san, Rick and Yoshi at a late night bar. It had been a totally frustrating evening with no action, no sighting of Jenny and, worst of all, no idea where she was being taken. Tanaka-san asked Herewini to remember the name of the place Jenny was going to as mentioned by the Japanese business man

'Sounded like Knacker Sue,' Herewini said.

Tanaka-san thought for a few moments, 'I don't know Japanese city of that name but at Fukuoka we have night life area called Nakasu so might be there. So I think Rick-san we should shift our search to Fukuoka. It's my home town and I have some Nakasu contacts so this might become easier.'

There was a brief discussion over the desirability of Flanker and Yoshi coming as well and they asked Flanker if he could get permission. A call to Inspector Mori updated him on the night's events and he gave approval for Flanker to go with them and act more than anything else as a liaison person between them and the Japanese police force.

Tanaka-san said he could cover Yoshi's costs to come as well. Inspector Mori was not so sure about having civilian extras involved in what should be an entirely police operation, but he liked and trusted the rugby people and gave specific instructions that they should leave the rough stuff and anything dangerous to the police and simply act as discreet eyes and ears to pick up whatever they could for him.

Tanaka-san pulled a poker-faced, hand-on-his-heart type assurance that they would restrict their role to a passive intelligence-gathering one, but Inspector Mori knew, if it came to a rough and tumble, Tanaka-san and his rugby mates would be in it like a rat shinnying up a drain pipe, with glee written all over their faces.

'Officially, Tanaka-san, you have given me the assurance I must have. Unofficially, I don't believe a word of it and be very careful. Some Yakuza are armed.

'I am now personally convinced Jenny is at risk but we still do not have enough facts to justify some sort of large-scale national search. Many a policeman has been down that track before to find the missing entertainer who was safely bunked up somewhere with a Japanese boyfriend, or just trying to elude the immigration laws,' Inspector Mori said.

⌘⌘⌘

Meanwhile Adam and Michiko's first day at Fukuoka had gone well so far. They filled in part of the afternoon strolling around Ohori Park, visiting the Art Museum, and awaiting Nishimura-san's return. There would be a meeting of the Fukuoka Record Club group in the early evening and, unknown to them at the time, a meeting set up by the Mayor of all the sponsors to determine whether the events should go ahead or not.

Nishimura-san and her boyfriend turned up on time and in the usual hasty Japanese manner she said they had just time to go to the Sea Hawk Hotel for a wash and brush up before the Fukuoka Record Club meeting. Adam groaned quietly to Michiko that everything seemed to have to be done in a rush in Japan. She nodded with a smile and added, 'You will get used to it.' Nishimura-san's tiny car seemed out of place in the huge courtyard in front of the Sea Hawk Hotel as smartly liveried bell-boys sprang to open her doors and remove the luggage. Adam was mightily impressed.

'This is a real hotel and what a setting right next to Hakata Bay and Fukuoka Big Dome sports centre. Modern Japan at its best!' he exclaimed. On their way to the lobby they passed a rain forest feature in the atrium.

'My God, it's got its own Amazon forest as well!' Adam exclaimed.

'It also has a thunderstorm everyday and tropical rain too,' Michiko added. They got a great room on the seventeenth floor with a magnificent view of Hakata Bay.

'This is the place where Kublai Khan and his Mongol

soldiers tried to invade Japan. He was driven back the first time and when he came back later with a big fleet we were fortunate to have a typhoon when he arrived, and many of his ships were wrecked. We called it kamikaze, or divine wind.' She pointed to the parts of the bay where his ships sank.

'I read that the first rice cultivated by man in Japan more than 2,000 years ago was also grown on the shores of Hakata Bay,' Adam added impressed by the history of the place. 'It's all very beautiful but the real treasure of Fukuoka is here!' he said.

'Where, what item do you mean?' she asked, looking around the room in innocence.

'You, you are it!' Adam grabbed her and planted a kiss on her lips. She blushed and hugged him back and then pushed him aside.

'I love your spontaneity but it's not really polite to do this in public in Japan. We are still old-fashioned in many ways, but our hearts yearn to be able to express ourselves a bit more like this,' she added. 'So we wait till later. Nishimura-san and her boyfriend are waiting for us in the lobby and we must get to the meeting on time,' she laughed.

He grabbed his small briefcase and a notebook and a camera while she dashed out to call up a lift. Nishimura-san was relieved to see them. She guessed they were very much in love and was a bit worried they might be side-tracked by each other and forget the meeting time. She apologised for the rush and added there was only limited time for free parking so her boyfriend was driving the car around and was parked outside. So another rush to the car and then some heavy commuter traffic to the meeting place which was a smallish community hall.

Adam was impressed by the number of people; it looked like several hundred at least and a typical selection of Japanese urban dwellers from many different walks of life. They all smiled and bowed deeply at Adam as if he was a visiting king from a foreign country. Adam was impressed as he had feared a rather hostile reception.

Nishimura-san led Adam and Michiko up on to the stage where they were seated next to several office holders of the club.

'The members of the Fukuoka club spanned several generations, with some of a similar generation to the Mereleigh Group, and the youngest being late-teenagers, Adam pointed out.

The small community hall was soon packed out and he could see a number of news teams including a couple of TV stations represented. Michiko followed his gaze and said the Nishi Nippon Shimbun had sent Sam and Kenny and she pointed them out and they waved back. She got a ring on her mobile phone from Sam at the back of the room just to say hi. He told her the newspaper's city hall reporter would go to the Mayor's meeting with the sponsors later and they should all meet up immediately afterwards and check notes. She agreed and told Adam.

While they were waiting proceedings to get underway Adam told Michiko he had seen a lot of small coloured paper birds at Nomura san's house and wondered what they were.

'Oh yes, there were hundreds of them bunched together and many, many bunches. It's a tradition in Japan when someone gets sick to make these paper cranes as it's supposed to bring good health, you must make at least one thousand. It's so sad his children had been making them when he went missing and the family received many of the bunches from their friends and other family members, but at the end it did not help him,' she said.

They were introduced to Ban-san, a pleasant smiling man of small stature with a resultant smile-creased face. He was the club's vice president and had been away on business until a few hours ago. He explained his wife had kept him posted of events but it was only after he got back to Fukuoka from Australia a few hours ago that the sad impact of it all struck home.

He bowed deeply to Adam, shook his hand fiercely and told him repeatedly in English it was so good of him to come. That finished, he brought the meeting to order and in Japanese expressed everyone's deep sympathy to Mrs Nomura over her husband's death and then he introduced Adam.

The group rose and gave him a solid round of applause. Adam was taken aback and spluttered that it was a privilege for him to be there and he and all other members of the Mereleigh Group were totally shocked by the death of Nomura-san and also passed on their condolences. As he said it he realised he had no flowers or anything to give her and expressed his embarrassment to Nishimura-san afterwards. She said she would fix it and got her boyfriend to go out and get some for him to give to Nomura-san's wife before the end of the meeting.

Ban-san then gave the group a full appraisal of the events that led to Nomura-san's death and drew no punches in his criticism of the national daily papers in their presentation of a very ill-balanced account of the events which wrongly laid the blame at Nomura-san's door. He saw their journalists wince at this and then he went on to praise the Nishi Nippon Shimbun in its accounts and stance over the matter, and he told the meeting that the two main subject they must discuss were ways and means of assisting the Nomura family in their time of need and deciding if they could or should do something for the Mereleigh Record Club group. Michiko quietly translated most of it for Adam's benefit.

You could hear a pin drop when Ban-san had finished, then a large middle-aged man stood up and said he would like to start a fund for Mrs Nomura-san and offered a large sum of money as a starter. There was a warm round of applause and many more wishing to put up some cash to help her. Ban-san said they would set up the fund and a special bank account and all wishing to make donations could meet later.

A young man in his early twenties said to cancel everything would be such a huge disappointment that he did not know if the Fukuoka Record Club could survive it. He said it did not matter to him that the film stars were not coming as he would really like to meet the real people and learn about their lives in Britain and perhaps one day go to Britain on a working holiday.

He also got a good round of applause, and then a housewife about Mrs Nomura's age stood up and said out of respect the group must consider her feeling in this matter as she had been through a terrible ordeal and her husband had done so much. Ban-san looked sympathetically at Mrs Nomura to try and catch her drift before suggesting she make any comment. He could see she was eager to reply so he invited her to the stage.

'Nobody can know the bad times we had last week. First we were all so excited as this visit was to be the high point of all our lives, and everyone here worked so hard for nearly a year and did so much that this thing was like a dream come true. Then suddenly there was disaster and so much worry about my husband and then it seemed he was recovering and we might find a solution and then total blackness   he is dead. I cannot believe it even now. It has all been so sudden.' She dabbed at her eyes and was assisted by Nishimura-san.

'When we read the newspaper reports we could not believe our eyes at the bad and very wrong things that were written about him. Could this be the same man who has been my loving husband for so many years?' She took an angry glance at the huddle of national daily journalists who were cringing under her withering stare. When all other members of the gathering also focused on them they wished they could vanish under the floorboards.

'Our own local paper has been so good but they destroyed the good it did. Maybe they don't want this city to raise funds for people with drug problems, if so they should say it in their columns and not try to kill this project as well. It is my and my family's firm wish that we do continue and entertain the Mereleigh group as best we can and if we only raise a few thousand yen for this cause that is good enough,' She sat down to a resounding round of applause.

'This is great stuff Michiko, fantastic, incredible, pure people power! Look at those national daily guys, they are crapping their pants now wondering how they can write this up. It's totally against the shit they wrote about Nomura-san yet they can't ignore it because the TV guys are here and they can't edit out the drama of Mrs Nomura's speech. I love it, I love it and I am going to file tonight with every word!' Adam was in raptures but Michiko reminded him there was the bigger City Hall meeting to come and that could take a completely different turn.

Ban-san decided to set up an emergency group to look at ways of running the event on a far smaller scale and asked Adam to convey their invitation to the Mereleigh group to come to Fukuoka.

'We can do homestays for them and they can see real Japanese life and go shopping with our wives and drink sake and beer with us men!' he said.

Mrs Nomura was surrounded by the TV journalists all wanting interviews and also scores of well wishers from the group. Nishimura-san and her boyfriend were vainly trying to organise things a bit in the hubbub. Sam and Kenny made their way across the crowded room to Michiko and Adam and said it was time to head off to the City Hall meeting.

'If we are quick we might get there before the end of the meeting,' Sam explained as he coaxed the taxi driver to put the pedal to the metal.

The City Hall had set aside a large meeting room for the bigwigs, and others who were going to sponsor the event. They tiptoed into the back next to a cluster of other journalists including the Nishi Nippon Shimbun's City Hall reporter. He told them things were not going at all well, as one or two large sponsors including the real estate development company were intent on pulling the rug from under the council's feet. The Mayor was heavily out-gunned and depressed and the real estate development company boss seemed to be holding forth most of the time.

The gist of it all, Michiko said, was the sponsors felt they had been intentionally or otherwise duped into this event and City Hall had failed to do a professional job in the vetting of the plans. In short, the disaster that had occurred was totally predictable and the best thing to do was to call a halt to it all, call it a day, save face and also money.

Michiko said it was apparent that the majority of the sponsors had not really followed events very closely themselves and had taken their viewpoint from the national daily newspapers, and were using the excuse that they had shareholders' money to think of as an excuse to pull out. The senior Nishi Nippon Shimbun City Hall reporter leaned over and whispered in broken English:

'It seems like dirty trick because most companies who support the Mayor are not present. I telephone one man I know from Mayor supporting company and he say some-body telephone many companies to say meeting has been cancelled so they did not come tonight!'

'So the Mayor is almost alone tonight, what can he do?' he added.

The inevitable happened: the majority of the companies present voted against holding the event. The Mayor got up, saying he had been seriously let down and it would reflect very badly on the city and in time everyone could live to regret it

'The fact of life is the city cannot do all these things without your sponsorship so, if you cancel, the city must also cancel as we do not have a prepared and approved budget to cover these things. I will say that I personally will do whatever I can for the Fukuoka Record Club group, Nomura-san's family and the Mereleigh group if they still wish to come to Fukuoka. We must remember the word "fuku" means happy. Finally I want to put my sympathies and condolences to the Nomura family on record,' he finished.

The Mayor walked out a side door drearily accompanied by several City Hall officials who knew they had many hard days ahead of them sorting out cancelled bookings and fielding political brickbats. Out in the streets and homes of Fukuoka, the account of the Mayor's visit to Mrs Nomura was splashed across the evening edition of the Nishi Nippon Shimbun and there was growing sympathy for her and her late husband and a warm appreciation of the Mayor's humility and good intentions.

Michiko, Adam, Sam, Kenny and the senior Fukuoka City Hall journalist made for a small restaurant to grab a quick meal and discussion before filing their stories. Sam and Kenny's report will cover the Fukuoka Record Club meeting, and the City Hall reporter the last meeting. They asked Michiko to get a reaction to both meetings from the Mereleigh Record Club group, who were encamped at a Kyoto ryokan totally unaware of the developments.

'It's a good news-bad news story and what do you want first?' Adam stated sarcastically.

'Don't you think we should get the Mayor's reaction?' Michiko asked. ' I know what he said at the meeting but I would like to contact him in about an hour and see how he feels after we have spoken to the Mereleigh group, and after he learns about the Fukuoka group's decision.' It was agreed. Adam added that he had to cover all the angles by himself for his own newspaper and the Guardian. 'At times like this we could do with a Japanese labour force!'

The Mereleigh group was relaxing over sake and nibbles when Adam rang through with the latest developments. He spoke to Andy and gave him the bad news about the sponsors first and then the good news about the Fukuoka Record Club.

'We have spent a lot of time on and off today discussing this and I can say for certainty that all members wish to continue to Fukuoka to meet our sister club and we will pay our own costs,' Andy said. 'If we can't make an official call on the Mayor, then we would like to make an unofficial one and also go to the Nishi Nippon Shimbun to thank the editor for his support,' he added. Adam passed the phone to Michiko who asked similar questions and noted it all down for her own report. She was about to hang up when Andy halted her:

'Just a moment, Chuck has something very important

to add. Over to you Chuck,' he said as he passed the phone to his old American friend.

'Hi there sweetheart, long time no see gal. Listen I been thinking a lot about this and you know I have a few bucks put away which are useless to an old cowpoke like me, so I want to tell your Mayor that I want to put up some cash towards this thing and replace those goddamn sponsors who chickened out on the deal!'

'So you tell your Mayor I want to know how much he needs, but also tell him I want to know the options, like does he want me to pay for a big hotel conference reception room and some cocktails. I'm going to look after the little guys from the Fukiyoka Record club, and I will be talking to them too!' he concluded.

Michiko was totally taken aback. She kept apologising at the end of every breath he took, and then kept saying, 'so generous so generous.' She told Adam in amazement and he just laughed and said,

'That is Chuck all over. Andy saved his life when they were both passengers on a cross-Atlantic liner. Chuck fell overboard. Andy organised a line of lifebelts and deckchairs to be thrown over so the ship could follow that trail back to Chuck. The two have been inseparable since and Chuck's loaded! He has about half a dozen big farms and ranches in Oklahoma.'

'That is incredible, this is a big story! So many angles!' She was agog at the developments in the last 12 hours. Adam decided to give Rick a ring and discovered he was not at the Shiba Park Hotel so left a voice message for him with the main developments.

The called a cab and headed back to Fukuoka City Hall to try and catch the Mayor. They were lucky he had another late meeting. At first he did not want to see them; he was tired, very irritable and just plain mad that the real estate development company torpedoed his effort to stage the event. His spirits rose as soon as Michiko was able to relay Chuck's offer to help. His political instinct told him he would win the last battle in this siege even though he had fewer troops and less financial resources. He eagerly gave Michiko and Adam the words they wanted, saying he welcomed Chuck's offer and, together with Chuck, the Fukuoka Record Club and the Mereleigh Record Club, they would do something.

When Michiko and Adam got to the Nishi Nippon Shimbun office they were immediately summoned to the editor's office. They found him striding up and down his office with impatience.

'Good, good, you're here. Please sit down now, tell me everything because by God we are going to stick it to the opposition with our front page story tomorrow.

'I also want a story on Adam-san and a photograph just to say who he is and what he is doing. When the bastards who are trying to shaft us realise we have a British journalist writing for the Guardian here, that will sober them up. They might realise they are insulting the Mereleigh Record Group in all this and it could annoy the British public to say the least,' he added.

'I won't ask you to write up Adam-san, you're a bit close perhaps.' Michiko dropped her head slightly in surprise and embarrassment at that and he continued, 'Sorry,

I did not mean any offence, but you have worked together for several days and I want a fresh view of Adam-san from one of our writers here, if Adam-san can spare about 20 minutes?' he said.

'No trouble, but I have to file for my papers in a few hours' time so must get back to the Sea Hawk as soon as possible after that,' he explained.

'Don't worry; I will get Michiko to take you by taxi to the hotel on her way back to hers.' He guessed she would be staying with him but did not want to embarrass her by suggesting it.

'It's OK, she is staying with….' He suddenly caught on it might be embarrassing to Michiko if her boss knew she was staying with him so quickly added, 'with a friend close by, I believe?'

He realised it was silly even just saying that, but he had dug her out of a big hole and created sufficient doubt to save her reputation. By this time Michiko was now totally embarrassed and decided to leave it at that.

'It's fine, I don't mind dropping him off,' she told her boss.

'Sorry, I hope I did not embarrass or offend you,' Adam said as they walked out of the editor's office.

'I think he already guessed we were lovers so what the hell? I just don't want to give anyone the impression that I sleep around with every foreign journalist who turns up. In Japan it's rude to be too inquisitive about other people's personal lives, we cannot be as direct about these things as you in the West can, even though we might do the same things,' she said.

'I am learning a lot about Japan from you. What other state secrets should I know?'

'Got a thousand years?' she replied with a smile.

'For you, I have a million years.' he replied.

Back at the Sea Hawk, writing and filing the stories was a piece of cake for Adam with Michiko at his elbow to prompt his memory and help with the Roman spelling of Japanese names. He had known a few girls in his time but none of them had such a physical and mental impact on him. The way she walked and her skirt swirled about her legs and over her buttocks. Her long, black, shoulder-length hair that shone, her smile that went to his heart, and her brown-tipped breasts. Phew, it was almost impossible to concentrate on the story with her so close and available but he managed, just!

She discreetly slipped away into the bathroom to take a shower and a bath and by the time he had filed his stories by email she had nothing on but a light hotel yukata. She snuggled up to him, gave him a big kiss and moved her body around his and then gently told him to take a shower first. It was probably a world record shower and Adam was barely dry when he came out grinning with a white towel around his waist. They kissed, hugged and fell on the bed and were wrestling in great passion when she whispered, 'what would you say if I told you I was pregnant?'

It was a bombshell. How could she know after just a few days, she must have been pregnant when they met? He was stunned for a moment and then she roared with laughter and said, 'You should see your face.' Then her voice took a serious tone, 'What would you think if I got pregnant?'

'I would think it a shame if it happened so soon in our relationship. For selfish reasons I want to enjoy you as you are for a few years, but if you asked that question a few years from now I would probably be delighted,' he said. 'Why do you ask, do you want to get pregnant now?' he asked.

'No, like you I want a few years with you as we are, but you know Japanese women are told to please men and if it's someone you love you feel you should do anything for them so I want to be clear about this at the beginning,' she said seriously. 'This is the most serious relationship I have had in my life, Adam!'

He touched her gently. 'And me too, I guess it's meant to be, will you come to Britain with me after all this?'

'If that is what you want, of course, but it might take me a month or so to finish up here and I want to introduce you to my parents.'

'There is also something you should know and you might wish to break the relationship when you know it. I am from Japan's untouchable class,' she revealed.

'What does that mean? I thought all Japanese people were the same. I can't see any racial differences,' he asked in innocence.

'There is no racial difference between Japanese but some families would not consider me a good bride and not allow their sons to marry me and some employers would not employ me if they knew this. In the old days we were supposed to live only in certain districts and do traditional jobs like being butchers and flower sellers,' she said.

'There is no stigma in being a butcher or flower seller where I come from, or the rest of the world, as far as I know. You look just like an ordinary Japanese to me, so how can anyone tell the difference?'

She told him there was no physical difference, nor any difference in names, but if you went for a job they might ask where you live and if the address is a wrong one they know, they might ask your parents' occupation, and know from that as well, and if you want to get married some people will research your ancestry to be sure you are not an untouchable.

Adam was visibly shocked and gave her a huge hug to reassure her of his love for her.

'Well, you did not have to wait a thousand years to tell me that and I am very glad as it makes no difference at all to me,' he said.

'But are you Jewish or a gypsy?' She looked deadly serious when she asked him.

It threw him for a split second.

'You're joking; I can see you can't keep a straight face.'

It made him realise there were so many things about Japan and Japanese culture he knew absolutely nothing about, and it was pretty humbling.

'In Japan I am an intellectually a kindergarten boy,' he professed.

'So I must rely on you to teach me everything. I don't think I could wish for a better teacher!"

She felt a warm glow inside her at his humility and flattery. 'You already understand one of the main facets of Japanese culture which is to be humble and self-effacing, and with that attitude you will learn fast.'

They made love, slept an hour or so and both woke wide awake not knowing why. They talked non-stop for a couple of hours, raided the minibar for wine, drank, made love again and slept soundly until dawn.

It took Adam several minutes to realise the hotel phone had been ringing for a few minutes. It was his office in Britain on the line. They were ecstatic at his coverage and gleeful that he had also got on to the Guardian's front pages with his story about the Mereleigh stuff-up. Michiko came back from the room doorway with the morning edition of the Nishi Nippon Shimbun and extensive coverage of same story with a break-out piece on Adam, and his photograph.

She asked room service to bring up a few national dailies. They all carried the Mayor's meeting prominently and the overtures from the real estate development company and its cohorts calling a halt to the program and blaming the Mayor and City Hall for the stuff up. They had no mention at all of the Mereleigh Group, nor even a whisper about Chuck's offer of financial assistance which the Nishi Nippon Shimbun had given prominence to.

'This is both good and bad. It's good because the Nishi Nippon Shimbun is getting all the breaks and is a day ahead of them all the time, but it's bad because everyone who reads the national dailies is going to be swayed by their negative angles,' Adam said .

'Quick, let's get the TV news.'

Michiko switched to a morning news channel and found the story about the fifth item down on the TV news, complete with some footage of the Mayor's meeting. The good thing was TV had given equal prominence to the Fukuoka Record Club's own meeting so its coverage was fair and balanced in some regard.

'What are the odds for public opinion forcing a change to bring back the sponsorship?' Adam asked.

'Hmm, aah soo. We cannot say for certainty, we are too close and biased, might be. I think the public will still be against it if the big companies will not support it, as it would mean lots of taxpayers' money. Even it being for charity is not enough as the public might as well give their money straight to the charity rather than pay through taxes which might cost them more because of administration costs. We have to consider this,' she said.

'So we better resign ourselves to a smaller privately organised affair with Chuck's money and the Fukuoka Record Club's generosity. That's OK, its fine. I am sure together we can raise some money for this charity and, as we know, if the big sponsors came in they would take all the credit and the Nomura-sans of this world remain anonymous,' he said

'Like black boys in a kabuki play,' she added. 'They do a lot of backstage work, always wear black and never get any credit.'

'I think there is going to be a very big fight between the real estate development company and its allies and the Mayor and Nishi Nippon Shimbun. I think might be we shall win but there will be much dirty work behind the scenes and people trying to create or drag up scandals. Adam-san, we must look after ourselves. We are in the front line getting all the news that the other side does not want us to publish. I am frightened, very frightened as reputation to Japanese is sometimes more important than money and we are making fools of the big bad boys!'

CHAPTER 11

At Tokyo Rick woke feeling mentally exhausted, wondering if they should have been bolder and made a private bust of the Otani Club or Jenny's apartment block to snatch her from the crooks. He felt the chances of freeing her were more remote than ever. The Mereleigh tour had proved a real headache what with the group identity mix up and this as well.

He took a shower, chucked his gear in his suitcase, and gave Herewini a call to join him for breakfast. They ate a full breakfast almost in silence, each with his own thoughts about the problem facing them, before making for Haneda Domestic Airport via the monorail. They were to meet Tanaka-san and Yoshi at the JL check-in counter for a flight to Fukuoka.

They caught the tail end of the morning rush at Hamatsu Cho Station and the monorail was crammed with people and suitcases. It was as uncomfortable as hell but at least the Japanese were always polite and did their best in a crush. Rick caught sight of Yoshi's beaming face near the check-in and Tanaka-san was standing close by. Yoshi and Tanaka-san grabbed their suitcases and insisted on helping them check in. The two Japanese friends only had carry-on over night cabin bags.

The flight to Fukuoka took about one and a half hours over the alpine spine of Honshu, Japan's largest island and it provided occasional spectacular views of this huge mountain range. During the flight Rick brought them up to date with the late night phone calls and his Japanese friends explained the latest national coverage of the Mereleigh affair in their Japanese language newspapers. They had been unable to buy a copy of the Nishi Nippon Shimbun so could only guess at its coverage. The treatment given to the Mereleigh affairs by the national dailies was very angled and biased in favour of the sponsors' statements.

Tanaka-san told Rick the newspapers loved this story because it was all turning into a matter of face and reputation, issues Japanese people valued highly, and while it was his belief that the public would ultimately recognise the moral right of the Nomura group and their efforts, there might be some nastiness from the real estate company and its cohorts before the end of the day.

'You must know, in Japan real estate companies sometimes have very close links to Yakuza and use Yakuza to get control of buildings and land and also to sort out problem people,' he said. 'It's a kind of what you say is a David and Goliath battle,' he added.

'We have to set priorities in Fukuoka Tanaka-san. Even though the Mereleigh group are my friends and customers, I am terribly concerned about Jenny, and I wish to make her my number one priority. Then, after that, we can do our best for the Mereleigh group, and then last, but not least, I want to catch up with Maggie, who I am supposed to be on holiday with!' Rick added.

'This is my idea. I have already asked rugby friends to meet us at Fukuoka Airport and for us to visit Fukuoka City Hall to discuss rugby support for the Mereleigh event. If City Hall does nothing for them we of course do it direct with Nomura-san's group and we also make call on this vice president Ban-san of the Fukuoka Record Club group to coordinate our support.

'After that we call on the editor of Nishi Nippon Shimbun to tell him we are supporting the event and hope he can mention this in his newspaper. There is also a very active Small and Medium Business Association at Fukuoka which is run by my good friend Hayakawa-san and I think he might come in on our side too,' he concluded.

'Ah, I forgot about Jenny, my rugby friends know some Yakuza involved at Nakasu nightclubs so these friends will discreetly try to find out if they know anything about Jenny. After we complete daytime schedule we start at Nakasu to speak to some people,' he said.

'Sounds like we need the constitution of a bull to get through today's agenda!' Rick exclaimed.

'That is why you see Japanese people always sleeping on trains, planes and buses, we have no time for sleep at our homes,' he laughed.

The plane circled Hakata Bay swooping low over Shinkanoshima Peninsula before landing. Two of Tanaka-san's rugby friends were there to meet him and also Adam and Michiko to see Rick. They took several cabs to a small coffee house; there the day's plans were discussed in detail in Japanese. After ten minutes of Japanese dialogue Adam said to Rick, 'Well, we might as well talk about the weather as I have no idea what they are discussing.'

'You just have to learn to be patient and wait until they mention your name, they generally get around to telling you what it's all about if they get stuck on something or reach a conclusion,' Rick joked. When they finished Michiko told Rick and Adam she would file a story on the rugby group's support for the event in time for the evening edition of the Nishi Nippon Shimbun and get a reaction piece from Ban-san as well.

'That should keep the pot boiling,' Adam commented.

She told Adam there was no need for them to keep the same schedule as Tanaka-san and Rick but just contact them about 6 pm to see what had happened. She also explained to Rick the appointment times to see some City Hall officials, Ban-san, and Hayakawa-san at the Small and Medium Business Association.

Tanaka-san was well received at Fukuoka City Hall by an official in charge of local sport and recreation. The official took him to another bureaucrat who had been handling the Mereleigh arrangements. After a twenty minute meeting Tanaka-san realised the City Hall could do nothing to help even by a discreet back door method so he rose, bowed deeply to the official and thanked him profusely, and then exited to meet Ban-san.

In the corridor he bumped into the Mayor, who knew about Tanaka as a famous local rugby player. The Mayor asked what he was doing at City Hall and gave Tanaka-san five minutes of his time to hear about his plan to support Nomura-san's group then complimented him, and said he would also give personal support and be at any events they organised.

'It was very good meeting Rick-san,' Tanaka-san said.

The meeting with Ban-san went well and was also attended by Nishimura-san and her boyfriend. Tanaka-san liked Ban-san from the outset and Ban-san insisted that they go and see Nomura-san's wife as she would be delighted at their support. It was an impulsive thing so they decided to go to her house immediately with Ban-san ringing her in advance. She was totally overcome by Tanaka-san's generosity and support and mentioned how she had heard an American called Chuck was also offering to help out by covering the cost of a venue and foodstuffs. Rick asked Ban-san who would co-ordinate it all and he looked a bit lost.

'My friend Hayakawa-san at the Small and Medium Business Association will, but he does not know it yet. He has a big face in the local business world and as boxers say can punch above his weight so he will relish the job,' Tanaka-san said.

Ban- san looked very relieved and thankful and suggested Nishimura-san and her boyfriend might want to help out as well. Nishimura-san nodded furiously in agreement. Before they left Nomura-san's house his widow told them they would have the funeral in two days time and hoped they could attend.

'God, how shocking, we totally forgot about this,' Rick thought to himself. He told Mrs Nomura that he was sure Andy and another one or two representatives of the Mereleigh group would break their schedule to attend. Then they took Hayakawa-san to lunch. He was a natural enthusiast for life with a permanent grin on his face and boundless energy. They could see he revelled in the challenge and told them he would organise a meeting of his board that evening and by 9 pm they should know about his organisation's support.

He grinned at Ban-san and said it would be OK. Ban-san looked hugely relieved.

Suddenly Tanaka-san noted they were several hours ahead of schedule so suggested Rick check in at the Sea Hawk with Yoshi and himself, as his hefty suitcase was proving a nuisance as they went from one meeting to another.

Adam and Michiko had meanwhile completed stories on the rugby support and filed. Michiko decided they should visit Daizaifu Shrine, Fukuoka's premier shrine set on a picturesque hillside amidst ancient camphor trees. They went to Tenjin to pick up a subway train to Hakata JR Station and while waiting on the crowded platform were jostled and parted, with Michiko getting violently pushed towards the platform edge just as a train approached.

She screamed. Adam tried to get to her but his way was blocked by two burly Japanese men and she looked certain to fall onto the track but fortunately another passenger waiting for the train was also shoved off balance and as he toppled he clutched at Michiko and hauled her to safety as he fell. Adam noticed a couple of burly men who seem to have instigated the move dashing out the exit as he went to Michiko's assistance.

'Did you see that? Stop them! Did you see that? It was deliberate!' she shouted at Adam. But he was too intent on picking up Michiko and too relieved to think of giving chase, though other passengers who had been shoved in the process agreed that there seemed to have been a deliberate push.

Adam decided to get Michiko up and onto the train. She was shaking with fear. Adam tried to calm her, but she kept saying it was not the fall that had shaken her but her firm belief the Yakuza were out to kill her. She broke into tears and clutched him and by the time they reached Hakata station where they had to change trains she was a bit more relaxed.

At first Adam felt her belief of being a Yakuza target was just the aftermath of shock, he could not believe they would have any reason to do this and after all, all the Fukuoka railway stations had closed circuit TV and the incident would be monitored. Who would risk anything like that on camera? He told her they should report it to the police at the first police box they found if she was still convinced it was a murder attempt. She told him she really wanted to do that.

During the day local talk back radio stations had picked up the Mereleigh visit topic and the lines had been running hot with calls for and against. Some callers had got personal and were damaging about Nomura-san and Michiko who had had several by-line articles supporting the visit. They found a police box near Hakata station and made their complaint. The young police officer meticulously took every detail down but they could see he was not very convinced. However he said they would run a check and take a look at the Tenjin station's CCTV video

Michiko was somewhat reassured and she managed to relax as they walked around the tranquil grounds of Daizaifu Shrine. She told Adam the legend of Tobiume, the flying plum which came to rest at this spot and indicated it was a desirable place to start a town. Adam loved the big wooden building, the gravel courtyard and the cobbled streets leading up to the place. The camphor trees he was told were more than 1,000 years old.

'This is the best of old Japan, so peaceful and beautiful.'

She told him how they could buy a fortune telling note so they did. Michiko smiled broadly after opening hers. Adam had no idea what his said as it was all in Japanese.

'It is unbelievable. It says I could meet the most important man in my life, if I am a woman, any time now! Can you believe that?' she said with a huge smile.

'If you bought another fortune note right now it might tell you to end a relationship with the man in your life now!' Adam joked.

'Don't make fun, these things can be serious. There is

no way I am going to buy another one now!' she told him. 'What does yours say?'

'It says, be careful of new friendships, they might destroy you!'

'What? Give it to me, that's terrible!' she grabbed the fortune paper from Adam and then put on pretence of anger.

'It says nothing of the sort   you can't read Japanese! Do you want me to tell you what it really says? It could be totally terrible,' she teased.

'OK, it's probably a load of rubbish,' he replied in a pretend bored fashion.

'It says tread carefully in your life now and big rewards will come your way!' she smiled broadly.

'I wonder what that could mean. Maybe I will get an ice-cream today if I am a good boy.'

'Don't be so flippant, you might not get even an ice-cream!' she threatened, but then continued with a more serious note in her voice, 'You like Japan I think?'

'Yes of course.'

'I am so glad. I don't think I could live with a man who disliked Japan, but we have our dark side too which you are discovering, so it's not paradise,' she said.

They strolled easily around the grounds both reflecting on the topsy turvy life they had lived since they had met and wondering what twists and turns were ahead of them in the next few days.

'What do you want to do tonight?'

'Go to a love hotel and hire all the leather gear and

have a video made of us,' she said looking serious.

'What, are you mad?' He was aghast.

'Only joking, you are a stuffed shirt like your Dad, but that is what a lot of Japanese couples do. They hire these rooms by the hour or two because they have got nowhere else to go. Actually Nishimura-san and her boyfriend want us to take some dinner with them sometime so maybe we can join them tonight.'

'How weird no-one is supposed to kiss or hug in public but it's OK to hire a fantasy sex room for a wild romp with all the gear and toys! What does that say about Japanese mentality I wonder?' He scratched his head, pretending to be confused.

'It says we have a lot of suppressed emotions and frustrations in this country of rules before feelings.'

'I can see the two qualities of life most absent are personal time and space. The long working hours and population pressure are the cause I suppose,' Adam said. 'OK, let's try a Love Hotel for an hour or so, it could be a bit of a laugh.' He gave her a wink.

They were on their way back to the Sea Hawk when an evening paper caught Michiko's eyes. It was not the Nishi Nippon Shimbun but a rival paper. She opened it in haste and Adam could see her picture and his on top of a story. She quickly read the article and exploded

'This is terrible, its dirty tricks, and they are trying to destroy me. What can I do about it?' she was almost tearful again.

'What's up?'

'The article is about me, how I have the lead story on

363

the Mereleigh affairs and am regarded as an up and coming columnist, but they have introduced a dark subject to destroy me! They have told the world I am an untouchable by giving my grandfather's address, everyone will know it's an untouchable area, and his occupation as a florist, which is another hint at my background. Everyone now knows that background and, to a lot of prejudiced Japanese, it will destroy my credibility as they will believe I have been writing all this to get back at society.'

'But surely normal intelligent Japanese will not bother about that at all?'

'Of course, but many Japanese still have a lot of prejudices. It's like they tried to torpedo me and destroy my credibility in an oblique fashion,' she explained. She also pointed to another human interest story on Nomura-san and was aghast.

'This story paints Nomura-san as some sort of eccentric with a possible family background of mental illness because his grandfather's father had experienced a mental breakdown. This is an organised campaign to try and destroy everything by discrediting the people. They will not print the facts, they are cowards!' she stormed. It took Adam a while to calm her down and also to calm himself as well.

When they got back to the Sea Hawk there were several messages for them from the Nishi Nippon Shimbun, from Rick and Nishimura-san. The one from the Nishi Nippon Shimbun editor said not to worry about the rival newspaper's article. He had total confidence in her and also in Nomura-san's reputation. Nishimura-san suggested a restaurant for the dinner that night and Rick just wanted to update Adam on the meetings and Nomura-san's funeral arrangements.

⌘⌘⌘

At Kyoto the Mereleigh group were revelling in being holiday makers: some had envisaged travelling through Japan as being similar to battling through Mumbai or being pestered by Italian street hawkers so were pleas-antly surprised at the smoothness and organisation of it all. Their first night sleeping on futons on tatami mats was universally acclaimed as a great experience and they felt they were really in the swing of things. The big trip of the day was to Nara, another previous capital of Japan from 710 until 784, noted for its Deer Park, the largest in Japan, and huge Japanese cedars and oaks and wisteria vines.

They were eager to see all this and Kofukuji Temple with its five-story pagoda construction set near Sarusawa Pond. The 360 metre circumference pond abounded with carp and turtles. All in all it was going to be another great day out and with the prospect of a bit of a knees up at Fukuoka with the Fukuoka Record Group things had taken a turn for the better they thought.

Maggie had received many phone calls from Rick and knew the truth of things and the nasty game of politics that was being played out, but she only kept Fran advised of Rick's fears and they decided not to bother Andy unduly. Peter had received the occasional call from Adam who had always sounded upbeat, particularly about Michiko, so he guessed things were moving on apace.

During their walk around some of the temples at Nara, Andy received a message via the JTB Tour guide to the effect that Nomura-san's funeral would be held in several days time in Fukuoka, and Rick felt it appropriate that perhaps one or two Mereleigh members should attend, and they consider a wreath or something appropriate. The group would be in transit via Space World from Hiroshima to Fukuoka at the time of the funeral so if Andy and someone else went then they would have to miss the visit to Space World and leave Hiroshima immediately after the sightseeing was done and only get a day there. He discussed this with the JTB tour guide and she said it could be arranged and once they decided who was going she could arrange for someone from her office to make the necessary bookings for them.

The group took a short break and it was decided that Andy and Fran would go accompanied by Chuck. Andy was glad to escape funfair activities at Space World and Fran felt she should be there as she had played a key role in the communications. Chuck was impatient to get things going for the venue they would use for the events. The news of the funeral cast a dark shadow over the rest of the day and, added to that, Adam rang in the early evening telling them about the shocking write-up a newspaper had given Michiko and how distressed she was.

⌘⌘⌘

At Tokyo Jenny awoke with a thumping head to a nightmare; she found herself in a strange room in a strange building. Like many Japanese small apartments it contained few furnishings: just a futon, a low dining table and several cushions for sitting on. Strangely there was nothing to cook or eat food with and no telephone.

She tried the outside door, a typical Japanese steel affair, and found it locked. When she was unable to unlock it from the inside, she knew that she was being held prisoner. The full realisation of the night's activities slowly came back to mind and she became aware they must have drugged her after they forced her into a car. A bruised right arm and a small pin prick of blood near the bruise was evidence.

She swore and cursed with anger. She was beyond self-pity, she wanted to get even. She found herself dressed in some of her daytime casual clothes so knew she must have been really out for the count not to have been roused by this. She was dying of thirst and there was no mug or glass so she drank straight from the tap and then her eye caught sight of a large empty vase, the sole item on a set of empty kitchen shelves and cupboards. She tried to open a window. It was locked so she threw the lamp at the window. It went clean through the glass and she could hear it clatter on the pavement outside a few seconds later.

She staggered drowsily to the window to see she was about six floors above street level. Below was a small collection of pedestrians, none of whom fortunately had been hurt by the descending lamp. Her door rattled as someone unlocked it in haste and rushed in. It was a tough looking mama-san and a Yakuza minder. They screamed at her in Japanese and the Yakuza said, 'Bad girl, will get big trouble!' She got the drift and decided there was little she could do for the moment.

'We go soon, you eat now. I come back one minute,' the mama-san said.

Jenny did not want to give them the pleasure of saying no to any of her requests and guessed they would not answer any questions anyway, so she desisted from asking where she was and where she was going. She decided to play it cool and quiet so that they might think her a pushover now and drop their guard a bit. She guessed what they would do, it would be to make her an addict of some kind so she would do what they wanted and thus she could repay them for all the time and effort they had invested in her.

She contemplated co-operation, but without drugs so she could stay alert and have a better chance of escape. It seemed to be the best way and maybe she should explain she was willing to do what they wanted and buy her way out of this fix. Would they believe her after last night, that was the question? Well, she told herself, she was a trained actress and this would have to be the best role play of her life, so she decided to back herself.

The door was unlocked again and the mama-san entered with food, accompanied by the big Yakuza. While the mama-san went to the kitchen Jenny brushed up against the Yakuza, smiled at him and fondled his prick. He was totally taken aback and clutched at Jenny to push her away when the mama-san came back

The mama-san cursed him and told him to leave the girl alone, 'She is not for you so keep your hands off.' The Yakuza started to protest but he could not sway the mama-san from the belief that he had made an indecent approach to Jenny.

'That was good for a start,' Jenny said to herself, correctly reading the situation, 'and he fancies me as he got a hard on straight away.'

Jenny then looked thankfully at the mama-san as if to say, 'thank you very much for saving me from this ogre.' The mama-san allowed herself a slight smile back at Jenny, who thought, 'Hey, maybe you like pretty girls, we shall soon see.'

As Jenny's mum had once said to her, 'being nice to people gets you a lot further than being a total bitch.' 'Good advice. I shall put it to the test.' she thought.

The food was budget convenience food bought from a nearby supermarket. Before they left her place Jenny managed to brush seductively past the Yakuza again and he allowed himself a smile. She also did the same to the mama-san out in the kitchen and got a similar response.

'We go in ten minutes time, be ready,' the mama-san said. Jenny smiled sweetly at her and said, 'OK fine.'

The Yakuza spoke in Japanese to the mama-san. Jenny figured they were trying to sort out if she would come without a struggle or if some medication was necessary. Jenny managed to wink at the Yakuza when the mama-san was not looking. He blushed like a small boy. She made a gesture like grabbing his prick. He got the message and he was again debating with the mama-san. Jenny hoped he was saying what she was hoping, and thinking she would give him a wank. If so they would not drug her or put handcuffs on.

She was spot on. Before taking her out to their transport he showed her his gun and indicated he would use it. She knew that was very unlikely. He would more likely drug her. The mama-san kept saying, 'be good, bad girl gets trouble.' She got the message. She was taken out into a heavily curtained minibus. Another Yakuza was at the wheel and she was pushed into the back seat with the mama-san by her side and the burly Yakuza sitting next to the sliding door.

She decided not to ask any questions as it would be a sign of weakness and concern and she did not want to give them any psychological advantage, but she tried to note and memorise significant landmarks through the dark tinted windows and curtains. It was almost impossible. Every Japanese building looked like thousands of others and, while the Roman alphabet was used on major road destination signs, they indicated places she had never heard of before.

Even looking at the direction of the sun was a problem. It was a dull grey overcast day and the sun could hardly be seen behind the thick cloud covering. Railways, bus terminals might be useful, as well as temples and shrines she thought, but the journey went on and on and then onto motorways which took the minibus out of Tokyo.

She figured it was going roughly south by the dull semi-visible glow of the sun behind the clouds. It was not long before she started to feel drowsy and dropped off to sleep. She had been deliberately sedated by the mama-san who had popped a pill into a drink. Her captors took the highway route to Fukuoka, making stops every few hours but being careful to make them in more remote parts and at approximate equal time intervals to allow for the effects of the sedatives to wear off.

She lost all track of time and hardly knew when she

was being asked to leave the minibus for a toilet stop or for food and had only a dim recollection of arriving at Fukuoka in darkness, probably in the early hours of the morning as very few people were about. She did not know that the Yakuza from Tokyo had been replaced by another gangster and there was a different mama-san in charge.

She was taken to a small tatami room in a nondescript concrete building, which could have been anywhere in Japan, and told to rest. She felt so lethargic it was impossible to resist the instruction.

⌘⌘⌘

Earlier the previous evening Adam and Michiko had enjoyed a pleasant dinner with Nishimura-san and her boyfriend. Adam discovered he had a common interest with her boyfriend in fishing. Adam loved fishing at sea in boats or off the rocks or in rivers or lakes and so did Nishimura's boyfriend. They discussed rods and reels, lures, bait and all aspects of fishing at great length until the two girls were bored stiff with their conversation.

Nishimura-san told Michiko and Adam they had to be positive about the function and get everything planned as soon as possible despite the raging media war and destructive noises made by angry sponsors who had pulled out. She gave Adam and Michiko a list of things the Fukuoka group would like the Mereleigh group to do such as prepare a list of sixties pop music they wanted to hear or dance to. There would be karaoke facilities and they had managed to get a good local band to play that specialised in rock and roll tunes of that era.

They had already identified a venue and set a modest catering budget. Nishimura-san did not ask how much Chuck would put up as she discreetly realised that Ban-san would probably work that out with Chuck and the Fukuoka rugby men, if the latter decided to put their weight behind the event. News that Fran, Chuck and some of the group were coming straight to Fukuoka for the funeral and to discuss the arrangements pleased her but she pointed out that Nomura-san's family would be fully involved first with the funeral rites.

'First they had the Tsuya on the day he died where everybody came to their house to pay their respects, like you did,' she explained, but there would be the funeral at the Buddhist temple in three days time, just a day before the fundraising event. Nishimura-san asked Michiko in Japanese to explain to Adam and the Mereleigh group what would happen at the funeral and the usual presentation of money in special black-edged envelopes by the mourners. Michiko in turn explained it to Adam who volunteered to brief Fran, Andy and Chuck on the procedures. Adam said he knew the group would have a whip around to provide cash for a gift and there would be no problem in giving cash if that was the practice.

Nishimura-san said the cash amount might be anything between 10,000 and 50,000 yen or more, and the family would return half that amount to the Mereleigh group in the form of gifts like towels, blankets, tea or plates. Adam suggested the Nomura family keep all the money as the group would not expect any gifts from them but Nishimura-san said they had to do something like that or lose face.

Adam said if they made a small cash donation towards the cost of the event that would be fine, but everyone appreciated Nomura-san was the main bread-winner and they would need every yen they could get for the family in the future. Adam told Nishimura-san it would be simpler if she dealt direct with Andy, Fran and Chuck on all things relating to the event and funeral after he had explained things to them. Michiko explained how they still had lots of follow-ups to make to their stories and how Rick and Tanaka-san were flat out trying to rescue Jenny.

Nishimura-san said, on her side, Ban-san would be in charge of the rock and roll party and liaise with the rugby men, and the S and M Business boss Hayakawa-san. Michiko said she had heard noises that the Nishi Nippon Shimbun would also help out with the event and that Ban-san could expect to get a call from the newspaper company tomorrow.

'You're a dark horse, you didn't tell me that,' Adam told Michiko.

'What do you mean a dark horse? I just overheard a bit of conversation the other day at the office and was going to tell you but forgot,' she explained.

Nishimura-san and her boyfriend ran them back to the Sea Hawk Hotel in their small car. It had been a very pleasant and successful evening on all counts and Adam and Michiko knew they had made new friends for life.

'We will go fishing together before you leave, I hope?' Nishimura-san's boyfriend asked.

'Of course, and you and Nishimura-san must come to

Mereleigh and I will take you river fishing in Britain,'
Adam responded.

Adam got on the phone in his room as soon as possible to contact Andy, Fran and Chuck at their Kyoto ryokan. They were anxious for his call and the briefing. Chuck gave an assurance that there would be a sizeable cash donation for the family and Andy said they had already received an average of about 20,000 yen per couple in from the rest of the group.

'As far as I can ascertain it will be a Buddhist funeral. They have a Tsuya, a sort of gathering of relations and friends who call to give their respects on the day of a person's death, then a few days after, the actual funeral at a temple. It might last an hour or two with prayers and people speaking about the deceased then the body is taken away for a cremation. The period of mourning goes on for a year, but with events about seven days and thirteen days after the funeral, and on the forty-ninth day the ashes might be buried.' Adam was rather proud of this newly-learned information.

Michiko managed to get a word in to Fran to verify the salient points and pointed out it would probably turn out to be a big affair with much media interest in who was attending and also the circumstances which led to Nomura-san's suicide. Adam and Michiko had lost track to some extent of what was going on with Tanaka-san and the others that evening but Adam decided if there was anything urgent they would surely contact them. Meanwhile he decided to file a short piece about the funeral, a sort of speculative thing suggesting something of a Japanese media fest.

The Guardian had told him they were really interested in Jenny's story as they had sent one of their UK reporters to Wales to interview her parents, who were now out of their minds with worry. The Guardian said they were also going to contact a few of the actors who appeared in the film about the Mereleigh tour of New Zealand to get personal reaction pieces from them over the present fiasco. Adam was advised that some of the tabloids might appear in Fukuoka to do beat-ups so he could expect competition! He excitedly related the call to Michiko who gave him a serious hard look.

'This might be the biggest story of your life, Adam, in fact two stories if we consider Jenny as well, but please let us keep our feet on the ground and remember the real people who suffer, Nomura-san's family and friends, and not sacrifice our ideals for some cheap journalism,' she pleaded.

'I hear what you are saying and agree but I think the real threat is from cheque-book journalism. You know the tabloids will stop at nothing to get the angle they want. We better advise Mrs Nomura and of course Nishimura-san to be on their guard,' he added.

Fighting weariness and a very strong desire to have sex with Michiko he decided he should try to contact Rick and Tanaka-san to tell them about the growing media interest in Jenny. He had no idea where to start until Michiko came to his rescue.

'There is a bar in Nakasu that the rugby men go to. I think we can find Tanaka-san by this bar somehow.'

A quick call to the bar brought instant results, the master of the bar not only confirmed Tanaka-san's presence at this very late hour but put him on the line. Clearly Tanaka-san and Yoshi had been lubricating fellow rugby men to garner their support for the rock and roll event. Tanaka-san's friendly slurred speech suggested they should instantly take a taxi to the bar so they could better understand how things were. Michiko conversed briefly in Japanese to get the details and gave Adam a wary old-fashioned look.

'Perhaps you should go without me?' she suggested.

Adam would have nothing of it, telling her, 'You are my right arm and also half my brain in Japan. I would be out of my depth trying to dig out some new facts in that atmosphere.'

'It's the atmosphere that worries me, these bars are not the sort of places that normal Japanese ladies like to visit, especially very late at night when the men are drunk!' she said.

'You're a journalist, you have to go anywhere to get a story, anyway I think we can trust Tanaka-san to protect your dignity,' he added.

The taxi took them past all the garish neon signs of skimpily-clad cowgirls, French can-can dancers and scantily-clad girls at front entrances with belts for skirts and minimal halter tops until they found the rugby bar. It was dead easy to spot as it had a neon sign of a most unlikely female rugby player in the shortest of hot pants and minimal bra clutching a rugby ball.

An anxious and excited Tanaka-san was waiting for them at the entrance and he instantly gave Michiko a few words of thanks for coming too and an assurance in Japanese that he would take care of her and make sure no one made any smutty remarks or groped her. She did not tell Adam this, only that he said everyone would be a gentleman to her.

They entered the crammed confines of the bar to the booming vintage voice of Elvis Presley belting out 'His Latest Flame.' Its occupants were nearly all burly rugby men with cauliflower ears, bent noses and buckled fingers, of an age group that would qualify most to appear in Golden Oldies teams. Almost without exception they were dressed in smart suits and insisted on age group music, that is the music of the mid to late 1950's, which featured the Ink Spots, the Platters, Frankie Lane, Jim Reeves and Hank Williams.

Almost to a man they raised themselves to their feet to press their business cards on Adam and bow deeply as he received each one in turn, and they cast polite looks at Michiko and also offered her their cards. She was impressed at this fine display of politeness albeit from a rather drunk collection of senior old men, and noticed almost hidden in a corner Rick and Herewini who had two scantily-clad hostesses sitting next to them, constantly offering to top up their drinks and get them finger food.

'I might have known you two could be found here,' said Adam with a grin.

Rick was barely able to stand up but had enough presence of mind to tell Adam, 'For God's sake don't tell Maggie you found me here, she might get the wrong impression!'

Michiko giggled with delight at the thought, and it made Rick flush with embarrassment. Herewini pulled himself together and extracted himself from the hostess who cleared enjoyed tangling her body around his.

'Sorry it's been a one-stop shop since we arrived in Fukuoka. All the best laid plans of man and beast, or rather Tanaka-san and Rick, to visit organisations and people came unstuck the moment we stepped inside here with Tanaka-san,' he explained.

'The most important thing is, the most important thing is,' Tanaka-san stated with repetitive emphasis, 'is that the rugby men will give us all their support for the Mereleigh group event, and just as I speak my friends here have their staff going out like octopuses gathering a big army to support you,' he finished his vital message with a huge smile on his face.

Adam smiled at his English and obvious good humour and expressed a very public thanks to everyone, which in turn inspired several rugby men to start a banzai cry and for Rick's benefit to mimic a New Zealand All Black haka. Michiko was splitting her sides with laughter at the carry-on, which resulted in Tanaka-san and Rick collapsing on the floor after the mock haka.

Yoshi had meanwhile ducked behind the bar to assist the Master. His staff maintained a steady flow of beverages to the customers. Adam found himself with a drink in each hand and yet more rugby men who wanted to present him with their name cards. The bar's mama-san came over, 'Michiko-san, please forgive their noisy behaviour. I am afraid rugby men are very noisy.'

'No, it's all right. I enjoy their jokes and they are really just big kids at heart,' Michiko said, giving her a reassuring smile.

Suddenly everyone quietened down and Tanaka-san asked Adam to address the gathering. It happened so suddenly that Adam was taken aback and thought he was joking at first then realised he was deadly serious.

'What shall I say? What do they expect?' he asked Michiko in desperation.

'Just thank them for their support and tell them how impressed you are and how welcome their support will be. That is all,' she whispered.

'First of all I have to thank you all for this totally unexpected and magnificent display of hospitality which caught Michiko and me totally unaware. It's incredible that you can agree to give your support to us at such short notice and I know that the Fukuoka Record Club and the widow of Nomura-san will greatly appreciate this.

'We have little more than a couple of days to get everything together, but for a country that can build tens of thousands of cars a day I suppose organising a party in two days must be a piece of cake. I presume Tanaka-san has presented you with the detailed instructions for the event,' he said with a big smile on his face.

It was met with a very worried look on Tanaka-san's face until he realised Adam was joking and that resulted in a huge roar of laughter and a round of applause. On that note Adam wound up his brief address, but then leapt to his feet again.

'There is another very, very serious thing and it is the Jenny Jones affair. She is the daughter of a good friend of Rick's and she seems to have been abducted by the Yakuza and that is deeply worrying to us all. Tanaka-san and Rick-san have been trying to rescue her,' he concluded.

It made Tanaka-san and Rick sober up very quickly. Tanaka-san was clearly disturbed by references to Jenny, and Rick felt a huge pang of guilt that he had wasted half the evening at this place when he might have been able to do something more constructive.

The rugby men were waiting for Tanaka-san to say more and he at first appeared to be reluctant. He kept his briefing very succinct but ended with the possibility that she could have been brought to Fukuoka. The rugby men listened in stony silence and waited for another senior rugby man to speak and sum up a collective view. The wrinkled old chap who looked as though his age twice qualified him for the Golden Oldies said it was a very serious matter and he would like to speak for them all.

'We must help you, and we will help you. It's no secret that we rugby men like to drink and we often move from place to place. Also some Yakuza like to play rugby and we know them and have our own discreet connections so please leave it with us,' he concluded.

Adam had no clear recollection of the rest of the night's proceedings apart from leaving the bar in some sort of massive convoy of taxis and private cars in a large entourage that seemed to include every rugby man who had been present at the bar. They all insisted on getting out of their cars to bow him, Michiko, Rick and Herewini into the Sea Hawk's lift. He noted Michiko clutched a huge bunch of flowers, and she was persisting in trying to get him to hold them for a photograph before they entered the lift. The drinks they had pushed at him made it impossible for him to comprehend the logic of any of this.

He let Michiko undress him and shower him and roll him into bed where he apologised for not being in a fit state to have sex, before he made a hasty but very wobbly run to the toilet to have a couple of decent chunders before cleaning his teeth for the second time and turning in. He had a bizarre dream before he woke which seemed to involve him being chased through a Japanese night life district by a couple of burly Yakuzas, accompanied by a scantily-clad Japanese cowgirl complete with lasso who was trying get a hoop over him with Michiko running beside him imploring him to take the bunch of flowers.

The dawn came all too soon, or at least he thought it was the dawn, but Michiko had let him sleep in to 10am and was shaking him gently offering a strong cup of coffee. She was already dressed and the hotel room tidied up. His mouth felt as though an aged vulture had sicked up its breakfast and deposited the contents in his.

She told him that the others felt they should be left alone to concentrate on the news stories but Rick had wanted a meeting at lunch time with them and also Andy, Fran and Chuck who were expected to arrive at Fukuoka by shinkansen late morning. Adam forced himself under a cold shower, got dressed, took a second cup of coffee and decided he could wait until lunch for any food. He stuffed his hands into his suit pocket to discover a huge pile of business cards accumulated at the meeting with the rugby men.

'My God, what do I do with these?' he exclaimed in mock horror.

'You buy some name card folders and keep them in the folders for future reference,' Michiko explained.

'Why does everyone in Japan have name cards? I ran out of mine days ago and everyone seems to know who I am,' he protested.

'Has it occurred to you that most places we go you are a very noticeable minority of one, the only gaijin at every meeting. Did you notice that I always presented my meishi and wrote your name on the back of it?' she said rather pointedly. She felt Adam was now in the need of a bit of education into the realities of Japanese life as the burden of translating everything for him and also conducting her own business was taxing.

'Look, I am so sorry, maybe I should order a few hundred cards to save you the trouble but I have to say it's impossible for me to remember all the faces that go with the name cards I have already accumulated. Look at these two rounded edge ones for starters, who the hell are they?'

'They are two of the hostesses at the bar we went to last night. If I was married to you and had not been with you last night to know your behaviour was innocent, I could have become angry to see those cards. All Japanese ladies have rounded cornered meishi,' she explained.

'Gosh, I have a lot to learn, but I guess you would have been really pissed off with me if you had found one of those cards the prostitutes put up in telephone boxes, in my pocket,' he smiled weakly and got a frozen stare in response.

'Tell me, everyone is Tanaka-san or Watanabe-san so how do you know if it's male or female if you don't actually see them?' he asked.

'If you talk to them on the phone it's pretty apparent by their voice and if they are referred to as a third party in a conversations then someone can mention "he" or "she" to clarify things,' she said. 'You must know that we also have grades of what you might call status and will call a senior person who we respect "sensei", which literally means teacher, and in shops and service industries customers are usually called "sama", but the important thing is you must always put san, sensei or sama on the end of their names. It is impolite not to do so.'

'You don't use given names very much,' he stated.

'It's true, but we often abbreviate them, and if the relationship is very close like in a family or boyfriend or girlfriend, or to a child, then you can use 'chan', she pointed out.

'So I should call you Michiko-chan?' he asked

'Of course it sounds so nice coming from you. You can shorten it to Michi-chan if you like,' she glowed.

Michiko took charge and had noted in her diary things they must do, which entailed calling their various newspapers within the next 12 hours, getting some name cards made for Adam and taking lunch with Rick and co. They would play the afternoon 'by ear' she said.

⌘⌘⌘

Andy, Fran and Chuck took an early shinkansen from Kyoto for the approximate four hour journey to Fukuoka. It was so much more convenient than flying and, of course, Andy would not fly in any case.

Andy was beginning to feel comfortable about how things were going. In his heart he knew the events at Fukuoka would go off OK, and doom-casters and critics be made to look foolish by the stand they had taken. However, he was no fool, and he realised the forces of big business and politics that had opted to be destructive to the cause would stop at nothing to save face, so everyone would have to tread very carefully.

He expressed his opinion to Chuck and Fran, who agreed, but Chuck added sagely that, as foreigners and visitors to Japan, they must tread very carefully with any public opinions and let their new-found Japanese friends take the lead.

'We are, goddamn it, the problem, not the solution, in the eyes of the detractors, so we gotta turn it around,' he told them.

They travelled most of the journey in silence, each reflecting on the current situation and Andy quietly tracing the various paths of Japan's main narrow gauge rail network which at times ran parallel to the shinkansen, even shared some stations, and then would curve off at sharp angles into endless suburbs or wind its way around mountains. The narrow three-foot six-inch gauge lines provided most of the bread and butter rail services, handling millions of rail commuters in brightly coloured electric train units, fast local and country trains and rail freight.

Andy looked for remnants of the steam era and found few, perhaps an old railway loco shed or water tower, but to all intents and purposes there was little left anywhere to show that steam was once king of the railways. Chuck was impressed by the rich paddies right up to suburban houses and streets and the tiny two-wheeled motor tractor cultivators that were used, and also the various fruit orchards and numerous polyhouses for growing pumpkins, tomatoes and other vegetables. He spotted tea plantations, and told the other two. Fran was busy snapping traditional Japanese farm houses and cherry blossoms.

'I ain't seen any critters outside in the fields since we been in Japan. No cows, steers, hogs or horses. They mush hav'm somewhere 'cause we send a lot of grain for cattle feed to Japan so I reckon they must all be indoors,' he exclaimed.

They saw glimpses of Peace Park before the shinkansen came to a brief stop at Hiroshima and were consciously aware of the train diving through the steeply graded rail tunnel under the Kanmon Strait that linked the main island of Honshu with Kyushu, the southern most of Japan's three major islands. All too quickly the shinkansen emerged in bright daylight amid the industrial morass of Kitakyushu with the busy port of Moji to the north-west of the line and large mountains to the south-east. There was a brief stop at Kokura, the main station for Kitakyushu, and Andy added knowledgably that the A-bomb that was dropped on Hiroshima had been destined for Kitakyushu but low cloud resulted in the

American A-bombers selecting Hiroshima instead.

'Kitakyushu was a great coal mining and steel town then as well as a vital port,' Andy explained.

'I bet they thanked their lucky stars the weather was bad after the bomb was dropped, and what a stroke of ill fate for Hiroshima,' Fran exclaimed.

The shinkansen drew into Hakata Station an hour or so before lunch and there on the platform exactly where their carriage stopped was Nishimura-san and her boyfriend to meet them. Andy could see Nishimura-san was so happy to see them. After all the troubles and effort it seemed the dreams of the Fukuoka Record Club would come true. She passed on apologies for Ban-san not being there to meet them but he was so busy making arrangements and meeting people he just could not spare a moment. He would meet them later in the day.

Nishimura-san had rather underestimated the amount of luggage they had and the rather larger dimensions of Europeans, when it came to fitting three adults in the back seat of her car. NEvartheless they managed to poke two large suitcases into the tiny boot together with a few carry bags and the three back seat passengers nursed one large suitcase while her boyfriend in the front had several other handbags and overcoats stowed on top of him. They headed for the Sea Hawk in this fashion and the front entrance bell hops were very impressed at how Nishimura had managed to get so many people and such a large volume of luggage into the tiny car.

Nishimura-san said a lunch had been arranged by Hayakawa-san and some of the key members of the Small and Medium Business Association at a rather select restaurant. She gave them time to check in and said they would all meet at the front desk and then go to the restaurant. Andy and Chuck were not particularly looking forward to another cramped journey in the back seat and were relieved when Nishimura-san said Hayakawa-san was there to meet them and had organised no less than three cars to take them.

'Gee, what overkill! We go from the ridiculous to the sublime, and I not complaining!' Chuck exclaimed.

They were taken to a very swish upmarket Japanese restaurant in Ohori Koen park where they were ceremoniously ushered into a very large, long, low banquet table set in a spacious tatami room with shoji blinds and flowering cherry blossom trees just outside.

'This is a picture, just too good to believe.' Fran was stunned by it all and then noticed everybody was seated waiting for them including Ban-san, Rick, Tanaka-san, Yoshi, Adam and Michiko. The two Nishi Nippon Shimbun journalists Sam and Kenny were also there together with the editor of the Nishi Nippon Shimbun and, to top it off, Hayakawa-san said the Mayor would arrive soon but would have to leave a bit early for a meeting.

'This is it I guess!' Andy exclaimed.

Nishimura-san and Michiko were strategically seated between the Mereleigh Record Club group members to provide assistance with translations, and the two Nishi Nippon Shimbun journalists were at the end of the tables so they could leap up and take some photos. The senior Fukuoka officials sat in the centre of the long thin table and Andy, Chuck and Fran were seated opposite for ease of conversation.

The Mayor, a man in his late 50's of shortish rotund stature with a beaming face, arrived offering apologies for keeping everyone waiting. Hayakawa-san and his top members would have none of it and insisted he was just on time. It was all a façade really, another court ritual. Kimono-clad waitresses scurried about in a discreetly unobtrusive way plying the diners with numerous dishes, and drinks in the form of beer, sake and whisky were provided for everyone.

Andy and Chuck were overjoyed to find the long, low dining table was set over a sunken pit so they could sit on cushions on the tatami mat and have their feet under the table in a normal western style.

'I can tell you that I don't know how I would have managed sitting cross legged through this meal if they had not got this place where we can put our feet,' Chuck stage-whispered to Andy.

The lunch started with pleasantries and inquiries about Nomura-san's widow and family. Nishimura-san said she was of course devastated but coping very well and sensibly in the circumstances as were the children. Nomura-san's wife had decided not to read newspapers other than the Nishi Nippon Shimbun, and not to bother with the TV and radio news as some of it was too distressing. However, Nishimura-san hastened to add that the Nomuras were full of thanks to the Nishi Nippon Shimbun Company, the Mayor and everyone else. She explained the family was in mourning and hoped they could understand her reason for not attending this lunch.

At an appropriate moment between courses the Mayor told them how he would attend the events and had requested that other councillors do the same. He had set up voluntary donation boxes for the Nomura family and said one of his senior permanent staff had volunteered to assist with the general arrangements.

Companies such as the Nishi Nippon Shimbun, which still wished to be involved, were going to work through Hayakawa-san's Small and Medium Business Association. The Mayor looked at Hayakawa-san and Hayakawa-san nodded in acknowledgement. The Mayor said he was personally very distressed at the opposition and what he considered as slandering of some key people involved.

'They have tried to besmirch the name of Nomura-san, but they will not succeed in the long run,' he concluded.

It was Hayakawa-san's turn to speak and he voiced similar sentiments and support. Then Tanaka-san got up and said he had been given unbridled support by the All Kyushu rugby association.

'We might not be so rich as key businessmen but we will do as much as we can,' he said.

Andy rose to his feet and said, 'My members had a whip around and raised a sum for the Nomura family in recognition of her husband's great efforts.'

No sooner had he sat down than Chuck got up and added, 'I personally want to cover the cost of hiring a ballroom venue at the chosen hotel.'

It drew an instant response from the Japanese audience who were clearly very impressed at his generosity, as five-star hotel ballroom hire does not come cheaply in

Japan. The rest of the luncheon was spent happily, with a few people, notably Hayakawa-san, Ban-san and others sorting out organisational details.

Rick inadvertently drew the meeting to a close with an announcement that he and Tanaka-san had a meeting with Herewini and others very shortly concerning Jenny. Tanaka-san organised transport and they picked up Herewini and Flanker at a Tenjin bar where they had been having a yakitori semi-liquid lunch.

Tanaka-san gave a briefing which simply said Emiko, his nightclub girl friend from Tokyo, had quit her job and come to Fukuoka, and she was convinced Jenny had been brought to this city. Emiko had a few names of clubs in Nakasu which might have a connection with her ex-boss in Tokyo. Flanker said that was a good start and he would contact the Fukuoka vice squad to find out what they had on these places and the masters and mama-sans who managed them.

Herewini said he had a customs contact at Fukuoka, a Japanese customs officer who had been sent to Auckland on a familiarisation programme and who had worked alongside Herewini for several weeks.

'Let's take a look at a possible breach of her visa requirements by her Yakuza bosses. We might be able to pin them down on that issue if we can't prove anything else,' Herewini stated.

'That is very good point, Herewini-san. Customs police immigration aspect and visa business,' Flanker agreed excitedly. The group dispersed with Tanaka-san, Emiko, Yoshi and Rick going to make some discreet checks on nightclubs, and Flanker and Herewini going to make calls on the local Police and Customs HQ.

Herewini was beginning to appreciate how the Japanese really liked to organise things properly and think out strategies at ordinary levels. No matter how smart the Yakuza were, the guys holding Jenny were up against some formidable determined locals who were not going to hang around and wait for the cops to do everything. He liked it and was glad to be part of the action. The old rugby guys were pretty special people.

The call at Fukuoka police HQ was pretty straightforward. Flanker's boss had already been in touch with them so Flanker only had to explain his current line of inquiry. He was told Fukuoka police could provide more resources if needed but he should understand there were always missing foreign hostesses who were inevitably found to have broken their visa conditions rather than being held anywhere against their will and, in any case, Jenny was still well within her visa term. It was only the suspicion that she might be held against her will that needed checking out.

That line was familiar to Herewini as it was a typical law enforcement organisational response to a situation which seemed fuzzy and unclear and would probably turn out to be nothing, or from lazy officers who either neither cared or knew how to get into a case, or from overworked officers who had a stack of major crimes on their desk to solve. Herewini was secretly pleased that the Fukuoka police were basically leaving it all to Flanker and his citizen support group.

As they walked out of the police station Herewini said,

'Well Flanker if we pull this bastard off and rescue her without their help, there could be a promotion or at least a good report and commendation in it for you!' Flanker smiled modestly at the prospect but, being Japanese, he had to say that, if it were successful, it would be entirely due to the efforts of his friends and not him.

The Fukuoka customs men treated Herewini right royally once they knew he was from Auckland, Fukuoka's sister city, and was in town to see his old friend who had been in Auckland. His customs officer friend Saita-san was all smiles when they entered his department, it was great for him to see Herewini again so unexpectedly and what was even better was that Herewini had come with a request for help in tracking down a foreigner who, not through her own accord, might be in breach of her work visa requirements.

It took about an hour of discussion with Saita-san and his bosses to work out a rationale which would allow Saita-san to assist Herewini in this search. At the end Saita-san's boss agreed they could make legitimate inquiries in that regard if there was reasonable suspicion and Flanker, representing the Japanese police, was able to satisfy them in that regard.

The customs boss said normally there would have to be a formal written request or else official transfer of information from the police to Customs but if Customs took their own lead on this matter and later 'found' the police were following similar inquiries, it could avoid going into too much formality at the beginning. It meant that Flanker should not make an approach directly to them, as the normal way was via the Fukuoka police, not a Tokyo detective. It was hard for them to take advice from Herewini as he was a New Zealander and the missing person British, so it would be best to come from a British person with the group.

Herewini had a brainwave and suggested that Perry, the British ex-cop with the group, could do it. He would come into Customs and make a formal statement on his arrival. The Customs boss was well satisfied with that arrangement and gave Saita-san approval to work with Herewini from then on to initiate some inquiries in advance. As they left the customs boss's office Flanker looked a bit puzzled and asked Herewini,

'Does this Perry-san know about this? I have not spoken to him and might be Rick only told him basic information. I had no idea there was an ex-policeman in the group?'

'As you say, I am sure he knows about Jenny but not about making any statements to Customs, but I will phone him today and he will agree because he is that sort of person. On the Mereleigh group trip to New Zealand he was signed on as a temporary New Zealand police constable to help trap a smuggling gang,' Herewini said.

'How about Rick-san, or Andy-san? Might be they should be the persons who take the lead,' Flanker persisted, as he did not wish anyone to be offended if they did the wrong thing.

'Well, Rick is a Kiwi like me so can't really take much on re a missing British person. Jenny is not even a member of his tour party and Andy will be up to his eyebrows in arrangements for the big event with the Fukuoka

Record Club,' Herewini patiently explained. Flanker was satisfied that Herewini had chosen the right path and relaxed.

'In Japan people can get very easily and greatly offended if we do not follow the correct path and it's really amazing that the customs boss is going to accept this arrangement,' Flanker pointed out. Saita-san totally agreed and said probably if a Japanese person had made the request to his boss he would not have been given so much consideration.

'You know, Japanese must be polite to foreigners and especially because you are from our sister city,' Saita explained.

Herewini was getting the drift of things very quickly and realised his normal piratical style might have to be contained somewhat out of respect for the special help they might need from Japanese customs and police. Saita-san said he might need an hour to search Jenny's visa details. They could be pulled up on the computer in moments but he wanted to do a bit of research on the persons and organisation that had vouched for her to see if they had previously breached visa regulations.

Flanker gave Saita-san a copy of the police file on Jenny and also the Tokyo nightclub boss who had brought her to Japan. He recollected that Emiko had mentioned several clubs in Nakasu that were thought to be associated with the Tokyo boss, and that he had asked the Fukuoka police for some details on them. Flanker said his boss, Inspector Mori at Tokyo, would expect daily succinct reports from him either verbally by phone or by email to keep himself up to date. He told Saita-san Inspector Mori was very proactive and would move quickly if and when a need arose.

'He is something of a Yakuza specialist,' Flanker added.

After a couple of hours' work they had Jenny's immigration file with full details of her sponsors as well as a list of properties owned, rented or managed by her boss which included several establishments in Nakasu, Fukuoka's night life district.

Flanker rang Inspector Mori to relate the events of the day and the inspector expressed a touch of surprise but pleasure that they had Fukuoka Customs chasing up the immigration angle. He told Flanker, 'That is good thinking,' and Flanker accepted the compliment with a glow as if it were his own idea, which he hoped Inspector Mori would think it was.

Inspector Mori then added he would email some background stuff on this Yakuza boss which might prove interesting. When it arrived they could see instantly they were not dealing with some minor player but a Yakuza boss of some standing who had real estate connections in Fukuoka and Kyushu as well as the Kanto area around Tokyo.

'It seems we are dealing with a big fish,' Flanker said in awe.

Herewini reminded his new mates that there was a kind of timeframe on this job, imposed by the amount of time he, Rick et al could spend in Japan.

'Let's realise that we are down to days, not weeks; we have to crack this bastard very soon,' he added.

CHAPTER 12

The past 24 hours or so had been little more than a haze for Jenny. She had great difficulty sorting out reality from hallucinations, and knew that, despite her best efforts, she was being regularly sedated. She found herself in some sort of VIP mini-bus with darkened and curtained windows, and the usual Yakuza and mama-san figure accompanying her. She found it impossible to work out where she had been taken since leaving Tokyo or the amount of time that had elapsed since. The 24 hours was an estimate as her watch had been taken and she found it hard to see the time on the Yakuza's wristwatch as his coat sleeve kept falling down over it.

From the speed of the vehicle and the noise of other fast-travelling vehicles, it was obvious she was on a highway. She was thirsty and not tied up, so quietly reached for the mama-san's drink bottle, which she was allowed to take without argument. She was so thirsty she risked it being doped and, after a gulp or two, realised it was some sort of patented spring water. 'Probably recycled sewerage water with a touch of blue dye,' she thought cynically. So far she had been quite unable to put into place any kind of escape idea, let alone practise the apparent co-operation plan, for while they were shifting her around like this they had all the co-operation they needed without her assistance.

After a while the vehicle turned off the highway on to a side road that she knew must be in mountainous country by the tortuous nature of the road. The mini-bus must have proceeded for a good hour or so before turning into what was presumably a very small side road as its speed dropped to little more than a crawl as it tackled sharp bends and some steep hills. It was a bit like going up some of the back roads in Wales but there would be no cosy Welsh farmhouse or cottage at the end of this run.

It was now dusk and she could see the occasional lights of other vehicles. Suddenly the mini-bus swerved off the sealed road onto gravel and crunched its way to the front of a building and stopped. She heard the gruff and guttural voices of Yakuza types, and the occasional smoke and booze-damaged tones of ageing mama-sans who were acknowledging her arrival.

The Yakuza inside the bus threw open the door suddenly and said, 'Outside doozo,' so she obliged and was surprised to see a very smart, traditional Japanese ryokan set before her, nestling picturesquely between high, steep cedar-clad mountains. The outside air was clear and conifer-scented, and she could hear the rush of babbling

~ The Mereleigh Record Club Tour of Japan

mountain streams cascading down hillsides. She guessed it was about as remote a place as you could find a ryokan in Japan and was clearly a very small select hideaway.

A mama-san told her to go inside and directed her to a tatami room. She pointed to an adjoining bath room.

'Take a bath, take a bath,' she ordered and pointed to clean clothes consisting of a new yukata and undergarments laid out for her use.

'So this is it,' she thought. 'They want me to be the plaything for some rich old fart of a gangster. Jesus, I knew it might come to this but what the hell can I do?' She thought frantically about a possible means of escape but realised she was in dire circumstances.

'Play the role, play the role,' an inner voice kept telling her. 'Remember acting classes, which is your strength. Use your talent to deceive them and then you will start to gain control. Keep them guessing.' Playing the screaming banshee had not really worked a few days ago, so she decided to play the role of a highly beautiful and talented courtesan, or at least act out an image of what they would want her to be.

She started by telling the mama-san, who seemed to have some grasp of English, that the clothes were not good enough to entertain important men in and the soap and perfumes cheap supermarket junk. She put on a hissy fit and demanded certain brands. From the mama-san's reaction it seemed certain she was being prepared to meet some big-noting Yakuza and that, if she told him they had provided cheap junk for her to prepare herself with, he would be annoyed.

Face was everything. Dressing up rather than down was the preferred style of most Japanese, particularly big-timing Yakuzas. Her demands delayed the proceedings by at least an hour until someone had organised a special delivery of cosmetics and a very expensive yukata. She examined everything in great detail.

'This looks like top quality Chinese junk straight from Hong Kong with imitation labels sewn on. Don't you have any taste or are you too poor to buy quality stuff?' It was an intentional insult.

The mama-san was clearly on the back foot with worry and anger but her national pride would not let her rest until she had provided the best, and in this case she was somewhat out of her depth, not knowing what was best in European terms. She snapped angrily in Japanese at a servant woman to indicate a transfer of responsibility for the imperfect arrangements to an underling, and indicated to Jenny that this was the best available at the time.

Jenny then realised her ploy had subtly established a pecking order. She was the boss, and the mama-san a servant who had to obey her commands, or else experience the wrath of the yet unseen Yakuza boss. She smiled to herself but was aware that the next step, trying to get the Yakuza to eat out of her hands, might be a heck of a lot harder at the very best, and perhaps impossible. She could only hope for some short-term advantage.

Gauge the audience as soon as possible, play to the audience, was what her drama instructor had told her, reach out to them and make them part of the fantasy and drama as though they are alongside you experiencing everything. She would have to work out rapidly what this meeting was about. It looked as though he wanted to sample the merchandise or at least estimate the value of his latest acquisition. This clearly was not going to be the man who came to Britain to recruit her, but probably the Yakuza clan chief or someone close to him.

The building was impressive with its traditional rounded river stone entrance floor, thatched roof and heavy timbered beams and supports. The somewhat flimsy shoji blinds and thin interior walls contrasted with the heavy weight of the primary structure. The furniture, if not antique, was built to look like it, all heavy and dark stained.

She caught a whiff of the sulphurous geysers and hot springs and realised this place had its own natural hot spring. It had in fact been built over a hot spring. She then twigged why she had been given a yukata (Japanese dressing gown) to wear. She was probably expected to bathe naked for the enjoyment of her captors.

The accompanying mama-san told her she was expected by 'Ichiban' boss so she must behave politely. Jenny treated the mama-san to a withering haughty look as if she was a mere peasant, which gave an explicit message to the mama-san that some role reversal might be about to take place! She was instead ushered into a small tatami room with the usual origami arrangement of flowers in a vase in a small alcove, a low-slung coffee table and orderly-placed floral cushions to sit on. The walls were bare except for a couple of framed pieces of ceramic art work depicting traditional cherry blossom scenes.

There was a small, expensive, gold-embroidered tablecloth depicting a religious festival with a couple of hundred loin-clothed Japanese in inscribed head bands carrying a large portable shrine down a very busy street crammed with people all wearing traditional clothes. There was a faint scent in the air which she guessed came from incense, and she noted a venerable and traditional Japanese-looking cupboard which she guessed might contain very valuable tea ceremony crockery and other such items for light snacks. She looked for names like that of a ryokan or a place on items, but all she could see in that regard was Japanese script and nothing that looked as though it was the marked property of a ryokan.

She was aware of a noise the other side of the translucent paper sliding door and could make out the image of a stooped, rotund man sitting cross-legged. What looked like a servant in a kimono was placing food on a small table in front of him and removing some articles. Suddenly he seemed to be aware of her, and after the female servant had left he called her to enter in almost perfect English.

She rose and carefully measured her steps to the sliding door and, with calculated dignity, made the grandest entry she was capable of. With a superior gaze she cast her eyes over all the surroundings for effect, as if he was just part of the furnishings and no more important than the pictures on the wall.

Only after she had measured the value and the extent of the surroundings did she glance in his direction. She had decided to do this without invitation and he probably guessed she was going to do so, and seemed to ask her hastily to be seated before she sat down as if to restore some sort of command of the situation. She took time to arrange herself before further acknowledging his presence. From his looks her entry had caused him both a degree of annoyance and respect and that, she knew, was first point to her.

'I have invited you here to my country house because, like Hugh Hefner, I am a great admirer of the female form in its many shapes and colours and am now indulging myself in a mulatto period.' He spoke with the gruff voice of a typical Yakuza but overlaid with what he thought was more than a veneer of sophistication.

'I should explain I have always greatly admired black singers and dancers, Ella Fitzgerald and Eartha Kitt for example, but they are of course an older generation than I, so I must satisfy myself with their recorded music and films and try to find the new young Ellas and Eartha Kitts.' He paused for effect to let it sink in, and Jenny knew then exactly where it was all leading.

He was a person perhaps bordering on 70 years of age. It was hard to tell with finely-skinned Japanese who never, or rarely, exposed their skin to the harsh sunlight. He was strongly built and looked very fit for his age like someone who regularly practiced judo and worked out at a gym. She was tempted to say something but decided against it. Peasants explained themselves to the aristocracy and the aristocracy waited and made the decisions. He did not get the comments he expected so continued.

'When one of my men told me about this British black girl doing Eartha Kitt impersonations and got me a DVD of your act, I decided to procure you. I am not sure if that is the right word? Anyway, I understand things went badly for you after arrival in Japan, and my staff was presumptuous, clumsy and rude. Please accept my sincere apologies,' he paused again.

She allowed herself the merest nod in his direction and looked beyond him towards a window in a bored fashion. She noted he had a handsome, smiling face that made people automatically want to agree with him just to see him beam back at them. It was nature's gift to him that he had this sort of hypnotic quality.

She could see men wanting to be cool like him just because of the smile, and women wanting to dive under the bed covers to bring the big smile to his face. She could also detect a very cruel crease or two around his mouth that could promise the wrath of hell to those who did not obey his commands. In short, a man to be taken very seriously but with perhaps a screw or two loose up top, that might make him vulnerable.

He was finding the dialogue hard going. She was one smart bitch, he could see, and that made her all the more attractive to him. He loved to break in smart bitches. They could all be broken one way or another.

'First you have to see my gallery.' He leapt up somewhat sprightly for a man of his age, straightened his yukata and led her towards a large adjoining room.

'You probably thought this place was a ryokan, a traditional Japanese inn. It was in fact built as one, a very expensive refined one in one of the remotest parts of Kyushu. I bought it, modified it for my convenience, and it is my country home.'

'Over the years I have entertained Marilyn Monroe, Sophia Loren, Julie Andrews, Madonna, Dionne Warwick and many others at my home here, as the whim took me.' He opened the door to a large long gallery bedecked with life-size photographs, Hollywood Hall of Fame style. Each big colour photograph was of a movie star lookalike with the lookalike's name inscribed on a brass plaque at the foot of the frame.

'Ahh, Julie Andrews, the Sound of Music, the King and I. An English lady of class. It took me years to find her. Julie is a perfectionist, so how do you find a perfectionist lookalike with the same culture and breeding? It does not come easily. We searched the world; England, America, Australia, South Africa, and found her performing at, of all places, a club at Nakasu, Fukuoka, singing to drunken Japanese businessmen. Of course I had to rescue her.' He paused again expecting an acclamation of some kind from her.

'How many men can claim to have had affairs with so many notable ladies from several generations? I have had more stars in my bed than anyone else in the world. I should be in the Guinness Book of Records, but then it would give the game away and all those people duped in believing I was taking out the real thing would learn my secret. There are only a few who know my secret and I know how to silence big mouths!' he boasted. 'Hugh Hefner might hold the world record for having more beautiful girls than anyone else but the film stars have eluded him, as you might say, like the plague.' He thought he had made his point.

'I understand what you mean, but there is a crucial

difference. I don't believe Mr Hefner threatens or disposes of his girlfriends when he finishes with them. In fact I believe he pays them very well and they are happy to put up with his wrinkled body in return for the cash!' she emphasised, hoping to sound tough and businesslike.

'You can have money, clothes, all these things beyond your wildest dreams for as long as I need you, but you will also be a lookalike as the real person is much older than you. That rather devalues you in some respects and changes you from the latest model, as it were, to perhaps something of antique value,' he replied sarcastically.

He barely got a glance from her. Jenny was morbidly impressed by his twisted and macabre obsession with unobtainable film stars and she was definitely not going to ask what happen to the lookalikes when he tired of them, as she knew that was what he was expecting. He knew what was going through her mind.

'You might wonder what happened to all these beautiful people. If this were an Alfred Hitchcock movie then I would say I had them all stuffed for eternal display, and take you to my basement where you could see their mummified remains. Ha ha ha…,' he roared at his own tasteless joke and ended abruptly when he saw her standing apparently motionless, and more interested in a small piece of furniture supporting another origami arrangement in a very expensive vase. She had seen a TV documentary on the SAS and learned that members were told to focus on an object and concentrate their mind on it when under torture. This was mental torture and she was not about to give way, even one inch to him.

'Yes, the vase is very expensive and very old, so be

careful not to knock it over,' he said.

'You and I are going to have to get along for quite a while, and two-way communication is a prerequisite. I find that after a stint of solitary confinement people like to talk to anyone. It saves them from going mad,' he added.

'I would have thought intellectual compatibility was an essential prerequisite for any worthwhile relationship.' She said this as though addressing a world audience.

'If I put you in a dog kennel for a week or two I imagine you would bark and chase any bone I care to throw your way,' she said icily.

'That's good, that is very good. You see we have begun to communicate. Maybe you are right but you are hardly likely to have the chance to put me in a dog house,' he added with a laugh.

She suddenly noted a small panel at the bottom of every picture. Within the panel were two samples of body hair, plaited neatly. Jenny shivered as though she had walked over someone's grave.

'Oh yes, I see what you are looking at. I insist on a physical memento of all my stars. You will see on the right hand side a hair sample from the head, and on the left a sample of pubic hair. It has always fascinated me how the hair colour of Europeans can differ between pubic hair and their hair on their heads.'

'Later I will take you to my theatre and show you films of all these stars performing and greeting me. You will be convinced I was received in Hollywood and other high places by the real people when you see it. I have fooled many of my business competitors and customers with this and you will appreciate there is a very strong business angle to this. It's is not what you call just personal titillation. There is a twin gallery to this one which is full of Japanese and Asian "film stars" but it will not interest you.'

'When anyone doubts my film star connections I bring my star of the day with me. You will come too, and perhaps meet senior Japanese Diet men in our Parliament, or foreign leaders from Asian countries. It is great fun! Of course these Diet men and senior businessmen are generally very old men who in their youth lusted after Eartha Kitt, and they will admire my ability to find someone who reminds them so much of their youth.'

'Eartha Kitt has been a very elusive lady. I searched the world for her lookalike 40 years ago all in vain. So now I intend to enjoy her company as she was 40 years ago in her prime. It will be a first for me, a journey into the past, as I have made a habit of always having a film star of the time. If it works out I might seek others from the past like Greta Garbo, Vivien Leigh, Elizabeth Taylor etc. It's a thought, they had a lot of style and class not like most of the scatter-brained stars of today,' he mused to himself.

'If you think about reneging on this arrangement I have to advise we have done our research. We have full details of your family in Welshpool. I am sure your parents will not want you to come to any harm, and you also will not want them to be hurt in any way, so the best thing is to co-operate and be rewarded for your efforts.' He gave her an icy, body-piercing stare to emphasise his point.

'I will give you the night to think about this and in the morning you will be free to call your parents, and I am sure they will confirm that it is best for you to be co-operative. There is of course a small reward in it for them too.'

He looked at his watch and said, 'This is enough for now, I have a business meeting. You can retire to your room for the night. I have had my staff lay out a complete wardrobe of Eartha Kitt's clothes and you will find a large file and DVD about her life. I expect you to read and digest it all so that we can have perfect performances.'

'What business do you have to discuss?' she shot at him, catching him unawares. He fell for it and replied, 'Oh some boring thing In Fukuoka in connection with a real estate company we have an interest in. The Mayor has proved a bit troublesome and has been trying to embarrass us.'

Jenny suppressed any inclination to ask more, which could perhaps compromise herself later. She was greatly relieved to be rid of him for the night. It would give her more time to think out an escape route and other means of fighting him off, but his comments about her parents were very worrying. She would do almost anything to see they were not hurt. He was a creep, a maniac obsessive, who wanted total control all the time, with a clear, cruel ruthless streak and most probably a serial killer. The mama-san appeared almost from nowhere to take her to her room and warned her not to think of escape as she would be guarded by a Yakuza all the time until 'ichiban boss' was able to trust her.

She wanted to cry in desperation but her anger overcame that desire. She recollected a few stories about female spies in the Second World War who became case-hardened by their experiences and hatred of the Nazis. They never gave up. She would be like that too, thinking always of getting even and escaping, that was positive. Deep inside her she knew some, if not all, of her predecessors must have been murdered. It was probably the only way this maniac obsessive could remove them from his mind. She shuddered but thought to herself, anger will keep me alive, and fear will kill me.

There was nothing so new about this creep. She remembered the legend of the Sultana Scheherazade who found herself possessed by the Sultan Schariar, who had the nasty habit of killing all his wives and mistresses after his first night with them. She was a smart lady and she told never-ending stories which he found so enthralling that he had to keep her alive, day by day, to hear the next episode.

She tried to remember who put this ancient, Middle Eastern legend to music, and easily remembered the music but not the composer. Then it came to her, it must have been Rimsky-Korsakov, or 'Rip-her-corsets-off,' as she used to remember him. She laughed to herself. Yes, Scheherazade would be her icon and when things got desperate, she would hum the some of the best-known parts to herself. Sleep came easily after that.

⌘⌘⌘

At Hiroshima, Perry and the rest of the Mereleigh Record Club had just checked into their hotel for the evening, and Herewini had given him a call to brief him about the need for Perry to make a request to Japanese

Customs at Fukuoka for assistance in tracing Jenny. Perry was a bit cool at first. 'I know Rick is well into this, and you too I can see, but doesn't Japan have one of the most efficient police forces and best customs services in the world? What on earth can I do to help?' he exclaimed.

'Just one thing an email will come through via the hotel to you saying what you should request. Just copy it, sign it and fax it to the Fukuoka Customs Department. I have a Japanese Customs contact, Saita-san, who can do all sorts of things to help if they get a request from a British national. You know how bureaucracy works, someone has to initiate things and that is going to be you,' he explained.

'Did you ever watch MASH, Herewini? If so you will remember the little clerk with glasses who used to hand his CO a sheaf of blank pages, and ask him to sign each one on the basis that the CO need not be bothered with the text. This sounds a bit like that to me,' Perry joked.

'Exactly right, you're quick on the uptake for a cop,' Herewini jibed, knowing Perry would comply.

'There is just one thing. If I do this, I feel I must also register concern with the British Embassy, even if Rick has already been down that track,' Perry insisted.

'It's OK by me mate, and it even sounds sensible!' Herewini added, 'I can even see Adam scribbling a line or two to the Guardian, updating the saga of missing Jenny saying "ex-Buckinghamshire detective now hot on the trail of the missing Welsh Girl." There is also a photo opportunity in this for you too.'

'Get off the grass, Herewini, don't push your luck or I

will pull out of it,' Perry warned light-heartedly. Herewini had got what he wanted from Perry and finished with a warm 'thanks' and 'spot ya at Fukuoka, mate!'

At Fukuoka, Tanaka-san had organised his rugby men to discreetly check out every nightclub known to be associated with the Yakuza clan that had kidnapped Jenny. He organised two rugby men per club and was glad that they all fitted the right age group of middle to senior businessmen and, of course, were experienced drinkers so they could quietly slip in and find out if any of them had acts or hostesses that resembled Jenny's.

Flanker had supplied the list of addresses obtained from Inspector Mori's research at Tokyo. It was a more extensive list of clubs than Flanker imagined and he was more than pleased to have the rugby irregulars helping out. Herewini was camped out at the Fukuoka Customs headquarter helping Saita-san, or rather waiting for Saita-san to get some results from computer searches. Saita-san was working unofficially and burning the midnight oil in the knowledge that his efforts would be approved the next day once Perry's fax had come though and been approved.

To be honest he had at first thought that Herewini's request was a bit of a wild goose chase, perhaps his personal search for a girlfriend who had erred from the straight and narrow. Saita-san had tracked Jenny's arrival at Tokyo and easily traced her sponsor to a well-known nightclub organisation with known Yakuza connections. Nothing unusual in that, he knew, and the addresses of the Tokyo establishments owned by it had, he had been told by Flanker, more or less checked out. This resulted in a lead from Tanaka-san's new girl friend, Emi, suggesting she had been brought to Fukuoka.

'So where do we go from here?' He was a bit flummoxed as his area was immigration and visas, not the vice circuit of Fukuoka. He was dabbling with the computer, basically amusing himself with miscellaneous searches trying to find an angle, when a couple of things fell out of the system so to speak.

By chance he had pulled a file on missing European women entertainers. He noticed that, over the decades, more than a few of them had worked for the Yakuza clan and overstayed their work visas, so he downloaded and collated that information. He had a baker's dozen, 13 of them, over a period of about three decades. He even had a file of their pictures and, there was something familiar about most of them, and it could not be that he had seen their pictures in the papers or on TV as most of them had disappeared long before he joined the customs service. He printed out the files and chucked the photos to Herewini.

'Herewini-san, what do you think of these, they seem a bit familiar somehow?' he suggested.

Herewini gave them a quick but careful appraisal.

'I don't know, except this one is a dead ringer for Julie Andrews, and that one the spitting image of Madonna', he observed.

'Hai soo desu, you are right they are, and in this one who is one of the exceptions, we have lookalike for Ella Fitzgerald. My father had all her vinyl records and the covers had her picture on them. I always remember a face. Might be we have a lead somehow?' he suggested.

'Only if this Yakuza group we are interested in employed them and specialised in lookalike film stars and entertainers. Perhaps Flanker could check that out with the cops tomorrow?' he said.

But this girl Jenny, is she a lookalike?' Saita-san asked.

'I don't know but Adam, or more likely Rick, should know as she is the daughter of his cousin's mate in Wales. I will try to call him at the hotel,' Herewini said.

Rick had just returned to the hotel after a long meeting with the Fukuoka Record Club group where he had accompanied Andy and Fran to sort out the events. As a travel agent, he was repeatedly made acutely aware of how a lot of people thought events and travel were easy to arrange, and just how complex, let alone time-consuming, things could actually become, especially when several parties were involved. The night's meeting was no exception. He had just walked into his room and kicked his shoes off when the phone rang.

'Hello,' he said irritably, but Herewini's news and enthusiasm soon overcame his tiredness and mild depression, and he agreed instantly to ring Jenny's parents to see if she had played any lookalike parts. His cousin at Welshpool had given Rick the number of Mr Ted Jones, Jenny's dad. The line was clear and the connection almost instantaneous.

'Hello, Ted Jones 'ere, what can I do for you?'

Rick got to the point before Ted could say, 'How b'ist 'ee,' a Welsh border greeting that he had picked up since his marriage to a Welsh lady. Ted sounded very tired and extremely anxious. He would clutch at anything which gave hope, and Rick could imagine Jenny's mum hanging on to every word, not wishing to miss the slightest nuance. Yes, he told Rick, Jenny had done some lookalike stuff, principally Eartha Kitt. She was very good at it and had won some acclaim at drama college in London, and also done a few Eartha gigs for cash.

'That's good, that's very good. It's the sort of lead we need just now. I don't want to say any more as we are getting very good support from the Japanese police and immigration officials, and we even have a Kiwi customs officer, an old mate of mine, Herewini, here on holiday helping us out,' Rick told them.

'You will ring us as frequently as you can please, to keep us posted, it's one hell of a worry, you see. You can't really imagine the hell we are going through and the distance doesn't help either, being so far away,' Ted pleaded anxiously.

'Of course, certainly, and if she should turn up okay out of the blue with a phone or text to home, please let me know too a.s.a.p,' Rick said trying to relieve them of some of the worry.

'Yes, yes. My God, don't we wish that to happen! There is one thing and I am not sure over the phone is the best way to tell you, her mammy here is glaring at me and is a bit worried about it, but anyway I want to tell you and you should know,' he hesitated.

'Okay, fire away Ted, I am all ears, the more info the better.' Rick assured him that it was unlikely that anyone would be listening on their call.

'Well, you see, it was all a bit strange. About three days

ago these strangers drove by in some swank car. I have to be honest with you, they looked like some East European gangsters, and we have plenty of Slavs now working in Welshpool just now so they could have been just local Slavs, so to speak. Anyway, they drove past twice, like they lost their way but came back a third time. I was in the garden with Mum here, and they came to our gate and asked if we were Jenny's parents.'

At the mention of Slavs, Rick's heart almost stopped. He recollected the dead Japanese at the Rising Sun Hotel at Newtown and Detective Inspector Roberts' comment that that hotel had been used by local Slav mobsters. He felt sick in his gut at the thought that by holding back on this information to his friends on the tour he may have in some way hindered the chances of finding Jenny alive. Before he could decide on telling Ted about this Ted cut in.

'Well, I can tell you our hearts missed a beat on hearing that, wondering what was coming next like. So we said "yes" to them and they simply said, "Don't do anything stupid, they know who you are," and left!'

'It put a great shiver down our spines, it did, and made us think perhaps Jenny has been taken to East Europe or somewhere else other than Japan. 'We been too scared to go to the police, there is so much at stake, you understand, but anyway we told you now...' he paused, and Rick cut in.

'This is just off the top of my head, but I am sure the police would advise the same. Get your bags packed now, and drive straight to the Welshpool police HQ and repeat the information, then go and stay at a safe house until we sort it out.'

'I can't let the cat out of the bag here as I don't know enough of what is happening, except I am told we are dealing with some very big fish in Japan who have tentacles reaching around the world. Promise me now that you will do this before I hang up?'

'Yes, yes, of course, we knew in our hearts we should do something like this, but we have been paralysed with fear. We will be out of here within an hour. Thank you boyo Rick, thank you and take care of yourself.' Ted hung up in haste, wishing to make as quick an exit as possible.

Rick could feel the adrenaline pumping. He was feeling guilty at not telling Ted about the Rising Sun incident but he had promised Detective Inspector Roberts not to talk about the dead Japanese man. He thought hard and long about telling Herewini about the Rising Sun incident, but decided against it because of his promise to the police, but it was gnawing away in his stomach like a cancer.

'What arseholes, what fucking arseholes! Jesus I hope we can bang these bastards up,' he said to himself.

He toyed with the idea of ringing Inspector Roberts but as Ted had decided immediately to go to the Welshpool police the local Welshpool cops would start putting two and two together very quickly, he believed. He could not imagine Jenny getting involved in local prostitution and frequenting the Rising Sun but he was sure in his gut that the dead Japanese man had a hand in this somehow.

He rang Herewini straight away to tell of the Eartha Kitt impersonations and threat to her parents. Rick could sense Herewini getting pumped up with anger as he spoke. Herewini let loose a string of obscenities and Rick cut in to say, 'I hope they don't let you off the leash too soon, or at least until we know exactly who we are chasing. In your mood you could trample hundreds under your feet in a search for an offender!'

Herewini blew off steam over the phone. 'I am out of here to see Flanker and hopefully get a bit more Japanese police action. Catch you later,' he said and hung up. Rick poured himself a single malt whisky and was about to step into the shower when the phone rang again.

'My God, isn't that enough for one day?' he said to himself.

'Hullo, is that Mr Rick Foster?' asked a very proper English lady's voice on an international call.

'Yes,' he replied, thinking that only the English call him Mr, to everyone else he was just Rick Foster.

'Please stand by, I will put Mr Birchall on the line,' she replied.

'Who the hell is he when he is at home?' Rick said to himself.

A pleasant and happy male voice announced itself as Adam Birchall, a director of UK Visions Movies, the company which had made a film about the record club's exploits in New Zealand. Rick vaguely remembered the man he had met but once. Adam was able to talk to Rick on first name terms and that cut to the chase a bit.

'Rick, I understand you are organising the current Mereleigh tour to Japan. First this is rather late. We apologise sincerely for the great communication stuff-up that was made and which appears to have given you all a lot of grief.' Rick grunted a cynical acknowledgment that it had caused the odd problem or two.

'Well, to be frank, we have been hellishly slow in sorting this out with our colleagues in Japan, and the upshot of it all is we want to help and we thought the best way we could help is to round up a few stars that took part in the film to come out and add some razzamatazz to the event?' he said, with what Rick imagined would be a big smile on his face and his feet up on a desk.

Rick was on the verge of telling him to get fucked when his better judgment took over. He explained in his most tactful, customer-conscious tones that without the studio's help and with heaps of obstacles in their way, the Mereleigh Record Club group and their Japanese hosts had put together most of the shattered pieces of an almost totally wrecked tour and had actually rebuilt their ship, so to speak, and were back in business with a big event coming up in two days in Fukuoka.

'The last thing they want is for someone to come down a red carpet at the last minute and steal their thunder. All these little guys, in fact the real people of this world that make things happen day after boring day, are on the point of achieving greatness in the face of much adversity. Please don't do something that will destroy their moment of glory. They bear you no grudges nor blame, and accept it was a human stuff-up but if you must do something please bear what I have said in mind.

'It's very late here in Japan, and I have already been helping friends in Britain find a missing daughter so am very tired. Can I suggest you ring Andy Cole at this hotel in the morning? I will talk to him and maybe we can find a way in which your stars can help?' Rick waited to hear that Adam Birchall had agreed to do that and to hear his 'sincere' thanks and 'total' understanding before hanging up.

CHAPTER 13

Andy woke early and greeted the day enthusiastically despite a wearing session with the Fukuoka Record Club folk trying to sort out the events for their big night. He learned that they planned to bring in a number of looka-like bands for the occasion plus have some invitation karaoke and a competition for the best singer. The looka-like bands and performers were not eligible for this.

Andy glanced at his watch, it was barely 6am, but he was wide awake. It was a bright spring morning with blossom on the trees. Ban-san said the day after the event they would experience sakura at a chosen park and be able to drink sake outside, and take many photographs of the cherry blossoms. After that they would be taken to the Arita pottery village an hour or so out of Fukuoka to see this traditional village with its many tiny streams, water wheels and shops.

Andy had already decided to extend his stay in Japan another few days so he and those who came to Fukuoka straight from Kyoto could visit Hiroshima. He hoped the rest would stay on as well, after all the tour to this point had been very stressful in many ways. He glanced down a newly printed programme of events for the big night.

To his surprise he saw that a local Mini Minor car club was going to chauffeur all the VIPs and also the Mereleigh Record Club guests to the hotel venue. He noted that there were a few stretched Minis that would be used for the Mayor and a few others. A local motorbike club that rode only classic bikes like British Triumphs, Norton Commandos, BSAs, and American Harley Davidsons was going to provide a motorised escort.

'My God, a lot of thought and effort has gone into this,' he reflected to himself. 'No wonder poor old Nomura-san topped himself when it all came apart.'

The lookalike bands included a local copy of the Beatles that had been given top billing, as well as the Beach Boys, Elvis, Del Shannon, Rick Nelson, Bill Haley and the Comets, and many other lookalike soloists. The Mayor of Fukuoka would welcome the visitors and the editor of the Nishi Nippon Shimbun newspaper would also speak. Andy would be called on to reply, as would Ban-san of the Fukuoka Record Club. That would be followed by the usual Japanese 'kampai' toast and things would really get under way.

There was a special note that the Mayor and not other VIPs would pay tribute to the Nomura family and pass on condolences. Andy noted it was normal for a widow and family to take part in this sort of thing so soon after a death in the family but Mrs Nomura-san wanted to come at least for a brief period to witness the efforts of her late husband and all his members. The note mentioned Mrs Nomura would sit at the Mayor's table, next to the latter's wife.

Andy approved this and noted that he, too, would pay tribute to the Nomuras. He could see why Chuck was so impressed after the meeting with the Fukuoka Record Club folk last night. He was just taking his first gulp of coffee when the phone rang. A super-polite English female voice asked if it was Mr Andrew Cole. He replied in the affirmative and was greeted by, 'Hi there, it's Adam Birchall here, you might remember me? I am from the film company that did the movie on your group.'

Andy listened rather cynically to Adam Birchall's excited tones and proposals and had only just hung up when Rick rang him. Andy told Rick that Mr Birchall said he, Rick, had approved his proposal to send a few movie stars to Fukuoka to help add to the occasion and he had already got them on a flight yesterday morning! Rick was somewhat stunned by Birchall's presumption and cheek, but he was pacified by Andy, who said he was sure they could control the situation and use the stars to good effect.

'I am not a great one for ideas but when Birchall was talking I had the thought that maybe we could do something in Ohori Koen park the next day for the public, a free thing, with voluntary donations to the charity and the stars could be there to sign autographs etc. Perhaps one or two lookalike bands will volunteer to put on an outdoor concert,' Andy said with a huge naïve grin on his face.

'Have you the slightest idea how much effort something like this takes? The Japanese like weeks, if not many months, to plan things. Planning is an essential part of the culture, they don't tend to be flash-in-the-pan, knee-jerk people. Suddenness and uncertainty tends to worry them,' Rick reprimanded.

Andy was undaunted. 'Anyway, Mr Birchall said he would approach Fukuoka City Hall about this and get his company's agents, the Universal Film company, to help set it up, and I was simply to ring the Mayor's office and let him know about the idea.'

'Christ almighty, can you imagine what the Mayor and his aides will think? If they don't die of shock, they will all go into blue funks and secret themselves away, possibly even into long-term hibernation!' Rick was staggered by the impossibility of the suggestion and Andy's naivety thinking it was easy to do.

'Well, all they have to do is make available or provide a sound shell at Ohori Koen, set up a lot of portable toilets, if they don't have enough already, and organise a clean-up gang to tidy up after the event, and of course notify the police so a few extra policemen can be on hand to assist with crowd control,' Andy added.

'You firmly believe this?' Rick was totally flabbergasted.

'As soon as it's 9 am, I will ring the Mayor's office and you can be with me to witness it,' he concluded.

'Witness yes, party to, very definitely not, so don't mention my name,' Rick mumbled. He was going to breakfast and walked out of the room shaking his head in disbelief.

Adam, too, had received an early call from Adam Birchall. It seemed Birchall had contacted the Guardian to tell them of his plan and obtained Adam's number from the Guardian. The purpose of the call was to organise some publicity for the four film stars he was sending. Adam was stunned into near silence and was only able to give monosyllabic replies. It was a fait accompli, what could he do but report on this new addition to the programme?

Michiko had meanwhile downloaded the Fukuoka Record Club's programme on her laptop computer, and was making those enthusiastic noises Japanese ladies make when expressing surprise and joy. It was a kind of high-pitched equivalent to Japanese males' belly talk. Adam felt he was about two days behind reality. The events of the past week had taken their toll, his mind had a kind of log jam of information. Japan was a major, life-altering experience for him. He had made commitments to Michiko and he had struck big-time national newspaper journalism with his newsfeed to the Guardian on the events of the Mereleigh Record Club, and a few pieces on the search for Jenny.

Michiko gauged his mood. 'You look like you need a holiday!'

'A holiday today means another three days to catch up on. No, this film star thing is a new angle, and I suppose it will all fall into place and add to the news value, but last night I was thinking about Jenny Jones and feeling that perhaps we could do more.'

He and Michiko agreed they would each run a piece on the Fukuoka Record Club's programme. They had some great ideas: the Mini Minor cavalcade, the lookalike bands etc that would go down a treat with the British public and really put Fukuoka on the map in Britain.

'Tomorrow we have the funeral of Nomura-san to cover,' she reminded him, 'and we must do our best for him and his family. I want to make that my priority and then after I think I can also do a story on Jenny based on the possibility she is somewhere in Kyushu. This is Nishi Nippon Shimbun circulation area and in addition to it being a worthy story, will also have local news value,' she emphasised.

'How many times have you a journalist sat down at your desk and wondered what you are going to cover tomorrow after you finish a big story? Depending on what happens to Jenny, we have a further three days work here on the Mereleigh story, then sadly it is back to the UK for me and an absence of some weeks or months before you can join me. Let's try to keep some special time for ourselves in the next few days even if it is just lunch together. The nights we have together, but I like being with you in the day time too.' Adam gave her a pleading look.

'My parents will come to the funeral tomorrow, you will have a chance to meet them, so please do. They will not kill you because you are a foreigner with a big nose,' she joked.

'Me, big nose, it's tiny, what do you mean?' he said in mock horror.

'All Westerners have big noses as far as Japanese and Chinese are concerned, just as all Japanese and Chinese have tiny slits for eyes in the Western view. That is traditionally how we cartoon each other. Of course it's totally racist. By Western standards your nose might be small but it is a tiny bit big by Japan standards, whereas my eyes are perfectly, what do you say, almond-shaped,' she giggled.

At this time Herewini and Flanker met at Herewini's hotel for a working breakfast. This was a kind of new concept to Flanker who never found eating breakfast work, but foreigners were strange in some respects. At breakfast Herewini told him of Saita-san's research which showed a number of film star lookalike Westerners had gone missing in similar circumstances over the last few decades, most if not all from clubs or establishments owned by the same Yakuza-controlled company.

To his surprise Flanker said Inspector Mori was already on to this as Saita-san had communicated this to him and also the fact that Jenny Jones was an Eartha Kitt lookalike.

'You mean I did not have to shout you this breakfast to tell you or get your support!' Herewini exclaimed in horror. 'That's one fully cooked American breakfast worth about four thousand yen down the tube!' he added.

'Someone told me you are not true Maori but brown Scotsman,' Flanker protested. 'Now I believe this, you are true, mean bastard Scotsman,' Flanker ribbed him.

'Yeah, I have some Scottish ancestry but the way you cleaned up your plates you must be descended from a Calcutta shitehawk in a previous life. There is not a crumb left of anything!' Herewini exclaimed.

'What is a shite hawk?' Flanker asked in wonder.

'It's the great-grandfather of all vultures and lives in Calcutta, where it eats anything and everything, dead dogs that have been lying in the street infested with maggots and flies, tape worms out of decaying pigs, you name it, it eats it,' Herewini told him.

Flanker roared with laughter, 'You not just a mean Scotsman, you are a bullshitting bastard, and I know what that is!' Flanker got a call on his mobile phone. It was brief with a lot of 'hai's and 'soo desu's'.

'We have some developments. Inspector Mori from Tokyo will arrive about mid-morning at Fukuoka airport. We are to meet him and will meet a specialist who can build a picture, or rather a profile of the sort of person or persons who might be kidnapping these girls.'

'You mean a profiler,' Herewini said.

Flanker said, 'My inspector does not want this information or the course of the inquiries to be disclosed to anyone else at this time except to Perry. As an ex-cop he might be useful in liaising with the UK police. In that regard we hope you can get Perry to come to Fukuoka as soon as possible.'

'He will love me for that, he is already pissed off that I dragged him into this to request Fukuoka Customs assistance in this inquiry. I told him it was just a matter of signing a fax letter and faxing it to Saita-san....' Herewini trailed off knowing Perry would agree but it might cost Herewini more than a few drinks for his voluntary contribution.

Inspector Mori's flight from Haneda, Tokyo was spot

on time. He travelled light, just a carry-on grip that contained some overnight gear and his lap top. Herewini was impressed by this mid-50s inspector of average height with a professional judo player's body and his wise, smiling humane face. He could see Mori could be very tough when necessary but was first of all an understanding person and his knowledge of human nature had probably helped him greatly up the promotion chain.

'So you are the world famous New Zealand customs officer who captured the big New Zealand smuggling boss. I saw the movie and wondered how someone so young could be so wise and tough,' Inspector Mori said with a twinkle in his eyes.

'Ohh, the film was just crap really, it was nothing that dangerous.' Herewini was genuinely embarrassed by the flattery.

'Let's take a taxi, we can talk in the taxi and save money and time. I take it you don't have a car here.' He shot a glance at Flanker, who nodded in agreement.

The Inspector had heard about the operation run by Tanaka-san and his rugby men, and asked Flanker to arrange a meeting as soon as possible with Tanaka and Yoshi, and he told Herewini he had been in contact with Saita-san so Saita-san was standing by as well. A meeting room at Fukuoka police HQ had been set aside for Inspector Mori, and Saita-san was already waiting there when they arrived. Flanker had been in touch with Tanaka-san and he and Yoshi, anticipating some debriefing, were on standby for the meeting.

Everyone exchanged name cards again as it was a first

meeting for a few of them, and took their seats, and were ready to go within about ten minutes of the inspector's arrival. Herewini told the inspector that if possible he would like to leave at midday as he had a special appointment at Nomura-san's funeral, or rather just after it, and while he had never met Nomura-san, he was going to do something there as a favour to Andy and the Mereleigh group in respect to Nomura-san. The inspector gave Herewini the nod and said that everyone would be out of the meeting room within ninety minutes as it was booked for another meeting.

The police profiler arrived. He was a man in his early sixties, of very academic appearance, balding with long grey side hair extending below his ears, and wearing a slightly aged Donegal tweed jacket and casual trousers. He had taken off a Breton beret as he entered, nodded to everyone, and absentmindedly forgot to present his own name card but received cards from everyone else. No-one pointed this out to him and Inspector Mori deferred to him as sensei throughout, using the term of respect with the literal meaning of teacher.

Saita-san opened the meeting, 'We have discovered there was a pattern of missing Western women over two decades all of whom seemed to have worked for clubs, or persons associated with a certain Yakuza sect. They were all dead lookalikes for well-known film stars. I have this file of photos of the lookalikes.'

The sensei profiler nodded throughout Saita-san's address and made a slight grunting noise at the end of it which indicated he would like to make comment. Inspector Mori immediately deferred to the sensei.

'I am sorry to have to interrupt now but Saita-san has already scanned and sent all relevant material to me late last night and it might save time if I spoke now as I have given some thought to the matter.' He had come to some initial conclusions.

'In the first instance, I believe we are looking for one man rather than several and this might make it much easier for everyone. Then it seems clear this man has a connection to the clubs and other persons connected to this Yakuza sect. I am sure everyone here has deduced this already but I have to restate the obvious as it my starting point. The other reasonable deduction is this man is both very influential and must be in his 60s as some of the first lookalike stars would have been at or near their peak 20 to 30 years ago if he still fancied them.'

'We can't say he prefers any particular type of women other than Western stars as they include blondes with big breasts, dark latin-type ladies, and at least one black American singer. Also these stars or lookalikes ranged in age from the early 20s to nearly 40. He does not seem to have an age preference either.

'So we can only say he likes to have glamorous film stars around him as they build his ego and make him feel important. He has, I am a bit ashamed to say, the Japanese 'copy cat' syndrome, that is if you cannot get the best you copy it, so we can say that, while he is rich, he is not so rich or desirable a person to be able to date or marry film stars, so he does the next best thing.

'Is he doing this just to satisfy himself or perhaps only to impress some people and deceive them, or else supply them to other people to exhibit at certain functions, private or public? We don't know if it is business and pleasure but it is logical for this kind of person as the leasing out of these ladies, or using them as escorts, could earn him money and help him secure business deals.

'If this is the case, it would account for the constant turnover and maybe we shall ultimately find more missing lookalikes on police files.' The sensei paused and glanced at Inspector Mori, who indicated his staff were doing this just now and had already turned up several candidates.

The sensei continued, saying the fact that none of these persons or their bodies had been found would seem to indicate that most, if not all, had probably been murdered, and if that was the case, they were definitely being shown off as the real thing, and thus would be a threat to this man's business interests if they blew their cover and identified themselves as lookalikes at a later stage.'

'Another thought, this man has a need to impress by showing off a steady stream of film star girl friends because he has some difficulty with female relationships. He is either ugly or has a strong personality problem that women do not like, or he might hate women because of their sexual influence over men. So maybe we are looking for an ugly man, or one with some big sexual hangups. He is a pimp of sorts but his prostitutes are involuntary lookalikes. We can assume involuntary as none has ever turned up afterwards to tell the tale!

'Like many pimps, he also probably sleeps with his girls. I think therefore it's possible he might have started his life as some sort of high-class Yakuza pimp, supplying girls to Japanese businessmen and politicians, and then hit on this lookalike thing. I suspect he is very powerful within the Yakuza sect and employs just one or two trusted employees to protect his business which is, of course, the girls. But he must also appear respectable and be a senior enough business man to mix with rich persons of influence, and gain access to some notable functions.

'I have one final comment. This Jenny girl does not really fit the profile of a victim. If she is an Eartha Kitt lookalike, she should be quite an old lady in her late seventies now but she is a young girl and only looks like Eartha Kitt when she was at the peak of her career.

'The other aspects fit a club and organisation which is run by the suspect Yakuza group. This man has already progressively updated himself. He even had a Madonna lookalike so why go for a retro look that is clearly not the star? That is the question if it is the same person,' he concluded.

'Oh, I can understand him,' Herewini volunteered. 'When I was a kid back in New Zealand, I always wanted a 1970 Chrysler Valiant, and when I grew up I bought one even though it's now about 30 years old. Maybe this guy had a thing about Eartha Kitt and could never find a lookalike when she was famous, and he is now doing it for personal pleasure.'

'That is a good point, and also some point in favour of an argument that says he only kept the lookalikes for personal pleasure and never showed them off. If we follow your line, Herewini-san, then maybe he has taken her for personal pleasure, and if he has, I feel the temptation to show her off, albeit as a lookalike, will be too great, if he has always done this in the past,' the sensei concluded and glanced at his watch.

Inspector Mori saw the glance and asked if the sensei had another appointment, which he did, that was to give a lecture at Kyushu University in about 30 minutes' time. The sensei was thanked profusely by Inspector Mori, and everyone rose with some going to the meeting room door to bow him out of the premises in the polite Japanese way. Inspector Mori took command of the meeting, saying he supported the sensei's arguments and also took into account Herewini's point.

'From the Japanese police point of view we now have perhaps thirty unsolved murders, discounting of course Jenny, just based on Saita-san's research and what we are now finding on police missing persons files so I have to act, and quite urgently, to solve as many of these disap-pearances as possible, realising the murderer might be still around.'

'That is a priority. Herewini, I have a feeling you might be right but there will be others more senior to me in the police force who might take the line she does not fit the age profile so therefore might just be a missing person who will turn up eventually with an expired work visa. With all this in mind we will continue the search for Jenny and in that regard I must commend the efforts of Tanaka-san's rugby men, you Herewini, and of course Rick, who is now at the funeral, for bringing this to our attention. This is one of the best examples of citizen support I have experienced,' he commented.

Tanaka-san then took the floor. 'I have organised about thirty-five rugby men to visit various bars around Nakasu and Tenjin to find out discreetly if a girl like Jenny was working there or has been heard of.' From this he had obtained two possible leads and the best was from his new girlfriend Emiko, who had made her own inquiries of one or two hostesses and mama-sans she knew at Fukuoka.

It seems one of the more aged mama-sans knew a local Kyushu businessman with alleged Yakuza connections who had taken one or two 'Hollywood stars' to some functions and she thought had even got his name in the Nishi Nippon Shimbun with a picture of the star.

One or two of the rugby men had found a couple of local clubs that had a strong connection with the Tokyo Club Jenny had been at, and said sometimes the Tokyo Club would send foreign girls down to them for a day or two to perform. Inspector Mori said that both leads were good, and instructed Flanker to get the details to see if any connection could be made between this mysterious businessman, his 'Hollywood Stars', and the two clubs. He would ask the Nishi Nippon Shimbun to search its files for any articles or pictures of the possible suspect.

Just then Herewini received a call from Perry on his mobile.

'Where are you?'

'I am at Hakata station and lost. I decided to join you chaps and get into this as soon as possible.' Herewini said 'hold on,' and gave the phone to Inspector Mori. The inspector took the call and told Perry to stand by the statue in front of the station and he would get a police car to pick him up in about ten minutes.' He told Flanker to get it organised.

Inspector Mori then said, 'I have received a file on Jenny from Britain and also some disturbing news that her parents have been frightened off by what looked like a couple of East European gangsters, and they are now staying at a safe house.' He added that he was glad that Perry was here now as he could liaise between himself and the Interpol connection in Britain and speed things up.

⌘⌘⌘

About this time Jenny was up and about and very frightened and depressed. She had slept until about 3am and then she began thinking about the terrible things that might be in store for her. She was certain her captors would get her hooked on drugs if she did not comply with their wishes, and then she would lose control of her life. It would likely be a choice between having to go along with everything, sex and all, with whoever, whenever etc; or being a drug addict.

She made up her mind the former was the better option, for keeping her sensibilities would give her a greater chance of escape no matter how shocking it was. She would have to become tough, very tough, very quickly but keep a veneer of innocence and compliance on the surface.

She was given a western-style breakfast by herself in a pleasant tatami room with big glass sliding doors and superb view of mountains, forest and fast-running streams. This would be an ideal place to honeymoon with the man of your choice but not this monster who had so far never disclosed his name.

Her breakfast was barely finished when the mama-san summoned her to another room where her captor sat looking cruel, smug and all powerful. With barely a glance in her direction he passed her a telephone and said she could ring her parents. She hesitated, suspecting some trick or sick joke.

'Go on, it will not bite you. You do everything. Ring international to be sure you get the right number, then you can speak to them yourself so you can be totally sure it's the right number!' he commanded. Jenny hated this. She knew there had to be a sick catch somewhere and she also worried in case the Japanese gangster had got to her parents some way, so she prepared herself for the worse.

After a second or two she could hear the phone ringing at her parents' small, modern detached house at Welshpool, and she knew it would be early evening and her parents could be expected to be home watching TV. The home phone was lifted and her Dad asked in rather worried tones who it was. He had been advised by the police to answer all calls as they had tapped his line to try and trace the calls.

His voice did not rejoice, as it should have done, at hearing his lost daughter on the line but gave a warm and weary acknowledgment and asked her if things were okay as there had been a few problems at home. Jenny could see that her captor had picked up another phone and was listening in, so she said she was OK in a kind of tired and worried fashion that indicated she was not, and was a nuance she hoped had not been picked up at her end.

Her father cut in briskly and said, 'That's nice,' in sarcastic tones and added, 'You must co-operate with your new boss. I think it might be in the best interests of everyone.' His tone was worried and concerned. She was about to ask why but guessed the phone line might be cut before any answer could be given. In any case her father continued and gave her the signal she wanted to know.

'We have had one or two problems here but we are okay after the storm. We have moved out for a day or so and had the phone diverted. That is all I can say for now, love. Hope to see you fit and well very soon,' and he hung up, or the line was cut. Her captor smiled at her in a boastful, bullying manner, revelling in the control he had over her life.

She was not so much interested in that but at the mention of a storm and the phone being diverted. She had seen the BBC TV world news and weather forecast on the TV set in her room, and there was no mention of any storms in Britain over the past few days. In fact it was the reverse; the weather had been unseasonably warm and calm. The question was, had they moved out of their own volition or under pressure? If it was the former maybe there had been some sort of tip-off from the UK police or others, if the latter then the Yakuza had them totally in their control. She wanted to believe the former but felt it was more likely that her parents had been got at.

She wanted to remain nonplussed by the news to keep the Yakuza guessing a bit in case her parents had deliberately moved out, and quickly decided she would try to indicate that she was not very close to her parents and that might take some pressure off them if they were being held captive.

'Oh, thank you for allowing me to make the call. It was not necessary, we are not very close. They did not want me to go on the stage at all and I have led my own life for the past few years. They only tend to think of the money I might earn for them,' she lied.

He seemed pleased and satisfied enough, but his demeanour was always snake-like, and totally untrustworthy, so he was probably cursing that she had not broken down and pleaded with him to let her go, she thought. If she was not disadvantaged in this situation she could have enjoyed this cat-and-mouse psycho game with him.

'This morning you are going to see some DVDs of mine and the other 'stars' who have performed for me so you can see what is expected of you. Also you might call me Dai. It's a sort of version of my given name which is Japanese and not Welsh, although it sounds like the Welsh Dai.

'You must learn fast as we might have a public presentation to make in the next few days which you will attend. In the meantime I will leave you here with my house guard, and the mama-san will take care of you.' With that he quickly withdrew and the guard came in to set the DVDs going.

The DVDs were quite professionally shot, obviously designed to be shown to select house guests to impress others. There were scenes of Dai at a ship launching at Nagasaki, with a Julie Andrews double, and at a Kyoto cherry blossom festival, with Marilyn Monroe on his arm. That seemed to be the most dated of them. There was a pretty recent one of him squiring Madonna around the

Hiroshima A-Bomb Peace Park and inspecting the hundreds of paper cranes hanging up to bring good health to the maimed radiation victims. They were all dead ringers for the real stars and it would take a forensics expert to pick out the differences on this DVD footage, she felt.

She wondered how the Japanese could be taken in by this. The media must have Hollywood columnists who would have some idea where the real stars were, and it would take only one exposure to show him up as a fraud. He must do some research to find out where the real stars are at the time and then make an appearance when the real person has gone bush or is totally incommunicado, she felt.

In her case she was going to be a clear lookalike, so where was the advantage in this for him? It would have to be a come down. She was confused and could not find the answer. She got bored seeing the rest of the footage but noted that his appearances with the stars were always in Japan and often quite brief, just short photo opportunities while people were on the move.

The important thing was that her parents must know of her plight. That was good and bad, good that someone else in the world knew but bad, because it seemed to have placed them under threat as well. She decided to play along and co-operate for the time being. There were no demands for her to hop into bed with him yet, and that was good.

⌘⌘⌘

At Fukuoka City Hall Andy and Rick had an early morning appointment with the Mayor before Nomura-san's funeral. As they travelled up in the lift for their appointment with the Mayor, Rick remonstrated with Andy about the impracticality of asking the Mayor to stage a one-off, outdoor concert in Ohori Koen.

'It's not only bloody impractical, it's also a kind of abuse of our friendship with him to ask him to do the impossible. You have to understand one thing about Japanese culture and that is it's is a big no-no to actually say 'no' to someone, and everyone in Japan will offer an answer like. 'It's a little bit difficult', or 'We might have to consult some more people', but the Mayor will be put on the spot by you and feel terrible just having to give you one of these polite 'no can do' answers. That is the point,' Rick said.

Andy was feeling somewhat chastened, and was having major doubts now about it. He admitted privately he really knew nothing of Japanese culture and should have listened to Rick yesterday before calling up City Hall.

'All right, no need to rub it in. Perhaps it was a misjudgement on my part but with barely a week in Japan I cannot expect to be an expert on Japanese culture and I thought it worth a try. So maybe we should pull out and cancel our visit, pleading temporary sickness or something,' he pleaded.

'Not a chance. In Japan you keep appointments even if you have to be carted in on a stretcher, especially with mayors. That would be even worse, and remember it's my reputation as well and I do business with Fukuoka!' Rick was taking control.

'We will go in there and I will lead the conversation

and try to think up another reason why we wanted to see the Mayor and hope he forgets your request. God knows what I will ask him but of course we have all of four minutes for me to dream something up between now and then.' Rick looked skywards in desperation and frustration as if pleading for heavenly inspiration.

Almost as soon as they exited the lift on the Mayor's floor, a neat, uniformed Japanese lady in her late twenties greeted them politely in slightly American accented English and took them to a waiting room. She was a distraction for Rick because she was beautiful and her movements so perfect.

'Have you noticed, Andy, how every human gesture in Japan is a piece of well-practised theatre. Just look at that lady who greeted us, her perfect, small, dark navy blue dress, sparkling white uniform blouse, not a hair out of place, shoes, stockings, make-up, as if she was ready to meet the Queen. And her body language was completely choreographed as if by a Hollywood director training a starlet for a short walk-on role. Her face the hand gestures and the words. Not one word too many, not one too few.

'As perfect as piece of Japanese porcelain. I bet if we went to City Hall in New Zealand or Britain some fussy old busybody would bumble over to us and treat us as some major inconvenience to her day. Everything in Japan is about style, doing things in style. See the businessmen accidentally meeting someone they know in a street. Many inevitably exchange business cards even though they already have each others' cards because they like to bow and the presentation ceremony which goes along with it. They bow on the phone to the invisible person at the other end. I often wonder if they bow to their wives before and after having sex,' Rick exclaimed.

'Give it a rest. For a man of your age it's pathetic, you only seem to have one thing on your mind. How about thinking up a reason for us being here? This lady will shortly send us in to see His Worship the Mayor,' Andy reminded Rick.

'Thank you for waiting, the Mayor is ready to see you now,' the office lady announced with a pleasant smile and slight arm gesture to direct them through an already opened door.

Rick indicated for Andy to go first, and Andy tried to insist that Rick went first

'You are doing the speaking so you go first,' Andy tried to insist.

'No, you go first as you are the leader of the group. I am the travel agent, and the person who speaks is often subordinate, like a Polynesian speaking chief. The paramount chief is allowed to remain silent and do the thinking,' Rick half pushed a reluctant Andy through the door.

The Mayor and one of his senior assistants greeted Andy and Rick with warm smiles and deep bows, and Andy responded by thrusting out his hand in a rather ungainly fashion for a handshake. The Mayor did not seem to know when to let go of Andy's hand and kept shaking it for a few seconds longer than necessary. When it came to Rick's turn the Mayor coped better and took a lead from Rick, who broke it off rather than wait for the Mayor to end it.

'I know from my visits to Auckland the Maori people

rub noses to greet but kiss ladies on the cheek,' the Mayor joked. 'I always worry I might get a cold before I go to New Zealand and have a runny nose as a result,' he told Rick.

'Yes that is the downside of hongi,' Rick added.

'Hongi…? Ah, soo desu, that is the name of the greeting,' the Mayor remembered.

They seated themselves around a long, low table with the Mayor and two officials (a second one had joined them) on one side and Rick and Andy on the other. Name cards were exchanged with the officials, and Rick was beginning to feel very uncomfortable as he still could not think of a reason other than Andy's stupid request, why they were there.

The picture-perfect, walk-on-role starlet of a city hall lady attendant returned with cups of green tea which she discreetly placed on the table, one for every person, and did so with surgical precision and absolutely no disruption to the bodies or movements of those seated. The only discord was Andy's obvious fascination with her, and her movements. He had taken on board Rick's impromptu lecture on the Japanese and their love of mini-ceremonies.

Rick had to give him a jab in the ribs with his elbow to bring Andy's attention back to the matters in hand. There was a slight embarrassing pause. Rick was still struggling with a reason why they should be there, and he had just opened his mouth when the Mayor cut in. A City Hall male translator had just arrived, a second or so late, to assist. It turned out the Mayor's English was quite good and he liked to speak himself, and only deffered to a translator if the subject was very sensitive, or if he got stuck.

'It is good you came this morning, might be you have a second sense or already know the news?' the Mayor asked.

Rick and Andy shook their heads wondering what was coming up.

'Oh, I am a little surprised as it's the British film company. Birchall-san contacted this office yesterday to say some of his stars are coming for the event and will support whatever we do. He gave me an assurance he had spoken to you and you agreed.' The Mayor looked puzzled and a little worried.

Andy was about to lunge forth with a rather critical tirade on this subject but Rick, second-guessing Andy, cut in. He explained to the Mayor in very diplomatic terms Mr Birchall's approach to them and their reaction, which was in essence that they would welcome the support from the stars but they really wanted the ordinary people of Fukuoka to take the limelight for their efforts and also see that members of the Mereleigh Group were not upstaged after all the turmoil they had been though.

'When I heard you made the suggestion about an open-air event as well at Ohori Koen, then I thought it would be the solution as it would give the stars more time, but you know the day after our planned event is too close. It must be a day or two later because we need to make full and proper preparations,' the Mayor added.

'Oh yes, yes, we totally understand, of course, yes of course,' Andy gushed, and Rick nodded in more cautious agreement.

'There is one thing, and that is the Mereleigh group was due to fly back a day or so after the main event so they would have to extend their visit,' Rick pointed out.

'Oh, that is not a problem,' Andy volunteered, then got a stage whisper in his ear from Rick that there would be an extra cost in hotel accommodation if they did. This was picked up by the Mayor, who said more to his aide than anyone else that he thought that City Hall could pay for their extra accommodation in view of the circumstances. His aide looked a little sickly but nodded in that submissive Japanese style, knowing they would have to find a budget very quickly and a legitimate rationale for the ratepayers' money to be spent that way.

Andy and Rick left the Mayor's office with a spring in their step and a smile on their dials, and were ushered into the lift again by the walk-on part starlet performing her office lady's duties. She bowed deeply to them as the lift doors closed almost as if it were the end of a big screen movie. As the lift made the ground floor, Rick brought them to their senses and pointed out they had barely 30 minutes to pick up Fran from the hotel and get to the funeral.

'Hell's teeth, are we going to make it in time?' Andy asked with concern.

'Do you remember the name of the temple?' Rick asked.

'No, I assumed you had it,' Andy rejoined.

'No, I don't,' Rick informed him.

'Oh this is great, how the heck can we get there at all

if you don't know the name of the place, and you a bloody travel agent to boot. My God, we will really lose face if we don't get there. This is ridiculous,' Andy was exasperated by it.

'Have no fear. I have the instructions to get there written in Japanese. We simply hail a taxi, give the driver the address and hey presto, we will be there in a flash,' Rick taunted Andy with a huge smile.

They arrived at a large Buddhist temple in the nick of time. The Nomura family and relations were staring to enter but they had tipped off an undertaker to assist the foreign visitors, and Nishimura-san and her boyfriend were also standing by to assist. Nishimura-san had already rounded up some of the others and it turned out that all the Mereleigh Record Club group had decided to abandon part of the tour to Space World and Hiroshima in favour of attending the funeral.

It was a clear, bright crisp spring day with a chilling wind which cleared the sky of any pollution. Nishimura-san briefly explained the happenings.

'Last night the family had their private funeral with the body and today the Buddhist monk or priest will officiate for a wider circle of family and friends. You have to wear these bracelet type things on your hands. When we enter, the monk will read some prayers from the Okyo, a holy book, and pray that Nomura-san is sent to heaven. There will be some chants and incense. After the funeral just the family and close relations will go to the cremation, so we leave off after here,' she explained succinctly.

They noticed a huge, gold leaf-embossed hearse; their

feet crunched over the gravel courtyard and they noted everyone was in black. Fortunately most of their group had at least one black garment on too. They were ushered into the temple with its many faces of Buddha and brass symbols and tapestries, before anyone could reply. Adam and Michiko were already inside and they smiled to the main group.

The proceedings were pretty much as Nishimura-san had explained it. Some of the more religious members of the Mereleigh Group recited Christian prayers quietly at appropriate moments for Nomura-san. The Mayor and editor of the Nishi Nippon Shimbun were placed next to each other and each man had a deep, serious look on his face.

There were some eulogies, and suddenly it was all over. As Nomura-san's widow and next-of-kin left they could hear a bagpiper playing the haunting strains of a Scottish lament. It was so unexpected but in a strange way exactly right for the moment. As they emerged into the bright sunlight, Andy was astonished to see Herewini, dressed in a kilt, playing the bagpipes.

'This man never ceases to amaze me, switching from Elvis Presley at our Mangawhai party in New Zealand to Jock MacSporran, or something like that, at Fukuoka in Japan. He should be on the bloody stage!' Andy was impressed. 'Where on earth did he get the kilt and bag-pipes from? He could not have planned for this.'

Herewini had the kit on complete with a sporran, tight short black jacket with military buttons, and a tam o' shanter. The Japanese were deeply moved and enthralled by this unexpected tribute to Nomura-san, and the media which had turned up for what they expected to be a routine funeral made a feast of it, with dozens of cameras snapping the shot and TV crews running around to get close-ups. As a result some of them almost forgot about interviews with the Mayor and other dignitaries.

Adam was impressed. He took half a dozen or so pictures and told Michiko that Herewini had ensured that Nomura-san's funeral would hit the front pages again thanks to this unusual gesture. Long, deep bows replaced the usual handshakes and hugs at a normal western funeral but Adam could see the emotions were the same. Michiko told him someone big must have helped the Nomura family pay for the arrangements as it was a huge affair for a regular salary man, and there was to be a reception as well especially for the visitors.

After 30 minutes or so everyone began to disperse and Herewini had by that time packed up the bagpipes and moved over to talk to Andy and Rick. He told Andy the clothing and bagpipes had been borrowed from a young New Zealand/Scottish teacher working in Fukuoka as an English teacher, who lived near Rick in New Zealand. In addition, Rick had known of Herewini's Scottish ancestry, and the fact that he had once been in a pipe band in New Zealand.

'It was Rick's idea,' he explained.

Ban-san had organised a small reception nearby for the Mereleigh group. It was an impromptu affair but served also as a means of welcoming the entire group to Fukuoka and having a discussion about the events so everyone could be fully briefed. Adam and Michiko headed off to the Nishi Nippon Shimbun to file some copy for their respective newspapers.

Herewini made his apologies and went to meet Saita-san and Inspector Mori at police HQ after doing a quick change back into his own gear. A discreet search of the Nishi Nippon Shimbun files had turned up a picture of a suspect that Tanaka-san's lady friend Emiko had referred to.

His name was Daisuke Yamada, a Kyushu property developer of some note. There were a couple of file pictures of him. One with 'Dolly Parton,' and another with 'Posh Spice.' The second was taken half a dozen or so years later. Both were social scene type pictures of the rich and beautiful and had no text other than a brief caption.

He was not particularly well-known to the public at large but only within somewhat select business circles through his real estate development company. Inspector Mori made a police check on him for any criminal records and found none except a note suggesting his company's connections with a Yakuza sect. There was no other comment. The inspector decided he should check with the Criminal Investigation Bureau of the Fukuoka police to see if they had anything informal on him, and got an appointment with the bureau chief almost immediately for late afternoon.

'This is our best lead to date, but first let us see if we can establish if the so-called stars in the pictures were the real people or lookalikes. I think we need to do this as soon as possible before we throw our full resources into this. It means we have to contact some film studios, or

Hollywood gossip columnists, to establish the historic movements of these ladies and also Saita-san might be able to pull out some visa information to see if they actually arrived and left Japan at the dates which would fit the pictures,' he said.

Saita-san nodded agreement and said he would get on to it straight away but he was not sure how far back the computer records went. Herewini suggested a third line of inquiry. 'If we can establish who their publicity agents were, surely those agents might have some records as they would be seeking publicity,' he suggested.

'Yes, Herewini-san, we shall do that too.' The inspector saw that Flanker was taking notes and made sure he had bullet pointed the three courses of action.

'Herewini-san, you are a brave and intelligent man, a man I would be proud to have in my section and today I heard how you played the bagpipes for Nomura-san's funeral, so I have double respect for you as a human being. For that reason and also because of possible legal problems I must give you my best friendly advice,' Inspector Mori began. Herewini was caught off balance by this sudden, unexpected attention and flattery, and was about to say something to the effect that it was all nothing when the Inspector continued.

'You are a serving officer with the New Zealand Customs Service on holiday in Japan. You have no official clearance by your own customs department, or any official Japanese law enforcement agency to be part of this investigation. If anything happened to you, it could cause great embarrassment to all of us here and a lot of questions to be asked in New Zealand too, that might badly reflect on your career,' Inspector Mori continued.

Herewini sighed and thought, 'This is it. They are booting me out of the loop for bureaucratic reasons.'

The Inspector continued. 'You see my dilemma and also Saita-san's. We are your friends, we really want you to be part of this but I feel we have reached a crucial, dangerous stage and we do not want to compromise you. Also someone senior might ask me what you are doing at our meetings as the missing lady is British and not a New Zealander,'

'I understand and was half expecting this days ago, but shit, you guys seem to be getting to the hot guts of this and how can anyone walk away at this point?' he asked.

'I have a suggestion. Your friend Perry, the ex-British policeman, made the official request to look for Miss Jones and this morning we heard from the British Embassy at Tokyo that the British police are happy for him to liaise with us on this matter. Perry-san has agreed, so he will take your place at our consultations and I have given him the wink — I think you say — to keep you informed so that you are aware of the developments and can make suggestions to him if you like.'

'It's the best we can do as we must also keep the British police informed. There is a final condition to this, and that is you must not impart any confidential information we give to Perry-san to anyone else nor compromise us by taking any unilateral action. Can you agree to that?' the inspector asked.

Herewini was clearly miffed that his wings had been clipped, but knew that common sense had to prevail. He knew they had done their best to keep him in the circuit, so he agreed, but found it nEvartheless very frustrating, and something of a piss-off. He shook the inspector's hand.

'So when do you want me to back out?' he asked.

'After this meeting I will take you to lunch as a provisional measure of thanks and then later, once we solve this case, I hope we can reward you more fully. So Perry-san will step into our next meeting, and I suppose he will contact you after each meeting.' The inspector put a finger to his lips. 'That I don't want to know about, but if anything should arise please inform Perry.'

The inspector, Saita-san, Flanker and Perry turned up for the lunch with Herewini the guest of honour. On the way to the lunch, Herewini's natural feeling of rejection and depression switched to enthusiasm when he realised he was now a free agent with no obligation to Japanese law enforcement agencies other than to respect the undertaking he had given to Inspector Mori and his loyalty to Saita-san. He believed he had sufficient information and enough Japanese contacts, apart from the two lawmen, to do some worthwhile private detective work of his own.

CHAPTER 14

Perry and Herewini left the thank-you lunch hosted by Inspector Mori feeling more than a little replete, so they took a stroll around Fukuoka's Bayside area to walk off the excess of food and drink and take in the tang of salt air.

'The strange thing is you don't look at all depressed at being dropped from the case; in fact I would say you feel rather pleased about it and that worries me,' Perry stated.

'The timing is just right. For starters I was never officially on the case in the first place. As you know, it was purely a grace and favour thing but now that I am under no obligation, I can flex my muscles a bit,' he said.

'I have a kind of sinking feeling coming on that I have been dropped in somewhat, but am not quite sure how or why,' Perry responded with a somewhat concerned frown.

'It's like this: the inquiry has reached a point where it has almost certainly identified a prime suspect. Possibly within 24 hours, after Saita-san has searched further customs and immigration records and folk in Hollywood have chased up agents for a couple of film stars, we will know if the so-called stars that this character Yamada squired about the place were the real ones. If the real stars were elsewhere, they will be no visa entries to Japan around for starters.'

'I have worked out a course of action we can follow that will assist Inspector Mori, on a hush-hush, de facto basis without him needing to know, except at a crucial point where he and his men can swoop in and make the arrests. I am going to organise a meeting of Adam and Michiko and Tanaka-san and his lady Emiko, and together I think we can take this investigation forward a few crucial steps.'

They paid an entry fee and walked into Bayside Aquarium, which was a huge, cylindrical glass-sided tank full of rather mournful looking fish.

'We need a bright, investigative Japanese person who knows her way about the place and is used to making inquiries. That is Michiko. We need as near as possible an inside source who knows Yakuza and some of the key players and can give us some direction. That is Emiko. We need a small team of private eyes who can get around the fleshpots of Nakasu again tonight, and check for more action and any clues relating to Jenny's whereabouts. That is Tanaka-san and his team…,' Herewini paused.

Roy Vaughan ~

'And when you have found this Yamada chap, the Mr Big of this case, you lead a charge on his place with a back-up of Tanaka-san's heavies and deliver the fair maiden from the dragon's den,' Perry said sarcastically, gazing at a very large fish with an even more mournful expression than his own on its face.

'No, don't discredit your intelligence by jumping to conclusions. By sending Tanaka-san and his rugby men in by themselves it would be like the charge of the Light Brigade against the heavy artillery of the Yakuza. The prime role of Tanaka-san's men is to be discreet, look like your average drunken Japanese businessmen and ask a few well chosen questions at night spots known to be owned by this Yakuza sect. No more, no less,' he explained.

'You know, sometimes you can get things wrong, it does happen to the best of us. I suggest you review each part of the plan and draw up a list of "what ifs" to cover everything that might go wrong. Also, how do you know if these parties will agree to it? It's a heck of an ask, as what you are talking of is a pure pirate operation, not something that Inspector Mori would approve of,' Perry stated. 'And where do I come in on this? Will you keep me in your loop, or is it the old mushroom syndrome where you feed me with horse shit and keep me in the dark?' Perry asked.

'Of course you will be an essential part of the loop,' Herewini enthused, 'but you will only pass on to Inspector Mori what I think he needs to know, and of course you keep me fully informed of what is happening at his end,' Herewini explained blithely.

455

'Jesus Christ, you are the bloody limit. I am to be your personal errand boy but when the shit hits the fan, I will be the sacrificial messenger that Inspector Mori and the entire Japanese police force and customs department will have for arse paper. That is not forgetting that po-faced, sour bitch of an Ambassador, our Miss Alsop-Smith, who insists I keep her posted as well as Interpol. All this for no pay and God knows how many days of my holiday sacrificed, and a wife who is already pissed off.' Perry shook his head in total disbelief.

'Stop being a drama queen. You're going to do it because you know it's worth the gamble if we can save Jenny and also, deep in your gut, the old excitement thing that made you join the cops is already moving into top gear,' Herewini chided.

'So, you're a bloody head shrinker as well and think you can read my mind. I know your type, Herewini. I have had to give fatherly guidance to many a young headstrong cop in my day. If this collapses around your ears, apart from being unceremoniously kicked out of Japan, when you get home there will be some "we fail to understand" and "it's been brought to our attention" let- ters in your email or post box from New Zealand official- dom wanting explanations as to why you have screwed up bilateral relations with Japan and Britain at the same time!' Perry stopped for breath.

'Yes, but it's worth a go…,' Herewini started.

'The one thing about you is you are totally compro- mising. I saw that even today. You did a magnificent job on the bagpipes at the funeral, won everyone's heart and

456

admiration, and are bound to be on the evening TV news in Japan and the UK not to mention the front pages of leading newspapers. You might even get an invitation to the Edinburgh Tattoo out of this, but there was one thing wrong,' Perry suggested.

'What? That I look like a Maori and not a Scotsman? That is racist, I have Scots blood and I am proud of it and my playing was perfect. I was in a pipe band for years as a teenager,' he said.

'Yes, but you told me you were a MacDonald and you were wearing a Campbell kilt. You're a bloody fraud or a complete sell-out. The MacDonalds will never speak to you again, they will probably have to bury you in a special Campbell graveyard for cultural lepers,' Perry suggested.

Herewini was genuinely taken aback for a second or so and tried to excuse this huge cultural insult to the Mac-Donalds by explaining it was the only kilt in Fukuoka that he knew of, and he was under obligation to play the pipes. Perry roared with laughter until Herewini, seizing an opportunity between his guffaws, said, 'Then you will help out with this plan!' Perry was brought back to reality with a jolt, but said in serious tones he would, if the others were willing to have a go and nothing illegal was done.

Herewini tracked down Adam and Michiko at the Nishi Nippon Shimbun's Tenjin head office. They had just filed reports on the funeral and were able to get to Bayside in about 15 minutes at a predetermined café venue. Tanaka-san and Emiko could make it in 30 minutes. When

all had arrived, Herewini swore them to secrecy and disclosed his plan. They all listened intently, but it was clear
Adam was the least enthusiastic of the group and Michiko
the most. Adam was hesitant because he did not want
Michiko exposed to undue risk and Michiko because she
loved the adrenaline rush of a thing like this.

Michiko was not going to let Adam kill the plan so
Adam made another rather feeble excuse, saying he was
going with Oswald to take part in a Mini car rally after
the main event. The Mini Minors would bring VIPs to the
venue and after the event their owners planned an out of
Fukuoka rally. Oswald had owned a Mark I Mini years
ago, and Adam had asked to go along.

Herewini said that, if Michiko and Adam were able to
start some research into Yamada's business interests that
afternoon and evening, they might not be needed tomorrow afternoon. It was agreed. Herewini then set about
drafting up a basic action plan, after Adam and Michiko
had pulled pages out of their reporters' notebooks to give
them something to write on.

Tanaka-san said he would have a dozen rugby men
out at the clubs that night, and Emiko would get together
with Michiko and Adam to help research the Yakuza
sect's business interests and a possible secret haven for
Yamada. Herewini warned them not to talk about this to
any of the others, and only to tell the Record Group members that they were doing a bit of research to help find
Jenny.

'So what do you plan to do now?' Perry asked
Herewini.

'Get together with Emiko, Adam and Michiko and see if they can come up with a better picture of this guy,' he responded.

'One final thing apart from being a messenger boy I don't seem to have a role, yet I am the only qualified and experienced detective in this group, albeit out of action for a year or so,' Perry said, sounding a trifle hurt.

'Perry, you are a decent joker, and I would like you in on the deliberations to guide me once we get some facts back, and also your advice on anything apart from Campbell and Macdonald tartans,' Herewini replied. Perry said he had a late afternoon meeting with Inspector Mori, so perhaps they could meet at the hotel in the early evening.

⌘⌘⌘

The post-funeral reception for the Mereleigh group turned out to be a pre-event briefing as well, and the Fukuoka Record Club was anxious to lay out all the plans for the events for them as soon as possible. It caught everyone unawares except Rick, who said it was quite normal for groups on trade missions etc to arrive in Japan after long and arduous flights to be dragged straight into tour or trade mission briefings.

'The Japanese want to be sure right from the start that the itinerary and all arrangements are correct so you have to suffer a while until it's done,' he told the group.

Ban-san read through the arrangements in great detail, and it took twice as long, as everything had to be translated by Nishimura-san even though she had gone to the effort of pre-translating it into a printed English brochure for them. There were others in attendance, a senior Fukuoka City Hall man, another official from the Nishi Nippon Shimbun and several other sponsors who had come back into the event.

Ban-san said, 'After deserting what they thought was a sinking ship the rats are now trying to clamber back on board as fast as possible.'

There was even an official from Universal Studios Japan to liaise with the UK film stars and the Fukuoka Record Club group. Yoshi came along to represent the rugby men as Tanaka was busy elsewhere, he was told, and an enthusiastic bespectacled young Japanese man, who looked like Ronny Corbett, was there to represent the Mini Minor Club. Andy noted that Adam and Michiko were conspicuous by their absence, but he saw a couple of other Nishi Nippon Shimbun journalists and other local and national media present.

It was all a bit daunting. The scale of events was going to be big, very big, and even larger than they anticipated under the original arrangements. Some of the women began to worry about the clothes they had chosen to wear for the events as they had already seen how Japanese women really dress up for occasions. Nishimura-san tried to put them at their ease and said their group was made up of just ordinary Japanese okusans like them. It would only be the top people who would boast their finery.

'Yes, but we shall be on UK TV and we don't want to look like a bunch of old fishwives and scrubbers,' a forthright and concerned female voice from the Mereleigh group explained. Andy groaned inwardly, more expense for late night shopping.

After what seemly like hours the briefing started and refreshments were made available, and the actual reception began. The Japanese Universal Studio man made a beeline for Andy. He started to apologise profusely for the mix up. Andy diplomatically pointed out that it was not the fault of the Japanese studio but just one of those things. Chuck came over to Andy with Fran in tow and said he was worried about the reception room booking for tomorrow.

'I paid the money days ago but I don't have a receipt or a goddamn confirmed booking. I want know what the hell is going on,' he explained.

Fran looked equally anxious and suggested they should go to the hotel straight away to get it sorted, and keep quiet about it until they knew what the situation was. Andy said they should get Nishimura- san to go with them. The others literally pounced on her and whisked her and her boyfriend away for another cramped journey in their tiny car.

Chuck was burning with anxiety and anger that he tried to control, and Fran were beginning to think this could be the last straw. Nishimura-san said it was very unusual as Japanese hotels were very efficient but, as they had been on the move for the past few days, perhaps the hotel staff did not know where to contact them.

The three of them were out of the car almost before Nishimura-san's boyfriend could stop it. They brushed aside the smart doormen and bell hops with Chuck leading the charge. Nishimura-san adroitly managed to insert herself between Chuck and the receptionist, knowing that Yankee anger was often a bit of a turn-off for the ever-polite Japanese. She took a breath and explained the situation in as polite and restrained tones as possible.

The receptionist called in the hotel conference organiser who was responsible for reception and conference room bookings. He looked at his booking sheets and said all rooms were taken, and there was no booking for a person with Chuck's name. Chuck got the gist of it and began to explode.

Fran then interjected, 'I am worried that Chuck might get a heart attack. Surely you have a correspondence file and should be able to trace the communications and the receipt of the money?'

The conference organiser bowed very deeply and said of course they could. He went to another desk and pulled out two large ledgers and meticulously thumbed through them.

'Ah so, we seem to have received a note to make a booking and a payment from Mr Chuck, but I cannot find at this moment what happened. Please give me a minute,' he requested, and disappeared through a door into the day manager's office. After what seemed an eternity, he and the day manager emerged. The day manager, clad immaculately in a black, well-cut suit, starched white shirt, corporate tie and lapel badge, bowed deeply and invited them into his office.

'This is it, they have screwed up and we are going to get the big apology, money back and no room,' Chuck lamented in anticipation of the worst.

Fran was also feeling very sickly about it, and Nishimura-san felt her knees going to jelly at the thought of a big event without a venue. Only the day manager seemed in possession of all his faculties.

'Please sit down.' They sat and a young lady hotel staff member brought in the obligatory green tea for guests.

The day manager proffered his business cards and Chuck struggled to find his, while Fran apologised for not having one.

'First I must apologise for our apparent lack of communication. I understand you have been travelling and our staff did not know how to contact you. There has been a change,' he began.

'I do hope you have a reception room for us,' Fran blurted out.

'Oh, I can understand your concern and must apologise.' They feared the worst by now and Chuck was beyond anger and feeling faint.

'There is a room for this function but I see it has been booked and paid for by another party on your behalf, so all that is necessary is for us to return your cheque,' the day manager said, smiling politely. He then waved to a staff member who came back almost immediately with a posh envelope with a ribbon around it containing a cheque, a thank you card, and the day manager's business card.

'Who the hell did this? It was my gesture, I am a rich dude. I can afford it?' Chuck was outraged.

'Rest assured, Mr Chuck, your gesture was greatly appreciated by the anonymous donor, and in reality your cheque was a kind of bridging finance or a financial guarantee that enabled us to keep this room for the event. It served a very good purpose as I know that, without your guarantee, the room would have been re-booked. Your service to us in Fukuoka was your trust that this event would happen, and it gave us the grace of time to find someone here to as you say, "pick up the tab." A matter of Fukuoka honour was at stake,' the day manager explained. 'If you have time, we have a few cocktails for you now as a means of apologising for the stress this caused you,' he added.

Back at the reception, Andy suddenly felt way out of his depth. This was a huge affair and a far cry from the rather modest fundraiser he initially envisaged, but the best thing was to sit back and go with the flow. It seemed there was little he could do or say that would now greatly influence events in one way or another. He expressed that to Rick who gave him a wry smile and said, 'Welcome to Japan.' Rick learnt that the group was going to be taken care of by various people that evening, so decided to make his apologies and try and track down Herewini to see what was happening about Jenny.

⌘⌘⌘

Back in Wales, the Mid-Wales police force had found a safe house for Jenny's parents. In fact, they approved a relative's house that Jenny's Dad had assured them very few people knew about. As an added precaution, they had contacted the Japanese police to pass on the allegations the Joneses had made about suspicious folk and then a day or so later, sent a plainclothes man to the vacated house and for a small chat in confidence with the nearest neighbour, to see if anything of interest had transpired.

The neighbour was a bit surprised by their sudden absence as they had a good relationship with the Jones family and it was unusual for them to go anywhere overnight without letting the neighbours' know. The plainclothes man told them why they had shifted out but all he could get out of the neighbours was that a British Telecom van with two technicians had been round the previous day and seemed to have tested some phone lines then left. The plain clothes cop said he would check that out with BT and see what was up.

When he checked with Telecom they had no knowledge or record of any technicians visiting the Joneses and all that BT had received was an instruction from them to have their phone diverted to another number. The plainclothes man returned to the Joneses' neighbours and asked if they had any descriptions on the men or the number plate details.

'Well, you know like, we don't really take that much notice of Telecom people. They had high visibility vest things on and both looked a bit dark like some of those Slav people, but there are four thousand Poles in Welshpool now. The van did look a bit scruffy for a BT van, that I can say, but otherwise I can't help really, can we Mum?' the neighbour deferred to his apronned wife.

'No not at all, really, if we had known to be on the look out, mind you, it would have been different, but even now you have not told us what is up.' She was now anxious to know the worst.

'I can't really tell you, see, other than they received a threat like, even I don't know the full story.' The plain-clothes man was cut short by an offer from the neighbour's wife to have a cup of tea.

'Well, I don't mind if I do. I was up really early today with some sort of cattle rustling complaint up beyond Llanfair. Some unknown stock wagon picking up stock, but nothing in it, the driver had just got the wrong farm,' he explained.

It was a house where the kettle always seemed to be on the boil. They were a retired couple, he an ex-shepherd and she with three grown-up kids. They raised the subject of Jenny, asking if he knew about their neighbours' glamorous daughter. She had been a TV star with a bit part on that TV 'Red Cap' serial about the military police. The plain clothes man played them along a bit, pretending to be ignorant.

'No, no, not at all. You see, I work shifts and off hours and if I am at home in time, I am often too tired to watch TV.'

'We think it's about her, it can't be the parents, they are just quiet and nice but you never know who these actresses mix with in London!' the neighbour's wife said.

'I have never been there myself, only as far as Coventry to see my cousin. Those two Telecom men, they did speak a different language. I have no idea what it was, but it was very strange!' she said.

'It was surely Welsh! You not being a Welsh speaker wouldn't know it from double Dutch,' her husband teased.

'Don't be so daft, of course it was not Welsh! I said a foreign language, Welsh might be foreign to you, your grandmother was English, but it is not to me!' she remonstrated.

The plain clothes man had finished his cuppa and was wondering if he should waste any more time here, but he asked a couple of questions.

'If you were to guess, what language do you think it might have been? Can you remember any sounds of words?' he asked.

'I think like my husband said they were some kind of Slavs from the south, and one had some shirt under his high visibility jacket and it had something like 'Slavic' written on it, and was red castles and things like a football supporters' shirt,' she said.

The plainclothes man noted the detail and said it could be useful. He then told them not to touch any door handles etc, at the Joneses' house as he was going to get fingerprints over to take some dabs.

'You won't be telling anyone about this conversation will you, as we can't let the cat out of the bag until we have trapped the rats?' he said.

They gave him an enthusiastic assurance that they would not breathe a word and asked if they should call him if anyone came to the place, and if they should also try to get some photos. He gave them his card and told them they must be very discreet if they took any pictures, but it was most unlikely anyone would return and they should be safe enough. He guessed correctly that the neighbours would tell one or two other locals, who would tell a few more, and within 24 hours everyone in the village would know but in a way that might help as only the outsiders would not know. He declined a second cuppa but took a couple of homemade scones for his lunch.

'It will do for my bait box,' he said referring to the plastic lunch box and then he drove off back to police HQ.

Later that day fingerprints turned up, as well as a plaster cast man, who took casts of some recent footprints. They were watched throughout the operations by the two neighbours leaning over the fence and the occasional passing villager who was told at great length and breadth what was going on.

If Jenny had been aware of the police work back home, it would have given her some reassurance that the process of law enforcement was on the move, albeit dangerously slowly for her. She was thinking of nothing other than escape and how and when she could try to make a break. She was also worried about the inevitable drugging to keep her pacified or else get her hooked so she would become a totally dependent slave to those who supplied the drugs.

After her captor, Dai Yamada, left her she was allowed out in the garden. It was a magnificent Japanese garden with fish ponds, sculptures, and strategically-placed clumps of bamboo and other plants. It was set in a small valley with a gravel track leading through light forest with a few directional signs in Japanese. There were a couple of aged gardeners at work and two large minders chatting and smoking near a fountain.

She decided to take a walk up the track and was

allowed to go unhindered but discreetly followed by the minders. It led to two large rock pools of naturally hot spring waters, and two changing sheds with neat, thatched roofs. She had a peep in one of the changing sheds to see it was really a sauna as well, everything made of wood and so neat and clean and long-handled spoons made of bamboo to toss water over your body. In different circumstances this could be paradise.

She was brought up with a start by one of the minders who had walked up silently behind her, and said in almost perfect English, 'Why not take a bath? You can if you wish.'

She blustered, 'But I don't have a bathing costume.'

'In Japan you don't wear a bathing costume for this kind of bath, ha ha,' he leered.

'I had a bath this morning. Why don't you take a bath, then I can see your strong muscles,' she teased, trying to turn the tables.

The minders were caught a bit off balance, but they managed to overcome the temptation of stripping off in front of her and impressing her with their manly bodies out of fear of getting a bollocking from their boss.

'Some other time when we get some free time.' They laughed in unison at the thought, knowing it would probably never happen but that it was a nice idea.

'You make the time and I will come and see you,' she provoked them further, and they were genuinely flattered by the thought and her cheekiness. This was a lady with spirit, and they liked it. Another little victory she had won partially over a couple of admirers who might think twice about being brutal to her if there was any chance of a bit on the side.

She asked them about the garden and the converted ryokan and was angling for a name of the place and its location, but all she got was an explanation of the things she could see and not even a name of a mountain. They claimed they did not know the names of any nearby mountains. It might be true if they were Tokyo boys.

'You are from Tokyo?' she led.

'Ah soo desu, you understand Japanese and know Kanto-ben,' one replied in impressed tones.

She just nodded to him which he took as a yes, but she was still trying to work out what 'Kanto-ben' was. She guessed 'ah soo' was 'yes' but had no idea if Kanto-ben was a person or another language.

'Here in Kyushu it is warmer,' she suggested, trying to get them to confirm this was still Kyushu.

'Hai soo desu, Sakura season comes earlier here than in Tokyo, and the dialect here Hakata-ben is different to Tokyo and its Kanto-ben,' one of them confirmed.

'Even warmer up here in the mountains?' she asked.

'Not necessarily in the mountain near Mt Aso because mountain area is bit colder but on flat by sea, hai, yes it is,' the talkative Yakuza explained.

So she knew she was in the mountain area of Kyushu and perhaps not far from Mt Aso.

'In your country you have onsen?' he asked.

'Onsen, what is onsen?'

'Hot springs like this,' he answered.

She thought for a moment, 'Yes, we have Bulth Wells and Llandridnod Wells,' and then seizing the initiative suggested they should visit her country, Wales, watch the rugby and try its springs. They were again flattered at the invitation and said they would like to very much but it was difficult, meaning impossible, for Yakuza like them who probably had criminal records and might never get visas to any decent countries without someone pulling strings and them getting false passports. They reflected on this aspect of a life of crime.

She knew prisoners could end up identifying with their captors but maybe some captors could be persuaded to identify with their prisoners and their former lives. These Tokyo clods knew stuff all about the outside world apart from Hollywood movies, she suspected, but everyone has some imagination.

'Have you got wives?' she asked.

'We got wives everywhere, too many,' they chuckled in unison.

She got the picture: bought women and what they could take among the pickings of hostesses. They were a kind of an international type, somewhat brainless heavies, employed for their muscle and lack of brain, who were tossed a few semi-reject hostesses from time to time to keep them quiet, as well as fancy American cars to drive. They were pretty easy to please really, bayonet fodder that made up the gangster world's front lines.

'I bet you don't have anyone special that does really good things in bed for you.' She spoke in a deep, Eartha Kitt voice, and flaunted her body to make her point. They were taken aback and admitted they wished they had someone like her.

'Where I come from there are a lot like me, plenty to go around for big boys like you…,' she lured them on. They had the hots for her and really wanted to screw her and were wondering if they could get away with it there and then. There was a sudden screech of a harsh Japanese female voice, and the mama-san came bobbing along the gravel in their direction as fast as she could and shouting abuse at the two minders.

If she had carried a broom, Jenny had no doubt that she would have hit them with it. Clearly they should not have let her visit the rock pools and certainly not without her being present. She knew exactly what they had in mind and a deep suspicion of Jenny's game.

The two big minders were instantly humbled into guilt, fearful she might tell the boss and they would get punished for breaking the rules. The screeching harpy of a mama-san grabbed Jenny by the arm to drag her back to the house. Jenny easily shook her free, then walked in a solitary, dignified manner in the direction of the ryokan after fixing the Mama-san with a haughty stare.

The mama-san kept yelling, 'Bad boys, bad boys,' but once they got to the house she instructed Jenny to wear some of the Eartha Kitt garb. 'The Boss come back soon. You be ready, be ready now,' she repeated impatiently.

No sooner had she changed than Dai Yamada appeared and told her he had arranged a rehearsal and audition in one. She was expecting a car journey out of the place but instead he took her down a corridor and into a small theatrette. There sat a couple of other middle-aged men.

'Just karaoke today, just Eartha Kitt karaoke, next time if okay, live band,' Yamada said.

She was given a menu of Eartha Kitt tunes to select a number from. She mused over the list. 'Under the Bridges of Paris' was top of the list with most but she wanted to create the impression she was really co-operative. 'Let's do it' was over the top. She hated the idea of sex with him. 'I want to be evil' might promote too much action too soon, so she hit on 'My Heart Belongs to Daddy' as a compromise.

He nodded in enthusiasm and agreement with her choice, and an attendant got the music rolling. The acoustics were spot on and her delivery perfection. She held the total attention of all present and she received a round of spontaneous applause at the end. Yamada nodded to his colleagues and boasted that she was tops, the real thing in fact, or better.

They made her sing another three songs. She did 'Just an Old-Fashioned Girl', 'Uska Dara - a Turkish Tale', and finished with 'The Day the Circus left Town.' Yamada-san was well pleased. He beckoned her down from the stage and said that evening she would rehearse with a band that would come to the studio.

He told her that, provided she co-operated and did not try anything stupid, she would perform before a live audience and he would reward her. If not he could not guarantee the safety of her parents. Knowing she had little option, she smiled sweetly at him and lied, Eartha Kitt-like, 'and why would I not cooperate, mon cheri?' He was won over at least temporarily.

She was asked to select four pieces of music for the band to play and told it was likely she would have to sing those items. Just to sweeten her, he organised a bunch of flowers and a mama-san to teach her some origami for the rest of the day. The mama-san was a crusty lady about the same age as Yamada and she seemed to have a close relationship with him. She was good at origami, and Jenny relaxed a bit and began to enjoy the lesson.

Her female instinct made her suspect something, so she took a punt and said to the origami expert, 'Yamada was your boyfriend a long time ago I think?' The origami lady paused for a while before replying, as though searching for an answer and some correct English words. The hesitation itself was intriguing and rather revealing.

'Many years ago Yamada took me for his girlfriend. He was not so important then and never had any Western girl. I was Japanese film star for just two years, but everybody forget me now.'

'But you're still here and still his girlfriend,' Jenny suggested.

Again the long pause then, 'You have smart brain but ask too many question so this is last question, and keep your mouth shut or you might die young. Not his girlfriend for long time, just servant. He had many girls like you from West. Don't ask any more.' Jenny was getting the picture, Yamada had surrounded himself with a handful of trusted employees who were vital to his plans and party no doubt to all the horrors he might have been engaged in.

She was given late afternoon refreshments, told to slip into another Eartha Kitt costume, and heard a minivan arrive with presumably a small combo for the rehearsal. The combo was dressed late-1950s style as if performing in a slick Parisian nightclub. The leader gave her a warm and friendly nod of approval and eased her effortlessly into the first number.

She was happy with her music. This was a natty neat combo, Japanese of course, but faultless. She would love to work with such a professional combo in Britain. It took her mind off other things including what the combo's relationship might be with Yamada. Were they totally innocent in the scheme of things or party to some or all secrets?

She noted when they arrived the leader had accidentally dropped a small chit on the floor when he dived into a pocket to get something. She wanted that chit, it could be something that might help her get out of this place. She spent most of the time between numbers thinking how she could get it without anyone seeing.

Yamada was enthralled with it all, living for a while on a different plateau, and she could see he was a perfectionist in many respects but a crazy one. He clapped enthusiastically at the end of each number, called for a few encores and seemed to have tears in his eyes at the end of the rehearsal. The combo started to pack up its instruments and he engaged in an enthusiastic conversation with its leader.

It seemed to Jenny that Yamada had agreed to engage

them for a gig or so with her. When she went over to thank the combo, he cut her short and guided the combo leader away. It gave her a chance to accidentally drop a decorative handkerchief and pick up the ticket on the floor.

No one seemed to have noticed her doing so. She made an excuse and went to the toilet to see what was on the chit. It was of course all in Japanese except for the word 'taxi.' She opened the toilet window a crack and could see the vehicle they came in. The minibus was in fact a kind of maxi-taxi and this looked like a receipt as it had the yen mark and some figures.

She quickly found she had no means of making an exit from the toilet window. It was too high off the ground and too small to get though but the chit might save her day later if she could give it to someone who could help her, and that was some reason to keep hope alive.

⌘⌘⌘

At Fukuoka, Herewini had decided to take a break and stroll around the Momochi waterfront and give his brain time to rationalise things a bit more. He knew he was overstepping the mark by setting up a de facto private investigation. The bureaucratic side of his nature told him this, yet his instinct was to go for it and step up the speed of the investigation. He could not wait for Michiko and Emiko to find some more leads, companies or persons that Emiko might know, or newspaper records that could throw more light on Yamada.

He hated waiting yet there was nothing to do for an

hour or two, no special lady back in New Zealand to call up, in fact no-one anywhere just now. 'I must be at life's turning point,' he thought to himself. He even felt a bit restless about his job with the customs department; there was no specific complaint about it, just a feeling he could do better somewhere else.

Hakata Bay, he noted, was a gem of a place, so much history going back before the failed Mongol invasion attempts, nice islands, nice hilly backdrop and next stop, Korea and China going west. 'I could live here happily for a year or two,' he thought. Still trying to put a perspective on his life he got a call on his mobile. It was Michiko in her normal enthusiastic tones, all bright and chirpy.

'Herewini-san where are you, I have got a lead on Yamada-san, and Emiko has prepared a bit more information. Can we meet soon?' she asked.

Herewini said he was about 20 minutes walking distance from Fukuoka Tower, so how about at the bottom of the tower? It was agreed, and he found Michiko, Adam and Emiko there waiting for him. They found a café and Emiko opened up.

'I went to the business section of the Nishi Nippon Shimbun, and there I found his connection with a certain real estate development company. In fact it was the same one that caused so many problems to Nomura and the record club people. You know, the company that pulled out of the sponsorship and organised a kind of public hate campaign against us all, which led to Nomura-san's death' she explained.

'Phew, that's interesting, very interesting,' Herewini said.

'Sure is, and that's not all!' Adam added.

'I managed to talk to a Fukuoka City Hall organiser involved in the event and he confirmed the company originally planned to sponsor an event like a lookalike band but withdrew because the big film stars were not coming,' Emiko remarked.

'OK, I get the drift. Yamada was in because he could set up a living lookalike star to add to the real ones from the UK and thus big-note it as a true in-crowd organiser, but when the real stars were not coming it killed his plan dead as there was no mileage in having a lookalike star when the ordinary folk from the Mereleigh Club were the only VIPs there,' Herewini said.

'Yes, I guess something like that, but we don't know for sure, just a guess,' Michiko said.

'Sure, just a guess but a reasonable one, but where does that leave us now? Has his company come back as a sponsor and joined the others who withdrew?' he asked.

'Yes and no, they wanted to rejoin but the Fukuoka Mayor would have nothing of it because of the problems they caused so we can't see them. I did find that they made their application to rejoin only after the UK stars' visit was confirmed,' she added.

'So they were still thinking of a current star lookalike at that time, not an old-time star lookalike from the 1960s, but now they are out in the cold,' Herewini noted.

'Yes, that seems correct and like me, I guess you were thinking we could find Jenny at the event tomorrow with

Yamada, but I am afraid it does not seem possible now, so perhaps back to square one,' Michiko concluded.

Herewini told her it was excellent research and certainly 'not back to square one. It's circumstantial but fits the picture we are beginning to get of this Yamada.'

'Emiko-san, she has something, and I will explain to save time. She talked to some mama-san she knew from Tokyo who knows this Yamada. He is a bit of a recluse by Japanese standards and only seems to appear at one or two high class clubs. He has a small, tight circle of friends and just a few people he trusts. She thinks he has a place in the mountains in central Kyushu, not so far from Mt Aso, but no one can say what his real address is,' Michiko said.

Herewini was contemplating his next move when he got another call on his mobile, this time from Saita-san, who apologised profusely about Herewini being dropped from the loop.

'I understand reasons very well but very unfortunate,' he added.

Saita-san said unfortunately they were having delays in getting to the periods that would cover the entry to Japan of the two alleged film stars, so for the present there was no way of telling if it was the real people or lookalikes that Yamada was showing off.

'It might be another 24 hours before we know,' Saita-san added.

Herewini thanked him and told the rest of them he felt obliged to ring Inspector Mori and also Perry. 'We can't sit on this alone when the Japanese police force has a hell of a lot more resources than us,' he explained.

He got Inspector Mori very quickly and the inspector was effusive in his thanks, but like the rest, had drawn similar conclusions. He told them that the police at Tokyo had begun to take fingerprints and look for DNA at the places it was believed Jenny went to and stayed at.

'We already asked the UK police to get Jenny's DNA from an old hairbrush or something, and also fingerprints from her bedroom or items she used regularly. If they match anything we find at Tokyo then we can say positively this girl is her. We must get absolute proof of that', he added.

'Perhaps the fish we are looking for here has unwittingly escaped a net we could have set to trap him, but we are a few steps closer to him I feel,' he concluded and hung up. Perry, too, was impressed and said he would have a meeting with Inspector Mori later in the day and get back to them afterwards.

'So what can we do now?' Michiko asked, hoping for a brainwave from Herewini.

He asked Emiko to keep Tanaka-san informed, as his rugby men might pick up more leads. Herewini was about to end the meeting and suggest they made contact with each other about 10 pm by phone when Michiko remembered that Hayakawa-san, the boss of the Small and Medium Business Association, wanted to meet Herewini for a private dinner with Adam and Michiko.

Herewini looked quizzically at her and Michiko said, 'I don't know the reason but it might be rude not to accept so if you agree, I will take you later. He is an important man here and has big face in this city as he knows a lot of people,' she added. Herewini a little reluctantly agreed to go.

Hayakawa-san had arranged a small tatami room in a select restaurant for dinner and he had with him one of his senior staff, Nakahara-san. Hayakawa looked like a traditional eighteenth century Samurai in a modern business suit. He was of slightly above average build but stocky, and clearly a man who liked to exercise. He had a pleasant face which smiled easily and seemed uncomplicated, and had a bald pate with side strips of hair on both sides and at the back, exactly like the shaved traditional head of a Samurai.

Herewini liked the cut of his jib. He came across as an energetic, can-do type of person being very self assured, and not at all arrogant or conceited; a person with a commonsense approach to life who could get on with anybody and could cut a swathe through senseless bureaucracy or cultural foolishness when necessary. Hayakawa-san began by complimenting Adam, Michiko and Herewini on all they had been doing for the Fukuoka Record Club and their private searches for Jenny. He told them he had a big face in Kyushu and many business contacts at all levels.

'Sometimes in business circles we know more than the police, especially about some shady personalities who never get caught breaking laws, but we know in our hearts what they must do to get so rich so quickly. In short, I want to help you, and of course that must mean I will help the Japanese police as well,' he told Herewini.

Herewini thanked him and wondered where this was

going and, if it was a good lead, why he had not brought Inspector Mori to the meeting so he could explain to the police at the same time. Hayakawa seemed to read his thoughts, and explained Kyushu was full of local people who shared confidences with other local people, but not necessarily the local police, for no-one really wanted to be the first person to mention another's name in a bad light to the police without having total proof.

'There is a certain business man in real estate development that we might see at some top-level functions from time to time. Now he must be about seventy years of age. I have seen him at some places with different film stars over the last ten to twenty years. He does not mix so well, just only to show off these ladies and then seems to disappear.'

'However, you have to know his company's senior staff seem to be so close to the Yakuza that we cannot tell the difference, and from time to time we have heard unproven allegations of dirty play and bribes to get contracts and also to expel ordinary people from their homes and shops so that his company can take over their land to develop it,' he added. There was a pause and Herewini could see an expectant look on Adam and Michiko's faces waiting for his response.

Herewini made a quick assessment. He trusted Hayakawa-san and decided to bring him into a police confidence, which was something he had never done before, but this seemed vital and might save time. He swore Hayakawa and the others to secrecy and revealed that profiling of suspects had brought one Dai Yamada into the frame. He mentioned the file of Nishi Nippon

Shimbun photos of him with 'stars,' and customs and immigration records which had thrown up about 20 so-called 'stars' who had overstayed their visas in Japan and seemed to have gone missing. Hayakawa pledged secrecy and was clearly very excited by this information as the candidate he had put in the suspect frame was the same person.

'Over the years my Small and Medium Business Association has organised many seminars and conferences, some of which, our research shows, Yamada-san attended. I asked Nakahara-san here, my assistant, to go through some records at random. Please note it is very hard to check so much historic information, so we only picked about five such events which I, or my staff, seem to think Yamada came to. We found three events and at two he had a 'star' with him so we copied our reference to that for you,' Hayakawa added.

'To be honest, I must say some of my members claim his company owes them a lot of money on some failed projects and promises so they want to find him personally, especially his residence, as then they could be better positioned to lay a civil case against him for fraud. We are small fish, he is a killer whale!' Hayakawa joked.

It was clear to Herewini that Hayakawa was prepared to join forces and his particular mission would be to find the kidnapper's lair. Because of Hayakawa's excellent local knowledge, he would have some advantage in that regard. They agreed this was the way to go, swore Adam and Michiko to secrecy, and promised the first news break to them when they had a result.

⌘⌘⌘

Back in Wales, the plainclothes policeman at Welshpool had been going flat out organising fingerprints and typing up the statements of the Joneses' neighbours when he got lucky. A local garage at Bettews had a CCTV record of a slightly battered Telecom van calling for petrol at a time that would fit the visit to the Jones' house of the two suspects. The plainclothes man had phoned a few local garages just on the off chance they might have something.

The video image did not show the number plate but gave some good shots of the faces of the two men. The garage owner was a bit suspicious as one of the men paid for petrol by cash, and to his knowledge, that was the first time he had struck an obvious company vehicle like this where the driver had used his own cash for this kind of transaction.

'When I looked at the van I thought to myself, I did, that maybe this van had just been sold by Telecom, and they had bought it. It was so rough and run down looking. It would be an embarrassment to drive it if you worked for BT,' the garage owner said.

The plainclothes man could see his point when he looked at the van, so he got on his mobile and asked traffic to do a check on all recently sold vans to see if any had been sold around Welshpool and to whom, and what make. He kept the video, thanked the garage owner, and said, 'Well, that could be a very significant lead indeed, and if traffic can pin it down, it might well help trace young Jenny Jones. But silence is the word, don't breath a word to anyone,' he cautioned the garage owner.

The plainclothes man's final call of the day was to the safe house where Jenny's parents were in hiding. He was glad he had a few titbits for them as, in most cases like this, he was often the purveyor of bad news or conducting inquiries so late in the piece that what was discovered was too late to help prevent someone being murdered. The lonely farmhouse set on a side of a hill where they were staying was guarded only by an over-eager Welsh sheep dog, a nice intelligent, shaggy haired black and white dog that made a lot of noise but was not in the least bit dangerous to humans.

Mrs Jones shouted at the dog, 'Shut up, sheep dogs are supposed to be quiet and just give the sheep the look, not make a hell of a lot of noise about the place.' Then she opened the door cautiously once she had seen the plain clothes man's ID.

'They told me you were coming. The police station rang but you're a bit late, we were expecting you about an hour ago,' she explained.

He could see the anxious look on her face as though he might be the bearer of bad news, and her hands were wringing nervously. Her husband also came to the porch to invite him in and he was aware they were fearful of asking the question.

'It's okay, it's not bad news, in fact we are making some progress, and I heard from Japan that they might even have a suspect. It's all hush-hush of course, so not a word to anyone please!' He noted their relieved looks and hoped this was not one of those false bits of good news which would turn sour very soon.

'I need a few DNA samples from you, just a swab from your mouths. Fingerprints has been to your house to get some traces of Jenny's hair but this might help as well. Of course we hope it's not going to be necessary but it can help us trace her movements through some suspect places so we can be sure we are on a definite trail.' The parents were glad of that titbit as otherwise DNA samples to their mind would only be used to identify a body. He looked around the small farm house and they explained it was a cousins' place and the cousins were on holiday for a month.

'You're Price the policeman, aren't you?' Jenny's Mum exclaimed.

'Yes, the other Price is the baker, he is my cousin. I often wish I had been a baker, better hours, you see, apart from having to get up so early every day. At least they are regular like.'

As he screwed the lids on the DNA samples, he told them about the BT van and promised the constabulary would be on to it very soon and, as no one had any idea where they were, they were not to work. In any case the local constable had been told to keep an eye on their present abode.

'He can see your place from his lounge down at the police house in the village. As a precaution he wants you to keep the front porch light on day and night and only take it down if there is a problem, also use this number to get him direct. He can be up here in about ten minutes by his car and as it's a one-way road, he could block it off easily enough. What's more he has a set of binoculars,' he explained. He could see they were still agitated and nig-gling each other over something.

'Look, if there is anything worrying you just let me know,' he said

After some further hesitation, they told him about the phone call from Jenny after they had been phoned by the criminals who had tapped their home phone and threat-ened them.

'We had to tell Jenny to go along with what they wanted! It was the best thing, and we have no idea what they will do to her or want from her. They did not even ask us for money which I think is usual in a kidnap cases,' Mrs Jones blurted out between sobs.

Ted Jones consoled her and said it was all very strange and frightening, but Jenny had always been a good girl so they could not imagine she had willingly got herself entangled in some crime. He looked very haggard after many sleepless nights and said he was frustrated that he could do nothing.

'If you think I can do something, I will be on the very first plane to Japan,' he suggested.

'No, no, Ted, not yet, at least. Let's play their game first, and make them believe you are co-operating.' Price the plainclothes man was then about to say, 'If you rush over they might kill her if they know,' but felt it cruel and unwise and just left it at that, but added he did not believe Jenny had been up to anything bad.

'We have had absolutely nothing from Japan to sug-gest she has caused any problems, quite the contrary,' he added reassuringly. 'That is also my belief. I am so glad you told me this about the phone call from her. We will make it a priority to follow it up. As for security up here, I am sure I have not been followed here, and anyway people always tell me I look more like a farmer than a detective because the car is always covered in cow shit, so there you are!' he smiled compassionately.

'We can get someone up here to be with you if you want, and that might be best,' he suggested.

Mr Jones produced an old but well-oiled .22 rifle and also a 12 bore double barrel shotgun and said he would use them if necessary. Policeman Price quickly reassured them that it almost certainly would not be necessary, and it was best they forget the conversation and mention of firearms.

'If it comes to firearms, we shall have someone up here as soon as you can say knife.' With that he took his leave, called Welshpool Police and relayed the mention of a call from Jenny. He was told to turn back and stay at the farm until they arranged a full 24-hour watch over the Jones.

'You might have to stay there a few hours until we can get this sorted. Don't frighten the hell out of them, just say it's a normal precaution,' his Sergeant instructed.

CHAPTER 15

The Fukuoka sunrise brought with it a realistic expectation of a fine, clear, sunny spring day. Rick, Maggie, Andy, Janine and Fran had arranged a brisk morning walk from the Sea Hawk Hotel to the Momochi waterfront to blow out the cobwebs, and take in all that could be seen of Hakata Bay. Now that the Nomura funeral was over, and with the Record Club events back in place on a grand scale, they were determined to enjoy themselves, except there was still the great burden of worry about Jenny hanging over Rick.

The other felt, perhaps misguidedly, more optimistic about her wellbeing than he did. Rick's only consolation was that the Japanese police and immigration authorities were hot on her trail, as was Herewini with his own private army consisting of Tanaka-san's rugby men.

The other four guessed his concerns, and Maggie told

him to try to put it from his mind today and enjoy what was coming up. He gave her a sick look of acknowledgment that said, 'Anything to please you but, not to worry, that is impossible.' Still he decided not to burden the others too much with it that day.

All members of the Mereleigh Record Club Group had stayed up late while the womenfolk in particular had sorted out clothes for the day. Peter and his wife Brenda had decided not to bring any Beatles era garb to this function. Peter said he had felt a bit of a wally wearing the Beatles suit in New Zealand.

Smart casual was the order of the day. Let the Japanese hosts wear hipster and flared trousers if they must. They were not going to risk any silly photographs of them in weird out of date garb appearing in their local paper, and Adam had been warned not to take any dodgy photographs of them and send them back for publication in the UK!

Andy and Fran reviewed the events of the day as they power-walked to Fishermen's Wharf and back, to be sure they at least knew where everyone should be at certain times. Ban-san and his Fukuoka Record Club group had already been at the hotel venue for a couple of hours working with the hotel staff and lookalike bands. The ballroom was huge and there really was no need for them to help as the hotel had it all sussed, and sufficient staff on hand to make sure things were in order.

Ban-san and Nishimura-san's main concern was Mrs Nomura and her kids. They had decided to put in an appearance but they felt a responsibility to see the Nomuras were not put under any stress and could back out whenever they wanted to. Ban-san was pleased that all the media were now hyped up about the events today plus the other happenings, including the big outdoor concert the next day at Ohori Koen Park. There had been some suggestions that the outdoor event should be at the ruins of old Fukuoka Castle but it could be pretty congested for a big event.

The Fukuoka Mini Car Owners' Club had been applying spit and polish to the vehicles for weeks as had the vintage motorcycle club whose venerable Triumphs, Nortons, Harley Davidsons and BMWs were in showroom condition. There were more than a few very worthy early models of Suzukis, Yamahas and Hondas in the ranks as well as a sprinkling of very ancient Vespas and Lambrettas.

There was more than a bit of rivalry between the Mini Car Club and the vintage motorcycle club, as the motorcyclists also wanted to carry a few VIPs to the main even in the opening cavalcade. In fact, there had been strong words and almost stand-up rows over this issue and over which group should take the lead. The motorcyclists claimed motorcycle escorts always preceded VIPs and flanked the important cars and the Mini Club owners said all the Minis should be up front and motorbikes behind.

In the end it took Fukuoka City Hall officials to make the rules, saying a few motorbikes should go in advance to clear the way, then the Mini Minors, and at the end the remaining vintage motorcycles. The Mini owners relented over exclusive rights to carry VIPs, and said if the Mereleigh Record Club members and other VIPs wished to travel on the bikes they could do so.

Peter, who owned a line up of ancient machines like a Vincent, Matchless and a Triumph Tiger Cub, was the first to switch to a motorcycle ride, Andy followed suit being an old Triumph man. Perry used to have a BSA Golden Wing, and Derek insisted on a Vespa ride because he used to own one and also because of his daring Vespa journey at Milford Sound in pursuit of another hostage taker. He pointed out to the Mereleigh group over breakfast that there seemed to be a case of déjà vu developing now and, if necessary, he would take the Vespa to find Jenny. He got a hollow laugh from some of the group in reply.

What they requested and what they ended up with was not always the same. Andy and Janine were obliged to take a stretched Mini and be at the head of the VIP group just behind the Mayor of Fukuoka, who would be in another stretched Mini. Adam Blount and his wife Jill were to travel in an old souped-up Mini Cooper with mag. wheels, wooden racing steering wheel and all the other bells and whistles.

Joan Round got a very early Mark I Mini with the old sliding windows, floor-mounted push button starter and manual choke. Rick and Maggie got a rag-top convertible Mini that would have its canvas top open on a good day like this. Some of them had Mini Minor station wagons with exterior varnished wooden framing and at least two Mini Moke 'jeeps' were to be used. Derek and Ann ended up with a Vespa complete with its own open-topped side-car, which Perry rightly pointed out, would not be the fastest vehicle in the parade.

'The theme song for your rig mate is "I'll walk beside you…",' he joked.

Peter was very pleased to find he would be riding pillion on a very early Vincent with coiled spring front forks like his ancient machine. Most of the ladies whose husbands had selected motorcycles knew three was a crowd on a bike and also nigh on impossible to accommodate, and were happy to travel by Mini Minors.

Adam and Michiko got a Mini with a sun roof near the head of the procession so they could see the main VIPs and take a few pictures. Oswald, who had owned one of the first Mark I Minis, rode with the chairman of the Mini Car Club in a smart customised Mark I Mini in dual-tone colours, and white-walled tyres. As his wife clambered in she commented that it seemed a lot more cramped than she remembered it back in his youth.

'You never seemed to mind moving into the back seat then,' Oswald said pointedly. He took a quick embarrassed glance at the Mini's Japanese owner and was glad he had not caught the drift of Oswald's comment, and added, 'Things were different then.'

The Minis and motorbikes had been split into three groups to pick up various VIPs and guests. The Mereleigh group members were collected from the Sea Hawk Hotel, another mixed group of Minis and motorbikes was sent to the Town Hall to get the Mayor and his councillors, and a third group to the Fukuoka Chamber of Commerce Building to collect some major sponsors.

A set rendezvous point was arranged, and the three groups met spot on time and reformed their ranks with the Mayor and top VIPs at the front in Mini cars being flanked by motorcycle outriders and a vanguard to take the lead and the rest behind. The four British film stars travelled in the middle of the group in open-topped Minis and waved furiously at the crowds.

A solid bank of TV cameras, press photographers and journalists formed a somewhat formidable barrier at the entrance to the hotel which would host the group in its large ballroom. Everyone was in fine humour, and the press got enough time to get their pictures before the police quietly asked them to move aside.

'This is incredible, there are more folk here than you would see at a Royal Variety performance in London,' Adam exclaimed to Michiko.

'It's just normal for us in Japan,' Michiko joked.

'I guess first the bad publicity and our problems, and then the good publicity, has made it a kind of media fest,' she added.

Out of the corner of his eye Adam caught a glimpse of Miss Alsop-Smith, the British Ambassador, stepping out of a brand new BMW Mini.

'Hey, that's cheating, it's supposed to be original 1960s Minis,' he told Michiko.

The rugby men, with Tanaka-san sitting up front with Emiko next to him, arrived in a large coach with huge rugby balls painted on both sides extending almost the total length and height of the vehicle. The rugby men were wearing the colours of teams they represented back in the 1960s if they were Golden Oldies, or for the younger ones, their current club colours. Adam noted that several of the Oldies had played for Japan in their hey-day and looked not a day less than 80.

The Fukuoka Record Club had organised lookalike stars of the 1960s to greet and escort the various groups into the ballroom. The Mayor and his group were escorted by Elvis, and the Mereleigh Group by the 'Fab Four' from Liverpool complete with mop-top Beatle haircuts. The huge ballroom was decked out like a mock café of the 60s, with several imitation juke boxes, coffee machines and bottles of soda pop. Several large strobe lights swept the floor. The MC for the night was an effusive, gushing Liberace lookalike standing next to a grand piano, with pictures of his mother and brother, George, alongside.

'Christ, where the hell did they get him from? He looks too like the real thing for comfort,' Perry exclaimed.

A huge banner was stretched across the back of the stage welcoming the Mereleigh Record Club and all VIPs with a big 'thank you' written beneath from the charity which would benefit from the event.

'I never dreamed this event could attract the sort of crowds that Elvis and the Beatles used to pull. It's fantastic,' Fran exclaimed.

'The great thing about it is that the young guys, not just the sixty-year-olds, are celebrating the sixties. A whole new generation, especially the 20-year-olds, are taking an interest. At least 30 per cent of those present must be in that generation,' Adam exclaimed.

'So we don't feel so bad like the only spring chickens here,' Michiko responded with a smile.

'True, true, you're not alone, and the sight of all the young Japanese sheilas in miniskirts will put fire into the hearts of some of the older jokers in our group,' Rick observed.

'Take a look at Perry and Andy, they can't keep their eyes off them, dirty old buggers, and the women are as bad. Lindsay Love and Brenda Green look on the point of swooning at the sight of the Mick Jagger lookalike and Elvis. Make sure you get some pictures of that, Michiko, and put them on the front page of the Nishi Nippon Shimbun, and you too Adam. Splash them across the front pages of the local rag in Buckinghamshire so all their neighbours can see them ogling the flesh!' Rick laughed.

'It's hilarious, really very funny, but I don't think the Nishi Nippon Shimbun will put that kind of shot on the front pages. It's a family newspaper, and we have to be polite to our foreign visitors,' she said with a chuckle.

Adam looked a trifle embarrassed that his Mum, Brenda, had been singled out by Rick and he was already concerned his Dad, Peter, might make a fool of himself, as he was inclined to be over-attentive to pretty young girls. The guests were still milling about while being shown to their various tables to the velvet tones of a seductive Karen Carpenter singing 'Yesterday Once More.'

'It's a 1970s song,' Adam said, with unconvincing outrage, as he tried to turn attention away from his Mum and Dad, noticing the latter had just caught sight of a group of mini skirted rockers.

'Sure it is, so what, it's called "Yesterday Once More" and that is supposed to take us back to the past,' Fran pointed out.

'By the way, your Dad is looking at the miniskirts, he is already well and truly in the past now!' Rick teased Adam.

They found themselves interspersed at tables with the Fukuoka Record Club members and some top Fukuoka VIPS. Andy, Janine and Chuck were seated with the Mayor of Fukuoka, his wife, and Ban-san and his wife. Rick and Maggie were seated with the editor of the Nishi Nippon Shimbun and his wife, and also Adam and Michiko, who made a polite pretence that she really was too humble a person to sit with the editor. This little charade lasted nearly a quarter of a minute before she accepted what she knew from the beginning was inevitable, and took a seat at the table with her boss.

Seating at tables and in cars and taxis defines status as almost nothing else except a very upmarket name card, and Rick was always amused at the charades that would inevitably be played out before people took seats at formal dinners with the most polite masquerading as the most humble persons. Fran was amazed at the speed and efficiency in getting everyone into the massive ballroom in such a short space of time. 'It's so military in its timing and precision, and everyone is so disciplined that the organisers only have to say something once and it's done. I would like to see them try to shift a British crowd as quickly and not get any backchat.'

The programme, in Japanese and English, indicated some drinks and aperitifs would be served, then introductory speeches with some responses from visitors, followed by the main courses to the accompaniment of more sedate lookalike bands and music, and then the big windup with hard rock, some demonstration dancing followed by open-slather dancing by anyone who wanted to take to the dance floor.

Perry noted that Tanaka-san and the rugby players had put on long black trousers over their rugby shorts and were now wearing black formal ballroom shoes. Tanaka-san was seated with Emiko beside him, and Yoshi and a rather plump and bubbly Japanese girl were sharing a table with Flanker with his girlfriend who could easily have been a twin sister of Yoshi's girl. Herewini and a very sophisticated Japanese girl made up the overseas visitor contingent at that table. Inspector Mori from Tokyo was also there seated next to Herewini.

It was clear that Inspector Mori and Herewini were deeply engrossed in more serious business, almost certainly discussing developments regarding Jenny, otherwise Herewini would have been all over the luscious-looking girl next to him like a rash. Rick felt he had dropped out of the loop where Jenny was concerned, and he was anxious to get over and talk about the search with Inspector Mori-san and Herewini as soon as possible. Maggie, noticing this, held his arm and whispered, 'Not now, you will get a chance to talk to them soon. I am sure if there is anything new or dramatic happening the Japanese police will have it covered and you will be the first to know.'

'Yeah, yeah, but I don't even know what has been happening in the past twenty-four hours and feel obliged to ring Jenny's dad sometime tonight with an update. They will be going out of their minds with worry,' Rick responded.

'You just look at Herewini and Inspector Mori. No one could be more focused and intense than they. You would even think they were about to make a major arrest tonight at this ballroom!' she observed.

'That is it. You have hit the nail on the head. Perhaps the creep who has kidnapped Jenny plans to put her on show here tonight. Hang on, I have to tell Inspector Mori! This would be just the right venue.' Rick leapt to his feet, very nearly skittled a waiter with a tray full of food, and dashed over to the inspector.

'Sumimasen Inspector Mori-san, sumimasen, is there a possibility that the man who kidnapped Jenny could bring her here tonight? Has anyone checked the guest list to see if she is coming?' Rick was breathless with excitement. In slow, reassuring tones Inspector Mori gave him an assurance that he had thought this quite possible and had some detectives posing as guests seated around the place to check.

'What we do know is this man who we suspect is a big, what you call, mover, in real estate development owns a company that was the principal one that wanted to pull out of sponsorship of this event when he learned no film stars would be present. Subsequent to that, he then wanted to rejoin when he heard some stars would come for the Ohori Koen event, but the Mayor refused to accept his company's sponsorship because they made so many problems which led to Nomura-san's suicide,' he explained.

'He is not an invited guest so he should not be here. However, we know he is very confident, but I think Jenny being half black could be easily seen, so I told my men to look for her. They have copies of her photograph,' he finished.

Rick was satisfied with that reply and was beginning to feel conspicuous standing when everyone else was seated, so decided he would try to have a chat with the Inspector later in the evening when the dancing started. He excused himself and carefully returned to his seat, apologising many times to the waiter he had nearly knocked over.

'There you are, dear, I told you they would have thought of everything,' Maggie reassured him. 'Let's have some fun tonight. They are going to let you know as soon as anything comes up, so no need to worry,' she tried to pacify him.

Rick knew he could not properly relax that night, or any time in Japan, until the search for Jenny had reached some conclusion, and he knew Maggie knew that too, but he decided to do his best to make it a fun night. Perry and Dick, with their wives, had arranged to be at the same table and had two senior members of the Fukuoka vintage motorcycle club with their spouses to keep them company. The women soon got bored with bikers' talk and started their own conversations with the Japanese wives.

'We arranged Jerry Lee Lewis lookalike to sing "CC Rider", and he can also do a good imitation of Charlie Ryan's "Hot Rod Lincoln", which is not exactly a motorcycle number but we like it very much,' the boss of the vintage motorbike club told Perry and Dick. He added that his members hoped they liked those numbers and beamed from ear to ear at their acknowledgment.

Michiko was looking around anxiously for Nishimura-san and her boyfriend and saw them enter late with Noumura-san's widow and children. Several other functionaries fussed around them and got them seated at a table next to the Mayor.

Liberace was clearly a man of somewhat larger proportions than the real Liberace, especially around the waist, and his movements were like those of a stately old dowager duchess. He took to the stage, called everyone to order and launched into the opening introductions and thanks to City Hall and all the sponsors with gusto.

It was clear from his occasional use of English that he did not need an interpreter, but he had one, as a matter of form, who was a man of diminutive proportions, no more than four foot eight, with a very serious countenance, who was given a set of steps up to a raised platform so that he could share the same set of microphones as Liberace.

It was a game of opposites. Liberace had a surprisingly natural high-pitched voice that struggled to reach the deeper tones of the real pianist of the 60s, and the tiny interpreter spoke in deep basso profundo tones. After some shilly-shallying that had the audience in fits, Liberace introduced the Mayor, who was almost on the move to the stage a split second before his name was called.

The Mayor launched into his address with great verve

and humour, and then brought everything to a dramatic, serious halt while he asked Nomura-san's widow and children to come to the stage. They had been prepared for this and agreed with it.

The Mayor asked everyone to give them a big clap and pause for a moment or so in memory of her husband who had made all this possible. She was then presented with a huge bunch of flowers and a large envelope tied with a black ribbon. She spoke bravely for a moment or so, expressing her thanks to everyone for the support they had given her and the children, and said her husband could never be replaced in their memories. As his death was quite recent she felt she could not stay too long but wanted everyone to have a good night out. She got a huge round of applause, bowed with great dignity and quietly walked off the stage with her children in tow.

'Phew, what an ordeal it must have been for her,' Andy said in admiration.

Liberace then summoned the Mereleigh group up to the stage and went into a long speech about how they formed their group several decades ago, but years on went to New Zealand, where they experienced some great excitement that led to a movie being made about them. It was the success of that movie that led to the group responding instantly to the Fukuoka Record Club's request to come to Japan and help with this fundraising do.

'Everything else you know, and we are sooo glad you came because many would have turned back at Tokyo because of the big mix-up. It's our pleasuuuure to have you,' he drawled.

They got a big round of applause, and then Andy was called on to respond. It was a moment he hated. This was like addressing the world and he had agonised for days about what he should say, written dozens of speeches and torn them all up. He even asked Adam, as a journalist, to give him some guidance.

'Just imagine you are talking to a few Japanese friends and write it that way,' Adam advised.

It took Andy a few minutes just to mention everyone of importance at the function and to thank to them for inviting his group. He paused. Michiko pushed up beside him to translate after every break into Japanese. It seemed an age to the other members who feared he was going to freeze up, but then he screwed up the scant notes he had and just ad-libbed it.

'For most of us it's the first time we have visited Japan. It's a fantastic place with the most organised, polite people in the world, and Fukuoka is the best city in Japan as far as I can see.' He paused and got a big round of applause which surprised him.

'We are here because our friends, the Fukuoka Record Club, invited us. We had no idea they had achieved so much with so few resources and are stunned by the magnitude of the civic and commercial support everyone here has provided to support the charity.' He paused and there was more applause.

'There was a mix up, but it is water under the bridge, except for Mrs Nomura and her family to whom our hearts go out. I hope the city can erect a suitable memorial to her husband, who was a truly remarkable person, as a tribute to his idea and efforts.' Another pause and more applause.

He whispered to Michiko, 'What next?'

She whispered to him, 'Whatever you want but you're doing fine and they don't expect too much.'

'The late 1950s and 1960s was a great period of change and my generation, I am proud to say, was right in the thick of it.' He paused and there was a silence. He had to mention the Second World War but was scared it would offend his hosts. Should he or should he not?

'Well, the possibilities for change came about at the end of the Second World War. We were war babies; most of our parents, if they survived the war, had been to hell and back in that period so we were lucky. We had food rationing to about the mid-1950s like you, and there was the Cold War and the Korean War, racial discrimination, big housing problems and most families had little or no money. Our generation became the first anti-nuclear protesters.' He paused and got a loud cheer.

'Our generation were out there in the streets protesting about racial discrimination in the United States and apartheid in South Africa. Bob Dylan was our prophet.' Another huge cheer.

'We protested against the Vietnam War, but the Hungarian uprising and Cuban missile crisis scared us stiff with worry, thinking a nuclear holocaust was about to start between the West and Communist countries.

'We had the new technology, first vinyl long-playing records and tiny transistor radios that were made in Japan.' Another huge cheer.

'Then we had cassette tapes and later of course CD's, but that is now. We experimented with drugs, LSD and cannabis.' The crowd was silent.

'And we made some huge mistakes which most of us fortunately survived but that legacy is still with us today, and we are here to fight drug abuse!' There was applause.

'What else can I say? We had fun as teenagers, great fun, the contraceptive pill was invented and AIDS did not exist, but now we have to be a lot more responsible about these things. We thought our world was totally renewable but we learned it's not, the sea level is rising, the climate changing and petrol is running out! The iron curtain no longer exists, man has walked on the moon, but the world still has many injustices. However, we are here tonight to celebrate rock and roll and pay homage to what we believe was the golden era of pop music,' he concluded.

He wiped some beads of perspiration from his brow. 'We hope this event can lead to some permanent connections and ways of helping the charity in the future. Really, it is totally overwhelming for us, we never expected anything as big ! Everyone of us will go to our graves with fantastic memories of this, thank you so much.'

Michiko just managed to translate the last bit before a final round of applause cut in.

'That was just right, Andy-san, they only wanted the simple truth from you,' she assured him.

'Great speech, Andy, just dandy,' Chuck said, pumping his hand and slapping him on the back. The Mayor stood up and shook his hand and the editor of the Nishi Nippon Shimbun told him it would be on the front page of tomorrow's edition.

Liberace then called Ban-san and his group to the stage and Nishimura-san stood by to translate for him. He first apologised for all the difficulties that his group had caused, as if he personally had been responsible for Nomura-san's death and the strife the major sponsors had created in pulling the plug on sponsorship. The audience was having none of it. There was a buzz of 'No, no, not your problem,' going around. He then launched into his speech saying Andy had stolen his very words and thanked Andy for saving him the time by not having to say the same things.

'My generation in Japan is a little bit too young to have been teenagers then, but I see the Mayor and many senior city men here, and we respect what their generation did to make the world a better place. In particular, the music, the fashions and everything. Thank you so much.' He bowed deeply several times and was followed by his group who also bowed and smartly fell in behind him. The events of the night then moved into top gear and for most it became a huge enjoyable blur of great music, fantastic companionship and for the British visitors a kind of surreal feeling seeing so many lookalike stars all with rather oriental features.

'If I wasn't pissed…….. I…I…… would say……… that all these pop stars are masquerading……masquerading……… as Orientals… for the night!' Perry exclaimed.

'Well, I am ….pissed….and I can say to you…. my friend……that this is all a dream, and…we are a figment of your ………bloody imagination,' Dick said profoundly.

'What...what...proof have you of that?' Perry demanded.

'Just... Just.... the fact...that you...and I ...for that matter... don't actually.....exist!' Dick responded as he wrestled his own body into a chair and then tried to guide Perry into his adjoining seat.

'It might....it might.. have possibly, just possibly.....come to your notice... that most of our Japanese hosts....the very people who invited us here....are pissed as newts and that creates ....it creates... a serious problem...for us... and might be a diplomatic incident...in fact,' Perry started.

'We don't.... We don't bloody well exist.... I tell you... so there can be no problem....... No problem at all ...me old mate,' Dick replied.

'There was, and it was solved several days ago,' a rather more sober Rick cut in.

'Yes....yes, if Rick-san says it's been.....solved...then it must have been,' Perry rejoined.

'I have no idea.......no idea...what you are talking about, but....as you don't exist...it does not matter,' Dick said.

'To put you both out of your misery our hosts have laid on some coaches to get everyone home, and had friends and family take care of the vintage bikes and Minis. So you will not have to ride pillion on the back of a bike or sit in the back of a Mini with a pissed driver in charge,' Rick explained.

It had been a full-on night for Adam and Michiko as they were both obliged to file a colour story on the event for their respective newspapers. They fitted in some key interviews with dancers and noted several TV stations were covering the event as well as a few other print and radio journalists.

Inspector Mori and a small team of undercover detectives appeared to have had a fruitless night. There seemed to be no sight of anyone looking like Jenny or Dai Yamada. The only titbit he had picked up that night was from Emiko who said she had heard on the local mamasans' network that Yamada had allegedly kept an old girlfriend or mistress with him for the past 20 years or so, who had once been a Japanese film star. Her movie name was Etsuko Suzuki. Out of the scores of 'stars' he had had, she seemed to be the only one who was still around, while the rest had disappeared, Emiko told him.

Inspector Mori thanked her profusely and told her to contact him, if any more information came to light. He told Flanker to check the files and see if Etsuko Suzuki was her real name and to check census records and electoral rolls to find out where she was living last, if she were still alive.

'Maybe she can lead us to Yamada's lair,' he told his subordinate.

Herewini's night should have been great fun with a stunning girl arranged for him as a dinner companion by Tanaka-san and his rugby friends, many good friends and great music. For all that it did not quite make it as a great night out for him and that was not due to any failings on the part of the organisers but a nagging feeling he should be out trying to find Jenny. He agreed with Inspector Mori's theory that Yamada might try to bring her to a function like this. The jigsaw puzzle profile of him was rapidly being filled in but a number of key parts, including the very evidence that she was in his clutches, were missing and no one seemed to know where he had his hideaway.

Herewini had spent much of the evening, to his Japanese partner's annoyance, checking out the females at the event to see if he could find Jenny. She must have thought him to be some sort of sex-starved pervert until he told her what he was doing. She warmed up a lot after that and he felt sorry for her. Her name was Yumi, and she was one of those perfect doll-like Japanese ladies who clearly had some expectation of meeting a foreigner who would take an interest in her that night.

Herewini lied and told her he had someone special who could not be there that night. He had no one special at the time, having just ended a somewhat longstanding and rather passionless affair a few weeks ago. He could see Yumi was great, but not exactly his cup of tea.

'If you come to New Zealand, I can introduce you to a lot of guys who would love to date you,' he told her thinking it must sound like the sort of line pimps used on unsuspecting girls.

'Yes, I would like that very much. I always wanted to visit New Zealand, can I stay at your place please?' she asked.

He felt touched and flattered by her trust in him, especially as he had ignored her half the night, so he agreed and immediately regretted it, knowing it could be a situation he would regret and make it harder to untangle himself from her great expectations. She immediately gave him her name card with her address and looked at him to give her his. He shuffled for a bit wondering if he could make a lame excuse and get out of it but the more honourable part of his nature compelled him to pass on his card.

She held his card like a trophy and looked deep into his soul to reaffirm that the young man opposite her was the person on the name card. He knew she would turn up and she was taking a long hard look so there could be no case of mistaken identity.

'Shit, I haven't even kissed her let alone screwed her, and she is starting to cling on like a newly pregnant girl-friend,' he thought to himself, not that he had made any girls pregnant to his knowledge, but he had seen that look in some of his mates' girlfriends' eyes. Anyway, she seemed a nice enough person, and he was confident more than a few of his mates would be happy to take her on. Hayakawa-san from the Small and Medium Business Association caught his eye and came over, giving Yumi a bow and nod of approval, and asked her to excuse himself and Herewini for a moment or two.

'So tonight I talked to some people about Yamada-san, and I think I know the place where he stays. It's very remote part of Kyushu in the general region of Mt Aso. Tomorrow, I have some time, but might be we have to stay overnight at some ryokan in that area,' Hayakawa-san offered.

Herewini jumped at the chance and asked if he had notified Inspector Mori, to which Hayakawa-san said the Inspector knew he was doing some digging around and indicated he did not want to be bothered unless he was fairly certain, so he decided it best that he and Herewini take a look first.

'If it's nothing, you will see some nice scenery and enjoy the trip, we might even find an onsen and take a hot spring bath,' he said.

They decided to see the first half of the Ohori Koen outdoor festivities and then take off. Herewini glanced around to find his lady friend for the night standing next to him and all the hosts lining both sides of the ballroom doorway to clap the visitors out of the premises.

'My God, I almost forgot everything starts and finishes exactly on the button in Japan. They have this polite way of giving the visitors the message to leave. When you see your Japanese hosts lining up at the door its time to go, but you must not leave until they are all there because they are going to clap you out of the venue.

Hayakawa-san said he wanted to invite Herewini, Yumi and Rick and Maggie to his club for a nightcap as the night was still very young.

'How could anyone say no?' Rick thought somewhat cynically, but Hayakawa-san looked a good sort and could be a useful contact in the future, and Herewini had no choice as he was off to Mt Aso with him tomorrow, though he yearned for at least eight hours sleep!

⌘⌘⌘

As she began to turn in for the night Jenny, still captive at Dai Yamada's place, reflected on the strange turn of events during her day. Things had started rather predictably except the performance she thought she might be asked to make that day did not eventuate. Instead she had been advised she would be performing tomorrow afternoon.

There was another rehearsal with the small combo to go through half a dozen old Eartha Kitt numbers. She had enjoyed that. It made her forget her current circumstances for a while. The combo also enjoyed the work-out but had to rush off just before lunch. The elderly origami mama-san, who seemed to be the boss, reappeared and ushered her into another lunch Japanese style.

She talked a bit about what was expected of Jenny and how she had to behave, or it would bring big problems for her parents. She gave Jenny what could only be described a killer look as she told her, and it sent a shudder down Jenny as she had an instinct that this old bird was totally ruthless when necessary, despite the niceties of origami.

Suddenly she choked on her food and was speechless. Jenny waited a few seconds for her to clear her throat, then realised she couldn't and was desperately fighting for her life. Without hesitation, Jenny jumped over to her side of the low table and thumped her on the back a few times but it failed to dislodge the food, so she spun her round to see if she could prize out the obstruction with her fingers.

Meanwhile the old woman was turning blue, so Jenny lifted her up. She was not a large person, and Jenny grabbed her from behind and with her arms around her midriff, gave her stomach a mighty squeeze. The first time there was no perceptible effect; the second there was a huge gulp and out popped the offending food.

The old lady gasped for air for it seemed like five minutes as though she might have a heart attack. Jenny squatted down besides her and made her take a drink of water once her breathing became regular. There were tears in the old woman's eyes, a mixture of delayed shock and relief. After about ten minutes the old lady regained most of her old composure and told Jenny.

'You save my life. Thank you, thank you so much. Without you I would be dead now. I never forget you know exactly what to do. Everything you do is right. Thank you, thank you,' she kept repeating.

Jenny was genuinely embarrassed by it all. It was an instinctive move on her part and, if she had thought about it, she might have let her die. 'If I had not saved her life, Yamada might have thought I killed her though,' she speculated cynically.

The old lady was quiet for about 30 minutes, reflecting deeply on something, it seemed to Jenny, and after this long silence she told Jenny to come with her. She took Jenny down a long passage to what seemed like an adjoining flat on the main building that was clearly her quarters. She made Jenny sit down, went to a large, antique Japanese chest and pulled out some large folders and albums.

For the next hour she showed Jenny photographs of herself many years ago as an actress. Jenny could see she was very beautiful then and spotted one sign in English behind her announcing her as Etsuko Suzuki. She told

Jenny she was the first actress that Yamada had. She was no impersonator of another star but things changed and went down hill from there.

'We had good relationship, might be five years, and then something happened to him. He went away, and I knew when he is away he has another woman, because he is Japanese businessmen, and that is the way of Japanese businessmen.'

'He was sick down here,' she pointed to the pelvic region, 'so I guess he got some sex disease and he no longer want sex for a couple of months. The first time we have sex after that, he is no good. He get erection but nothing else. I worried a lot because might be he got tired of me so, I have idea which I hope can please him and get him better. I say to him, "I find you new actress girlfriend and she get you going again," and he agree.' She stopped for a breath and Jenny was beginning to get the picture as to where this was all going.

'So I get him another actress, a Japanese girl, you know, just one movie hit and nothing else, so she comes cheap and not against will and get some pay. We try her slowly but after he takes her out a few times he takes her to bed, and nothing, so he get very angry and tell me get rid of her. So I get rid of her and tell him I will find someone else. I get someone else and same thing.'

'During this time he likes to appear in public with these film stars but they are expensive, so I have idea to find lookalike girls. It's cheaper and nobody knows difference except him and me and the girls. He gets reputation as ladies' man in business circles. He likes the flattery but still not have any sex capability, so I say we try west-ern lookalikes.' She paused.

'How do you get the Western girls, same way as me, get someone to find us and bring us to Japan under false pretences?' Jenny asked angrily.

'Basically yes, gomen nasai. It's quite easy as theatri-cal agents have lists we can get on internet now and we have men you can go to make the deals,' she explained.

She then opened up a photograph album crammed with lookalike stars and about 20 or so were underlined.

'Why did you underline these ones?' Jenny asked.

'Because they are the ones we hired, look we got you on the final page...,' she said, showing Jenny.

She then produced another album with newspaper clippings and photographs showing Yamada-san at vari-ous functions with the lookalikes next to him.

'So for all these years he has been doing this and no-one has ever guessed?' Jenny was astounded at the cheek of it all.

'That is right, just him and me and the two guards,' she explained.

'So after I have done a couple of gigs, I have to hop into the bed with him and when he fails to perform I am sent down the track!' Jenny was outraged.

The old mama-san tried to calm her. 'It will be differ-ent for you. You must go to bed with him but after that because you save my life I will make it different for you afterwards,' she assured Jenny.

Jenny was about to ask why when one of the guards

came in and told the mama-san they were both needed now by Yamada to discuss tomorrow's show. Jenny did not have a chance to talk to the mama-san after that, she had to dine with Yamada-san and gazed at him in a different light. He was really a very pathetic figure, a vain bastard who liked to strut his stuff but could not walk the walk.

She hated to think what happened to the rejected girls. The old nightmare of a cellar crammed with bones came to her mind but she did get some solace from the old mama-san saying she would make it different for her afterwards. 'Christ,' she thought, 'does that mean a bullet to the head instead of some horrible slow death by torture?'

She was tossing and turning on her futon when she heard the sliding door open to her tatami bedroom and the old mama-san came in with a small portable music centre, radio and CD player, and said she had one CD Jenny might like to play. It was a CD an English girl had left some years ago, 'The Very Best of Acker Bilk.'

'Jesus, just what I need, Dad's era stuff, still better than nothing,' she reflected. She thanked her and the old mama-san was gone before she could ask her any questions.

As she could not sleep, she popped it on and eventually cried herself to sleep after hearing the haunting tones of Bilk's clarinet and orchestra playing 'Stranger on the Shore' and the evergreen Beatles number 'Yesterday', and the piano and clarinet rendition of 'That Lucky Old Man.' It was the music her Dad played incessantly until it drove his wife mad. She was so anxious about her parents and terribly homesick for the green valleys of Mid-Wales and familiar sound of Welsh voices.

⌘⌘⌘

Back at Fukuoka, Herewini gallantly insisted that Rick, Maggie and he drop off Yumi at her place by taxi before going back to the hotel. Rick looked quizzically at Herewini wondering why his old mate was not making some excuse to take Yumi home himself and bed her. She looked willing enough. After they had dropped her off he said, 'That was a bit out of character, have you decided to start leading a life of celibacy?'

'God isn't he the limit.' Maggie cut in humorously 'It's none of his business Herewini. Just because you are a gentleman, unlike him, he has to try to bring you down to his level.'

Herewini laughed. 'I admit it's a bit out of character. Perhaps I am in love with someone else and don't quite know it yet.'

Back in his hotel room, he reflected on himself and the statement. It was partly true. He had fallen in love with a girl in a photograph at very first sight, and couldn't let it rest until he saw her in the flesh, but knew he had to rescue her from some strife before he could do that.

'Christ, this is the stuff of ancient schoolboy annuals, it does not happen in real life. What if she turns out to be ugly as sin, has bad breath, hates men or has a bloke of her own, or she is dead when we find her?' He mused over all the possibilities while trying to get some shuteye and came to the same conclusion he made when he first saw the picture. 'I have to find her to find out.' He was about to get some shuteye when he noticed the red message light on his bedside phone flashing. In fact two voice messages awaited him.

The first was a terse one from his Customs Department boss at Auckland saying he had heard that he had got involved in a search for a British girl and it would be best if he kept out of it so as not to blur the edges of his responsibilities to the New Zealand Customs Department and upset relationships with the Japanese Customs and Immigration Service. He was pissed off and angry. It was his own time, and he was acting out of social responsibility and had actually helped the Fukuoka Customs service. 'Who is this cretin?' he said to himself.

The second message was from Adam, who said he wanted to join Herewini and Hayakawa-san on the trip tomorrow and bring Michiko. He was not too sure it was a good idea but decided against getting into a lengthy debate with Adam at this late hour in favour of taking it up in the morning.

The dawn came too soon for many of them. In fact it was about 9.30am before most of the Mereleigh group rose. Herewini had been up an hour or so and decided on a lengthy jog along the waterfront. He was joined by Adam who was not as fit but did his best to keep up. The unexpected company of Adam on the jog made Herewini agree that he and Michiko could come provided Hayakawa-san agreed. To his surprise Adam said Hayakawa-san had invited him providing Herewini agreed.

'We are only going to suss out this joker's eagle's nest, no rough stuff, and if there is a sniff of it, you and Michiko are to clear out PDQ,' Herewini told him

'PDQ?' Adam asked.

'Pretty darned quick, get the message?' Herewini stressed the point.

When they got back to the hotel, most of the group was poring over English language editions of Japanese national daily newspapers. The Fukuoka event had made the front pages. Michiko was jumping with joy at the Nishi Nippon Shimbun's coverage. All the national dailies proclaimed what a great success story the event had turned out to be and what a coup for Fukuoka city to get behind it. They all mentioned the Ohori Koen park concert and the reports were matched by TV and radio coverage.

Surprisingly, there had been hardly any mention of Jenny in any Japanese newspapers. A missing hostess was hardly news in a country where they regularly went missing to dodge immigration requirements. Adam went on to the internet to check out British coverage of the event. He was pleased to see the Guardian gave it good coverage and the local Bucks paper had gone overboard with his story and photographs.

⌘⌘⌘

Jenny woke feeling totally washed out and lacklustre. She knew she had to try to build up her own morale to cope with things and keep her eye on the ball should a chance to escape emerge. Etsuko Suzuki, came in with breakfast and told her she had a vitamin for her. Jenny took it without thinking and realised it was something to put her on a high, and cursed at being tricked so easily.

The mama-san told her the Eartha Kitt clothes were laid out and she would be picked up by Yamada in an hour and taken to the concert venue. She unbent a little and wished Jenny luck.

'I know you perform very well but today the audience might be very big,' and that was all Jenny could get out of the old lady before she was left to her own devices and to get changed. She remembered the taxi chit and decided to take it with her but before placing it in her bag she found a pen and wrote in as large a letters as she could, 'Help me, I am Jenny Jones, a prisoner!'

She just hoped she could find someone, preferably a European; she could pass this to quietly, without raising the attention of Yamada and whatever Yakuza guards were there. She needed to find someone intelligent who would realise the taxi chit was the key to her where-abouts.

She had thought it all through. If she made a fuss in public the minders would probably drag her off, saying she was having a fit or something, and then her parents might be punished in some way to make sure she behaved in future. The taxi chit idea seemed to her to be a discreet way of getting help without alerting Yamada and his cronies.

⌘⌘⌘

Back in Wales, it was evening and Price, the plainclothes policeman, had completed a fairly hard day checking up on some local crims when he would rather have spent more time sorting out the mysterious British Telecom stooges. However, forensics had done most of the legwork. Having found the van to be an ex-BT one, they discovered a new owner with a Slavic name who gave a false address, but they had the CCTV footage from the local garage and had gone to immigration to see if there were any photo matches with recent Slavic passports. He related this discovery to his boss, Detective Inspector Roberts, who thumped his table and proclaimed it looked like the link to the dead Japanese man at the Rising Sun Hotel.

'God, we have been working on this bloody dead Japanese for bloody ages, and just a couple of days ago Interpol traced his Yakuza connection to Fukuoka, Japan, where you're missing girl is.

'We know from Japan that our dead Japanese friend was Hiroshi Kameda and a so-called agent of a big Yakuza boss who had this penchant to hiring foreign actresses. Now you have these Slavs in the frame over Jenny, and it my guess Kameda was the one who did the legwork towards getting her hired. Kameda was murdered, poisoned in fact. Pretty brazen stuff right on our own doorstep almost. The question is by whom: the Slavs, his own boss or someone else?'

'Just leave it to us and Immigration, Guv, we only have a few thousand Slavs to check out,' Price said with heavy sarcasm.

'Well, get into it fast man, this bloody Japanese body has been hanging around our necks so to speak for far too long and there has to be a connection.'

Price nodded in a rather reluctant subservient way. Well, that was a joke; Immigration laughed him out of court. 'Did he have any idea how many male Slavs from Eastern Europe were entering Britain by the day? It was not just a case of a needle in a haystack but a needle in the universe,' he was told.

He decided to get back to the computer to see if there were any police updates on crims and wanted men, particularly any East European crims who might be needed for something. He got an instant new different result.

'Well my goodness, indeed to goodness, have they ever?' he mumbled when he checked out an e-mail reply. 'Here we are! Just the boyos, wanted in connection with smuggling in prostitutes from Romania, and what glamour boys they are too, a couple of right tough-looking thugs. How on earth could anyone think they could be working for BT?'

There were a couple of pages on them: when they were believed to have entered the UK, who they allegedly worked for and the current likely whereabouts.

'Hey, and what's this? Some local tart at Newtown picked up for drugs was a known acquaintance of them and has been identified by the Rising Sun receptionist as the person who was last with the Kameda chap. My oh my, Mr Roberts will be pleased and it's hot off the press! What a surprise, Mid-Wales, my own back yard! '

'What's up with you Price, you going mad or something? They say talking to yourself is the first kind of madness, but of course we 'ere already know you're bloody mad,' a colleague at the next desk observed.

'I have to put the DI in the picture now as our inspector can get the quick action and resources we need to move this one along.'

Without further explanation the plain clothes man headed off to track down Detective Inspector Roberts who he knew had headed off to the local rugby club's bar for a couple of pints. It was near the end of the day and a nice bonus for him after the time-consuming business of dealing with small-time crims and schoolboy offenders. Forensics matched up some fingerprints they had taken at the Jones house with the fingerprints the police had on two Slav pimps.

'All we have to do now, Price, is find them,' Inspector Roberts said with enthusiasm, clearly meaning Price rather than 'we'.

'Yes sir,' Price replied.

'And where are we going to start?' the DI asked.

'Up your arse,' is what Price wanted to say but without any specific ideas in mind, he resorted to a usual acceptable reply. 'By routine police methods, known acquaintances, associates, no family here in this case for these boyos, but if they've been around our manor for a while I expect they have been in a few clubs and pubs. We don't have too many of either in Welshpool, should only take a couple of hours to check the town out but Shrewsbury, that's different, a bit bigger and more exotic so to speak for these chaps,' Price volunteered.

'What you (the DI did not use 'we' here) are saying is we have no idea at all where they might hang out, not even the teeniest hint!' the DI said sarcastically.

'Well, not that bad, we might find someone who knows them in town and possibly be able to lean on them a bit to find out,' Price offered.

'You mean some drunken farmer who has come out of the hills to sell a few sheep at the market and then shagged some local Slav prostitute and is boasting about it around town,' the DI said.

'Well, not quite as vague as that, we do know some Slav prostitutes. I don't personally, just heard of them professionally, and that is where we could start,' Price suggested.

'Okay Price, but don't think for a moment these two Slav crims will be hanging about in town or taking in the country air around Tregynon. If they have done a job and got paid for it, they are more likely to be hitting the bright lights at Birmingham, London, Manchester or Liverpool. Who knows? You do your local checking, and I will go out on the network and ask other centres to keep a look out for our possible kidnappers, or whatever they have been up to.'

'I have to say it does seem Jenny Jones went to Japan completely voluntarily so our Slav friends might only have played a minor role in whatever nefarious crime is being played out.' The DI stood up, saying while it was a priority with them the two suspects would hardly be a priority at other police centres as their only crime at Welshpool was posing as BT technicians and making threats to a local couple with a missing daughter.

Price always got pissed off at having to be polite to

sarcastic bastards like the DI. The bloody problem with the likes of them is they became removed from the grieving victims and forgot it was the DCs like him that always did the spade work and other things to a point where the DIs could play at being sarcastic schoolteachers.

The DI didn't come from Mid Wales but was from the valleys down south. He had married locally but wasn't quite local in the way that Price was. Roberts would say, 'I am from Welshpool,' but everyone knew he was not 'from Welshpool' but simply 'lived at Welshpool.' Price smiled to himself. You had to be born at a place to be 'from' it and Roberts would never be 'from' Welshpool. 'You might well joke about sheep farmers coming to town for a bit on the side Mr Roberts, but we up here are a bit more clannish and nothing strange goes unnoticed,' he thought to himself.

He knew DI Roberts would also be sending off an e-mail to Interpol at Japan to boast of suspects being identified as if he had done it all himself. He was clearly an OBE candidate, meaning Other Bastards' Efforts. Price did the rounds of a few pubs favoured by visiting farmers and found a landlord who knew of one or two of his regular customers who had boasted about a couple of Slav girls on the game.

Price took note and then found a couple of phone numbers and posed as a punter and got what he wanted. The two girls were shit scared they would get beaten up by the Mid-Wales police for their sins and, without being too explicit, said their pimps were Rumanians who had moved out of town for a few days. He got the address of a flat in Welshpool the girls gave him after he assured them the police were not interested in them provided they co-operated, and even found a neighbour who had seen a battered BT van parked nearby.

'Just a piece of cake, sir, let's hope the girls don't warn off their pimps. Most likely they will, but my guess is if we watch the girls, the pimps will contact them some way, some time,' he told the DI later that night.

Detective Constable Price gave Ted Jones a ring and got him out of his bed.

'This is just to reassure you, Ted, we are onto something. Can't say much more on the phone, but we are making progress,' DC Price said.

A bleary-eyed Ted Jones thanked him and said it would help keep their spirits up.

⌘⌘⌘

Most of the Mereleigh group were far more relaxed after their main event and well prepared to enjoy themselves at Ohori Koen Park for the open-air festival. They had chummed up with the four UK film stars at the event the previous night and would meet up with them again at a set time at Ohori Park for a set piece photograph for the media.

Rick was waiting at the coach at the Sea Hawk Hotel. It was a fine, sunny warm day with clear air. Everyone made it to the coach on time and was making the usual post-party wise cracks about the previous evening. A uniformed young lady coach assistant bowed them all on to the coach, the driver closed the automatic door, and the coach cruised on to the main road. It was a short distance to the park and by pre-arrangement the coach was admitted to a temporary fenced-off area near the main rostrum in time for the opening.

They were met by a Fukuoka City Hall official and his female assistant, both with clipboards in hand, and also by Nishimura-san and her boyfriend. Hayakawa-san was also on hand to make contact with Herewini, Adam and Michiko. A large, good-natured crowd clearly out to have fun had already assembled ready for the opening, and thousands of others were progressively making their way into the park. The park's lake waters sparkled in the sun and the large mountains of interior Kyushu made a tremendous back drop. As they got off the coach, Rick, to his dismay, noticed the record club group was one short so he did a name check,

'It's Ewan Perth; does anybody know where he is?' Rick said in exasperation. A somewhat embarrassed Fran stepped quickly over to him and, in a low voice, said he had made an arrangement with Liberace last night and she, Fran, was to tell Rick that Ewan would be coming to this event with Liberace.

'Well, that is fine by me, but I wish someone had told me earlier,' he replied to Fran.

She apologised again, and Rick told everyone, 'It's okay, we know where he is, he will see us here sometime,' and left it at that.

The open-air event was far less formal than the previous evening's festivities. A local DJ from a 1960s rock station took charge and made informal gestures and thanks to all and sundry who had made it possible, but emphasised strongly the efforts of the main sponsors whose banners bedecked the rostrum, and several other smaller stages that were positioned around the park.

It was a great day out for grandparents, mums and dads, teenagers and babes in arms. The music was mostly 1960s rock but with many modern re-mixes and more recent versions of old pop standards. There were lookalike bands but mostly they were modern rock groups playing traditional numbers.

At the appointed hour, the Mereleigh group and the Fukuoka Record Club group were summoned to the main rostrum for formal pictures with the four UK stars. It was a long and testing process to satisfy the visual needs of all the media present and everyone was glad when it was over.

Helena and Foggy Night were in raptures. She had taken her usual sketch pad to Japan and throughout the tour had made numerous sketches along the way of people and places. They had deliberated a lot about joining this tour but decided it would be rude if they did not as they had only met again as a result of the first tour to New Zealand. They told the rest of the group this was their first reunion party. Maggie Moss said it was the same for her and Rick.

'Next time we go on a tour somewhere with the record group it will be Adam and Michiko's first reunion,' Maggie pointed out.

Michiko glowed at the thought and Adam smiled. Rick said he would have thought everyone would have had enough, but he was jumped on by the others who would have none of it. After the photographic formalities were over, it was decided everyone would go their own way and muster at the bus. That was the cue for Hayakawa-san to take Herewini, Adam and Michiko in hand, and make for his parked car and the trip to Mount Aso.

'I am sorry, you will miss the closing,' he apologised. They assured him it was okay as what they had to do was far more important. His air-conditioned, curtained limo was parked next to the exit and they were en route within a moment or so.

Inspector Mori was following his hunch and had a few detectives around the various stages to see if they could spot an Eartha Kitt lookalike. That morning he had struck trouble with his lap top computer's internet connection, but had not worried much as he planned to be out in the field most of the day.

Jenny was ushered into Yamada's limo and sat next to a large Japanese lady and a Yakuza. Unusually, Yamada took the front seat, which in Japan is usually relegated for use by the most junior person who is expected to act like a footman. The drive to Fukuoka was long, but would have been pleasant in other circumstances. Yamada just told Jenny they were going to a big city for an open-air performance and she would have to sing a few numbers with the same combo she had practised with, and then they would return.

If she were absolutely satisfied her parents were safe, Jenny told herself, she would make a dash for safety at the city but she had no idea where they were and certainly did not want to be the cause of their death or injury. As they came closer to their destination, she could see Fukuoka signs along the road and then guessed that was where they were going. She also tried to note the signs pointing to where she had come from. The only certain one was Kumamoto, but she knew her journey had begun an hour or so before they passed that city. They made a comfort stop and the large Japanese female followed her to the toilet like some prison warden.

Some apparent employees of Yamada's were awaiting their arrival at Ohori Koen by a minor entrance to the park. They took over the car and waved them towards the waiting combo, who were carrying their instruments, aided by several other non- musicians. The combo's leader told Jenny they would set up immediately at one of the smaller stages and play within the hour. He reconfirmed the numbers and checked if she was okay. She felt pretty dreadful and thought she must look it. That pill she had been given did not really agree with her digestive system and she hated feeling woozy.

The combo set up, tuned their instruments and within moments they were introduced to loud applause, and she rattled through her numbers. It was an excellent performance and thoroughly enjoyed by young and old. It was the biggest audience that Jenny had ever performed her Eartha Kitt numbers for, and for a while she forgot her circumstances and just became the total dedicated artist.

Yamada was seated nearby and his face was lit with smug pleasure. He was the first on the stage at the end, cameras flashed and a few key media photographers had been tipped off at short notice to come to the performance. Yamada got the pictures he wanted with Jenny on his arm. Then in a flash it was time to go, and before she could gather her senses properly, she was almost raced back to the limo and in transit again for his home.

She did however manage to thrust the taxi receipt into the hand of a respectable looking middle-aged Japanese man who was walking with his wife, and she also managed to cast a pleading look at him several seconds later as she was being walked away, just to reassure herself than he had not thrown it away. He was clearly a bit bemused and was still gazing at it when she lost sight of him.

She prayed to herself he would do something and once again had highs of optimism and great lows of depression. She found it impossible to keep her moods on a level plane. It was far worse than waiting for the results of an exam. You know you might just pass or just fail, but this was life in the balance stuff and she had no control over the situation.

Inspector Mori had given himself the task of watching the stage where Jenny performed but he had no idea she would be there, let alone at the Ohori Koen event at all. He missed her appearance because of a call he received from Fukuoka Police HQ on his mobile. He had to walk a short distance from the stage and crowd in order to hear the voice on his phone. It turned out merely to be a routine call and a message from Tokyo asking him to e-mail his office as soon as possible. He told the police caller his internet link was down and he would try later.

As he walked back to the stage, the performance had finished, but he could hear people taking of Eartha Kitt so he quickly found out he had missed an Eartha Kitt lookalike performance. He grabbed a pressman who had been at the events and asked to see his digital photos. He then knew it was Jenny, He asked what direction they had gone.

The pressman did not know. He made a call on his mobile to Fukuoka police saying a possible sighting had been made of her but he had nothing to go by, no car registration nor description of any vehicle, and had no idea if she had left or was still milling around. He requested all other detectives and unoccupied policemen to man the exits from the park to see if they could see Jenny. At least the detectives had photographs; the rest would just have to look out for an Afro-European lady about 25 years of age. But where was she?

CHAPTER 16

Inspector Mori cursed his luck, knowing often in cases like this there might be just one chance and if there was, he had blown it by taking the phone call. He had lost Yamada and he had lost Jenny, and he knew that unless he found them again, he was in grave danger of losing face. Such a serious prospect was unthinkable. Time, then, to redouble his efforts.

By chance he came to the same exit Jenny had been taken to and saw a European lady and her husband waiting there. The European lady had a sketch pad and was furiously filling in a sketch. He noted it was a sketch of a part Afro-European woman. It turned out to be Helena who knew about Jenny and had seen the tail end of her act and recognised her as the missing person. She had managed to follow her at some distance to the exit, and had seen the car she was driven away in.

Inspector Mori recognised her and Foggy as being group members and introduced himself, asking if they had a description of the car and its number plates. She apologised and said she was confused by some Japanese script and had tried to copy it as well as the numerals. It was all hastily noted and impossible to decipher with any certainty, but the car was a late model white Nissan limo and her description of Yamada fitted.

'I am sorry, we don't usually carry a camera as I like to take my impressions from my own eyes and not through the lens of a camera.'

He praised her and her artistic talents and presence of mind.

'Much better than a camera, much better than a camera, as you have the circumstances in your head, and a bigger picture,' he told her. The inspector desperately needed a car as he had guessed the route they might take if they went via Mt Aso to Yamada's secret hideaway.

There was another stroke of good fortune. Helena and Foggy told him they expected one of the Mini Car Club people to pick them up in a few minutes at this exit. They had to wait barely a minute but the owner's wife had to cram in the back with Helena and Foggy and give up the front seat to the rather portly inspector. The Mini owner was overjoyed that his car was to be used in a police chase.

'This is Mini Cooper. Mini Cooper is very fast Mini, might be fastest Mini in the world,' he boasted.

The inspector got on his mobile phone to request the police look out for a white Nissan limo with occupants matching Helena's sketch. He knew it was pretty hopeless without a number plate. One in a million chance, he told himself quietly, and the Mini held a thread of hope if his guess was correct. It would also be nippy in the city traffic despite its heavy load.

Hayakawa-san, Herewini, Adam and Michiko were well up into the central volcanic plateau of Kyushu and Hayakawa started to open up and expand on his interest in finding Yamada's eagle's nest. It seemed a number of the Small and Medium Business Association members had been diddled by Yamada's major real estate company, and if they could get access to some of his files and discs they would be able to prove it.

Herewini was mortified. 'I don't know that I can help you. Rescuing a kidnapped person is one thing, but unless we can prove she has been staying there or is there, there is no reason for us to enter and risk our necks. What happens if she has never been there and we go in to pinch these company records and get caught? We can be convicted of burglary and I, as a customs officer, apart from a prison sentence, would lose my job if there was the slightest hint of criminal behaviour!'

He spoke directly to Michiko so she could translate in exact terms. She, too, was somewhat aghast. Hayakawa-san pondered a few minutes, saying he understood totally, and it was too much to ask of Herewini so he would do it himself, and they could absent themselves while he did it. If he found any traces of Jenny then he could call them.

Herewini was silent for a long while. He did not really

like that idea either as it seemed a bit unsporting to let Hayakawa-san do all the dirty work. He told the rest of them he also felt uncomfortable at leaving Hayakawa-san to take all the risks and he would have to think things over a bit more. There was silence in the car for a while, everyone was desperately thinking of a solution.

Michiko broke the silence. 'We, Adam and I, as journalists, can go and knock at the door and tell them we are journalists doing a story of special Japanese houses for a British magazine. You know most rich Japanese love to show off their homes and have them in influential foreign magazines, so perhaps they will agree.'

'With respect Michiko, do you think they will show you the inner sanctums of the house, a room where she might be kept prisoner? To say the least, it's most unlikely,' Herewini said.

'I can make excuse to go to the toilet, or something and take a look while Adam is with them. At least we might discover this is Yamada's place and that is a good first step,' she added.

They all thought it over for a moment. Adam was stuck for words as he was rather shocked at Michiko's audacity, and thought it could be bloody dangerous if their ruse was uncovered.

'I have to say I don't want Michiko taking great risks, and we must think of something we can do to keep safe. Perhaps I can leave my mobile phone on so you can hear us in the house and give a key word or two if it's an emergency and we need help to get out,' he suggested. Hayakawa-san said that sounded sensible and a good compromise, and Herewini said only if they had fail-safe communications.

'My suggestion is that first we establish where this place is according to Hayakawa-san's information, then we park the car somewhere discreetly away from the place, not too far, and Hayakawa-san and I check out the perimeter of the property, fences, other points of entry and exit, and then when we have it sussed, Adam and Michiko try to gain legitimate entry by the front door,' Herewini suggested. They all agreed and spent time organising a code of emergency words to be spoken over the mobile phone.

'I am obliged to keep Inspector Mori informed; it is a kind of gentleman's agreement. Now with Hayakawa-san's need to filch files, I certainly can't say that is part of our expedition! Quite clearly, if the coast is clear and an opportunity there, Hayakawa-san needs to pick up his files before the police arrive. It's rather complicated things,' Herewini pointed out, adding, 'The thing is if there are a load of heavies about the place we have no police back-up to hand.'

'I actually thought of that,' Hayakawa-san said in perfect English, 'so I arranged for Tanaka-san and some rugby men to come up behind us and stand off the place a few hundred metres and then rush in to help if required.'

'And if the Yakuza are armed? We went through this kind of scenario with Inspector Mori before when we thought we might have to bust open a Nakasu nightclub. It was agreed we would leave the heavy stuff to the police for that reason,' Herewini pointed out.

'As a matter of fact Tanaka-san's group is now coming behind us but we have no police back-up, so it might be best that we accept what we have and call in Inspector Mori if need be,' Hayakawa-san responded.

'Well, as I am the only person here with any sort of law enforcement experience, albeit customs work, I have to say the whole thing is total madness, and if you accept my advice, we back off. That is official! If you wish to continue against my advice, I will have no recourse other than to help you, so please call it quits. I don't want to lose my job and end up in jail,' Herewini concluded. Michiko translated the lot to make sure Hayakawa-san understood and she detected a devil-may-care note in Herewini's voice, so she smiled broadly at Hayakawa-san as she spoke. He caught the drift and said it was far too late to turn back now.

Their journey progressed steadily uphill, gaining a few thousand feet before they diverted off a main highway on to a tortuous secondary road, heavily forested on both sides. The road clung to hill sides, dived through numerous short tunnels and over bridges. The traffic progressively thinned out. It reminded Herewini of some of the back-block roads between Nelson and Westport, and Adam was trying to find British comparisons but all he could think of were the wild, almost treeless moorlands of Scotland and Wales. The climate control on the car showed about a seven degree Celsius temperature drop from their start at Fukuoka, and Hayakawa-san said it would get cooler still as the final stretch was all uphill.

The sky had clouded over and looked stormy. Michiko called for a comfort break and plunged off the road into the forest to relieve herself. The men waited patiently and then all but Adam did the same. He took the opportunity to tell her it was not too late to pull out as it could be very dangerous. She insisted on continuing and he knew it was impossible to change her mind. He was the most cautious of all of them: he did not lack courage, but with a new-found girlfriend he was much in love with, he wanted nothing to endanger it.

While they sat and waited, a largish mini-bus ground its way past with a dozen or so men inside. Adam did not pay too much attention but as soon as Hayakawa-san returned, Michiko told him in Japanese she thought a group of Yakuza had passed them going in the same direction. She asked him not to tell the others. He nodded agreement and looked worried, but said nothing.

After a further thirty minutes or so driving, and a few country lane junctions, their road was almost down to single traffic proportions with passing bays and clearly looked as though it would peter out at a dead end in some blind valley. Hayakawa-san said he anticipated this from a road map and therefore would stop about half a mile short of the place and try to conceal the car, and then they could check out the perimeters of the property. They found a passing bay that had a short unmade forestry road spur with a sharp bend which put the car out of sight from the road. It looked little used.

Once they stopped, Hayakawa-san called up Tanaka-san. He had a GPS on him and gave Tanaka-san the co-ordinates. He told the others, 'He is about 50 minutes behind us with his rugby men, and he asked about the weather here because the forecast is for a storm. He told me it's not unusual for heavy rains to flood the roads and cause big landslides, so we better hope it does not happen.'

Herewini got a call on his mobile phone. He recognised Inspector Mori's number, thought about it and decided politically it was best for him not to reply otherwise he might have to lie. It would be easier to say he must have been out of range, but he did not like this. It was unprofessional, and Inspector Mori was a friend. Adam asked him who called, and he said some joker he met at a bar whom he would rather not see again.

Hayakawa-san pulled out a rough map with pencilled-in boundaries and one or two footpaths. It was agreed that Adam and Michiko stay with the car. They could look like a loving couple if someone drove past, while the other two checked out the boundary to see what access or escape routes it might provide. After what seemed an age but was only about 30 minutes, they returned and pointed out two overgrown paths leading to the property from a steeply-wooded hillside, like old woodcutters' tracks.

'We have to go up to come down, whichever way we go, either into the place or out of it, and there are several small, steep mountain streams, so we will have to watch our footing,' Herewini explained.

Hayakawa-san suggested both he and Herewini wait under cover in the forest a few hundred yards from the front entrance to the residence while Adam and Michiko drive up in the car and try to gain entry as journalists. The couple were expected to suss out the layout and try to ascertain if there were any traces of Jenny and also Yamada. He also wanted Michiko to find out where his office was so that he could try to gain access later and pick up the company files.

The weather was getting worse and rain imminent. Hayakawa-san came prepared. He had umbrellas for Adam and Michiko and some heavy wet weather gear for himself and Herewini. In addition, he had carefully thought out another guise that he and Herewini could adopt if it were decided that they made a frontal respectable approach. To Herewini's amusement it consisted of two white shirts and formal blazers and a couple of name tags in Japanese and English declaring one person as Brother Shimada and the other as Brother Kawazaki.

'We will be Mormon missionaries and you will be a Japanese Hawaiian because you are not exactly Japanese-looking but can pass as a mixture of Japanese, Polynesian and European, and that will account for you not speaking Japanese. You will be Kawazaki. It's easy to remember, same as the motorbike,' Hayakawa explained.

'The outfits are fine but I am no Mormon and don't know anything about the religion, do you?' Herewini asked.

'No, not at all, except no alcohol is allowed and famous tablets left in the desert, and their HQ is at Salt Lake City. But I have a Japanese-translated Mormon Bible and got an English one for you.'

'Very few people listen to what they say, they just want to get rid of them civilly so we can just say a few polite words and refer to some section of the Mormon Bible and read from it. I also have clipboards which look formal. They will be impressed we travelled so far to this place. Anyway we might not need to make formal entry. We just wait until Adam and Michiko have finished,' he said.

'If any of my rugby club mates back in Auckland hear about this I will be the laughing stock of the team for years afterwards,' Herewini shook his head with disbelief at the proposition.

They donned the Mormon gear and put the wet weather gear over the top and drove up to within a few hundred yards of the house, and then let Adam and Michiko drive on to the entrance. The rain by now was starting to bucket down and there was no shelter apart from under the rain-doused dripping conifers.

Herewini checked his watch and estimated Tanaka-san's rugby support group would only be about 20 minutes away. Hayakawa-san guessed his thoughts, picked up his mobile phone and called Tanaka-san to advise him to pull over at the same slip road into the forestry cul de sac and remain out of sight until needed. He also told him about the two partly-formed paths over the hill to the property. Herewini told Hayakawa-san that he felt obliged to ring Inspector Mori. It would take the inspector at least three hours to get to this place going flat out in police cars, so that would give them plenty of time to do what they needed to do, he figured. Hayakawa-san agreed.

Inspector Mori was very pleased to get the call. He told Herewini he was about to arrive at Kumamoto in the

Mini car and had arranged a larger unmarked car to proceed from there. He mentioned Helena's sketch of the suspects and told Herewini that a member of the public had been slipped a taxi chit by Jenny, called the police and a duty constable had the presence of mind to link it with Jenny. Things had happened very quickly, and Inspector Mori was notified almost within thirty minutes of Jenny passing on the taxi chit to the middle-aged couple, he told Herewini.

Herewini confirmed that the four of them were at the address and he decided to tell the inspector about the role playing to get entry. There was a long silence at the other end while Inspector Mori thought about it.

'Your plan has its risks but providing Adam and Michiko keep strictly to their roles and avoid being obviously inquisitive, they should be in no danger. But there is a problem; a small bus with some Yakuza was heading for that place. Kumamoto police keep track of them and advise us. We don't know the reason as we never seen that size group of Yakuza go to that place before.'

'Be very careful, we have no back-up for you, not even a police helicopter, as we heard the weather has closed in and cloud level is below the mountains. By car might be we are about 40 minutes away but roads in that area are subject to landslide in big storms. I am worried, don't take risks.'

'Finally, and this is the most important thing for you we believe, Yamada and Jenny are returning to that place and they might arrive within about 10 minutes at the earliest as they left Ohori Koen Park about twenty minutes or so before we got under way,' The inspector's voice sounded concerned but he was very methodical and his advice very sound.

When Inspector Mori reached Kumamoto Police station, he picked up four burly detectives, thanked Helena and Foggy for their efforts and assured the Mini car owner the police would pay full hire costs for the use of his car. As soon as the inspector got under way, the Mini car shot out at a safe distance behind. The owner, Helena and Foggy were not going to miss the action for anything and knew better than to ask permission to follow Inspector Mori to Yamada's place.

⌘⌘⌘

Back at Welshpool, the plainclothes man had hardly any sleep. After tipping off Ted Jones and his wife that they were on to something, he got a surprise call from the pub owner where the sheep farmers hung out.

'There has been a development I think you should know about, on the quiet of course, no names…,' the pub owner started.

'Yes, yes, of course,' Price said impatiently.

'Well, do you see, just before closing these two rough-looking Slav chaps turned up with a couple of prostitutes. I reckon they were prostitutes as they looked like it and dark and swarthy they were like gypsies. One had been here before with a farmer so I think I am right. And the skirts, well more like a thick belt than a skirt, you could just about see their name plates, you could!'

'Anyway, they had an intense conversation but I overheard a street name, just can't remember it for the moment but you will know off the main street. It's really an alley where the old narrow gauge line for the Welshpool and Llanfair light railway used to traverse to get to the old mainline station. Number 32a they said.' The publican was cut short by DC Price who said he was on his way.

He contacted the Welshpool police station and arranged a nearby rendezvous, and within 15 minutes they were rat-tat-tatting at the door. It was opened by one of the girls in a belt for a skirt and without formality DC Price and his colleagues invited themselves in; saw the two Slav men whose faces fitted the frame, and the other girl busily packing. They had been packing in haste and were probably one minute or so away from making a quick exit.

There were no arguments. It was all too sudden for the Slavs, and a few burly Welsh coppers were enough deterrent to stop them trying to chance their luck. DC Price was on a roll. He decided to arrest the two males on the spot for a breach of the immigration laws, and he detained the two women on the same account. It was pretty matter of fact from them on. Inspector Roberts was at home tucked up in bed and the duty sergeant was more than happy to have a bit of decent work to do on an otherwise quiet night. It only took about thirty minutes of questioning for the two men to confirm their identity, little realising there could be a far bigger charge coming up, that of conspiring to threaten bodily harm to the Joneses and being a party to kidnapping Jenny Jones.

Once he had them nicely pleading guilty to the Immigration Act charges, the sergeant dropped the subject of Jenny Jones to them, saw a furtive look on their faces and told them, 'Well, we will do the decent thing and let you sleep on that one over night in the comfort of our cells as there are some more important policemen than me coming over to interview you on that tomorrow!'

'That is a fine night's work DC Price, a good tip-off too, don't know how you do it!' the Sergeant stated. 'Mr Price the publican wouldn't be a relation of yours at all, would he?' he asked.

'Price the Pub they call him. Now you ask, he is a second cousin, born on the wrong side of the blanket, bit of a black sheep in the family but he knows where his loyalties lie, so please keep quiet about it otherwise you will dry up my snout,' DC Price confessed.

'Mum's the word, I will be very happy to see the inspector's face in the morning when I tell him you have it all sorted. He seems to think we are a pack of yokels up here, but there you are, he's from South Wales, so what can you expect!'

Inspector Roberts would be seeking more on the Slavs' link to Kameda in the hope of obtaining a murder charge. His latest advice from Japan was that Kameda's boss may have had him bumped off as it was known that more than a few lieutenants of the Yakuza sect had died mysteriously, apparently for either knowing too much or failing to do their job properly.

⌘⌘⌘

In Japan, Herewini and Hayakawa-san stood shivering in the wet under a tree and had only been there about 10 minutes when a large white Nissan limo cruised effortlessly up the road. A glimpse through the trees at the occupants was enough to tell them what they wanted to know.

'It's Yamada and Jenny Jones,' Hayakawa-san whispered in Herewini's ear somewhat melodramatically.

'No need to whisper, they can't possibly hear you and even I have difficulty it's raining so much!' Herewini responded. He had caught a glimpse of Jenny looking a forlorn figure surrounded by her captors.

The two of them had a quick conversation, wondering if it would be safe to call Michiko on her mobile and alert her but decided against it. She could not answer if they were there and she and Adam still in the house. It was all the proof they needed, though, and Herewini lost no time in passing that information on to Inspector Mori.

Michiko and Adam knocked at the front door spotted a bell and rang that also. It certainly was an ex-ryokan, she told Adam, a very upmarket traditional country inn, in fact, but walled off now like some high security millionaire's residence, which of course was what it was now. The old lady with the severe face who opened the door was Etsuko Suzuki, accompanied by a very large Yakuza minder, who looked like Odd Job from the old James Bond movie.

It sent a shiver down Adam's spine but Michiko was unmoved and gaily told them they were fashion and lifestyle magazine journalists and were interested in seeing the conversion job to this former ryokan. They apologised for not making an appointment and lied, saying they rang a few times but there were no answers. Michiko was very convincing and had actually stepped right into the place where the old lobby and front desk had been, and began to 'goo' and 'gah' about the furnishings etc.

'It's so traditional, so tasteful,' she purred in that flattering Japanese female way, being ever so polite and complimentary. Adam took her lead and added similar statements in English guessing what Michiko was saying in Japanese. Michiko kept it up and told Adam in English what a privilege it was to see such traditional magnificence.

It was very borderline; they could see Etsuko Suzuki was very flattered, and she even admitted to having played a large part in organising the renovations, and furnishings, and she knew Yamada's ego would be flattered by such compliments, but not so sure he was ready to tell the world about his hideaway. She realised she had to be very careful with these two journalists. There was no question of roughing them up or being overtly rude, yet she guessed Yamada would return with Jenny quite soon and she wanted them out of the way before he arrived.

'I will give you both a very quick tour as we expect some friends very soon but there is one condition. The owner is a very rich man and you must not disclose the location of this place as he does not want rubber-neckers and tourists up here. If you agree I will give you a brief look around.'

Adam showed her his UK Journalists pass and Michiko her Japanese press pass and she was convinced they were legitimate, and they gave her the undertaking she asked for. The rooms were very traditional, nearly all either tatami or smooth, stoned, thatched roofs over many of the rooms with big, dark stained beams, little charcoal braziers set in the low dining tables and tasteful cushions. It could almost have been a samurai's residence of two hundred years ago apart from the electricity and modern flush toilets.

Michiko could see the old ryokan office was still an office and probably the one where Yamada stored his things. They were handed umbrellas and led out into the garden though it was teeming down with rain and a gale tugging at their storm sticks.

Etsuko Suzuki wanted them to see the natural thermal hot pools. While gazing at a pool Adam very nearly fell over with surprise. He caught a glimpse through the bushes of Hayakawa-san and Herewini crouching low behind a bush. Herewini quickly indicated for Adam to shut up and look away but not before Hayakawa-san mouthed the words 'office.' Well, that is what Adam guessed as it was the only reason why Hayakawa-san was there, so under the pretence of scratching his nose; he managed to point in the general direction of the front office without drawing any attention to himself from Etsuko Suzuki.

'Phew, they must have decided to change the plan and come over the hill', he said to himself. It did not please Adam and seemed to have added to the risk as their plan could be compromised and surely there were other 'Odd Jobs' about the place. Herewini was not too pleased either at Hayakawa-san's insistence that they start to check out the place before Yamada returned. It could mean they might be better positioned to grab Jenny and make a break for things if they were already inside the place.

Herewini also had grave doubts about the logic. With Inspector Mori on his way, plus the rugby men, it should be like hitting a smallish enemy platoon with a brigade of troops. There was merit in trying to take Jenny out of the scene and away from the action in case firearms were being used, and now that Hayakawa-san had told him about the small busload of Yakuza that had come up to this place, it really made it all the more confusing.

He had agreed to go along with Hayakawa-san's plan on a step-by-step agreement basis. First, get into the wooded gardens and see who was about. Only Etsuko Suzuki, Adam and Michiko so far, but a glimpse of at least one Yakuza minder inside and, from the hill through the rain squalls, they had seen the minibus used by the Yakuza parked around the back. That was the real worry.

He insisted that they check that out first, so despite Adam's hand signal indicating the location of the office, they decided to creep around the side and see if there were any signs of the other Yakuza. They got within fifty feet in dense shrubbery. Fortunately, the heavy rain helped conceal them and no one in the house wanted to spend time outside in the wet gazing at the scenery. The saw half a dozen or so Yakuza loading boxes, and small cartons into a covered van. They were obviously moving out a lot of paperwork and computer files plus some computers.

Hayakawa-san said, 'I think the stuff we need might be going in the van but if we can see the office from outside and check if there is anything in there like files, we might still have to get inside.'

Hayakawa-san said he would make a check. With his dark wet weather gear on and hood up he did not look unlike some of the Yakuzas, so he took a chance and boldly broke cover and walked across the court yard. He followed a few Yakuzas in the luggage carry trail, went into the office with them, was handed a couple of boxes and took them out to the van. He then mumbled an excuse about needing a piss and disappeared into the bush again.

'This is it. It's our lucky day. We just wait until they finish and drive off in the van,' he said with a huge, beaming smile.

This is what Herewini found so likable and also so bloody annoying about Hayakawa-san, that smile could talk you into deep shit but also when things were really crap, the smile would convince you that it was all a bed of roses and escape was easy. He had met a few Kiwis like that, he knew the type! He tried to make light of it but in sarcastic tones said, 'Okay, you belt the shit out of the six big Yakuzas down there, and I will ask the one in the cab for the driver's keys and take over the driving after he politely hands them over.'

'Whatever happened to the Mormon missionary angle? Here we are with the dark jackets, white shirts and Brother what's-its-name badges on all to no effect at all!' Herewini added.

'You know you got to be flexible in the field, think on your feet, be prepared to change the plan,' Hayakawa insisted.

'You know, I never ever thought a Japanese person would lecture me on that, it's not supposed to be a natural trait in Japan, but we Maori in New Zealand have always followed the ways of the late great Maori comedian Billy T. James, a man whose characters were so flexible they could actually change physical form, and identity.' Herewini knew when a situation looked very tough a bit of humour was sometimes the only way to get through.

'That is what I will do, like your Billy T. James in this heavy rain. when the time is ready I will assume personality of Yakuza foreman and take charge, send them all into the house, keep the truck keys, you will drive and we will be gone,' Hayakawa-san said with a kind of childlike innocence.

'It might work, it's so outrageous and cheeky, but what about Jenny? I am here for her, not the bloody files,' Herewini stressed.

'That is, what you say, a piece of cake. She comes back to the house first with Yamada, you get down close to the house and attract her attention some way, get her into the garden or road outside and off we go,' Hayakawa-san said.

'My God, you're the frigging limit, Hayakawa-san. You've got me in fits of laughter. Look, my shoulders are shaking with mirth, but no, it's stark raving fear. These guys must have firearms and we have nothing. I am not ready to die yet.' Herewini was mortified at the thought of it.

'OK Herewini-san, like we decided when we got into

this garden, we go one step at a time and always have an exit from the situation for every step. Then if chance happens, we take chance, okay? That is fair, I think.'

'For you and me the first priority must be to keep Jenny from harm. Her life is more important than any amount of money you might recover for your members,' Herewini emphasised.

Hayakawa-san's face looked deadly serious. 'That is exactly so, and I thank you for reminding me. It has to be her first, then the files if we have a chance.'

During this debate, Adam and Michiko's brief tour had ended. They lingered as long as possible, asking more questions and looking for traces of Jenny's room but Etsuko Suzuki now wanted them out quickly and away from the place. As they walked to their car, they could not see or hear the Yakuza shifting boxes behind a walled tradesmen's entrance, and had no idea what was going on. Adam said to Michiko, 'What next? We can't really telephone Hayakawa-san and Herewini when they have changed the plan and gone into enemy territory, so to speak. It might blow their cover if they have forgotten to switch off their mobile phones.'

They decided to motor down to the slip road and concealed woodcutters' track where they were supposed to rendezvous, and just wait. That is what the two men would expect them to do. Adam said they should try to phone Inspector Mori, Tanaka-san and the rugby men. They contacted the inspector first and found he was very concerned about the weather and landslips. They told him they had been in the house and that Herewini and

Hayakawa-san had changed an agreed plan and had gone in to suss the place out in greater depth.

The inspector was annoyed, and asked if they had seen any signs of Yamada's white Nissan limo which was ahead of him. They said no. He asked if they could have missed seeing it, and they said only perhaps when they were being shown around the garden. It was possible Yamada could have arrived at the house when they were out in the garden, and that could account for Etsuko Suzuki's insistence that they look at the natural thermal pools in the pouring rain. Inspector Mori sucked his breath and let out some Japanese belly talk to indicate things were getting too dangerous and confused for words, and he had no immediate ideas.

'You just wait where you are, keep in touch with me regularly. I just hope this road stays open so we can reach the house, also the rugby boys should be coming up ahead of us as well so when they do, you can stop their small bus, take them to the slip road and insist they contact me before doing anything. Either Tanaka-san's mobile is off, or he is in blind area with no radio signal, so try your best to contact them,' the inspector instructed. Michiko promised to do so, and then tried Tanaka-san's number without success.

The small bus carrying Tanaka-san and the rugby men was grinding its way painfully with the steep hill, and Tanaka-san had tried to use his mobile a few times without success. He, too, was very worried about the weather and their chances of getting through, but the rugby men were keyed up with excitement at the possibility of a punch-up with some crims. He cast his eyes over them;

they were mostly his home club of middle-aged and elderly players, nicknamed 'troublemakers' within the rugby world.

They were tough and fit for their age but no spring chickens. Cunning yes, he could rely on that, but no one had any weapons, and he realised he should not have gone ahead with this. It was beer talk that had made him rashly accept the challenge at a late night drinking session. Luckily, he had Yoshi on board and also Flanker. Unknown to Tanaka-san, Flanker had got wind of the scheme and told his boss, Inspector Mori, about it. The inspector had laughed and thought it a joke at the time and something that might not happen. He just told Flanker to go with them if it happened and keep him posted.

The bus was down to about ten kilometres an hour in low gear, and there were jokes about having to get out and give it a push from the back seat occupants. It rounded a corner and the driver came to a sudden halt, having been waved down by a rain-sodden Adam and Michiko. They quickly told the driver to park off the road in the concealed slip road, and then briefed them on what was happening.

Michiko said she should be able to reach Inspector Mori on her mobile before he entered the dead broadcasting zone. She got the crackling tones of his voice and a broken-up reply that a large tree had fallen across the road. It was much too big for them to shift, so they would have to walk the rest of the way. Inspector Mori insisted they stay put and do nothing until he arrived. They estimated it might be thirty minutes at least on foot!

Flanker said he wanted to reconnoitre the place. Tanaka-san said he also wished to join in, and Adam and Michiko offered to go. It would leave Yoshi in charge. However, it was also decided to keep some sort of watch on the road to check on any outgoing traffic from the house. No one had come prepared for the storm, and none had rough trekking clothes for tramping the old loggers' trails. The rugby men had piratical rigs of training jerseys, jeans and old zip-up jackets ready for a rough and tumble but nothing resembling any oilskins.

It was freezing outside but the brisk walk up the hill and down to the fringes of the garden kept the four of them warm for a while. Flanker caught a glimpse of Hayakawa-san and Herewini in the bushes not far away, and told the others to go back. He would join them as he had a police pistol and they were at risk doing what they were. He would try to talk them out of it and to await police reinforcements. The other three were glad to get back to the warmth of the bus and play a waiting game.

Herewini and Hayakawa-san welcomed Flanker's appearance and an update of the situation, but they refused to budge. They quickly worked out that if Michiko and Adam did not see Yamada's car on the road, they must have arrived while the couple were outside inspecting the thermal pools.

Meanwhile, Flanker was shaking with wet and cold; Herewini was able to find a pile of used plastic rubbish bags and did the old farmer's trick, cutting a head hole in the bottom and two slits for arms on the sides. It fitted okay but stank to high heaven of compost. He then found another one and carefully folded half the base inside out

556

on itself to make a sort of Robin Hood top and grabbed some old garden string so Flanker could tie it up.

'You look like some old scarecrow,' Herewini laughed.

'What is scarecrow?' Flanker asked, not very amused at what must be some sort of mild insult, and then added, 'Anyway, its okay and keeps me dry but smell is very terrible!'

'I think maybe it had pig shit in it before,' Hayakawa-san said, holding his nose and moving away.

Herewini said he wanted to check out the rooms to find Jenny's and would creep around the outside. The gloomy late afternoon light was fading and all the house lights were on, making it easier to move around outside without being detected. The other two would remain where they were. It didn't take Herewini too long to find Jenny's room. She had not drawn the blinds properly and he spotted her there sorting out a few personal effects.

In another part of the house, Yamada was telling Etsuko Suzuki that they were shifting house immediately. He had got wind the police were on to him and they would be going to new premises along with all the files he had ordered his men to pack up and shift. She had suspected that was his plan when he said earlier in the day he was sending men to shift the files. It had happened before and they would most likely go to a luxury Tokyo apartment.

Etsuko Suzuki had told Jenny to pack her things, and Jenny was busy doing this when Herewini came snooping around. He made sure there was no one else in the room, and then tapped gently on the window. She thought at first it was the storm rattling something, went to investigate, and got the shock of her life seeing his face pressed against the glass.

She was about to withdraw and scream when he told her in English to shut up. She paused furiously trying to make out who or what he was. His English had a bit of an accent, he looked a little like Japanese, someone who was might be part European, but he was well built and bigger than the average Japanese.

'I am a Kiwi. I am here to rescue you, just do as I say,' he told her hastily.

She was like a stunned mullet, unable to fathom it all out. He told her to open the window, grab a heavy raincoat and tough shoes. She obeyed, as if in a daze, and athletically slipped through the window to join him. He grabbed her arm and adroitly hopped back into the bush, making sure she closed the window afterwards.

'We don't have too long. This place is full of bloody Yakuza, but the cops are not too far away,' he told her.

She gathered her senses. 'Who the hell are you, how do I know I can trust you?'

'Just look deep into my face.' He smiled kindly at her as he said it, and added he was a holidaying New Zealand customs officer who was a mate of Rick, a man she might know. She confirmed knowledge of Rick, and Herewini explained how Rick had got involved in the search for her at her dad's request.

'Rick is at Fukuoka with his group now. With a bit of luck we should all be safely back at Fukuoka in about three hours' time,' he told her, saying he had two Japanese friends hiding out who were helping with her escape. He bundled her into the small couch area they had made in the bush to shelter from the worst of the rain. First of all she smelt Flanker.

'My God, something stinks here!' she exclaimed.

The other two men rocked with muffled laughter. Flanker was furious, but apologised and explained why. Herewini suggested that Flanker could perhaps wander into the loading courtyard where the van was, then distract the Yakuza who had nearly finished packing the van. He would pretend to be a tramp looking for some food or something. Then Herewini and Hayakawa would overpower whoever was in or near the driving cab, grab the keys, fire it up and take off, first making sure Flanker was able to get on board.

The first part went well; most of the Yakuza were in the house leaving only a few to sort the remaining packages. Two of them seemed to fall for it and were trying to tell a tenacious Flanker to piss off, but Flanker was a big guy and pushed his way towards the kitchen. It left just one Yakuza in the cab of the truck. Things went a bit wrong. Herewini, Hayakawa and Jenny were making a dash for the truck when two Yakuza started to emerge from the building with Flanker, who they were attempting to throw out.

Herewini, Jenny and Hayakawa dived into the back of the truck and hid among the boxes. The two Yakuza, thinking they had dealt with Flanker, then slammed the door of the truck and jumped into the front seat with the driver. He fired it up, and Flanker made an unseen gallop to the truck, opened the back door and scrambled in to join the others. The truck rounded the courtyard and took to the open road.

'Now what?' Flanker asked.

'Just move away from me please,' Herewini said. Jenny had regained her composure and was very impressed by the appearance of her handsome saviour.

'You live up to your picture even more than I imagined you would,' Herewini told her and explained how he had been stunned by the picture. 'If you were ugly maybe I wouldn't have rescued you,' he teased.

'What sort of a Kiwi are you? If you're a Maori, where are all the tattoos and things?' she asked.

'I keep them concealed, I only reveal them to ladies I love,' he joked. Hayakawa-san reminded them what they were there for, and suggested they might as well stay for the ride as he wanted these documents in one piece.

'When truck finally stops we overpower two Yakuza in the front and then get to police as soon as possible,' he outlined.

'I am the police,' Flanker reminded them.

'What are you going to do?' Herewini teased him.

'Take a bath at first opportunity,' he said.

'No, before that,' Herewini continued to tease him.

The truck was bouncing down the road and seemed to have swerved off the main road on to a rough track as they talked. They tried to raise Adam and Michiko and Tanaka-san on their mobiles without success and also had a similar lack of success in trying to get Inspector Mori.

'Telephone coverage is not so good here,' Flanker observed.

'That is classic Japanese understatement for, and excuse the language, "it does not fucking work,"' Herewini explained to Jenny. 'In Japan, if they tell you there is a small problem, it translates to "it's a bloody huge disaster,"' he amplified.

Back at Yamada's house, Etsuko Suzuki had found Jenny missing, so a hue and cry was in full force, with Yakuza being sent all over the place to hunt them out. They soon suspected Flanker the tramp as being the abductor, but there was no trace of him or Jenny. That raised suspicion that they might have somehow got onto the truck so a car with four armed Yakuza was sent in pursuit to check it out.

The driver of the truck had been instructed to take a little-known and used track through the dense forest to Kumamoto which was less prone to landslides. As it was downhill all the way, they were not so worried about loss of traction on its unsealed surfaces. The turn-off was before the slip road where Adam, Michiko and the rugby bus were parked, so they had no idea that any vehicles had left the house.

The van stopped suddenly, and it became apparent that part of the track was submerged beneath flood waters. The driver and his companions got out. Flanker sprang into action. 'Okay, let's do it now!' He told Jenny to stay put, and told the others it would be three on three.

The Yakuza were taken by surprise but put up a good fight. Herewini realised he would need all his strength to overcome his opponent who was pretty skilled in martial arts, Hayakawa-san's judo skills and fitness came to the fore. It was beautiful to watch, if you had time! Herewini noted the slick moves he made with envy.

Flanker was the first to overpower his man, and he had one of those nasty single handed grips on him. Then Herewini and Hayakawa came in equal second with their opponents under control. Jenny was out of the truck by then and gave a few claps of encouragement. They disarmed two of the Yakuza who carried pistols. They found some strong sticky brown packaging tape in the cab of the truck and trussed them up as best as possible, threw them in the back, and left Flanker there to keep an eye on them.

'They will really enjoy your smell,' Herewini teased him.

It was now dark. After inspecting the flooded portion of the road with the headlights full on, they decided to give it a go, and Hayakawa-san cautiously eased the laden van through about two feet of water. They were tracking on downhill when they became aware of the headlights of another vehicle behind. It was the car with the Yakuzas trying to catch up, with everyone on board ready for action.

Herewini made a snap decision. He ordered everyone out of the truck, including the three strung-up captives they had just taken, placed them next to a tree and they took up positions a few car lengths behind the truck. After careening down the mountain at breakneck speed, the car looked like a rally car that had just completed Rally New Zealand. It pulled up sharply once the driver realised his quarry was at a halt. The Yakuza men jumped out hastily, pistols drawn.

Flanker told them this was a police operation, and they were to lay down their arms as they were surrounded. The Yakuzas decided to take their chances, dived for cover, and started shooting randomly at where they thought Flanker and the others were. It was very wild shooting, and it gave away their positions to Flanker and the others who responded quickly with more accurate fire. Herewini and Hayakawa-san had both taken the pistols from their own Yakuza captives. Hayakawa-san had never fired a pistol in his life before and got a few seconds' tuition from Herewini, interspersed with some incoming bullets.

Flanker told the others he was going to live up to his nickname. They were to keep their positions and he would try to outflank the Yakuzas. After sneaking around the bush, he managed to get three telling shots away which wounded two of the Yakuza. The other two had the spirit knocked out of them with two wounded companions, and not knowing where the fire was coming from; they gave up and walked meekly towards Flanker after first throwing down their firearms.

The two injured Yakuza had only mild flesh wounds, one in the right upper arm and the other in the left thigh. They were quickly bandaged with torn clothing. It was decided to abandon the Yakuza car where it was after seeing nothing of interest or value was left behind. The injured Yakuzas were patched up and put in the back of the van with the other prisoners under the guard of

Flanker and Herewini. Hayakawa-san then took the wheel with Jenny beside him up front. Hayakawa-san warned Jenny it would be a long and tortuous drive, and with that got the rig rolling again downhill.

Back at the slip road, Adam and Michiko and Tanaka-san's group were getting increasingly anxious with no sight of Flanker, Herewini and Hayakawa-san. Tanaka-san looked at his watch and calculated Inspector Mori and his detectives should be on the scene soon and made a quick decision.

'I think we should use Hayakawa-san's car to drive down as far as we can to pick them up, even at the risk of being seen by some of Yamada's men,' he told the group. They agreed, and one of his group was picked to drive it. Tanaka-san felt a bit stupid at not thinking of this sooner for depending where the fallen tree was, it could save a lot of time. He then selected two of his rugby men to take the woodcutters' track over the hill to see if they could spot Flanker and the others but told them they should keep out of the house and make sure at least one of them came back to him with an update as soon as possible.

When the two rugby men approached the garden boundary, they almost ran into a small group of Yakuza out searching for Jenny, and they heard them complain that she must have escaped in the van with the weird desperado who bumbled into the garden. They were trying to fathom out how just one desperado and a girl could overpower three Yakuza who had been loading the van at the time. It was a puzzle to them and they obviously had not seen Flanker and the two other men.

There was a lot of activity at the house with all outside lights on and small groups all over the place searching by torchlight. They could hear Yamada shouting but the wind and rain was so strong they could not make out the words. They also spotted the small bus and Yamada's white Nissan limo parked near the rear service entrance. Some gear was being taken out to the bus and suitcases being put into the car. The rugby men felt they had seen enough, so trekked back and reported to Tanaka-san. Shortly after their return, the car with Inspector Mori and his detectives arrived. He was quickly briefed by Tanaka-san and was clearly not happy about the situation.

'It would seem that Jenny, Flanker, Herewini and Hayakawa-san are missing and can be presumed to have escaped some way in the van, possibly hidden in the back with three Yakuza in the cab. But by what road? This road is the only formed road to the house so the van has either broken down or there must be some logging track out of that place,' he assumed. When given the description of the Yakuza small bus, he estimated the maximum load it could take, and added to it the possibility of a few other Yakuza housemen who stayed at that place.

'There may be about 25 of them, and we have to assume they are armed. Everything indicates that Yamada is making a hasty exit and taking all the evidence with him.' He paused and thought for a while and continued, 'We will take a chance. Two of my armed detectives plus three rugby volunteers should take Hayakawa-san's car, continue up the road and look for a logging track the van might have used. There will be fresh tyre marks, of course, that should be followed. A car should be faster

than a van, and I imagine it's many miles before it con-
nects with another sealed road.

'I will keep a small base group here in this bus. Adam,
Michiko, please stay here and two rugby volunteers. The
rest of us are going in on foot, half of us up the road, and
the other half up the loggers' track over the hill. One of
our major problems will be communication, but fortunately our police radios can keep us police in contact with
each other. Remember we have just five pistols between
us, and two of them will go in the car, so we only have
three at our disposal to take on the main group. If we can
bail them up some way and prevent their escape until
more police come in, it will be successful, and the best
way is to try to disable their bus and whatever cars they
have. So disabling the vehicles is the first priority,' he
ended.

CHAPTER 17

The big day out at Fukuoka's Ohori Koen Park had gone far better than expected. The four UK film stars had the exposure they wanted and the film company felt it had regained its reputation after the big communications mix-up. The only anxious folk were the Mereleigh Record Club group now back at the Sea Hawk Hotel minus Adam and Michiko and Foggy and Helena. They had received a brief message conveyed to Rick from the latter two that they had seen Jenny and were now in hot pursuit to her captors' hideaway.

Ban-san of the Fukuoka Record Club made some phone calls to Fukuoka police on their account and they guardedly admitted Inspector Mori and others were now involved in an active search for her. The group's concern was focused on the absence of Adam and Michiko and also Herewini, as someone remembered a meeting

Herewini had with Hayakawa-san and Tanaka-san. A call to a Fukuoka Small and Medium Business Association member confirmed Hayakawa-san was taking friends for a ride in the country and would be staying overnight somewhere near Kumamoto.

Rick was furious at not being let on this. Knowing Herewini, he realised that Hayakawa-san must have had something up his sleeve. He glanced at Peter who, with the rest of the group, was lounging in a bar. Peter and his wife had an anxious look on their faces so he strolled over and put on a brave face and said Adam and Michiko were probably just following the police to get the news first. Peter nodded in agreement, saying 'No doubt, that young Michiko certainly seems to have fire in her belly.'

They had heard about the storm forecast and the dark clouds began to gather over Fukuoka. In somewhat weird circumstances they watched the Sea Hawk's regular rain-storm and lightning feature in the hotel's own rain forest as the real thing started to take place outside. Rick was desperate to do something so he called Ted Jones in Wales to tell him Jenny had been sighted.

It was early morning and Ted had just helped his wife hang out the washing. It was a grand spring morning with plenty of sporting lambs baaing all over the place, and the daffodils out and all. He did not know why, but he was feeling a bit more relaxed. It was not just the call from Price the plainclothes man confirming some arrests of those who had threatened him and jiggered with his phone, but something else he could not put a finger on.

Rick was surprised at his relaxed tones on the phone.

He was heartened by Ted's news of the arrest of the Slavic thugs and when he told Ted about the sighting of Jenny and police follow up it brightened Ted's day even more, though Ted did say, 'I do hope the Japanese police are not trigger-happy like the Yanks and if guns have to be used, make sure they shoot the right people.' Rick gave Ted an undertaking he would stay up all night if necessary and keep him posted.

'In that case I will phone in sick today and do some gardening within sound of the phone. Thanks a lot Rick, it's much appreciated. I see I am going to have to buy you a few pints when you are over next!' Ted ended.

After Tanaka-san had switched to a police car at Kumamoto, the Mini Minor driver, with Helena and Foggy on board, had lost sight of him after he turned up a side road. They made the same turning but the Mini, although pretty nippy for its years, was no match for a modern fuel-injected multi-valve V6 engine.

All three aboard the Mini were eager to get to the action even if it was a case of a late arrival. Foggy offered a cautionary note. 'We must remember we are essentially rubber-necking and should be careful not to get in the way and hinder the police.'

'It's a bit like "Goodbye Pork Pie",' Helena said. No one knew what she was talking about, so she told them about a funny New Zealand movie that featured a group in a Mini Minor on a big chase.

The Mini came more into its own on the steep hill climbs and hairpin bends, things it could take at almost full tilt. Eventually, like Inspector Mori's police car, they came to a halt at the same tree which had fallen across the road but, unlike the Inspector, felt no huge necessity to proceed beyond it on foot. They spent a moment or two deciding what to do and ended up making a decision to hang about for a couple of hours. The weather was getting worse but the owner of the Mini had some classic 1960s CDs to play to keep all amused for a while.

Inspector Mori's men who had been assigned to take Hayakawa-san's car and track down the van had found the logging trail with fresh tyre marks and were racing down the now very muddy trail in a rally-like fashion, trying to avoid any crippling damage to the car in the process. They had to drive past the house to find the trail and were sure they had been spotted by one or two Yakuza, but there was no attempt to stop them as they had bigger fish to fry in the van.

The two other police and rugger groups sneaked around the house, but they soon realised they had no chance of getting near the vehicles and disabling them without the risk of being seen and having a shoot-out. Tanaka-san therefore told them to play a waiting game. When the moment came, it seemed everyone had been summoned back into the former ryokan's main hall for some kind of briefing. It was in fact a furious Yamada calling off the search for Jenny and deciding it was time to hit the road. He gave final instructions to his men, most of whom would go in the bus and he in the car, and they would take the logging track in case of being cut off by the police. They had no knowledge that the proper road was blocked.

The briefing gave Inspector Mori and his detectives

just enough time to disable the vehicles and take cover again. From their hiding places in the adjacent forest they could see and hear the anger of the Yakuza as they tried to start the vehicles. The Yakuza somewhat recklessly flashed high-powered torches around the place, easily identifying themselves and what they were doing.

Inspector Mori had told everyone they should move into deeper forest rather than confront the Yakuza as they were greatly outnumbered. Most on Inspector Mori's side were unarmed so they probably lacked enough fire power to win if it came to a shoot-out. Yamada made a decision. They would all walk out down the proper road, take cover in the forest if necessary, and either try to find a vehicle they could steal or arrange for someone to pick them up. The phone lines were down and mobile phones were near useless at that location.

'We will walk all night if necessary and then, when we find a phone, we will arrange our transport.' He glanced around and could see Etsuko Suzuki was quiet.

'I will stay here. No one can accuse an old lady of anything. I am just the housekeeper who knows nothing,' she told Yamada.

Yamada agreed. 'They will question you but possibly they have nothing, so after a few days they will leave you alone and I will contact you in about five days' time unless you reach me,' he told her.

Yamada and his private army of Yakuzas marched out into the stormy darkness, and after about 20 minutes one of then stopped for a piss and saw Tanaka-san's bus. It was vacant except for Adam and Michiko, and the two rugby players left behind with them. Within a few minutes it had been commandeered by Yamada, and the four of them forced into the back seat with burly Yakuza minders.

One of the Yakuza shouted at them, 'Get into the back seat and don't give trouble or you're dead meat.' Adam and Michiko had been taken completely by surprise. Michiko told Adam, 'we must move to the back seat and they threaten to kill us if we move.' Pistols had been brandished by the Yakuza to show they meant business.

The bus took off downhill at speed. Adam whispered to Michiko, 'You'd better tell them about the tree across the road.'

She thought for a second and said, 'We know about it but we are in the back and there is an emergency exit near us. If we brace ourselves tightly between the seats we should avoid major injury and be able to escape.' Adam told her to let the two rugby men know. They estimated the tree was about ten minutes away but in a split second they saw a large, dark shadow across the road. They dived between the seats and braced themselves.

The bus driver jammed on his brakes, but with almost no room to turn, he locked wheels, and simply burned rubber. The bus hit the tree almost front on with a horrendous crash, buckling the steel bodywork and sending particles of safety glass and other debris flying. The scene was pure mayhem with many injured, possibly some dead, and the headlights, or what remained of them, gazing skew-whiff at the night sky.

The four in the back seat were badly shaken up but

among the first to gain their composure. They quickly prised open the rear emergency exit and took to the forest. They clambered around the fallen tree and were amazed to see a small car parked on the other side, and even more surprised to find Foggy and Helena inside. Without any detailed explanation, they forced themselves in, thus breaking some record probably by having one driver and five passengers in a Mini Cooper in the quickest time possible.

The car's owner almost literally had his feet around his ears as he fired the Mini up did a quick turn and took off downhill at speed. He was still driving like a lunatic long after it was necessary. About forty minutes later, the passengers insisted on a comfort stop to tend to their bruises and cuts, and to have nervous pees to relieve the shock of it all.

Everyone started to talk all at once, trying to explain or figure out what had happened. Then they boarded the Mini again with greater care and the benefit of experience to get as comfortable as possible. The owner was also convinced that he need not travel so fast. There was a further 80 minutes' driving before he came to a lonely village and managed to raise a couple of locals, who then contacted the police to let them know what was happening.

Adam and Michiko, ever the journalists, decided to alert their newspapers with an eye to getting a scoop if the police found Jenny and arrested Yamada. They both sent scene setters leading right up to the present that could be topped off with any further action. Adam's office in Britain was very excited about it all as they had already picked up news of some arrests in Welshpool in connection with the kidnapping. About the same time, Hayakawa-san and the van had found a way back on to a sealed road, and he pulled out his GPS and worked out where the formed road was.

'Might be just thirty minutes to Kumamoto from here, and I prefer to go there to big police station first, so we can use our mobile phone again soon and tell them we are coming,' he told Jenny.

Jenny had resumed her normal self after the shock escape, and rescue, and she was beginning to have fun. 'You can dine out on an experience like this for the rest of your life and, hey ho, aren't the Sunday newspapers going to pay heaps for an exclusive story?' she thought to herself.

Herewini and Flanker were finding the unventilated back of the van more than a bit stifling, but their mood lifted as soon as it hit solid tar-seal road again. The last part of the trip to Kumamoto police station went very quickly and when the van swung into its brightly-lit courtyard, it was immediately surrounded by two dozen armed Japanese policemen in full riot gear. It was a bit of overkill as the Yakuzas in the back were still well trussed up and glad to get out without fuss.

Once the prisoners were sorted and the other four seated in a comfortable police room, Jenny went around and gave each of them a huge hug and a kiss, especially Herewini who, she said, was the real hero. He loved it all but feigned modesty. Jenny was allowed to ring her parents but told to restrict the call to saying she was safe and at the Kumamoto police station and unharmed.

'Once we have your statements and more details, I expect you can have more contact with your family, but please understand we must quickly evaluate the situation so we can capture the kidnappers and not give them any knowledge that could help them escape. So please tell you parents to, what do you say, "keep it under their hats," I think,' the police officer ended with a smile.

Herewini told Jenny about Adam and Michiko, and asked her if she could give them a scoop as they had been very helpful. 'I am sure they can arrange megabucks for an exclusive story,' he added. She agreed, she could agree to almost anything, she felt so good now.

When the phone rang up at the small farm near Welshpool, Ted was expecting Rick, and he was anxious as he knew these things could go bad at the end. His confidence had drained from him in anticipation of the worst when Jenny burst out that she was free and okay. There were tears at both ends of the line. Her mum came on too, and then she had to end quickly to help the police.

The Kumamoto Police had heard from Adam and Michiko by now, and had a good idea what was happening, so they dispatched a busload of SWAT-squad police up the mountain to sort out Yamada's private army, and also several four-wheel drives back up the logging track to block off any possible exits there. The four-wheel drive group soon ran into Inspector Mori's detectives, who could barely see out of the mud-splattered windscreen, and they immediately joined forces.

The bus crash had been both chaotic and bloody. Yamada had escaped with a broken arm and many cuts and bruises. He had grabbed a few Yakuza with only slight injuries and they had headed off into the night down the road, leaving the others to sort out the dead and injured. They had heard the sound of vehicles racing up the mountain and had taken to the bush until a police bus and ambulances roared past, then they continued on down the trail.

Earlier, once the Yakuza had left the old ryokan, Inspector Mori and the rugby men had taken over the building and found Etsuko Suzuki and another old mama-san. 'Small fish,' he thought. He carefully checked every room and was well into the work when one of their number who had been sent down to the rugby bus at the slip road reported it missing. It was his worst nightmare. He imagined that Yamada had got four of the team captive including Adam and Michiko and were well off into the night somewhere.

He sent four of Tanaka-san's rugby men off on foot down the road, suspecting the bus must have come to a halt at the fallen tree if it went that way, and told them simply to get back and let him know as soon as possible if that was the case. The bus could have gone down the logging track but he guessed that in these conditions, if it did, it would never be able to get back up again on such a muddy, slippery road. He posted some of the rugby men at the doors as lookouts, and then took statements from the ladies. They were very tough old birds who knew when and how to be quiet, and they were not giving up anything that night.

The night drifted on and eventually two exhausted rugby men came back to tell of the coach smash and no sign of Adam, Michiko, and the two others, and they described a scene of horror with smashed bodies, and with the injured wandering around in a daze. The inspector then grabbed half a dozen or so men and took off on foot at speed hoping he might be able to apprehend Yamada.

He got to the scene about the same time the police bus with the SWAT squad arrived. Inspector Mori quickly organised a group to head down the road and try to cut off Yamada who he rightly believed would be on foot sticking quite close to the road. He called for sniffer dogs to hunt him out. It was a very long, cold night, but about daybreak the dogs had been in action for an hour or so and hit a trail that led to a very damp and disoriented Yamada and his cohorts. To Inspector Mori's surprise and pleasure they had no fight in them and came along quietly.

⌘⌘⌘

By midday the centre of the inquiry and interviews had been shifted to Fukuoka, along with the vanload of documents which Hayakawa-san would not leave out of his sight. Adam and Michiko had already arrived at Fukuoka Police Station, as had Inspector Mori, by the time Herewini and Hayakawa-san turned up. There was a roar of laughter from Adam and Michiko when they saw the duo, with Adam telling the world in general, 'This is one for the record. Take a picture Michiko, you might never see Herewini and Hayakawa-san looking like Mormon missionaries again in your life.'

'You promised not to take a picture of us like this,'

Herewini protested. Jenny was looking the most composed of the lot. It was her first meeting with Adam and Michiko.

'I have heard about you both from Herewini, he was full of praise for your support and he told me I could trust you with my story, but please I am too shaken up to say anything now and must help the police first. I promise to give you first shot,' she said. Inspector Mori was still very anxious to control what information they gave out to the public. 'We are still interviewing Yamada, and he will admit to nothing, so we have to prove everything step by step,' he explained.

In her interview Jenny told the inspector about Etsuko Suzuki and asked if she had been arrested too. It had not been done. The Inspector was shocked and surprised by Jenny's tale of how Etsuko had been an old lover who procured the lookalike stars for him. She said Suzuki might also know what happened to them afterwards.

After a very lengthy interview, Jenny was allowed to go to a local hotel to clean up and sleep for about 6 hours. She was woken by a policewoman who said Inspector Mori was heading back to Yamada's old ryokan almost immediately with a more technical forensics team, and Jenny was needed on site as Suzuki had said she would make a confession to her.

'It was because you saved her life,' the policewoman said.

The trip back was much quicker. The weather had cleared and a police helicopter was laid on. Jenny felt a shudder of fear at having to go back to that place, but she also felt a small pang of sympathy for Suzuki, who looked a broken woman not far from death. Suzuki greeted Jenny politely and explained again how Jenny had saved her life. She had therefore promised Jenny her end would be different from the other girls'.

She confessed to recruiting many girls over the years in the hope that they could give Yamada the physical love and satisfaction he could not find with her. It had all been in vain. No woman had been able to satisfy him after her, and he was always so embarrassed and shameful about it that they made a pact to keep it a secret.

'There was only one way to keep it a secret. The girls had to die!' she said.

'So he killed them all?' Inspector Mori asked.

'No, I did it for him. It was quite easy for me, a kind of revenge to get rid of these young bitches who thought they could give him something I could not,' she stated.

'But they did not do it willingly?' Inspector Mori persisted.

'That is quite correct, Inspector, none of them came voluntarily when they knew what it was about, but each one was a deep personal shame for me. They had to go, you must understand that,' she added.

'But Jenny was different. These other girls treated me like rubbish, beneath their fear they hated me and could never understand the love I had for Yamada. Only Jenny was kind, she saved my life so I am telling you this so she can understand how deep and compelling a woman's love can be for a man.' She stopped and breathed deeply.

'I owe Yamada nothing any more, nor anyone else except Jenny. Doomo arigatoo gozaimashita Jenny-san.' That was all she would say until gently prompted afterwards by the inspector for details of how she actually killed them and how they disposed of their bodies.

'Poison in the drink. It was quite quick. As soon as Yamada told me they were no use, they would go within about 24 hours. Around the back his two most loyal retainers and I would put their bodies in the big garden incinerator. It has gas booster burners about as quick as a normal crematorium. Their ashes are in the garden.'

She ended showing no signs of remorse, as though her punishment over the years was the humiliation of having to produce all these girls to try to perform a function that she could not. No one could punish her any more. In her mind she had existed in a living hell for a few decades, wrestling with her emotions and hatred for the young girls.

There was a stony silence for more than a few minutes as the inspector, Jenny, and all others present absorbed the magnitude of her crime, and pondered over a love that would drive a woman to those lengths. Jenny sat with tears in her eyes. She did not know if she was crying for Suzuki or all the girls who had been killed. It had to be the girls and the parents who had lost their daughters.

A burly Japanese policewoman next to Jenny whispered, 'Only in Japan we can see this kind of stupid loyalty to a man. A woman who hates to lose face in front of her husband will do anything to keep face!'

'Not so,' Jenny replied. 'Anywhere when love gets so

deep, a woman will do some irrational things, but this has to be at the very extreme irrational end of it.'

Inspector Mori left forensics in charge of the crime scene. He formally arrested Suzuki and arranged for her to be transported back to Fukuoka by car, and then he flew back by helicopter with Jenny, and a few other police officers. During the flight he confided in her.

'I think we can arrest Yamada OK for being a party to all those murders. He would have known. It was his property and his employees, so to my mind he is the prime culprit. He could have stopped this happening right at the beginning. He clearly also got some economic benefit out of the lookalikes as well.'

He continued, 'I think Suzuki will testify against him, certainly her statement is enough to put him away. Then we must consider the suicide of Nomura-san of the Fukuoka Record Club. Yamada was the man who pulled the rug from sponsorship of the Mereleigh group when, in a fit of rage, he realised he could not use his lookalike, you, at an event which did not have film stars at it. It totally wrecked his big ego trip and Nomura was the victim of such a barrage of slander that he took his own life. We will level a manslaughter charge at the very least,' he said.

'The vanload of documents that Hayakawa-san procured in one piece should have lots of paper and computer trails for that and many other things, I imagine,' the inspector added.

Jenny knew nothing of Nomura-san and the early misfortunes of the Record Club until the inspector explained it all. She was staggered by his revelation and her planned role in it. Jenny was booked in at the Sea Hawk Hotel along with the other Mereleigh group guests and was warmly received with huge relief by everyone.

A very big press contingent had amassed to interview her and to take photographs. A middle-aged Japanese man, who spoke excellent English, introduced himself to her and gave some official ID proclaiming he was the official police media affairs officer, and asked her if she was willing to be interviewed at a joint press conference with Inspector Mori. She looked to Adam and Michiko. They were the cats who had already supped the cream so they had no fears as their stories were well en route to their media organisations. They nodded in agreement, and offered her a few tips.

'Please sit with me, Adam, and help me, and you too Michiko. I don't want to say anything dreadful,' she pleaded.

Inspector Mori took the lead and told the media Yamada and Suzuki had both been arrested on a variety of charges, the principal of which was the murder of some twenty girls over the past few decades. He praised Hayakawa-san, Herewini, Tanaka-san and the others who had played such vital roles, and also Jenny for keeping her head. Before finishing he hinted at further manslaughter charges being levelled concerning the suicide of Nomura-san. That drew a sigh of surprise, but he would not amplify on the details until further investigations had been made.

He also indicated possible multiple charges of fraud arising from the discovery of the vanload of documents and CDs. All this Adam and Michiko already knew and had filed stories on, but only they knew the full inside story and the full picture of events leading up to the arrests.

Jenny handled her interview with the confidence of a natural actor on opening night. No hesitation, short correct answers, and a winning smile. She was going to be plastered across the pages of all major Japanese and UK newspapers, and Herewini's involvement meant the New Zealand media would put him and Jenny on their front pages as well.

Those who had been out rescuing Jenny were dead on their feet, it was only the adrenaline of the pursuit that kept them going now, and Jenny was rapidly coming down from a high. Fran took Jenny under her wing and got her tucked up and told the hotel front desk not to put any calls through to her room until 8 am. Herewini sank a few stiff rum and cokes with some of the other males in the group and felt a huge wave of tiredness sweep over him, and was fast asleep a second after he hit the sheets.

There was a huge buzz about the Sea Hawk the following morning. A big media contingent was hanging about to re-interview the major players in the rescue with the addition of Japan and Far East correspondents for many British publications seeking updates and features. Fran was in her element playing matron and keeping the media away from Jenny. Once the 8am phone curfew was lifted, Jenny found herself fielding call after call after call. Several of them were from film companies offering her auditions for new movies, all on the strength of her interview yesterday.

She rang her parents to say she would probably have to stay in Japan a few more days at least to help the Japanese police. Ted Jones said, 'You're all over the papers and TV here, and our phone has never stopped ringing with people wanting to contact you for interviews or promising film jobs. They have even been filming our house and talking to the neighbours about you, and they interviewed old Mrs Evans, the teacher, to get an angle on your childhood. You're bloody famous, girl!

'We've never seen the like of it. Mum and I are coming over. We guessed this would happen so we've been in touch with the local travel agent and he can get us on an overnight flight to Osaka tomorrow night from Heathrow by Japan Airlines, and then, I believe, we transfer to Fuki oka, that place you're at with a rude name . So we will give you our flight details and hopefully you can meet us at Fuki oka airport?'

'It's Fuu-kuu-oh-ka, Dad. Break it up into separate syllables. Yes, I will meet you. Tell Mum she should see one of the guys who rescued me, a real hunk, and a Kiwi Maori guy. I hope to see a lot more of him!' She was already thinking of an excuse to see Herewini that day.

'Rick and all the Mereleigh Record Club people have been fantastic to me. Several of them got involved in my search and took personal risks, it's absolutely amazing,' Jenny poured out the information for at least fifteen minutes before Fran tapped her on the shoulder and said Inspector Mori would like her to ring him after breakfast.

To her delight, Jenny saw Herewini at the restaurant, and they had breakfast at the same table, but with no privacy as most of the Mereleigh group were there and everyone was butting in and talking at the same time. As she went up to get her cooked breakfast from the breakfast bar she managed to say to Herewini she would dearly like to spend a day looking around Fukuoka and hoped he might join her before they all parted.

'Great minds, my thoughts entirely, it was on the tip of my tongue, but today I fear Inspector Mori will have a big chunk of our time one way or another. But let's make it tomorrow and, if circumstances permit, how about dinner together tonight?' he asked.

It was agreed, and she asked, 'What is your full name? Is Herewini a first name or family name?'

'Ohh, everyone just calls me Herewini. It's actually my first name taken from my Mum's side of the family which is Maori. Dad is also part Maori but granddad was Scottish, a MacDonald, so some smart arses in New Zealand call me MacHerewini,' he laughed.

'But you're part-African or something I believe?' he asked.

She told him about Ted, her Kenyan Dad, who had lived in Wales most of his life, and her Welsh Mum, and how Rick and her dad had met though Rick's Welsh cousin, and how they had hit it off because Rick had lived and worked in Kenya and Tanzania as a young man.

'You're my Jimmy Jones, without you and your courage I wouldn't be here now,' she said with laughter in her voice.

'Who the heck is Jimmy Jones? Some relation of yours?' Herewini replied with a degree of confusion.

'Have you never heard of this tune?' Jenny asked, then sang

'Oh you need good timin' a tick a tick a tick a

Good timin' a tick a tick a tick a tick a

Timin' is the thing

Its good timin' brought me to you

If little David hadn't

Grabbed that stone

A lyin' there on the ground

Big Goliath might've

Stomped on him

Instead of the other way

But he had

'Oh you need timin' a tick

A tick a tick a

Good timin'…

'Yep now you've sung it of course I do,' Herewini grinned back at her.

'I thought you would be an expert on rock and roll like the rest of them. Jimmy Jones made it a huge hit back in the golden age of rock.'

'I wasn't around then of course but my dad had the tune on a CD. You need a falsetto voice to sing it, or tight pants.' He gave the tune a go in a high falsetto voice. Herewini was then caught short by the realisation that this was the girl he could fall in love with. His emotions surprised him as he wrestled with the thoughts of where this was going. Was she being serious or just grateful for being rescued? He paused not wanting to appear pre-sumptuous. There was a moment's silence as Jenny caught the drift and wondered if she was running too fast into something that her instinct told her could be the start of something big.

'Well, I am Herewini MacDonald, not Jimmy Jones, a pretty ordinary guy really, not a rock star.' She felt a rush of confidence come over her, 'Well you are Jimmy Jones in my eyes,' and gave him a big hug and a kiss.

'Hullo, hullo, hullo, another budding romance. I thought one on this trip was enough.' It was Perry, the ex-British cop, being his normal, slightly rude, intrusive self. He had a message from Miss Alsop-Smith, the British Ambassador, congratulating Herewini, and the others who had helped rescue Jenny, and also complimenting Jenny on the calm, sensible way she had handled things. Herewini explained how Perry had been made unofficial liaison officer between Inspector Mori and the British Embassy during the search.

Inspector Mori had arranged a large briefing room for his afternoon meeting with Jenny, and he had also asked Hayakawa-san, Herewini, Tanaka-san and Adam and Michiko to attend. He had also assembled the key police-men who had been involved with this operation. This was to bring everyone up to date regarding the arrests, and to officially inform those who would be needed as wit-nesses. It was also to thank everyone for their fantastic co-operation and to point out to Hayakawa-san that it would take some days to sort out the documents taken from the van.

'The Japanese police are not in a position to offer any rewards but we can cover out of pocket expenses for all of you, so after this please see the clerk at the door and tell him what you need to cover your costs. However, I think there might be some other rewards. Jenny, might be you will get the big break in movies now. I hope so. Herewini and Tanaka-san, I believe Hayakawa-san has something to say.' The inspector nodded to Hayakawa-san to continue.

He got up and bowed very deeply to everyone and said, 'All my members asked me to convey their deepest thanks to you for the recovery of Yamada's documents. Collectively several of our companies have been defrauded of many billions of yen over the past few years by companies owned by Yamada and his associates.

'I am convinced we will have documents now which prove this, so we intend to set in motion legal action to gain compensation from Yamada's assets, which is very extensive. It is going to take time, maybe 12 months, because court processes are involved. However, my members have instructed me to make an ex-gratia payment to Herewini-san because, without him, I would not have had the courage to go to Yamada's place alone, and also to Tanaka-san and his rugby men for the back-up. This, I am afraid, will be small, but when the settlement of Yamada's assets are finalised, I have been instructed to see that Herewini and Tanaka-san personally get the usual debt collectors' percentage of the takings,' he concluded.

Herewini and Tanaka-san were stunned. Herewini calculated it; if it were ten percent between the two of them then even five per cent each of a few billion yen would be a hell of a lot better than a kick in the pants.

'I think, Herewini, it could be at least NZ $5 million for you, so when you get it please invite me to New Zealand for a holiday,' Hayakawa said with a broad smile

Herewini got to his feet and thanked everyone profusely, and said no doubt Hayakawa-san would get a big pay rise and a bonus from his organisation, and it might one day care to take him on a world tour! Inspector Mori had the final word. He told the group that he had informed Mrs Nomura about the Yamada estate and his intention to press manslaughter charges against him.

'That should leave Mrs Nomura with a very good chance to seek damages from the Yamada assets, and if we get a conviction on that charge I am sure the judge will deal very generously with Mrs Nomura's claim.'

Herewini did not have his chance of a candle-lit dinner with Jenny that night because the Sea Hawk put on a special celebratory banquet for all the Mereleigh Record Club members, and all those who had taken part in Jenny's rescue. There was just one condition, and that was a select group of TV and other media be allowed in for twenty minutes for photo opportunities. They were going to cover the dinner's cost in return.

The final few days in Fukuoka went too quickly for everybody. Jenny and Herewini found themselves doing a lot of sightseeing with Adam and Michiko, aided by Nishimura-san and her boyfriend, in a large luxury limo hired for that purpose. For both Jenny and Herewini, the final days were taken up with rounds of clubbing and parties all over the place. It was like some fantasy but both knew time was short and reality around the corner: Jenny with the promise of new film work, Herewini with new-found wealth and a responsible job he was supposed to go back to.

There were a couple of nights of passionate love-making which frightened Herewini to the core. He had fallen hook, line and sinker for the dream girl of his imagination who had turned into a reality. She was about to escape in a day or so if he could not find a way for them to be together. She had said in the early hours of dawn one night that she would never forget him and there was that deep trusting look into her eyes that led right to her soul, so he thought, and he felt he was not wrong.

They grew closer as time started to run out, neither of them wishing to possibly risk the relationship by suggesting something more permanent. It all seemed so delicate, yet they agreed on everything. Just before dawn on their last night together in Fukuoka, Jenny said with tears in her eyes that she had to return with her parents to Wales and see everyone including the local police at Welshpool who had helped track her down.

'What can I do? I want to stay and be with you but I have to do this, and also I really want to have a crack at a couple of movies.' She clung on to him almost with the urgency of a drowning person fearing what separation from him could bring.

'I understand. Perhaps I am on the verge of being fired from the NZ Customs service because of the French leave I took, and now I have a swag of money coming my way and Hayakawa-san saying he might have a big job for me.

It's a major turning point in my life with you and perhaps my job. It would be fantastic if I could just go to the nearest travel agent and get you a ticket to New Zealand but let us both sort out our immediate career moves with an view to spending more time together as soon as we can. That is what I want!' he explained, knowing that a new-found relationship like this could vanish very quickly if one partner became so engrossed in some other thing or person during a period of absence.

'I trust you, Mr Jimmy Jones, and you can bet every day and night I will be thinking of you and working out ways for us to get together again.' She was almost sobbing as she spoke. 'You have been to hell and back, take it easy it will work out fine,' he tried to reassure her.

They made love once more then she had to leave to meet her parents and get ready to fly back to Britain with the rest of the group. Adam and Michiko were at their hotel lobby talking to her father when she arrived. The three of them had been discussing Jenny and Herewini's new romance. As Jenny arrived, Michiko could see the tears in Jenny's eyes so went to her immediately with a big hug and some warm consoling words telling her that, as far as they could tell, Herewini would do his utmost to make it all happen for them both.

Jenny's dad read her like a book. 'Don't worry, Herewini is welcome at our place anytime but we all have a few things we all must do first, Your mum is so looking forward to taking you back home with us for a while but she will not stand in your way if you want to go overseas again and neither will I. It's your life.'

Adam advised Jenny that there would be a big media

turnout to see them off , as if they had been left alone by the media since Jenny was released from the clutches of the Yakuza. She had been all across the front pages of the major national dailies in Britain and Japan and also New Zealand, because of the Herewini connection. She was good with the media; as a natural self-effacing person, it did not bother her but the farewell would be hard and emotional and the media would be deep into her personal life and feelings.

Michiko guessed her thoughts and said, 'You are like Princess Diana at her peak, they love you to bits and every Japanese person wants to say sorry for the difficulties you had. They are not thinking about your love affair with Herewini and you're having to part, but if you don't cry about your ordeal, they will think you are an unnatural cold person. I am going to be with you at the airport on the same plane and I can speak to the Japanese media in the same language so don't worry; you don't have to say much at all. Soon I want to be welcoming you and Herewini to our place in Britain. Oh my God, I never been there before and I too feel so sad leaving my parents behind so please help me too.' Michiko wiped a tear from her own eyes.

Herewini, Rick, Maggie, Foggy, and Helena were at the airport to farewell Jenny and the rest of the Mereleigh group on their return to Britain before they took another flight to Auckland. The Fukuoka Record Club had turned out in force; the Mayor, and civic dignitaries, and all the other newfound Japanese friends were also there. The airport officials were beside themselves with worry at the congestion mounting up at the check-in desk. There were tears all round, extra presents being laden onto the departing members of the group, and last minute hugs. Andy and Janine and Chuck were also at the farewell as their ferry to Russia did not depart until the late evening.

'I never imagined the Japanese were so warm and emotional. There is not a dry eye among their womenfolk and the men are behaving as though they were saying goodbye to their dearest relations. It's incredible,' Andy observed trying to keep a firm dispassionate note in his voice.

'Shucks, this about beats it all. You did invite the Fukuoka Record Club people back to Mereleigh and I guess they are all very excited at the prospect. You know they would not take a cent off me in sponsorship after the Mayor sorted the mess out, so I diverted it all to a mental health society. There is no way I could leave this place without contributing something and Nomura-san's widow, well, she just would not take anything from me, but at least we know she will be taken care of by the Japan side,' Chuck explained.

'Chuck, we are going to need you if they come to Mereleigh, my God we are going to need you. It's OK for Andy to invite everyone, but how the heck are we going to pay for them all? The ratio is about 200 to 1 in their favour,' Janine pointed out with a degree of horror.

'Don't worry, gal. I will simply sell one of my many ranches to bankroll you guys,' he laughed.

Janine butted in, 'I nearly forgot the Hotel receptionist gave me this letter for Andy when we checked out.' She handed Andy a plain white envelope with a UK postmark.

Andy paused for a moment before opening it wondering who it had come from.

'Come on open it up we are al;l waiting to know whio its from,' Janine prompted.

He pulled out his reading glasses and carefully opened it al most as though he was scared something may fall out of it. There was a single pieced of paper inside neatly typed.

'Its from the Ministry of Foreign Affairs. John Russel it seems he is back in London after his posting to Beijing.'

Andy read it a couple of times before saying, 'It's a short note thanking us very much for our help, regarding Boris, but he does not mention Boris by name just refers to him as our Russian friend. It says he is now in the UK and they say he had a rough time before some friends were able to get to him and assist him with a safe passage to the UK. The artist fellow who we saw at Moscow railway station is in the care of a Russian support group and his work is now in favour with the current Russian Government.'

Andy handed the letter to Chuck and said, 'It seems this Russel chap would like to see us in London, on our return, to thank us all properly and we will meet Boris again then.'

'What an amazing turn out. Its almost unbelievable I was sure we would never see Boris alive again once those thugs got hold of him,' Janine dabbed her eyes with a handkerchief.

'You got to take your hat off to your 007 guys Andy. They must have pulled a few rabbits out of the hat to get Boris out of Russia,' Chuck handed the letter to Janine.

'Yes and I have to admit it Andy you did the right thing though we had our doubts about you with all that secrecy about the envelope, and my shorthand notes,' Janine gave him a hug as Andy shrugged it all of .

'Alls well that ends well. We know have something very pleasant to look forward to when we get back home,' Andy added.

Rick was busy trying to round up his group and could see Jenny and Herewini were very distressed at the parting. He had never seen Herewini so emotional before. 'You know, it takes a parting like this to realise just how much you love a person,' Rick told him

'That is only too true. I should have gone with her to Britain. She asked me but I would have to quit the customs service if I did, and I am already on thin ice for extending my leave here,' he said emotionally. 'It's probably a very selfish thing and I regret it, but I tried to work things out properly and not rush anything, for her sake as much as mine,' he said.

'Did you ask her to come to New Zealand?' Rick asked.

'Of course, but like me, she said she had to sort a few things out first and have a bit of time with her parents. It would be rude and heartless for her not to go back now,' he explained.

'So what is the problem? You will see her, I suppose, when the court case opens in Japan, if not sooner in New

Zealand?' Rick asked.

'Yes, but I am going to miss her like hell until we get together again and that can't be soon enough,' Herewini said. 'The Mereleigh Record Club of yours has certainly changed a few people's lives. You know, Jenny called me her "Jimmy Jones".'

'Oh you need timing, a tick a tick a tick of timing, a tock a tock tock .... good timing is the thing,' Rick sang the opening lyrics. 'I thought I had good timing meeting Maggie a thousand years ago when she was about fourteen and me fifteen but it's taken us a few decades to get together. Grab it while you can, mate, that is all I can add,' Rick said. 'I heard Hayakawa-san has some possible big assignment for you in the South Pacific if you want to quit the customs service and go private?' Rick then quizzed Herewini.

'He mentioned it, but I was frank with him, saying a first priority was trying to bring Jenny into my life permanently and then sorting out my career with the customs service one way or another.'

Herewini continued, 'I almost forgot. Can you ring an Inspector Roberts at Welshpool collect? Here's the number. The local cops passed it on to me for you.' Rick's heart sank. A feeling of guilt had remained with him ever since he found the dead Japanese man.

'I will do it now. Hang about, I hope it does not take long.'

Rick returned within ten minutes with a strange look on his face.

'Well?' asked Herewini.

'I think you heard I'd found a dead body in a New-town hotel?' Herewini nodded.

'He was Japanese and apparently the man sent to hire Jenny. Someone murdered him and I was first on the scene.'

'They don't think you did the job?'

'I don't think so, as they found a connection between him and the Slav gang. It seems it was a contract killing of Kameda by poison. They don't have anyone yet and I am definitely not a suspect, they tell me,' Rick finished.

'So why are you looking so po-faced about it? Should be a cause for celebration! Herewini gave him a playful punch in the arm.

'If I tell you, you must swear not to tell anyone?'

'OK, scout's honour, fire away.'

Rick shuffled his feet 'Well I had booked in, rather in haste, at this damned brothel place by mistake called "The Rising Sun." It was an internet booking sight unseen...'

Herewini roared, 'The poor boy from "The House of the Rising Sun." What's it worth not to tell Maggie?'

'You promised, you bastard!' Rick protested.

GLOSSARY OF JAPANESE WORDS USED

bento	traditional Japanese lunch box of foods
(doomo) arigatoo gozaimashita	thank you (very much)
gaijin	foreigner
gomen nasai	sorry
hai	yes
Hakata-ben	the dialect spoken in and around Fukuoka
ichi ban	number one
okusan	wife
onsen	hot spring(s)
otosan	father
ryokan	Japanese traditional inn
shinkansen	bullet train
soo desu	indication of agreement
sumimasen	excuse me
yakitori	grilled chicken on skewers
Yakuza	Japanese mafia or gangster
yatai	street stall selling alcohol and simple food
yukata	Japanese dressing gown

Printed in Australia
AUOC010933290113
255078AU00001B/1/P